THE GUNS OF ZANZIBAR

Marcus Baxter Thrillers
Book Four

Tim Chant

SAPERE
BOOKS

THE GUNS OF ZANZIBAR

Published by Sapere Books.

, 24 Trafalgar Road, Ilkley, LS29 8HH
United Kingdom

saperebooks.com

ISBN: 978-0-85495-359-2

CHAPTER ONE

The city of Zanzibar was as far a cry from London as Marcus Baxter could imagine. While it was winter in the southern hemisphere, the island of the same name basked in tropical heat, the East African sun beating down on the pale coral stone of the small city. London had been cool and damp, the great stone palaces of commerce, industry and government dark grey under a sky of racing clouds.

Baxter turned away from the open window, but remained close to it and the hint of a breeze. He hadn't had an opportunity to acquire a tropical-weight uniform before leaving England, and now he sweated in the dark blue woollen uniform he'd changed into before reporting for duty. Commander Parker, the senior officer of the small Royal Navy contingent on Zanzibar, struck a match and leant back in his chair as he sucked life into his pipe. Skeins of blue smoke drifted through the humid air.

"A survey?" the commander asked doubtfully, looking up at Baxter from under bushy white eyebrows. His tone betrayed his scepticism, though Baxter wasn't sure if this was due to the concept itself or the man who had been sent to undertake it. "To see about bringing our humble little coaling base up to the standards of a naval station? You don't look much like one of those hydrographic chaps that are sent to us on occasion. Engineer, are you?"

Baxter resisted the urge to glance at the Royal Navy Volunteer Reserve insignia on his cuffs, marked out in wavy lines of gold rather than the straight lines of the regular service. "No, sir. I just have a lot of experience, particularly with coaling."

"Hmm." Parker puffed on his pipe. "Well, that's what we do here. Five thousand tons of coal in covered storage, ready for the occasional visit from the Cape Squadron. Sadly not the finest Welsh stuff. Well, all this seems in order, and you may go about your business of seeing if we can be turned into a proper naval station."

There was a certain amount of sourness in Parker's voice. He was old for a man of his rank, and had no doubt seen men of his own generation and younger already pass him by to the rank of captain. He was surely under no illusion that if the small coaling station here *was* to be upgraded, then he would not be promoted and retain command.

"Thank you, sir," Baxter replied as affably as he could.

"A six-month assignment, I see. The war-planning chaps must be taking this seriously." Parker nodded to the reservist insignia on Baxter's sleeve. "Must be a bit of a pain for you, Mr Baxter, being taken away from your civilian life."

"Not at all, sir," he said. The commander's wondering conversation confirmed Baxter's suspicion that he'd already been at the gin, but he couldn't really blame Parker, assigned as he was to an out-of-the-way backwater of a station. "Happy to serve."

"Well. You'll have to pardon me, but I don't have the necessary office and staff requisitioned for you just yet. The Admiralty telegram indicated you would be arriving in a fortnight's time."

"The fault is mine, sir," Baxter said. "I made my own travel arrangements. Keen to get started, you understand."

That was true as far as it went. The British Naval Intelligence Division, or 'Room 39' as it was nicknamed, had put him on the Union-Castle ship RMS *Edinburgh Castle* to travel here via Cape Town. He'd jumped ship in Gibraltar, then made his own way from the Rock through the Mediterranean, the Suez Canal and the Red Sea. He had travelled the interminable, sweltering journey down the west coast of Africa before, back when the machinations of another NID operative had ended with him being made a prisoner of the Russian 2nd Pacific Squadron on its way to a fateful engagement with the Imperial Japanese Navy. It had been hellishly hot and humid, exacerbated by the constant need to coal at sea, and Baxter hadn't relished the prospect of making the trip again, even in the relative comfort of a passenger liner. Now that he had a task at hand — orders, no less — he was impatient to be about his work.

"Keen one, are you?" Parker grumbled. "Well, I'd see someone about a tropical-weight uniform, first thing. I expect the officers of my command to be ship-shape and Bristol-fashion, none of this changing into mufti at the first opportunity."

"Very good, sir." Baxter caught a flash of steel in Parker's pale grey eyes, as though he suspected some insolence.

"How much have their Lordships deigned to communicate to you about the situation in East Africa, Mr Baxter?"

In fact, very little had been communicated to him beyond what was in his official orders, but he didn't want to admit that this was a rush job. "Some, sir, but I'm a firm believer in hearing from the officers who actually know the situation."

This seemed to mollify Parker somewhat, and he relaxed in his chair. His eyes wandered over to the sideboard, and Baxter found himself hoping a cool drink would be offered. His new commander, however, obviously decided it was still too early in the day to be seen drinking.

"What do you know of our status here?"

Baxter didn't let the sudden change of tack put him off his stride. "That this island is a British protectorate, under the overall authority of the Governor on the mainland and a Resident; Major Pearce is the senior British official in Zanzibar, I believe."

Parker snorted. "I see you've read your briefing, which is accurate as far as it goes. His Highness Sayyid Khalifa-bin-Harub rules these islands. He has graciously accepted our protection and has deigned to allow us offices in his palace. The Resident's office is, of course, on the top floor. And, just over there —' he pointed towards the coastline — 'are the Germans. They are the reason we are here, and why the Sultan was keen to accept us. He gets to keep his crown, and we gain control of a trading and refuelling hub without the expense of running a Crown colony."

"And how are relations with our neighbours, sir?" Baxter asked.

"Cordial, of course," Parker replied absently. "Dar es-Salaam is barely fifty miles from here, and there are not infrequent social calls. I'm sure you'll get to meet our opposite numbers in due course. We may have been relegated to the role of a coal base for the East Africa squadron, but we're well situated to keep an eye on our German neighbours. That's what approaches a main naval base for them in these waters, though you could hide an entire squadron of cruisers in the Rufiji River Delta. Why we haven't already been reinforced is beyond me."

Baxter didn't offer his own opinion. Just as the Royal Navy contingent here was in a position to attack German forces if hostilities did break out, the reverse was also true. There was a powerful RN squadron in these waters, based further south where it could strike anywhere along the coast.

"I imagine you might be interested in the comings and goings of German naval forces?" Parker went on. The question, asked in an entirely innocent tone, was clearly intended to trip him up.

Baxter shook his head. "Entirely outside my role, sir," he said. That was true enough, but the question struck a little too close to the bone for Baxter's liking and suggested Parker was perhaps sharper than he liked to present. He *was* under strict orders not to reveal his true mission to anyone in the small naval contingent here, which would make executing his orders complicated, though not impossible. "Survey and hydrography, that's me. If I might ask a question, though?"

Parker sighed and linked his hands across the front of his tropical uniform tunic. "Certainly, *Lieutenant*," he said.

Baxter didn't miss the emphasis on his rank, and knew he had to tread carefully. For years, he'd worked in spaces without a formal structure to a greater or lesser degree. Now he had to adapt to it afresh.

Not that he'd ever been particularly good at operating within military structures when he'd been a regular officer, he had to admit.

"You speak of the Germans as an enemy, or at least a potential one. Have you seen or heard anything to suggest that's likely to become a reality?"

Parker levelled a cool gaze at him. "One of the benefits of being stuck out here on the edge of the world, Mr Baxter, is that one gets a clearer perspective on many things. The Kaiser eyes our possessions hungrily. He may not be ready for a fight just yet, in the way we are, but mark my words — he's working on it."

Baxter didn't know if the commander was talking specifically about the station here at Zanzibar, or Britain in general. That was, at best, debatable.

"You mentioned the possibility of visits, sir?" he asked. "The German colonies, I mean."

"Bit of tourism, is it, Mr Baxter? Or are you looking for something more specific?" Parker asked, a suspicious gleam in his eye.

"Well, as busy as I'll be, I'm sure I won't spend my entire time here working, and it would be a pity to miss the opportunity."

From Parker's noncommittal grunt, Baxter thought perhaps he'd managed to sound innocent enough. The commander had come altogether too close to the real reason for Baxter's presence, as communicated to him in his secret orders. "It's not unheard of," Parker said at last. "Just go in mufti, d'you hear?"

"Of course, sir," Baxter said smoothly. Changing out of the wool frock coat and trousers was to be his first order of business, anyway, followed by investigating the best way to get across to the African mainland and start pursuing his quarry.

Baxter felt one hand start to clench at the thought of the man he'd been sent here to find. To *hunt down*, was the wording used by Lieutenant Saunders, the Naval Intelligence officer who had given him the task. The man was George Arbuthnott, the rogue intelligence agent who had set the course of Baxter's life by involving him in the plot to raise tensions between Britain and the Russian Empire in 1904, the train of events that had led him to Tsushima. Baxter had last seen the rogue agent in Odessa in 1905, by which time he was working with the

Tsarist secret police, and had thought never to see him again after he'd shot the traitorous bastard in the knee and made good his escape.

Baxter had barely thought of Arbuthnott in the intervening years, being somewhat busy with any number of little wars. But when he did, he'd hoped that Arbuthnott had died of his wounds, or been disposed of by the Russians. That had changed when Saunders had approached him with an offer he had found very hard to refuse. He was to find Arbuthnott in German East Africa, bring him out, and earn his commission back.

"Well, that will be all, Mr Baxter," Parker said now. Baxter forced himself to release the tension in his arm. "Just let my adjutant know what you need in terms of staff and provisions for your, ah, survey work."

"Thank you, sir." Baxter snapped a smart salute as Parker turned his attention to the papers on his desk.

Baxter was relieved to step out of the office and into a cool and shaded corridor. Parker's adjutant, a harried-looking sub-lieutenant, popped his head out from an adjoining cubby hole. "Everything top-notch, Baxter?"

"Fine, thank you," Baxter replied. The fellow had introduced himself when Baxter had arrived to report for duty, but he hadn't registered the name. "In terms of a billet?"

"Catch as catch can, I'm afraid. As I'm sure the chief explained, we weren't expecting you for a fortnight. I can recommend a couple of hotels in town for the short term, clean and all that."

"And can you also recommend a tailor?"

The sub-lieutenant brightened perceptibly. "Why, I most certainly can — everyone here goes to Perito. Italian chap —

he can whip you up something suitable for the climate in a matter of hours. Well, days, maybe, for a chap your size."

Baxter sighed inwardly. The British Naval Intelligence Division had provided an allowance to cover his activities, but he guessed tailoring appearing on his statement of accounts would raise a few eyebrows. Officers were expected to be gentlemen, after all; the modern Royal Navy seemed to expect them to be gentlemen first and officers second. "Thank you. If you wouldn't mind writing those details down, and perhaps suggesting a bar where one might get a gin, that would be splendid."

The chap grinned. "Thought you'd never ask! The English Club should be open," he said cheerfully, then grabbed his white cap from a hook by the door. "Hensley, by the way."

Baxter allowed the young sub-lieutenant to lead him from the palace where the British presence kept their offices. Hensley seemed eager to please at least, if a little overly familiar. Baxter would no doubt learn the lay of the land from him.

Stepping out from the cool of the palace into the midday sun was almost like a physical blow. Baxter had experienced baking heat before, during his time with the Russian fleet, and while running the Italian blockade into Tripoli, but he knew it would take him a while to reacclimatise after a couple of years spent in cooler climes. He desperately wanted to open his frock coat and loosen his stiff shirt collar, but he didn't yet know whether Hensley was the sort to tattle to his superiors. The RN put a lot of emphasis on the correct dress.

Hensley grinned. "Don't worry, the Club is on the waterfront and has a sea breeze," he said when he caught Baxter's sour expression. "It's not so bad when you get used to it."

The rooftop bar had a view across the broad harbour. The water glittered in the sunlight and a cooling wind brought with it the tang of salt. That smell, so familiar and comforting to Baxter, mingled with the land-based scents of grilled fish, tropical fruit and, underlying everything, the spices Zanzibar was so famous for. In the distance, Baxter could hear the musical tones of a muezzin calling the Muslim faithful to prayer. He sipped his gin and tonic, delivered by a French waiter who seemed oblivious to the heat, and felt himself relax for the first time in a while.

The walk from the palace to the English Club had been through the labyrinth of narrow, busy streets of the Arab quarter, noisy with shouting traders and artisans working in cramped, dim shops. They'd narrowly avoided being run down by a train that shot through the crowded streets without any sort of safety barrier, which had amused Hensley enormously, and Baxter had noted that the whole town appeared to have electric street lights. The European quarter, marked by the twin spires of a cathedral, was quieter and more spacious, providing some measure of relief.

"There's golf, if you play, and cricket at the sports ground," Hensley said after a few moments of contented silence. "And the pleasures of Dar es-Salaam and the mainland are barely fifty miles away."

Baxter glanced across at him, trying to decide if he was labouring under the delusion that as a newcomer, he knew nothing at all about the area, or navigation in general. While it was true that he hadn't spent a lot of time in these waters, Baxter had passed through on more than one occasion and could certainly read a damn map.

"What's the approach to the harbour here like?" he asked.

The sub-lieutenant was eager to please and visibly relaxed when asked for information. "I wouldn't exactly call it treacherous," he said. "But you do need to have your wits about you, what with the shoals and sandbanks. Shallow a lot of the way, as well."

Not exactly treacherous, but with hidden dangers. It summed up perfectly the job Baxter been sent here to do.

"And how do I get across to the mainland from here?" Baxter asked. "Seeing as relations are still cordial between us and the neighbours?"

"An official visit, do you mean? Or, um, a spot of tourism?"

Baxter wondered why Hensley had emphasised the word 'tourism'. He did seem to be a bit of an odd fellow, overly earnest, which might explain his posting to this backwater. "Oh, I'd just like to have a look around. Given you weren't expecting me, and therefore don't have a staff and office, I thought I might go and see how the other side lives."

How the other side lived, Baxter discovered when he landed a few days later, was not so different to the people of Zanzibar. The German Empire had held sway over that part of Africa longer than the British had controlled the islands just off its coast, and it showed in the greater prevalence of colonial architecture and the fact the main street was named *Königstrasse*. The small city was, perhaps, slightly more orderly than the older and more vibrant Zanzibar, and the signage was, of course, in German. The town wasn't a bustling metropolis, but nor was it a quiet backwater.

A cargo ship had just arrived and the docks were busy with African workers offloading the latest European imports, while merchants nearby haggled over prices or negotiated fees to ship their exports. The streets beyond the dock were quieter, but Baxter still passed Arab merchants and stallholders, porters going about their business, and more than a few Europeans abroad despite the midday heat.

There hadn't been much in the way of border control when he'd disembarked from the small fishing boat, hired for the short hop between island and mainland. It had taken the local fisherman three hours, with a favourable wind, to bring Baxter into the harbour. He'd relished the simple pleasure of being aboard a sailing vessel, undisturbed by the thump of a steam engine or the smoky cloak coal-fired vessels in particular carried with them. The crossing had been relatively calm, the sheltered waters not getting much beyond a heavy swell.

Arriving by sea had shown him just why Dar es-Salaam had been chosen as the centre of German East Africa. The harbour was deep and sheltered, with a narrow mouth that could be controlled very easily with the proper siting of light coastal artillery. Zanzibar's wide harbour was more accessible, but also more exposed to the weather, not to mention hostile action. A German light cruiser lay at the far end of the harbour, long and sleek; that would be the SMS *Königsberg*, he guessed.

Even though Britain and Germany were at peace, it still felt oddly like enemy territory, perhaps because of what he'd been sent here to do. The mission would almost certainly take him deeper inland, up the Rufiji River or one of the other waterways that wended their way down to the coast. That, at least, he was qualified for. Baxter was a blue-water sailor at heart, but he'd had plenty of experience of riverine steaming. Right now, as he'd told Hensley, he just wanted to understand the lay of the land and get a feel for the people opposite him.

He had no idea why Saunders had picked him for the job of hunting Arbuthnott. He wasn't one for sneaking in and out of places. The information contained within his secret orders had mentioned contacts in both Zanzibar and Dar es-Salaam, but they would be expecting him in a fortnight or more, and he had no notion of how they'd react if he was early. In truth, he had no real idea how to go about this mission.

He would not let that stop him from trying, hence coming here to get the lay of the land. There was little point in trying to keep a low profile, of course — he was aware of how much he stood out in the crowd. He made no attempt to disguise his presence or his nationality, checking in at the main hotel on *Königstrasse* and generally doing his best to give the impression he was a tourist.

Baxter had already assessed the state of the port on arrival, being careful not to do anything obtuse like use his field glasses or make obvious notes or sketches. Now, as the day started to draw towards it close, he wandered the bustling streets of the city, making a mental note of landmarks as he went and generally enjoying the novelty of being somewhere new.

As he strolled through the city, snacking on fried plantain eaten out of a twist of German newspaper, he started to get a prickling sensation on the back of his neck — a sense that someone was in his wake and keeping him under observation.

Baxter slowed his pace, pausing to finish off his plantain, and then stopped and looked around, as though contentedly taking in the scene. His watcher was clearly too well trained to do anything obvious like dash down a side street or look away in a hurry. But among the crowd he thought he saw a familiar face. But that was absurd. There were more than a few European faces around, alongside Africans and Arabs, which probably explained that fleeting impression.

Baxter may have been wrong about recognising someone, but he knew he wasn't wrong about being watched. It made sense, he supposed — he was a newcomer, obviously British, at a time of heightened tension between Britain and Germany. He'd be astonished if the German colonial authorities followed every new face around a busy harbour town, however.

"Well, nothing I can do until they show themselves," he muttered, and headed for the hotel in the centre of town. He walked briskly, now, dropping the casual saunter of a tourist and adopting one of a man keen for a drink. He had to fight the urge to glance back over his shoulder, knowing it would give away the fact that he knew he was being shadowed.

Assuming he wasn't just imagining the whole thing.

CHAPTER TWO

"Entschuldigung, dürfen wir uns anschließen?"

Baxter looked up from the cup of excellent coffee he was nursing. The hotel's breakfast room, bright in the morning light pouring in through the large windows, was relatively crowded with both guests and German colonists; this was obviously the place to be for the German gentleperson at leisure in East Africa.

Before him stood a young man with a broad, friendly face and round glasses. Like Baxter, he wore a linen suit, but one that suggested considerably less wear and more care for his appearance. Baxter's gaze was drawn beyond him to, presumably, his wife. She was a tall woman, and dressed in what had been the latest European fashion several months ago. Her pale blue eyes were challenging as she met Baxter's look.

Baxter started to reply in his somewhat rusty German, then stopped with a self-deprecating smile. "My apologies — I'm a little out of practice. Please, take a seat."

The gentleman's smile returned as he held the chair for his wife. "Ah, a pleasure to meet one of our *Englander* neighbours," he said in relatively unaccented English. "Mr...?"

"Baxter," he supplied, then smiled. "And I'm Scottish."

"My apologies. I am Dr Masing, and this is my wife, Esca."

"Herr Doctor, *Frau* Masing," Baxter greeted them both, as a waiter came to take their order for breakfast.

"And what brings you to our fair city, Mr Baxter?" the doctor asked once the waiter had moved on to the next table. "Business, or leisure?"

Baxter had already guessed that the doctor would be direct in his enquiries — he had that particularly German manner about him. "Oh, leisure," he said easily. "I'm on business in Zanzibar, and decided to take the opportunity to visit somewhere new."

"And Africa, in her enormity and variety, certainly offers many new places," Masing said contentedly.

"Do not be so quick to tell a British man of new places," *Frau* Masing said, speaking for the first time, her tone sharp. "He will want to occupy them."

Masing laughed. "You must forgive my wife, Mr Baxter. She is from the Transvaal."

Baxter resisted the urge to point out the irony of her statement, given they were sitting in what could have been a Berlin hotel transplanted to Africa. "There is nothing to forgive," he said, keeping his tone light. Esca Masing's eyes narrowed slightly, perhaps surprised that her barb hadn't provoked a reaction. "And what brings you both to German East Africa?" he asked, adding only the slightest emphasis to the word *German*.

Masing seemed oblivious to that. "I have just taken a post at the *Europäisches Krankenhaus* — excuse me, the European Hospital — as a surgeon," he said, sounding quite pleased with the prospect. The German doctor's smart suit and relatively pale skin made more sense to Baxter now, knowing that he had likely only just arrived in warmer climes.

"I met Esca in Berlin, as her family was, well…" Masing trailed off. The subject of how he had landed a wife from what was now part of British South Africa when he was new to the region had obviously come up in conversation before, and he clearly felt compelled to explain it.

"In exile," Esca said coldly. She clearly wasn't happy that her husband had managed to seat her with the enemy of her people, which Baxter couldn't blame her for. The fact that he wasn't rising to her various provocations was also clearly irritating her.

He swallowed the last of his coffee and took a final mouthful of his eggs and bacon. "Well, Doctor, *Frau* Masing, I hope you do not think me rude, but I must be about my day," he said briskly.

Masing looked slightly crestfallen. There were, Baxter guessed, only so many Europeans in the city and the doctor's exposure to the locals would be limited by the relatively strict segregation he'd noticed. He was, if Baxter was any judge of character, a man who enjoyed company and relished meeting new people. "Are you staying long in Dar es-Salaam?" he asked as Baxter rose.

"Another day or so, I think."

"Well, perhaps you might consider joining me for a drink in the Club this evening?"

"That would be most agreeable," Baxter said smoothly, realising he had — perhaps — started to cultivate his first contact in German East Africa.

The German Club was not dissimilar to its counterpart in Zanzibar, and the two operated a policy of polite friendliness that gained Baxter entry, vouched for as he was by Dr Masing. The bar was busy, a long room decked out in polished mahogany and brass, the air thick with pipe and cigar smoke. It was filled with uniforms that managed to be both familiar and alien. Baxter saw plenty of *Kaiserliche Marine* officers, with whom he would have more in common than the army officers. He paid more attention to military matters than many men in his profession, who only cared about matters naval, and knew local defence here was provided by the colonial *Schutztruppe*, though the officers were exclusively German.

There were plenty of civilians around as well, which seemed to be the circle Masing preferred to move in. While Baxter was generally more comfortable around military men, no matter the nationality, Masing's choice of company suited him better right then, given the nature of his mission.

Baxter was onto his second stein of lager when the military presence made itself known in the circle of businessmen, doctors and local plantation owners Masing had introduced him to. A young man in a somewhat disarrayed uniformed dropped onto the sofa beside Baxter, the seat recently vacated by a Bavarian who had gone to relieve himself.

"Apologies, old chap, don't have much in the way of German," he said cordially after the German shouted something cheerfully unintelligible at him.

"My apologies, *mein Herr*!" the young man exclaimed, the flush of drink deepening slightly. "I had thought you were a replacement officer for *Königsberg*, but I was clearly mistaken!"

Masing seemed to know the young man, but then, as Baxter had noticed earlier, the doctor was gregarious. "This is Mr Baxter, from Zanzibar," he said, leaning across and raising his voice above the hubbub to join the conversation. "Mr Baxter, *Leutnant zur See* Kleiner."

"Are you with the Cape Squadron, *Herr* Baxter?" Kleiner asked cheerfully as they shook hands. His English was accented, but fluent.

"*Herr* Baxter is here on business, and is not a naval man," Masing said, sounding slightly bemused.

"Come now, Doctor, I know a naval man when I meet one. Even the vaunted Royal English Navy is not so different from us."

"I was in the RN," Baxter admitted, as it was always best when a lie was salted with truth. "I'm still a Reservist, in fact. I'm in Zanzibar on business, though, and visiting your fine city for pleasure."

"And what business is that?" demanded a more clipped and considerably less slurred voice. Kleiner straightened up in his chair without quite coming to attention. Like the English Club in Zanzibar, the German Club seemed to operate a policy of informality between men of different ranks and services, but the newcomer exuded a stiff, formal air that had taken some of the cheerfulness out of Kleiner.

Baxter rose to his full height, looking down on the newcomer, though not by much, and offered his hand. The fellow was probably about his age, polished and slick in a way Baxter would never manage. His tan *Schutztruppe* uniform was neatly pressed, his handshake firm and brief. "Import-export primarily, Captain…?"

"Schiller," the officer replied. His tone remained frosty, and he clearly spoke English reluctantly. "Attached to the Tenth Company here."

They stood staring at each other for a moment, Schiller with obvious hostility, though Baxter couldn't decide if that stemmed from him being British or ostensibly a civilian. Perhaps both.

Schiller broke eye contact first, turning to Masing. "*Herr Doktor*," he said in German, followed by something Baxter only caught the gist of. He was clearly asking after *Frau* Masing. From the doctor's somewhat uncomfortable response, Baxter could tell that he wasn't happy with the attention.

Another officer approached, equally smartly turned out and with a senior officer's insignia. Kleiner actually stood up, though not quite at attention and swaying slightly on his feet.

This officer — a colonel, Baxter thought — ignored the civilians and spoke sharply to Schiller. His eyes, cold and hard, met Baxter's only briefly, before he was dismissed as being of little or no interest.

Schiller didn't make his excuses; instead, he said something to Masing about visiting him and his wife in due course, and left with his commanding officer.

"Interesting pair," Baxter said.

"That was von Lettow-Vorbeck, the commander of the *Schutztruppe*," Kleiner said, some of the bonhomie draining out of him. "A fine officer and a gentleman, who did much to save our colony from restless natives."

Baxter knew what that meant, and while Kleiner used the right words, his tone indicated he knew as well. "Well, let's not worry ourselves about what the military gets up to," he said cheerfully, picking up and draining his beer. "Who wants another?"

CHAPTER THREE

Baxter arrived back in Zanzibar two days later, slightly later than he'd intended or indeed told Hensley, who seemed to have taken it upon himself to act as Baxter's aide.

"Where the bloody hell have you been?" the young sub-lieutenant demanded, intercepting Baxter as he headed back towards the rooms he'd taken in the Arab quarter of Stone Town. It was one of the stranger buildings he'd ever stayed in, constructed out of coral stone that gave it a smooth texture and light colour. Like many of the buildings in the town, it had an ornate doorway, beautifully carved and reinforced with brass studs.

"Tourism," Baxter said bluntly. He didn't like Hensley's suddenly sharp tone, a far cry from the personable young man he'd had a drink or two with on the day of his arrival. "As we discussed."

"Apologies, old chap," Hensley said, backing down somewhat under Baxter's hard glare. "Parker was in high dudgeon when he realised you weren't on the island. He had something for you to do."

Baxter maintained his stare for a second longer. Something about Hensley's tone had put him on edge — particularly as he was senior to Hensley. He knew he'd have to work with the local staff once he was sure he could trust them, however, so there was no point burning his bridges just yet.

"Not a problem, Hensley," he said. "I'm not under Commander Parker's orders as yet, but I'll go and report. Do you know what it was he wanted me to do?"

Hensley grinned. "Oh, pick up some drunken lout of a sailor — old Navy, unless I miss my guess — blethering on about the Germans being up to something over in Dar es-Salaam. He thought it might be of interest to you, given you're here to see if we can put onto a war footing."

Baxter quirked an eyebrow at Hensley, wondering if he could really be that naïve. He doubted Parker was doing anything other than demonstrating his authority over Baxter, even if he wasn't technically on staff yet.

Hensley blethered on regardless, missing or ignoring Baxter's expression. "Looked like he'd been in more than a few fights in his time. Cauliflower ear and a broken nose. Parker ended up losing his temper and sending the fellow on his way, but there'll be the Devil to pay for you, I'm afraid."

Baxter grunted. Drunk or mad ex-sailors weren't exactly an uncommon thing, particularly in these sweltering regions. But there was something in that description that caught his attention. "Did you get his name?"

"Chap didn't want to provide it. Something awfully rum about him, if you ask me. Left in a hurry as well."

"Do me a favour and let me know if he resurfaces, would you?"

"Oh, I wouldn't worry about that — old Nosy will make sure you're the first to hear of it. He's decided to take full advantage of you while you're under his command."

Baxter knew he should probably reprimand the junior officer for speaking in disparaging tones about his station commander — not least for the obvious nickname. He was too hot and tired, though, and in truth his head was still slightly sore from the overproof rum he'd been drinking with Dr Masing the previous night.

"Lovely," Baxter said. "Look, I'm going to get cleaned up and change into uniform, then I'll go and pay my respects to Commander Parker. After that, assuming he hasn't found something else for me to do, we should talk about the assessment I've been sent to do."

If Hensley was going to be under his feet, he may as well make use of him.

The sub-lieutenant brightened at that. "I'd like that — I have some notions myself of what needs to be done to bring this station up to operational status."

As it turned out, Parker's bite was nowhere near as bad as his bark. Baxter had served under some tartars in his time, including Jackie Fisher and Tich Cowan: men who could put the fear of God into even seasoned officers with just a glance, but who also inspired respect from the men under their command. Others had been brutal tyrants. Parker was neither a tartar nor a tyrant. He'd clearly forgotten why he was angry with Baxter by the time he reported to the palace, resplendent in the surprisingly well-cut tropical service uniform he'd been measured for before heading to Dar es-Salaam. Parker obviously remembered that he was angry about something, though, so a perfunctory dressing down had been delivered.

"And from now on, do think to ask permission before sojourning among our, ah, neighbours," was the parting shot after Baxter had duly weathered the slight squall of his temper.

"Yes, sir," he said smartly. "Very good, sir."

"Very good, indeed." Parker sighed. "Well, I have no other duties for you just now, so you may as well make a start on your survey. But be sure to be available as and when I require you."

"Yes, sir."

"Dismissed." Parker's attention was already on the stack of papers on his desk.

Baxter marched smartly from the room. Even though he was now dressed in the white tropical uniform, he found himself overly hot, the clothing still far more restrictive than he'd like in this climate. He waited until he was well clear of the station commander's office, situated in an upper storey of the magnificent old palace, before he let himself breathe out the lungful of air he'd been holding since Parker had started speaking.

He unclenched his hands and flexed them. He'd known that he was going to have to take orders from difficult senior officers. He'd worked with plenty in the past, both during his short previous career as a regular RN officer and during his time as a mercenary. During the latter, however, he'd been free to speak his mind — even if that did carry the risk of being shot at. Now he had the uniform back on, even as a Reservist, he had to be more careful.

Baxter shook his head and grinned.

Hensley was approaching along the long, wide entrance hall. He paused a few paces short, looking concerned.

"Went better than expected, then?" he asked.

"No, it went exactly as expected," Baxter replied.

"Well, it's good to keep a sense of perspective, I suppose," the sub-lieutenant said cheerfully. "Time for lunch, I think — what do you say to Pierre's? I've got some ideas about putting the base into order that I'd like to go over with you."

Baxter had thought Hensley to be competent but unimaginative. However, as they ate grilled mackerel and drank India pale ale, Hensley soon disabused him of the notion.

"Now look, old chap, I know you can't talk about why you're really here or even confirm what department you're from,"

Hensley said after a few minutes of eating in companionable silence. "It's pretty clear that your primary purpose isn't to do this survey."

Baxter stared hard at him, a forkful of fish halfway to his mouth. He knew that he should ignore or deny that statement, according to the letter of his orders, but his work here would be untenable without some form of assistance.

Hensley rattled on, blithely unaware of his scrutiny. "You've probably worked out that the Commander has too much on his plate to be of any help to you. I've certainly never seen him make any attempts to cultivate friends and contacts across the water."

"And you have?" Baxter asked.

Hensley smiled diffidently. "Wouldn't be my place, and I've not been on the station that long myself. What I do have is a sense of what needs to be improved around here so that we can function as a proper naval base, not somewhere for a cruiser to pop in when the coal bunkers and drinks cabinet are getting low."

Baxter kept his face impassive. "I assume you've put this work to Parker?"

"Not interested," Hensley said flatly. "And I have orders to drop it, on the basis that it's not proper work for a line officer. Better left to technical qualifications, apparently."

Baxter nodded. The officer class of the RN was far more hidebound than it might once have been, not open to new ideas. Fisher had had quite a fight getting them to accept engineers as fellow officers, and he knew there were many of Parker's generation who hadn't really accepted the new, technological way of waging war.

What was interesting was the fact Hensley had thought to undertake the work off his own bat and remained interested in it despite orders to the contrary.

"That doesn't surprise me," Baxter said after a long drink of his beer. "I take it you have a thought on how we can proceed?"

"As I said, I know full well you're not going to be doing the work, and old Parker up there in 'Admiralty House' isn't going to assist you in your real work. He's not a bad chap, really, but he is going to get underfoot. I'd be more than happy to assist you with the survey work and generally keep old Nosy off your back."

"That seems a lot to take on with the duties proper to a line officer," Baxter said.

Hensley waved that away. "Oh, I am bored to tears here, so it really wouldn't be an imposition." He paused, looking at Baxter speculatively. "All I ask is that when you put the report in, you just let the right people know who compiled it. Perhaps put in a good word?"

Baxter had no qualms about agreeing to that. He was a firm believer in giving credit where it was due, though he didn't feel the need to point out that his good word would carry very little weight indeed. More to the point, he needed allies here. Saunders had been clear that he needed to be low-key in his real mission and would need to be careful about who he brought into his confidence. Having someone who thought he was indebted to Baxter on side would be helpful, given that Parker clearly wasn't going to be of much use.

"That sounds like an eminently workable solution," he said, raising his glass. "But enough shop talk — let's save that for after lunch."

Hensley was as good as his word. Parker had agreed for a few Royal Navy ratings to be put at Baxter's disposal, along with a Chief Petty Officer called Dalton, who was almost certainly well past retirement age, and some African workers. To go with his small staff, he had been assigned what he guessed what the smallest office in the entirety of Admiralty House. This wasn't a house as such, rather a suite of offices in the Bet-el-Ajaib Palace — the House of Wonders, as the locals called it – that was now the seat of governance in the city. Custom and military stubbornness meant the RN personnel insisted on calling it Admiralty House, however.

None of these details worried him, of course, as he intended to spend as little time as possible in Zanzibar. While Hensley wasn't directly assigned to him, he'd managed to extract a grudging agreement from a distracted Commander Parker for the sub-lieutenant to liaise between Baxter and the establishment here. As far as both of them were concerned, that was sufficient cover for Hensley to spend his time expanding and refining his ideas.

Which left Baxter free to consider how best to achieve his mission. That remained seemingly intractable to him as he tossed and turned in the baking night and spent his days doing his best to appear busy while pursuing the necessary contacts and information.

As he went about his business, Baxter couldn't shake the feeling that he was being observed. It was the same feeling he'd got in Dar es-Salaam, the prickling on the back of his neck that came from someone staring at him for too long. It came with a general sense of unrest and unease; that he'd been sent here with limited expertise and resources to do a seemingly impossible job.

"Bloody Arbuthnott," he muttered as he paused on the port's main wharf. HMS *Pegasus*, an old protected cruiser assigned to the Cape Squadron, was steaming in to resupply, her clean if slightly old-fashioned lines and plume of dirty coal smoke reduced to stark silhouettes against the rapidly setting sun.

"What's that, sir?" asked Dalton, the silver-whiskered CPO assigned to his office. He had a broad Yorkshire accent and looked more like he should have been sweating under English skies on a farm, not on a baking-hot quay in Africa.

"Oh, nothing," Baxter said. "Just an old ... acquaintance, who sort of got me into this line of work."

"Well, this isn't such a bad line of work to be in, is it, sir?" Dalton asked. Like Parker, he belonged to another time, and his advanced age and the fact Baxter was a Reservist clearly made him think he could speak more freely with him than he would another officer.

Baxter took a deep breath. The air tasted of coal smoke and jasmine, spices and tar. "No, no, it isn't," he admitted. He'd found himself warming to Dalton, who, despite the fact he was essentially comfortably retired while still technically in service, had thrown himself into his new work as fast as his arthritic joints would allow.

"If you don't mind me saying so, sir," Dalton went on, his voice dropping to what he probably thought was a confidential murmur, "I think there are some undesirable types giving you more than the usual amount of attention."

Baxter tensed, expecting the older man to point or nod in the direction of the watchers. Dalton was clearly cannier than that. "Don't go looking, sir," he said. "They're over by yon water barrel, not far from that ugly tub of a French steamer. Couple of shifty-looking types."

"Locals? African?"

"No, sir. Look like European types to me. Germans, maybe."

Baxter half-smiled at the disapproval in Dalton's voice. Clearly cordial relations between the neighbouring colonies didn't extend much beyond the officers — if it even existed there. "Get a lot of Germans here, do you?" he asked. He couldn't discount the possibility that the men watching him — assuming Dalton wasn't just imagining the whole thing — were just innocent tourists.

"From time to time," Dalton said. "They come across to look at the docks here or try to get information out of my boys. Not very good at it, though, sir — they get short shrift from us."

Baxter was slightly taken aback. Neither Parker nor Hensley had mentioned anything of the sort happening — that would have been useful information for him. But then, it was entirely possible the small, close-knit crew of sailors hadn't even bothered reporting it to their commanders.

"Well, Chief," Baxter said after considering this information. "Carry on."

Dalton saluted smartly. *Pegasus* had just dropped anchor and raised the signal to indicate she was ready for resupply. Baxter was supposed to be observing the work of refuelling the cruiser to inform his official work. He'd had more than enough of coaling a ship during his time with the Russians, and in truth had little appetite even for watching the evolutions. Hensley was here to oversee the work, but their presence would hardly be necessary if Baxter was any judge. Dalton would be better left to his own devices, as experienced petty officers were.

Baxter turned smartly on his heel and started walking briskly back towards the tall edifice of the palace, easily spotted by the clocktower that had been added after damage inflicted in the short-lived Anglo-Zanzibar War of the last century. He was careful not to look directly at the two European men loitering nearby, beyond a quick glance to fix them in his mind.

Baxter thought fast as he walked. He didn't have the resources or experience to tail them, and had no cause to have them arrested. He could have them taken up anyway and deal with any repercussions when they came, but he didn't fancy another dressing down from Commander Parker.

He scanned the crowd of people at the harbourfront, checking to see if the two watchers had any companions. Baxter's stride faltered as he again caught sight of that oddly familiar face in the crowd, the same one he'd seen in Dar es-Salaam. This time he looked straight into features that he hadn't seen in a very long time. They'd lost the roundness and softness of youth and had gained an angular, lean look only slightly undermined by an attempt at a goatee beard. The face wore an expression of surprised recognition.

"Tommy!" he bellowed before he could stop himself. The two watchers jerked upright, startled, before taking to their heels and disappearing into the crowd.

The Scottish boy — or the young Russian man, as he appeared to have become — froze for a moment, then he too turned and ran for it.

CHAPTEN FOUR

As Baxter started running, he caught sight of the two Germans sprinting towards the European quarter. Tommy Dunbar was going in the opposite direction.

"Bloody typical," he muttered. The lad had always had a knack of doing exactly the wrong thing, as far as Baxter was concerned. He paused, torn between running down the two German agents or going after Tommy to find out ... well, everything, he supposed. Where he'd been for the last nine years. What he was doing in Zanzibar, and who else was with him. Was *she* with him?

Baxter realised that his hesitation meant Tommy was well out of his reach. While he could get up a fair head of steam, he knew that he wouldn't be able to maintain it for long in this heat. Tommy, on the other hand, was running like the wind and already had a good hundred yards on him.

He went after the Germans. One was a corpulent fellow who was already eating his companion's dust. *No honour amongst spies*, Baxter thought grimly as he pounded after the two men, ignoring the shouts of startled onlookers as he plunged down the narrow alleys. It didn't take him long to close the distance with the slower of the two men, who was pouring sweat and barely going faster than a quick walk.

"Why don't you just give it up?" Baxter called after him, slowing as well in order to conserve his strength. "I just want to talk."

The fleeing man turned, faster than Baxter was expecting, a Luger in his hand. Baxter hesitated briefly, adrenalin flooding his system as he tried to decide if he was close enough to charge the man down before he managed to chamber a round. That moment's calculation could have killed him, as the German agent brought the weapon to bear.

Baxter dived sideways, into the lee of one of the small stone buildings that lined the landward side of the road. The German held his fire, either wanting to save his ammunition or not wanting to draw too much attention. Once that trigger was pulled, the cat would be out of the bag.

Baxter pressed his back into the cold stone, feeling the sweat trickling between his shoulder blades. He'd had guns pointed at him before, been shot at more than a few times. It *had* been a couple of years, though, and the unexpected potential violence had set his heart thumping in his chest. He slid down into a crouch, calming his breathing and listening hard. He could hear the other man's wheezing breath, his heavy footfalls creeping closer. Baxter tensed his muscles, knowing his only chance was to ambush the agent.

An incongruous screeching noise startled him, the whistle of the train that plied a route between Zanzibar and a nearby village. Baxter hadn't even noticed that he'd run across the tracks. He heard the German swear explosively, and the shouts of African and Swahili shopkeepers and passersby. When he stepped out of cover he could just make out the panicked agent fleeing up an alleyway on the other side of the tracks. The train was seven carriages long, and even at that pace he'd be long gone by the time Baxter could restart the pursuit.

Baxter stood in the street, oblivious to the people giving the him a wide berth, as he turned the rush of events over in his mind. Tommy Dunbar's presence on the island was too much of a coincidence. And if Tommy was here, there was every chance that others from his past were also on Zanzibar. He felt his heartrate quicken slightly, as he realised that Ekaterina Juneau might be here.

That was ridiculous, of course. He'd last seen the countess in 1905, in the aftermath of the great clash of Russian and Japanese battleships in the Tushima Straits, and there was no reason to believe she was here. Tommy was an adult, and though he had no doubt that he was still working for Ekaterina, just as he'd been when Baxter had found him in Odessa, it was entirely possible he was here by himself. Or perhaps Koenig, his sometime friend and comrade, was lurking somewhere on the island. From what Koenig had said the last time the two of them had met, Ekaterina had set herself up as some sort of fixer for the rich and influential, having left her semi-official position in the Tsar's secret police. Baxter knew, deep in his bones, that her agents would be here for the same reason he was — to run down Arbuthnott. That would be personal for Ekaterina, not business.

Baxter's scowl deepened. He'd let himself get distracted by the thought *she* was here, instead of the more pressing matter of why the Germans were paying him any attention at all.

Hensley trotted up, and Baxter realised he'd been stood scowling in silent contemplation for some seconds.

"Are you going to tell me what in blazes is going on?" the sub-lieutenant asked once he'd caught his breath. "I assume this is to do with your ... work?"

"All in good time," Baxter said, his voice hard and flat.

"You could at least tell me whether you're in Zanzibar for something ... specific?"

Baxter sighed. That much couldn't hurt, and he needed allies. "Not something," he said at last. "Someone."

Hensley nodded, obviously deciding this was good enough for now. "Well, we'd best lead by example," he said. "We have been ordered to oversee *Pegasus*'s coaling. Unless you want to organise a manhunt for those two? Or the other chap you were shouting at?"

Baxter was beginning to suspect that Hensley was considerably sharper than he liked to let on. "And what do you think are the chances of the local bobbies actually catching them?"

Hensley shrugged. "Unlikely," he admitted.

"There we are, then."

"I take it you knew the other fellow? The one who left in a hurry by himself?"

"Never seen him before in my life," Baxter said, knowing perfectly well that the lie would be unconvincing.

"Drink later, old chap?" Hensley asked diffidently as they walked back towards the harbour.

"This *is* going to be thirsty work," Baxter said. "The Club?"

"Where else?"

The sun was making its rapid descent towards the horizon as Baxter and Hensley arrived at the English Club and made their way up to the rooftop bar. Baxter had become used to how quickly the light went at this latitude, after years plying these seas, but as the sun disappeared into the dun mass of the African continent, he was struck again by how extraordinary the sight was. A far cry from the long grey twilights of the northern climes he'd grown up in.

"Something the matter, old chap?" Hensley asked nonchalantly.

Baxter shrugged. "Just wondering what the bloody hell we're doing here," he said.

"Bringing the *Pax Britannica* to the natives, of course," Hensley replied wryly. He clapped Baxter on the shoulder.

"Come on — if we wait too much longer, all the tables will be taken. *Pegasus*'s officers are a thirsty bunch and they'll be ashore soon."

It was fully dark already, beyond the pools of electric light, but still warm and there were already more than a few Europeans scattered around the tables, including most of the coaling base's officers. Hensley exchanged cheerful greetings with his colleagues as he headed across to join them. Baxter was suddenly tempted to slip away quietly, a dark mood threatening to overcome him. Lieutenant McSwain, an engineer who was in charge of coal storage and machinery maintenance, beckoned him over. As he approached, Baxter realised they had a civilian guest in amongst the sea of uniforms.

"*Herr* Doctor," Baxter greeted Dr Masing as he settled into one of the wicker chairs.

"*Herr* Baxter!" Masing exclaimed. "What a pleasant coincidence! You had said you were not a naval officer."

"Well, you see, Doctor, Mr Baxter here isn't what you call a *proper* Naval officer," one of the other men at the table said. "More of a part-timer, as you can tell from his cuffs."

It took Baxter a moment to dredge up the skinny sub-lieutenant's name. He was a sallow young man, still pimply and clearly someone who'd only just received his commission. Greaves, that was it. A few years ago, he would have bridled at the undisguised condescension. Now he just shrugged as Masing raised an eyebrow.

"I'm a merchant sailor by trade," he explained. "His Majesty requires some of my time every year or so."

"You English are strange, with your hierarchies," Masing said. "In my country, if a man wears the uniform, he is considered — what is the word? — *ja*, proper, no matter the circumstances."

Greaves flushed slightly, but Hensley spoke before the evening could descend into unpleasantness. "What brings you to Zanzibar, Doctor?" he asked, unconsciously echoing the question Baxter had been asked more than a few times since his arrival. "Pleasure?"

"Oh no, sir, business, serious business. That of medicine. I am here to talk with the doctors in your English Hospital and see what agreements can be made for co-operation."

Baxter nodded thoughtfully.

"A worthy enterprise," McSwain said. He was a dour Irishman whose demeanour never seemed to lighten even when he was deep in his cups.

"Good healthcare should transcend borders, and indeed race," Masing said with cheerful earnestness. "It is, after all, one of the great benefits we have brought to Africa."

Baxter raised an eyebrow. "I believe the establishment you work in is referred to as the 'European Hospital'?" he said mildly.

"Well, some of my countrymen are … particular," Masing said, with an expansive gesture that was obviously meant to clarify what he meant without him needing to say anything. Baxter nodded. A lot of the colonists wouldn't want to be treated in the same establishment as the people they ruled. Baxter had known officers who would have insisted on a separate sickbay on board naval vessels if they thought they'd get away with it.

It was, of course, ridiculous. Any man who thought like that had clearly never been in a serious action where immediate attention trumped the niceties of rank or station. Baxter could see Greaves and one or two other officers nodding as though they agreed with the attitude, which didn't surprise him in the slightest. McSwain's scowl had deepened, suggesting that they were navigating shoaling waters.

"And is *Frau* Masing joining you?" Baxter asked, reaching for the first thing that came to mind.

The German doctor shifted very slightly. "Esca is on Zanzibar, but has other engagements," Masing said. The ice in his glass rattled against the side as he raised it to his lips. "The company of men mixed with gin does not appeal to her."

"Sensible woman!" McSwain growled. Baxter kept his peace, knowing that what the doctor actually meant was the company of *British* men.

The *Pegasus*'s officers arrived not long after, a small tidal wave of chatter and white uniforms. Fairly rapidly, the Club became something not unlike an exclusive officers' club, the handful of civilians there either pushed to the edges or leaving. Masing seemed completely unconcerned by the RN officers, and even appeared keen to track down Hewitt, the ship's surgeon.

"A man as good as his word," Hensley commented as the doctor wondered off in search of his counterpart, chatting amicably with anyone who crossed his path.

"Rare type, these days," McSwain grunted.

"I say, have you chaps heard the news?" a newcomer asked, dropping into the seat Masing had vacated. He wore lieutenant-commander's stripes on his sleeve, which probably made him *Pegasus*'s executive officer.

"What news would that be?" Hensley asked.

"Some bloody Serb lunatic has killed the Archduke Franz Ferdinand."

CHAPTER FIVE

The news quickly spread around Zanzibar. HMS *Pegasus*'s crew had been the first to break the news to the town at large, having received a bulletin via wireless telegraphy, but the word soon pulsed along the telegraph cables and was followed by the newspapers from Britain and the rest of the world.

"I remember a time when news like this would take weeks to reach us," Baxter commented wryly after Hensley had passed him a copy of the *Manchester Guardian*. It had an illustration of the assassination of the Archduke and his wife Sophie, Duchess of Hohenberg, front and centre, a dramatic and probably highly unlikely rendering of the shooting. "And yet here we are. Barely days after the event, and we've already received the broadsheets."

"I'm still not entirely sure what the fuss is about," Hensley said. Baxter had heard the same from other officers and the handful of civilians he had encountered. "Obviously it's bad for the Austrians, and one feels for the family, of course. Dashed uncivilised to boot, shooting the Archduchess. No call for that. But as the *Guardian* says, it's hard to see how their murders will have a major impact on world politics. I mean, I assume there may be some local ructions…"

Baxter twitched an eyebrow upwards. "I can't pretend to know much about Balkan politics," he said. He did, in fact, know more than most, having been caught up in the various wars in that part of the world. He wasn't much inclined to tell Hensley his history, though. "I have worked in the area, though, and mark my words, it's an absolute powder keg."

"Well, if anything does come of it, I'm sure it'll be another local war — like the skirmishes that started a couple of years ago," Hensley said. "Nothing for us to worry about, particularly not here at the edge of the world."

Baxter grunted noncommittally.

"No, no — worrying about this won't do at all, old chap," Hensley said firmly. "We have another full day of ensuring sacks of coal are properly counted and accounted for. I'm sure this will be excellent information for your report."

The younger officer's voice was shot through with wry humour. Baxter looked back at the lurid illustration on the frontpage: the almost comical expression they'd given the Archduke and the determined look on the driver's face as he lunged to protect the doomed royals. The report on whether the coaling base could be easily turned back into a full naval base suddenly seemed more pressing than his assigned task.

Baxter folded the newspaper and stood up.

"Where are you going?" Hensley asked.

"I need to send a telegram," Baxter replied. He'd last contacted Saunders, the closest thing he had to a superior officer, not long after he'd arrived in Zanzibar. Although the telegraphy network was entirely controlled by Britain, Saunders didn't want too much going back and forth between them, and in truth there had been little to report. Now, though, was probably the time to see if there were any fresh instructions.

The orders, when they did come, were sufficiently succinct that Baxter was forced to wonder why they had taken more than a week to arrive, even allowing for delays as the dots and dashes made their way along undersea cables and through various overseas post offices, before finally being translated and delivered to his lodgings by a breathlessly enthusiastic Arab boy who was sent on his way with an extra few pennies in his hand.

Proceed as previously instructed.

Baxter scowled, crumpling the sheet of yellow paper in his hand. Then he shrugged. *I've got my orders, and should really get used to following them.* He'd never had an issue with following orders during his last stint in the RN. He'd been drummed out of the service with the threat of a conduct unbecoming charge, not insubordination. His time bouncing between the different wars that had been bubbling away for the last decade had been slightly different, though, with less strict discipline and more risk of disputes being settled through immediate and bloody violence. The ache in his shoulder, mercifully abated now he was in warmer climes, attested to that.

Baxter's reverie was broken by the sound of a creaking floorboard on the landing outside his room. That wasn't unusual, as the building was subdivided into lodgings, all of which were occupied. But there had only been one creak. And that told Baxter that someone had frozen almost immediately outside his door. He imagined the sweating German agent or perhaps Tommy Dunbar, listening intently, wondering if he'd been heard, and deciding what to do next.

Baxter didn't give him the opportunity to decide. He was light on his feet, something that had served him well in the past, and he moved silently across to the door, ears alert.

The *snick* of oiled metal parts working told him what was waiting on the other side of the door. He knew from personal experience that there was no sound quite like a gun being cocked.

Baxter moved fast, wrenching the door open and reaching out. He caught the briefest impression of startled eyes, a mouth opening to shout, as he got both hands on the man —

one on his collar, one on the wrist of his gun hand — and hauled him off his feet and into the room.

The fellow was wiry, but stronger than he looked, and recovered quickly from the surprise of Baxter's ambush. He lashed out with his foot, trying to catch Baxter's knee, but mistimed the blow, the toecap of his boot thudding into his thigh instead.

Baxter grunted with pain, his anger blossoming. He still had a firm grip on his assailant's gun hand, and had the satisfaction of eliciting an agonised cry as he twisted up, forcing the pistol's muzzle away from him and towards the ceiling. The gunman was strong, but not as strong as him, and he kept the pressure up until the attacker was on his knees. Baxter squeezed his wrist until the pistol clattered to the bare floorboards.

"Who the hell are you, and what do you want?" Baxter snarled.

The man said something unintelligible through his gasps of pain, though Baxter thought it sounded like Afrikaans.

"Let my friend go," a new voice said from inside the room. Baxter's head snapped round to see a similarly lean, tanned man pointing a pistol at his head. He'd clearly come in via the window, which stood open to admit the cool sea air.

Baxter gave his assailant's wrist a last squeeze then let go. The man fell forward, gasping and clutching his wrist.

An icy calm washed over him, replacing the hot rage. He took in every detail of the two intruders, from their crumpled suits and battered caps to the well-maintained pistol that remained trained on him.

And the slightest tremor in the hand holding the weapon.

Not enough to do anything with, across the few feet between them.

The second gunman stared at Baxter, his eyes angry and his knuckle white on the trigger. A bead of sweat trickled from his temple down the side of his face.

"Well then," Baxter said. "What now?"

"Now you tell us what you're doing here, Britisher," the gunman said. He had a definite Boer accent, a fact that didn't escape Baxter. "And why you're so interested in Dar es-Salaam."

Baxter smiled at him. "It's a beautiful city," he said. "And I'm here following orders, on a posting from the Admiralty."

"Of course you are." The other man couldn't hide the sarcasm in his voice. "You look like a clerk."

"You realise that, right now, you're probably looking at a few nights sweating in the local gaol," Baxter said conversationally. "Assuming we just call this a case of burglary gone wrong. They hang people for murder."

The smile he got in return was thin. "Perhaps we hate you enough that we don't care," he said, in that odd clipped accent. "Or perhaps we think we can get off this cursed island before we're caught, and you with us."

There were more footsteps on the landing. Baxter tensed to spring. If they had one or more compatriots — and he'd seen no sign of the corpulent man with the Luger from a few days ago — there would be little he could do. But if he was going to act, it had to be...

"If everybody could stay calm," the person approaching the room said. Baxter felt a tightening in his guts. It was a British voice, and one he recognised. "I'm not about to burst in guns blazing, but I think you may want to hear me out."

That thin smile was back. "Well, come ahead, *friend.*"

The man who ducked under the door lintel was tall, though not as tall as Baxter, and while he was running to fat he still carried himself like a prize fighter, with a broken nose and cauliflower ear to prove it. He'd been middle-aged when Baxter had last seen him in 1905, but he had one of those craggy faces that was probably never going to look any older until he was dead.

"Billings," Baxter spat, at the sight of Arbuthnott's henchman. "You look like you've come up in the world. As I recall, I left you unconscious on the bridge of a Japanese auxiliary cruiser."

The former RN petty officer gave him a gap-toothed grin. "That you did, sir, and it was fair enough."

The first intruder had finally managed to recover himself, staggering to his feet and scooping up his pistol to train it on Baxter.

"Both guns pointed at me?" he said, though at this point, Billings was almost certainly more of a threat to him. There was no way his presence here was a coincidence.

Not considering who Baxter had been sent here to run down.

"Yeah, does seem unreasonable," Billings commented. He appeared to have done well for himself. He was dressed in a white linen suit, with a straw boater held in one hand. "How about one of you gents points one of those shooters at me?"

"How about you both shut up?" snapped the man who'd come in via the window. He seemed like the one in charge, or thought he was.

"Why not do something sensible, like put those away and bugger off?" Billings said. The genial bonhomie had disappeared behind the flint-hard mask of a veteran petty officer. "If you hurry back to that hovel you're staying in, you may reach your mate before the local constabulary gets there. Chatty little blighter, that one."

The two Boers exchanged looks, obviously trying to decide whether they should believe this craggy man who seemed utterly unconcerned by the guns being waved around. "Well, go on then," Billings said, as though he was speaking to unruly midshipmen. "Off you trot."

The one who'd come in through the window muttered something in Afrikaans. The one Baxter had tossed around like a ragdoll backed slowly up towards the door, glaring at the two British men. As soon as he was out, his companion slipped after him, and a moment later Baxter heard running feet retreating down the landing.

"Well, that's them seen to for now," Billings said, moving to the door and peering out briefly. Baxter moved quickly to the table next to his bed and pulled out the .38 Smith and Wesson he kept stashed there. He didn't cock it or aim it at Billings, but he felt a lot better with it in his hand.

Billings' bushy eyebrows went up as he turned round and saw the weapon. "Well, no need for that Mr Baxter, sir," he said. "We're all friends here."

"Are we, Billings?" Baxter asked. "I don't recall our last interaction being overly friendly. Or the one before that, come to think of it."

Both times had, in fact, involved violence. The first had been on the pitching deck of a doomed yacht Billings had stranded him on, and the second on a Japanese auxiliary cruiser in the Tsushima Strait.

"That was just business, sir," Billings said carefully. "There was nothing personal to it, and I can promise you that we're on the same side on this one. At least, we will be once you hear me out."

Baxter stared hard at the big man. He sounded sincere, but from previous experience Baxter knew that many petty officers in the RN had a knack for appearing entirely honest in the face of a senior officer or regulators' inquisition.

"All right," he said. He lowered the muzzle of the pistol. "I've already guessed that you're still working for Arbuthnott. So why should I listen to a word you have to say?"

The former petty officer ran his tongue over his lips. He seemed more nervous about Baxter being armed than the two agents they'd seen off. "Well, I imagine you've been told that Mr Arbuthnott has turned proper traitor, sir, and I can see how that view might have some purchase with you, seeing as you've been on the receiving end of his ... plots."

Baxter maintained his level look. "Spit it out, man," he said.

"Well, sir, the truth is that he's not been working with our enemies. I hope you know that I wouldn't have any truck with him if he was, seeing as we used to serve together."

Baxter was running out of patience. "Well, assuming my mission here has anything to do with Arbuthnott, what difference does this make to me?"

Billings seemed slightly taken aback. "Well, sir, the thing is, Mr Arbuthnott has got himself into a bit of a sticky situation. He's in need of a rescue, sir."

Baxter swore under his breath. "From German East Africa?"

"From the very same, sir."

CHAPTER SIX

Baxter felt like he had been dragging his feet for weeks in Zanzibar, trying to find a way to tackle the seemingly impossible task that he'd been given. The package of orders, opened once he was on his way, had boiled down to a simple directive.

Find Arbuthnott, formerly of the Royal Navy's Intelligence Division and now perhaps working for a potentially hostile foreign power. Take him into custody if possible and limit any damage he might be doing.

Now he had to balance that against what Billings had told him. Baxter knew actual world events could appear very differently to the view seen by the Admiralty, thousands of miles away in London. The telegraph cables that now criss-crossed the world, often through the deep oceans, had brought reality closer to the halls of power, along with the more recent arrival of wireless telegraphy. But there was only so much Saunders could realistically know, and Room 39 often worked on the basis of speculation.

"You seem troubled, old chap," Hensley said, appearing in the doorway of the tiny cubbyhole Baxter had been assigned in Admiratly House. It was more of an arched entryway than a doorway, on account of the lack of a door.

"Troubling times, Hensley, troubling times," Baxter replied thoughtfully, then nodded at the sheaf of papers the other officer was holding. "Anything new?"

"Very little," Hensley said, dropping onto a rickety stool that was the only other seating in the stuffy office. "There are rumours that Austria-Hungary is about to mobilise against Serbia — these are from the official dispatches, of course. The

Habsburg Emperor is still insistent that he just wants to see justice done for his son, and most of the papers agree that if war does break out it'll just be in the Balkans."

"There's nothing we can do about what's going on in Europe, except make ready here."

"I've been thinking about that," Hensley said cheerfully. "As far as I understand it, even if there is a war in Europe, everyone's agreed that it would be a dashed bad show to kick off in the colonies as well. Might give the natives the wrong impression."

Baxter snorted. "Wars have a nasty habit of spilling out of control, even when you think it will be a nice quiet local affair," he said. "If this does turn to bloodshed and our government deigns to get involved, we'll be up to our necks in it before you know it."

"Well, jolly good!" Hensley declared, though there was a brittle undercurrent to his tone. "I'd hate to miss all the fun."

Baxter shook his head in despair. He couldn't remember if he'd thought that way when he'd been Hensley's age, but it was a common attitude among younger officers that rarely lasted beyond a first brush with a hostile force.

Hensley seemed oblivious to his disapproval, which suited Baxter fine. He didn't want to have to explain exactly how he knew that there was nothing fun about war.

Baxter sat back, thinking through the latest developments. Things should play out exactly as the newspapers and commentators were predicting. Austria-Hungary would continue to posture, demanding concessions from Serbia. While international opinion seemed to agree that the latter nation was probably responsible for the assassination, the Habsburg Emperor seemed determined to provoke what they no doubt thought would be a limited war.

He sat forward decisively. He could ruminate all he liked about what might happen, but he had to plan for the worst. It didn't even matter if Billings was telling the truth, and Arbuthnott was not in fact a willing guest of the Germans but a prisoner. The only way he could find out and progress with his mission was to go to German East Africa. If Europe did stumble into war, for his purposes it didn't matter if the conflict was kept confined to the old world. Even if the colonial authorities restrained themselves to eyeing each other warily across the artificial borders they'd drawn across the continent, he would no longer be able to come and go from a belligerent colony.

"Off to Dar es-Salaam again?" Hensley asked. His voice had lost its boyish enthusiasm for the potential of conflict and sounded considerably more professional for it. Then he went and spoiled the impression. "Well, having seen *Frau* Masing, I can't really blame you."

Baxter gave him a flat stare. "Take my advice, Hensley, and avoid getting involved with other men's wives — it's been the downfall of better men than you. And yes, I am off to Dar es-Salaam. While I'm gone, keep at the report. I suspect I'm going to need to submit it soon. And perhaps see if you can find that young chap we spotted watching us, down on the docks. I want a word with him when I get back."

"Anything else?" Hensley asked.

"That should be it. Oh, and see if you can keep Parker off my back — I should only be gone for a few days."

Baxter was surprised to see a customs official approaching along the dock as he arrived back in Dar es-Salaam in the closing days of July 1914. He'd made the short journey in his usual conveyance, a fishing boat operated by a local Arab and his three sons. They seemed keen to be away, and no amount of money Baxter offered would tempt them to remain in Dar es-Salaam until he was ready to return.

Aldo, the captain, eyed the officious-looking German. The appearance of a uniformed official had hardened Aldo's determination to be away. "Three days," the fisherman said. "As agreed."

Baxter nodded, but Aldo had already turned away and was murmuring orders to his crew as they prepared to cast off. While the fishermen had shown themselves to be honest and trustworthy, a lot could happen in three days.

Just for a moment, Baxter hesitated. He was launching himself into the unknown, with an uncertain route back out and a brewing international crisis that could make his presence in a German colony most unwelcome. He took a deep breath, filling his nostrils with the smell of fish guts that hung around the fishing boat, and grinned. It wasn't as though he hadn't thrown himself into these situations before.

"Business?" the customs official demanded as he ran up the steps and onto the stone quay.

"Business," Baxter confirmed.

The German tilted his head back imperiously. "What is your business in Dar es-Salaam?" he asked in English. Baxter had briefly toyed with the idea of pretending he wasn't British, or trying to slip ashore somewhere along the coast, but that sort of behaviour couldn't be explained away if he was caught.

"I'm here to see *Herr Doktor* Masing at the European Hospital," he said, matching the brisk business-like tone of the official. "Old injury I'd like him to take a look at."

"You do not have English doctors in Zanzibar?"

"None with Dr Masing's reputation."

That seemed to please the customs official, who nodded firmly, as though this was the answer he had expected. "Welcome to Dar es-Salaam," he said, before turning smartly on his heel and marching away.

Baxter watched the man head back along the quayside. It took him a moment to realise that the port was very quiet indeed. He looked along the length of the harbour, which was normally busy with commercial shipping, and saw there was actually very little going on. One thing, however, did catch his eye — the long, sleek shape of a warship lying much further up the long narrow inlet, where she couldn't be readily observed from the sea. It was almost certainly the SMS *Königsberg*, a protected cruiser on the German equivalent of the RN's East Africa Station. She wasn't a powerful vessel, from what he remembered, but she *was* a power in these waters.

Well, she'll have to go if they want to maintain the pretence of this being an open port, he thought. More to the point, while the harbour was eminently defensible, it would also be absurdly easy to bottle any warships up here.

That was assuming that war even broke out, which was still highly uncertain. Even with modern communications and regular deliveries of newspapers that were only a week old, Baxter felt dangerously out of touch. He knew no more about what was going on than what he read in the broadsheets: that negotiations were under way to resolve the crisis, to bring Serbia to the negotiating table. Most confidently predicted that the long peace that had reigned across the world would not be brutally disrupted because of the actions of a lone gunman in a forgotten corner of Europe.

He'd know more if he was back in Britain, of course, and be better placed to find himself a meaningful posting, rather than undertaking this mad scheme to try to capture a traitor. Or rescue a double agent, if Billings was to be believed.

It was late July, the coldest month of the year in these parts and not unlike the summers of Baxter's youth in Scotland, albeit slightly more humid. This was his fourth visit to Dar es-Salaam, and he found the atmosphere in the sleepy colonial city somewhat changed. When last he visited, there had been plans afoot for a giddy celebratory week to mark the anniversary of the *Schutztruppe* — the local forces — and the connection by rail of the city to Lake Tanganyika, far to the west. Dr Masing had told him excitedly of the plans, which would even include an aerial display, and of the arrival of a merchant ship weighed down with supplies and delicacies. War had seemed a long way away then, but there was little in the way of a festive air now.

Despite the threat, no-one appeared to be overly concerned about the prospect of war. There were a few more uniforms in evidence, both officers of the colonial soldiers and the cruiser in the harbour, but just as in Zanzibar, the atmosphere suggested nobody thought that they would come to blows.

Baxter stayed alert as he made his way through Dar es-Salaam to the northern coast, where they'd built the European Hospital to take advantage of the cool sea breeze. It was a whitewashed two-storey building which had, according to Dr Masing, many of the advancements you would normally expect to see in a modern hospital on the continent. Baxter had little idea what that meant — the last doctor he'd seen had been a

Greek man with shaking hands on a sweltering island in the Aegean.

"I have to say, I am surprised to see you here, Mr Baxter," Dr Masing said cheerfully as he ushered Baxter into his office.

"Or indeed at all?" Baxter said as they shook hands. The German doctor gestured him to a chair in the light, airy room.

"You are referring to the tensions on the continent?" The doctor waved a dismissive hand. "It will come to nothing."

"You sound very sure of this," Baxter said.

"You are as bad as my darling Esca. She is certain, of course, that your government wishes to provoke a war in order to demonstrate the effectiveness of your Navy over ... well, everyone else's." A smile took the sting out of his words. "Even if there is some tension, there is no reason why we colonists cannot remain friends. The people here probably have more in common with those in your English colonies than they do with the Prussians who rule us. Now, enough of this talk of politics — what is it I can do for you, Mr Baxter?"

"I took a bullet, about two years ago. A thirty-two, to be precise, in my right shoulder. Never got it out, and it causes me some problems."

"I see," Masing said, slightly disconcerted. "It aches when it is cold and damp, I imagine?"

"Got it in one — though it's not been so bad here."

Of course, while it would be good to get the bullet out of his shoulder, it wasn't his reason for visiting Dr Masing, just a useful pretext. Baxter's mind flashed back to January, when London had been in the grip of a particularly bitter winter. He'd been down on his luck, out of funds and about to give up on any hope of getting back into the RN. So when Saunders had offered him this job, he'd taken it, keen to get back into the service. He was starting to feel that it had, in fact, been a mistake.

"I find it odd that you know the size of the bullet. Tell me, would you say it is a, ah, large one?"

It took Baxter a moment to realise what Masing was asking, and he laughed. "Not really, *Herr Doktor*, though just between you and me, when you're shot at close range the calibre of the round doesn't make that much of a difference." His ruminations on London were replaced by a memory of Connie, her dark eyes intense over the sights of the small revolver just before she'd shot him. Mostly to save his life. "And I know the calibre because the woman who shot me told me afterwards."

Masing blinked behind his round glasses. "I must confess I have never dealt with a gunshot wound before, but I imagine it is not unlike a kick from a particularly angry mule."

"You deal with a lot of those?" Baxter asked.

"More than you would think; in fact, the last case I saw was exactly that injury. Aside from that, my work mostly revolves around diseases both tropical and…" He coughed, looking suddenly embarrassed. "Well, one might say private in nature."

Baxter laughed. "I've been a sailor damn near all my life, Doctor — you don't need to worry about offending my sensibilities."

Masing smiled as well, though Baxter thought he seemed more embarrassed than he should for a doctor. Perhaps Masing had moved in more refined circles and was finding colonial life more robust than he'd been expecting.

That would make him somewhat more naïve than Baxter was expecting, and he suspected the real decision maker had in fact been Esca.

"Well, anyway," Masing went on brightly, recovering his composure. "At the very least I can have a look and see if there is anything modern surgery can do. Remove your shirt, if you please."

Baxter left Dr Masing's office with a slightly more painful shoulder than when he had arrived. For all that the doctor had an amiable manner, in a professional context he was business-like. His grip as he'd probed and prodded the offending area had certainly been a lot stronger than Baxter had expected. The doctor had sent him on his way with instructions to come back tomorrow once he'd consulted his books and, perhaps, some of his colleagues.

He followed an orderly through the cool corridors of the hospital. It was whitewashed and smelled strongly of bleach. Baxter could hear murmured conversations and, somewhere close by, someone lost in a deep delirium, moaning and muttering to himself. His shoes sounded painfully loud in the hush, particularly compared to the almost silent tread of the orderly.

Baxter paused briefly at the end of a small side corridor. A uniformed man was stationed outside a door, armed with both a holstered revolver and a sabre. "Someone dangerous being kept under lock and key?" he asked his escort. He kept his tone light, not wanting to give any sign of particular interest in the sealed ward.

The fellow shrugged. "Criminal," he said. "Or a lunatic. One or the other."

The guard sat in a somewhat rickety-looking chair with an unlit pipe clamped between his lips. That suggested he'd been there a little while and the novelty of his duty had worn off. Baxter also thought it probably meant he wasn't relieved that often or even inspected by an officer.

"Your English is excellent," he told the orderly. *Never hurts to keep on good terms with the lower decks,* an old mentor had told him.

The same shrug, but a slight smile. "I worked as a waiter, in London," he said. "And then again in Zanzibar, before I got a job here."

Baxter nodded. The interconnectedness of Europe made even the threat of war seem absurd. Everyone from the royal families down was in some way related to or knew the countries that even now eyed each other suspiciously across contested borders or the cold grey water.

"This way, if you please, sir," the orderly said, gesturing him onwards. Not wanting to attract any suspicion, Baxter started walking again and didn't risk any more questions.

Tonight, he knew, he would have to risk a lot more than suspicion.

CHAPTER SEVEN

The streets were quiet, but not completely deserted, when Baxter left his hotel that night. He'd spent the day as he normally would and made no attempt to sneak away from his lodging. If asked, he'd decided to appear as a British eccentric taking a nighttime constitutional.

There were still merchant sailors in town, not to mention soldiers and what appeared to be men in from the *veldt*, determined to extract as much of a good time as possible before they left. Baxter didn't have any trouble with them, and once he was as certain as he could be that he wasn't under observation he quickened his pace and walked with more purpose. He retraced his steps from earlier in the day, back towards the hospital.

The streets emptied out as he neared his objective. He was well away from the residential areas and their attendant pleasures now, with less of an excuse to be here. On the plus side, it would make it easier for him to spot any tails.

He paused at the edge of the hospital's grounds. There was no perimeter wall to speak of or a fence, and why would there be? The colony was secure, and any rebellions were hundreds of miles away in the deep country. Baxter forced himself to breathe easily as he carefully examined the hospital and its grounds, looking out for any guards. Under normal circumstances, he knew, there wouldn't be any. But there was an armed guard inside, which suggested they might take further precautions.

It was time to make a decision. He had no reason to suppose that it was Arbuthnott under guard inside the hospital, beyond the intelligence he'd received from Billings. The former petty officer hadn't given Baxter any reason at all to trust him and had turned down the opportunity to accompany him.

"I'm a known face amongst the Germans, so to speak, so it's probably best that you're not seen with me," the fellow had said when pressed on it.

But there had been the guard on what appeared to be a private room, and from what Billings had said Arbuthnott wasn't in the best of health. Baxter knew he should feel a pang of guilt about his own part in that, given that he'd shattered one of the rogue agent's legs by dropping him from the bridge of a Japanese auxiliary cruiser. He'd also shot him in the other knee in Odessa. He didn't feel guilty, though. Arbuthnott's machinations had almost got him killed on at least two occasions, and endangered people he'd come to care about.

Nothing else for it. One way or the other, he had to know if his target was in custody here or whether he was a guest of the German authorities. He stepped out of the deep shadows under a palm tree and walked quickly across the ground toward the hospital. It wasn't completely open, with low bushes and more palms here and there. He didn't dash from cover to cover, as that would have looked more than a little suspicious, but he took a path that kept what vegetation there was between him and the building as much as possible.

The night was quiet, with just the rustle of the wind in the trees and the rumble of surf not so very far from him, underpinned by the ever-present whine of insects. Being close to the sea was strangely comforting, even though it would offer no escape for him unless there happened to be a boat tied up at the jetty on the ocean-side of the hospital.

Baxter paused as he got closer, leaning against the broad trunk of a massive tree. He crouched, staring hard at the building, noting where there were lights showing through the shutters. He had no sensible explanation for his presence. His only defence, therefore, would be to avoid detection. That probably meant going up the side of the building and in through a window; no great struggle for a man who'd grown up on sailing vessels.

But which window? He closed his eyes, trying to match what he'd seen of the building's interior with the whitewashed exterior so he could determine the likely location of the guarded room. Since he hadn't been able to hear the Indian Ocean from the corridor outside the guarded room, he'd already guessed that it was on the landward side of the building.

He opened his eyes again. There was a large window on the second floor, one he was pretty sure gave onto the landing near his objective.

Baxter tensed himself to move, feeling his heart starting to thump harder in his chest. He'd done his fair share of creeping around on shore, usually at night, during the late war between Italy and the Ottoman Empire, and before that in Odessa. It always felt far more immediate, more personal, and a revolver would make him just as dead as a hit from a battleship's main guns.

As he slid out from the cover of the massive tree, a flicker of movement in the corner of his eye stilled him. Baxter pressed himself back against the rough bark of the tree, sweeping the area in case he'd missed a guard, or maybe just a patient or member of staff out for a walk.

It wasn't entirely dark here; a crescent moon and the stars were bright in a clear sky, and light spilled out from the windows and doorways of the hospital. Baxter knew from experience at sea that these sorts of half-light conditions could be as difficult as full darkness. Where a pitch-black night would hide possible threats and targets, half-light played tricks on the eye.

Not a trick of the eye this time. His gaze found the movement, a figure — no, two — darting across the lawn towards the hospital. They weren't aiming for the same spot he'd been about to go for, but clearly intended to scale the wall and go in through a different window. They were close enough that if Baxter had moved a minute earlier, he would have been the one under observation.

The sensible thing now would be to retire from the scene, given there were clearly others with an interest in the same man. It seemed unlikely that someone would be trying to break into the same hospital for a different reason. Even if this was completely unrelated, someone else blundering around the hospital increased his own chances of being caught.

Baxter had a good notion of who else might be after his quarry, and why.

Instead of listening to the voice of reason, telling him to avoid this lee shore, he stole forward. He crouched behind a bush about five yards from the two men who had reached the wall and were busy preparing a grappling iron, feeling a growing annoyance with them. Not only were they getting in the way of his own investigation, they appeared to be making a hash of it. The grapnel was utterly unnecessary given the nature of the climb, and would make altogether too much noise.

Best put a stop to this caper before we all get caught. He started to move forward but was brought up short again, this time by the snick of a pistol's hammer being drawn back behind him.

He froze in an uncomfortable half-crouch, not turning or raising his hands. He knew without needing to turn who it was behind him. "Hullo, Tommy," he said quietly.

"*Dobryy vecher*, Marcus Alexandrovich."

The voice was the same, just a bit deeper, and the Russian was unaccented.

"Have you forgotten how to speak English, Tommy?"

"I have not, Mr Baxter, and it is Tomas." A slight pause. "Have you forgotten your Russian?"

Baxter didn't rise to that. He shifted round to face the young man, taking a knee to keep his head low. Tommy Dunbar was pointing a Nagant revolver at his head. It was a weapon Baxter had become very familiar with during his time with the Second Pacific Squadron, and he knew how heavy it was. The muzzle was unwavering, though.

Baxter realised that his fleeting impression that the boy hadn't changed that much was far off the mark, now that he saw the young man up close. He remembered a slightly freckly, sandy-haired youth who had just been entering his gangly years. Baxter was now confronted with a lean young man, perhaps a touch shorter than he might have expected, who wore a neatly-trimmed goatee and moustache and small round spectacles.

It was the eyes, more than anything, that showed the difference. Tommy Dunbar had been an exuberant, excitable boy, much given to mischief. Tomas had a serious face and hard eyes. He wondered what had happened to him in the intervening years, though given Ekaterina Juneau had apparently put him to work he could guess at some of it.

"My Russian is a bit rusty," he admitted. "Can't even remember enough to tell you that if you don't stop pointing that gun at me, I'm going to take it away from you and smack you around the head with it."

Baxter wasn't quite sure what response he expected. Fortunately, Tomas just smiled and raised the muzzle, lowering the revolver's hammer carefully. "You are here for Arbuthnott?" he asked.

Baxter desperately wanted to know what the other two Russians were up to but couldn't risk a glance over his shoulder. He kept his eyes on Tomas and nodded. "Though I'm surprised you … Ekaterina, that is … haven't already caught up with him."

He wasn't quite sure why he'd stumbled over that name. It was all ancient history, even though he still kept the unopened letter from her that Koenig had delivered to him in Vladivostok, not long after they'd finally made it to the far side of the world.

Tomas shrugged slightly, a studiedly nonchalant gesture. "We have had other business," he said. His English had lost its glottal Scottish accent, which didn't surprise Baxter; Tomas been living amongst Russians for close to a decade. "And he is a slippery character to pin down."

Baxter wanted to ask how he knew for sure that Arbuthnott was here, and if so, how did he come to have that information? And the really burning question — was Ekaterina somewhere in Dar es-Salaam? There was no time for any questions now, though. Not with Tommy's compatriots about to make a mess of breaking into the hospital.

"What's your intention here?" Baxter asked instead. "I assume you're not here to murder the man?" He wouldn't necessarily put it past Ekaterina to shoot a man in cold blood, but he would be surprised if Tommy — even if he was now Tomas — would.

But then, a lot can change in just a few years.

Tomas shook his head quickly. "I'm to capture him and bring him back to Russia for a long overdue, fair trial," he said.

Baxter suppressed the urge to snort derisively — Imperial Russian courts were not exactly famous for their fairness. "You seem to be in a bit of a rush to do it," he said.

Tomas glanced away briefly, his expression becoming guarded. "It is perhaps likely that we will not be welcome here for too much longer," he said at last, indicating that his thoughts matched Baxter's own impressions of the situation in East Africa. "The last message we had from … the countess, is that the Empire may be about to mobilise."

The 'Empire' could refer to any number of potential combatants, of course, but Baxter suspected that Tomas meant the Russian Empire. He'd also given away, without Baxter having to ask, that Ekaterina wasn't here in East Africa. He felt a stab of disappointment but suppressed it quickly.

"You are here to capture him as well?" Tomas asked, glancing over Baxter's shoulder then muttering something in Russian under his breath. Baxter remembered enough of the language to know he was cursing the two men breaking into the hospital.

"In all honesty, Tomas, I didn't know for sure he was here." He didn't want to lie to the young man, not directly anyway. Baxter knew he was a bad liar, and Tommy had always had a nose for falsehood.

"Perhaps we can work together, *da*? Like in Odessa. Justice is justice, whether it is meted out in London or St. Petersburg, and we are all allies now."

Baxter mulled that over. He'd be happier working with the Russians, even if they weren't an official arm of the Russian government, rather than having them constantly getting underfoot. There *might* be a conflict of interest if it turned out that Arbuthnott hadn't turned traitor, but he'd deal with that if it ever came up. "Well, given how much of a mess your lads are making, it's probably safer if we work together."

That earned him a poisonous look. "I would be doing it myself if you hadn't been crashing around out here," he snapped. "But yes, we should go and…"

Before either of them could move, though, there was a resounding crash from the direction of the hospital. Baxter whipped round to see the rope dangling from the balcony Tomas's compatriots had been trying to get in through. A second later, lights came on throughout the building and raised voices were heard. There came another crash, then the sound of a pistol shot.

"How close are you to those two?" Baxter asked, indicating the two men.

Tomas sniffed dismissively. "Local hires, and not competent either. They know nothing."

"Then I suggest we get out of here."

The young man nodded. "I concur."

As they turned to go, something occurred to Baxter. "Your local hires, they're not South Africans are they? Boers?"

"*Nyet.* Both German, in fact, petty criminals who thought we were just breaking and entering."

"Find better help next time," Baxter muttered, as they jogged into the safety of the night.

"Now we are working together, I think I have."

It felt a little odd, sitting in his hotel room in Dar es-Salaam drinking schnapps with Tommy Dunbar, not far from the German Club where he knew that not only would Dr Masing be drinking but probably also a range of officers from the

German colonial forces, navy and constabulary.

"It is not vodka, but it'll do," the younger man said, crossing his legs and staring intently at Baxter. "You are prospering, Mr Baxter?"

Baxter leant against the wall next to the door, unsure what to make of the situation. The last time he'd seen Tommy, he wouldn't have been allowed anywhere near hard spirits. Now he was quite comfortably sipping a glass of German brandy and complaining it wasn't what he was used to.

"I'll take a decent rum or gin over either. Or a Scotch for that matter. And yes, I'm well."

"Back working for the British government?"

Baxter felt his brow furrow into a scowl. He wasn't sure he liked these probing questions. "What about you, Tomas?" he asked instead. "Working for the Okhrana, or whatever the Russian secret police is calling itself now?"

Tomas looked annoyed by the question. "No, of course not," he said scornfully. "We work for a number of clients, including the Tsar. The government finds the services that we provide most excellent for certain discreet tasks that need undertaking, but then, so do any number of *boyars* and the wealthy."

That matched what Koenig had told Baxter when he had run into him during the Italo-Ottoman unpleasantness. Tomas was looking at him expectantly. Baxter briefly considered saying nothing further, but he knew that if he wanted any sort of co-operation with the Russians then he would need to be at least a little forthcoming. And he needed that co-operation if for no other reason than to keep them from getting underfoot.

"To answer your question, yes, I'm back in the Royal Navy. That's why I'm after Arbuthnott."

That seemed to please Tomas inordinately, and just for a second there was the hint of the old Tommy in his beaming expression. Then he mastered himself, and returned to the quietly watchful young man he seemed to have become. "For us, it is … personal."

Baxter nodded. "Well, I may be here on orders, but that doesn't mean I'm not going to enjoy bringing that bastard in."

A silence fell between them. Not strained as such, but Tomas seemed to have developed a capacity for patience that Baxter knew would become galling after a while. "So," he said at last. "How do you want to tackle getting Arbuthnott out of that hospital?"

There was the slightest flicker of uncertainty in the young man's eyes, perhaps surprise that he had even been consulted. That was one of the reasons Baxter had asked the question in the first place — he knew Tomas would be expecting him to think their relationship hadn't changed in the years since they'd last seen each other.

Not that Tommy had ever done as he'd been asked, even back then.

"I had hoped … you might have an idea?" Tomas said finally.

Baxter took a swallow of the fiery schnapps — rough, even by the standards he'd come to expect of the drink. "Well, they will probably have guessed by now that *someone* is trying to get to him, so they're either going to move him or increase the guard."

"Well, as I said, my two employees didn't really know what we were doing…"

"Never assume your opponent is stupid, lad, unless he's shown himself to be. Whoever's running the operation here hasn't done that yet."

"So we must assume that the opposition will work out what we're doing," Tomas agreed. He opened his mouth to say more, then closed it again when they heard the rumble of running boots coming up the street.

"That doesn't sound promising," Baxter murmured, moving to the window. "Turn the light down, would you?"

He waited a moment after Tomas had turned down the gas lamp, allowing his eyes to adjust to the gloom before twitching the curtain open slightly. Just in time to see what looked like a full platoon of *Schutztruppe* double-timing past the hotel, Mauser rifles in hand. "That seems a bit excessive for someone trying to break into the hospital," Tommy murmured, craning his neck to look round Baxter's shoulder.

"They take that sort of thing quite seriously here, I think," he replied, "having dealt with quite bloody rebellions. But you're right, it does seem a bit over the top. Wonder if there's something else going on?"

"When is there never *something* going on?"

The troops — native *askari* under the command of German officers and NCOs — were splitting up by sections and fanning out into the surrounding buildings. Five men under the command of a burly corporal made their way up the steps to the hotel.

"Do you think they could be here for us?" Tomas asked.

"It would be a little heavy-handed to arrest every foreign national just because someone tried to break into the hospital, even for German authorities. Particularly if the men actually caught were locals."

Tomas made an unconvinced noise. "It may have nothing to do with the break-in at all," he said. "It may be because we are foreign nationals — the wrong sort of foreign nationals."

That decided Baxter. It could be an exercise in rounding up anyone who looked suspicious after an attempted break-in. And, though he didn't say it, Tomas Dunbar did look somewhat suspicious.

"Where are you staying? And do you have anything you care about leaving behind?"

"Down by the docks, in the native quarter," Tomas replied. "And yes, there are one or two things that it would be inconvenient to leave behind."

Baxter heard the door to the hotel bang open. There were raised voices speaking German, which he couldn't make out.

"They are looking for Russians," Tomas said. When Baxter glanced at him with a raised eyebrow, he said, "I am twenty years younger than you, my friend, and have not been around naval guns being fired as much as you have. You sent me below at Tsushima, if you recall."

"I'm beginning to regret that," Baxter said, not unkindly. "And it can't be more than fifteen years between us. Your friends at the hospital could have blabbed about your nationality."

There was another gale of shouting, louder this time, and the sound of boots on the stairs. "Only Russians," Tomas said bleakly, tilting his head. "Something about 'enemies'."

"Time for you to go," Baxter said firmly, unlatching the window. "If I were you, I'd leave German East Africa. You know where to find me on Zanzibar."

He wanted to say more, give Tomas advice on how to get out, what to do, what to avoid. But he guessed that wouldn't go down well — the lad he remembered had grown into a capable young man, and probably knew more about such matters than he did.

"You should come with me," Tomas said. "The hotel staff may have told them I came up here with you."

"Hell mend them if they try to take me," Baxter said, his tone growing dark. "Old Nosy back in Stone Town may not like me, but he won't stand for an RN officer being imprisoned without cause, and it won't take long for the Resident to get involved. Now go!"

Tomas needed no further encouragement, and nor had he forgotten any of the skills picked up at sea. He went out of the window without fear or hesitation. They were on the second floor, high enough that a fall would be dangerous but nowhere near the heights Tommy had used to skylark in the *Yaroslavich*'s auxiliary rigging. With a scrabble of shoes he managed to get up onto the building's flat roof and disappeared into the darkness.

Baxter quickly closed the window as he heard boots on the landing outside his door. There was nothing more he could do for Tomas now; he just had to trust that the lad knew what he was about. A loud hammering on the door distracted him from his concerns.

He was confronted by a short, barrel-chested German in a *Schutztruppe* uniform. Ginger whiskers bristled at Baxter. He knew the fellow, or at least the type: an officious little man who'd been given a uniform and the slightest bit of power, which made him think he was far more important than he was.

He did have a pistol on his hip, though, and two African soldiers behind him with rifles held across their chests. Baxter looked at their impassive faces, and again wondered what the locals here thought of the doings of the white men who'd seized power here.

"Papers!" the German snapped. Baxter guessed he was a corporal from his insignia.

"May I ask why I've been disturbed?" Baxter asked, instead of producing his documentation. He didn't want to cause too much of a scene here or provoke the non-commissioned officer, even if his instinct was to kick him down the stairs. The longer he kept them occupied, though, the more time Tomas would have to get clear.

"Papers!" the German snapped again, thrusting out his left hand and dropping the right to the automatic pistol on his belt. Baxter felt a trickle of sweat down his back. While he was confident that the Germans would have no reason to detain him and wouldn't want to provoke an incident with the British authorities in Zanzibar, these men appeared as though they meant business.

"Of course." Baxter fetched his documents from the small bag that he kept packed at all times and handed them over.

"*Englander?*" the German enquired, shooting him a suspicious glance. Baxter repressed the urge to correct him, and merely nodded.

"Any Russians?" the man snapped. "Have you seen any?"

"I don't think I've seen a Russian in a couple of years," Baxter replied, adopting the somewhat officious tone he'd heard from men like Parker altogether too often. At least that was the truth, albeit only if the question was very literally interpreted. Tomas very much appeared more Russian than Scottish. "Now look here, what is this all about?"

The tone seemed to have the desired effect. "*Russisch* are now enemy nationals," the soldier said stiffly. "The *Reich* is now at war with the Russian Empire."

CHAPTER EIGHT

The war, of course, was a very long way from German East Africa, and while rumours abounded, there was no concrete news. It seemed Austria-Hungary had declared against Serbia, no doubt hoping to keep it a conflict limited to the Balkans. That plan had clearly failed. Aside from the area around the Danube, Baxter didn't know much about the vast land that the two great empires were going to fight each other over.

It was, for the most part, of very little importance or interest to the local people. The German colonists might find themselves called back to serve, but only if the conflict lasted more than a few months or a year. To the majority of the Kaiser's subjects, it was a white man's conflict and excited little passion. There had been an attempt to round up any Russians in the colony, though Baxter had been relieved to hear that none had in fact been found. Life, it seemed, was determined to continue at its sedate pace.

"This is the consensus," Dr Masing said unhappily. They'd met in the light, airy breakfast room of the hotel. Although the Masings had found more permanent lodgings elsewhere, the doctor had been waiting for Baxter when he'd come down. He had a nervous air about him. "Though there is some talk that the Russian navy might raid us."

Baxter snorted derisively. "Unlikely — they'd either have to come from Vladivostok or all the way down from the Baltic, and the Russians don't have the best track record with that sort of long-distance operation."

Masing blinked myopically at him. "Well, I trust you are right, and moreover that more sensible heads prevail in Russia.

They should leave this matter to the Austrians, as should the French and your own government. Then we can all remain friends."

Baxter watched Masing fidget uncomfortably, picking up and putting down his now-cold cup of coffee. He didn't offer an opinion on who was responsible for the escalating conflict. He knew a little about the last time the Russian Empire had gone to war, as he'd found himself caught up in the middle of it. The fact the Tsar had been encouraged by his cousin, Kaiser Willhelm, to provoke war with Japan suggested that there wasn't a wise head in Berlin either.

"I'll drink to that," Baxter said, raising his own coffee cup.

"I thought your military gentlemen were not so averse to conflict? What is it you say, something about sickly wars..."

"A bloody war or a sickly season," Baxter supplied with a smile. "It's a toast often heard in the wardroom, as either offer a route to promotion. I doubt there are many who have seen action who would subscribe to the notion, though. But if it comes, well..."

"Let us hope not," Masing said unhappily.

"And what is *Frau* Masing's take on this?"

That earned a wan smile. "Oh, my lady wife is looking forward to the *Schutztruppe* sweeping down to South Africa to liberate her people."

Baxter felt his mood start to sober, and decided a change of subject was in order. "Is something amiss at the hospital?" he asked. "I had expected to see you there as agreed. Eleven, I believe."

"There was a break-in at the hospital last night, or at least an attempted one," Masing said, and Baxter realised from the discreet wording that this was a rehearsed speech. "The local police have therefore decided that only staff are to be allowed in and out for now, until the culprits have been caught."

"I trust no one was hurt?" Baxter asked.

"One of the men who broke in was killed," Masing said. "The other was caught. As you can imagine, it has caused a great amount of distress amongst both staff and patients."

"So the culprits are no longer at large?"

"The two who entered are not, of course, and I imagine the one who lived will hang in due course. I understand, though, that the belief is that they were not acting alone."

"You seem remarkably well informed, Doctor," Baxter said evenly.

Masing flushed slightly. "My wife is a confidante of the Resident's daughter. We also see Captain Schiller not infrequently."

Baxter had a sudden flash of intuition. "Doctor, if there's something on your mind, I suggest you spit it out before it gives you a heart attack."

Masing looked so uncomfortable that Baxter started to feel genuinely sorry for him. "Well, *Herr* Baxter, *mein Freund*, there are questions being asked about all foreigners currently in Dar es-Salaam. My wife in particular suspects all British people of being up to no good, and she is … forceful enough that many will listen to her."

Baxter found himself wondering about this match between Masing and his wife. The doctor seemed like a decent man, obviously skilled at his job, if a little naïve. Esca Masing was a striking woman who drew attention as much through her poise and manner as her looks. But then, from what Masing had said, she'd been a penniless exile when they'd met.

"Doctor, you should have realised this by now," Baxter said. "A British man abroad is never a foreigner. He is merely *abroad*."

Masing laughed, a surprisingly light sound for a man already running to corpulence. "Indeed, I have heard similar said about my countrymen." The laughter died. "But, in all seriousness…"

Baxter smiled to show he didn't take any offence. "I can assure you, Doctor, that I wasn't involved in last night's incident." He didn't want to lie to Masing, who he'd come to regard as a friend, and while it technically wasn't a lie, he didn't like to skirt that close to one. "Can I assume, then, that we must cancel today's appointment?"

Masing welcomed the change of topic. "Alas, with the situation at the hospital, even if we were able to identify an approach to your problem, I do not think now would be the right time to undertake surgery."

Baxter nodded. He had not had any real intention of going under the knife, either here or on Zanzibar. He knew how long recovery took, and he had no desire to be out of action if there was the opportunity to achieve his mission. He had hoped to gain admittance to the hospital again, though, with a view to reaching Arbuthnott.

Masing broke into his thoughts. "How long are you planning on remaining here, *Herr* Baxter?" he asked.

"I should probably get back to Zanzibar soon," he replied, not wanting to commit to anything; his arranged pick-up wasn't for another day. Not that he thought Masing was fishing for information, but he was the sort of man who would tell his wife everything. "I have duties to discharge."

"While I hope you understand that under normal circumstances I would be more than happy to treat your infirmity, I think it might be best if you did return as soon as possible. To avoid any … unpleasantness."

"I understand entirely, Doctor, and I do indeed feel the tug of duty as we speak."

"Speaking of which, it is almost time for my rounds." Masing drained his cup, and the two men rose at the same time. The doctor offered his hand. "Well, *Herr* Baxter, I hope to see you again, when we both have more time."

Baxter took the proffered hand and shook it firmly. "A sentiment we can all agree with," he said.

Once Masing was on his way, Baxter headed back up to his room with a sense of urgency that he didn't allow to show in his movements. There was something about the interaction that had put him on edge. Even if the German had not deliberately given anything away — and there was no reason for Baxter to expect him to — he couldn't escape the impression that he was concerned that something was going to happen. And soon.

Baxter went to the window of his room and peered out. The *Schutztruppe* were still on patrol, as well as men from the local police. It was probably more activity than this quiet little colonial town had seen in some time, and it had brought the local residents out. Not only that, he realised, but the same sort of shady character who'd been watching him in Zanzibar. He may have convinced Masing that he was no threat, but clearly someone else believed he was.

Time to go. He hadn't unpacked his bag, and as always travelled light. He didn't want to give the impression he was checking out of the hotel, so most of what he'd brought would have to be left in his room. He took his papers and extra money. He hadn't brought the revolver, and briefly regretted it.

Baxter checked his appearance in the mirror which hung over an ornate, old-fashioned wash basin. More presentable than usual, close to the expected image of a British man abroad. He grinned at that, and briefly wondered if he was on the verge of making a complete hash of things.

Well, too late to worry about that now. Whether or not he was out of his depth, he was where he was.

The heat hit him like a wall as he stepped out onto the street. "Good morning, *Herr* Baxter," the old porter greeted him, starting to pull himself up from the wicker chair he occupied on the veranda. Baxter waved him back down, then took off his straw hat to fan his face.

"Hot today," he said, which got a chuckle in response.

"This is the cool season," the old man said from the comfort of his repose. Baxter was surprised he got away with sitting down while on duty, even here — the management of such establishments prided themselves on maintaining European standards. The porter — Otto, he thought the man's name was — seemed to have something of a sixth sense for when the manager was in the vicinity, however, or when guests at the hotel were likely to cause him trouble. "You should come back around Christmas."

"Well, if I'm still in this part of the world come December, I'll be sure to drop in," Baxter said, although he dearly hoped to be reinstated to the regular service and on a posting somewhere cooler by then.

"Are you with us for long, *mein Herr?*" Otto asked.

Baxter shook his head. "Another night and then, alas, back to my duties."

Otto smiled, then slowly drew himself up from the chair. He grumbled something in German about never being *off* duty just as the hotel manager hove into view, marching briskly down the street towards the hotel. *Herr* Ritter had black hair oiled to one side and a thin moustache.

Ritter also appeared to have a couple of rough-looking individuals trailing after him, cut from the same cloth as the Boers who'd dogged Baxter in Zanzibar. It was probably nothing, but given he didn't much want to get caught up in further conversation anyway, Baxter turned and headed towards the harbour while they were still several yards away.

He avoided the appearance of hurrying, merely lengthening his stride slightly. He heard Ritter call something out that might have been *"Herr* Baxter!" but feigned not having heard him, and started whistling jauntily as he increased his pace.

He didn't glance over his shoulder, but the prickling sensation that ran up his neck told him the two men following Ritter had sped up as well. There wasn't the sound of running feet, so he guessed they didn't want to make a scene right here in the middle of the street.

That meant they weren't about official business, otherwise they'd involve the *Schutztruppe* still in evidence on the pavements.

Baxter turned sharply between two white-stuccoed buildings, so intent on keeping ahead of those men that he almost ran directly into Esca Masing. He managed to sidestep her, and only realised it was *Frau* Masing when she turned deftly and took his arm. *"Herr* Baxter," she said, her voice icily polite. "Just the man I have been looking for. Walk with me."

Baxter didn't quite know how to extricate himself without making a scene. They fell into step, though he had no intention of going very far with her.

"Good morning, *Frau* Masing," he said evenly, not giving her the satisfaction of seeing him glance over his shoulder as he heard the two men coming up behind him. He suspected they were in her employ, a suspicion confirmed when she glanced back and tilted her head very slightly to them. "I trust the day finds you well?"

She glanced sharply at him, obviously trying to decide if he knew what was happening and was brazening it out, or whether he was just an idiot British man abroad.

"We shall speak plainly, I think, Mr Baxter," she said, obviously deciding it was the former. "Contrary to how you have presented yourself, I think you are a man of many parts. And you are up to no good, as I believe you British might say."

"Very well, though 'no good' does depend a lot on your perspective."

That earned him a thin, humourless smile. "I am glad you do me the courtesy of not lying further."

"I doubt it would do me much good."

They were walking further away from the main street, between the large airy buildings of the European quarter. Baxter suspected that Esca was steering him towards the commercial district. It would be quieter, with fewer people to take note of them — at least, people who mattered in her mind. Baxter suppressed a smile. He knew he was in danger, but Esca and her cohorts had perhaps underestimated the danger they were putting themselves in.

"You are not a bad liar, Baxter, but I am good at telling liars from honest men. Most of the men here, they are honest in their way. Too honest to suspect you of being a spy, or to do anything about it if they did."

Baxter nodded. That confirmed his suspicion that she was operating on her own, no doubt drawing on private resources. Or perhaps with elements of German officialdom, he thought, remembering Captain Schiller's obvious interest in her.

"This does not surprise you?" she asked, when he made no response.

"Not at all. I've been around long enough that very little surprises me. And you're not the first woman I've met who does this sort of work."

Esca's expression remained neutral. Perhaps she was aware of Ekaterina Juneau and her interest in Arbuthnott. He didn't think there were many women involved in this sort of business, though probably more than his superiors in London might think. Baxter decided to try a different tack.

"What's your plan?" he asked.

Esca glanced sharply at him, taken aback by his directness. "Well, I think it should be clear. I have two rough men at my call, and we will go somewhere quiet to ascertain what it is you are planning."

"Do you think two men will be enough?" he asked.

"I am also armed, of course," she said coldly. "And I have more men nearby."

He was fairly sure that was a lie. Her resources could not be unlimited, any more than his were.

Baxter stopped, and detached her arm from his.

"You would do well to come along quietly," she said. "We are not barbarians. No harm will befall you…"

Her voice trailed off as he struck. There was only one place she was likely to have a gun, the small practical bag slung over her shoulder. He snagged the strap and pulled it away from her, knocking her off balance. He didn't bother rummaging around for the weapon, but instead threw the bag as far away as possible as he turned to deal with the other two threats.

He went for the one on the right first. He'd reacted faster to the surprise, which meant he was probably the more dangerous of the two men. Baxter's toecap went into his crotch just as he was dropping his hand to the revolver in his belt, the kick landing hard enough to lift him off his feet and then deposit him in a crumpled heap, in too much pain to do anything but gulp air and whimper. Baxter struck the second man with a backhanded blow to his temple, bouncing his head off the neighbouring building and dropping him like a poleaxed ox.

Turning to run in the direction they'd been going, Baxter realised he'd made a miscalculation. Esca may not have had more men nearby, but she did in fact have one. He was a tall man, lean, the skin of his face dark but not weatherbeaten or scarred. He held a long hunting knife with a casualness that spoke volumes about his ability to use it.

Baxter backed up, keeping some distance between them. His opponent came forward without hurry, assessing him with predatory eyes, weighing him up. He was clearly a man who enjoyed his work.

Esca eased away from Baxter and behind the knifeman, her eyes darting as she tried to see where her bag had landed. She didn't look scared, more angry that the situation had spun out of her control.

Esca's voice was triumphant as she spoke from safety. "I am afraid I cannot promise no harm will come to you now, Baxter. Not now that Henrik has smelt blood."

He glanced left and right, assessing their surroundings. They were in a narrow alley that restricted Henrik's ability to circle him. Even so, he wasn't sure if he'd be able to deal with his opponent, and even if he won the fight he'd be badly cut up doing it. His prodigious strength would only help so much against a man with a knife.

Baxter was only a few steps from the end of the alley, a bright rectangle of midday light that held a false promise of safety. There was no way he would survive turning his back on this man if he got any closer. It was quiet here, with just the hum of insects and the slight creaking of a shutter moving in the gentle breeze. Baxter closed his eyes briefly, trying to recall the frontage of the buildings they'd passed between. A house and a workshop, both of them in need of some work but obviously not a priority.

He grinned suddenly, the cheerful expression giving Henrik slight pause. Baxter took a step backwards, then another, and another, before launching himself from the end of the alley as Henrik snarled and threw himself forward, blade first.

For a gut-wrenching moment, Baxter thought he'd made another poor choice. Squinting into the hard light, he cast around for what he *knew* must be there as he saw Henrik sprinting towards him with a low, animalistic snarl. Then Baxter spotted the loose shutter. He reached out and grabbed the rough wood, and with sheer brute force he ripped it from its mounting. He turned on his heel, maintaining the force used to tear the shutter free. He'd timed it perfectly, the section of stout wood intersecting Henrik's path as he exploded from the dark alley and took the full weight of the improvised weapon square in the face.

Baxter didn't hang around to see if he'd killed or seriously injured the knifeman. Just slowing him down was enough. He turned and sprinted away before the noise of the altercation drew too much attention and before Esca could lay hands on her weapon. He could hear the woman yelling in Afrikaans, anger and frustration in her voice, and he guessed she was haranguing Henrik to get back on his feet. He didn't look back; he just kept running to put as much distance as possible between himself and his would-be captors.

CHAPTER NINE

Baxter spent a tense day keeping on the move around Dar es-Salaam. He wasn't exactly skulking, as that wasn't his forte, and he didn't exactly blend in with the local population. His brief interaction with Esca, however, had provided him with a certain amount of useful information — not least the fact that it was unlikely they would try to grab him in broad daylight from a public space. The rule of law still applied in German East Africa, and the men she would send after him would have no claim to any authority to take him into custody.

He avoided places like the hotel and the German Club, instead walking until his feet ached and dropping into bars and coffee houses to keep himself fuelled. As the sun rose higher in the sky he found himself doing that more and more often, sticking to pleasantly refreshing German lagers for the most part; he needed a clear head to work his way out of this problem. He stuck to establishments with verandas in the busier streets, making sure that there were always people around.

Baxter knew he couldn't keep this up for long in these sweltering conditions. He'd stood watches that lasted more than a day, that much was true. Along with every other sailor aboard the *Yaroslavich*, he'd worked more hours than he'd known to keep the Russian cruiser afloat and underway after her engines had been sabotaged during a great cyclone. He was on land, though, baking land. He was out of his element, and by the late afternoon more tired than he would have thought possible.

It was then that he finally saw Esca Masing again, watching him from inside a *Kaffeehaus*. He was on the other side of the street, pausing to shake a pebble out of his shoe, and when he looked up their eyes locked. She made no move to rise, but just glared at him over the rim of her coffee cup.

Baxter shivered slightly despite the heat. He'd come up against some nasty pieces of work in his time, and had even left one or two of them dead in his wake, but the sheer venom in her gaze was new to him.

While he felt a certain amount of satisfaction when she broke eye contact first, Baxter soon realised that she'd wanted him to see her. She wanted him to know that she was on to him and, what was more to the point, keep his attention on her. Glancing around, he realised that at least one of her men was in the area.

This wasn't the disaster it could have been; after all, he knew they'd find him eventually. They would know that his main route of escape would be by sea, and therefore the harbour was where he would end up eventually. He had considered slipping out of the city and escaping overland, but he had next to no knowledge of the hinterland beyond Dar es-Salaam and he would still be deep in potentially hostile territory. Even though his appointed transport wouldn't be here for another day, the sea remained his only way out.

He glanced up at the sky. It was still bright, but he knew it would be dark soon. The sun would plunge towards the horizon and disappear in the blink of an eye. That was when things would get dangerous.

It was a fight he couldn't win. But he'd be damned if he was taken prisoner again, after his experience of more than a year with the Russians. He'd fight his way out across Africa if he had to.

Baxter looked back to the coffee house and saw a small triumphant smile on the Boer woman's face. It was an ugly expression, and he merely raised an eyebrow in response. He looked around again and saw another thug had appeared and was loitering nearby.

Baxter was just considering making a move, when raucous singing broke the tension developing on the street. He realised at once that it was sailors singing. They may have been in full throat in German, but there was no mistaking the mix of drunken bawdiness and the desperation of men who knew that their run ashore had come to an end.

Looking up the street, he saw a *Leutnant zur See* leading a group of dishevelled German sailors in something approaching a marching formation that was constantly disrupted by one of the men tripping and having to be propped up by his comrades. There were a couple of sober sailors accompanying the sorry parade, looking more than ready to use the truncheons they carried. Not out of any real malice, Baxter knew, but because they were the ones on escort duty instead of having enjoyed the delights of Dar es-Salaam.

He knew instinctively what was happening here. While *Königsberg* had put to sea the day before, she must have left behind a party to round up the miscreants who were enjoying a last shore leave a little bit too much. They would no doubt be brought back to the cruiser for punishment and a return to duty.

And that meant they would have a vessel in the harbour.

"*Herr* Baxter!" the lieutenant leading the procession called out cheerfully, despite the embarrassment he no doubt felt on behalf of the Imperial German Navy.

Now that he was closer, Baxter recognised him as Kleiner, who he'd met on his first visit to the German Club. That was a stroke of luck.

"*Leutnant* Kleiner!" he replied. "I see you've got the round-up duty."

He couldn't remember if he'd exchanged many words with Kleiner, but was relatively certain his English was good. Better than Baxter's German, certainly. It seemed his recollection was sound.

"Alas. We are ordered to cruise points further north… A second, *bitte*." Kleiner turned and roared something in a tone of command that belied his youth, sending one of the escorts to round up a sailor who was trying to slip away from the party. Baxter doubted many of these men had a real desire to depart the service, as they were still in uniform and had been caught. It was more a sense of mischief that motivated any bad behaviour, that and hard liquor. It didn't make them any easier to control.

"Listen, old chap," he said casually, as Kleiner turned back to him. "It looks like you've got some rough customers here, and I've got plenty of experience dealing with drunk sailors. I'd be more than happy to trail along behind and kick any who get out of hand in the arse."

Kleiner opened his mouth to decline, but then one of the men staggered out of line and threw up copiously in the gutter. That surprised Baxter — it didn't matter what navy a sailor was in, he could generally handle his liquor. The ashen-faced man looked to be a new recruit and was subjected to some good-natured ribbing by his compatriots. All of them would regret this by the morning; Baxter knew exactly how brutal a hangover at sea in these hot climes could be. Right now, though, the men were in the sort of cheerful mood that would either lead to hijinks that could get out of hand, or would turn sour and mutinous once they'd sobered up and realised they were in trouble.

The junior officer gave him a wan smile. The stink of regurgitated spirits was starting to fill the air. "That would be most kind, Mr Baxter," he said, before turning to the senior warrant officer accompanying him and saying something in German. The veteran sailor gave Baxter a suspicious look, but he had his orders and saluted smartly in acknowledgement.

The sorry procession was kicked into motion again, the escorting sailors growling at the defaulters under their guard. Judging from the way a few of the men cast apprehensive looks his way, Baxter guessed they had just been threatened with a few minutes alone with the giant British man.

Baxter looked back towards the *Kaffeehaus* and saw Esca still there. Her triumphant smile had dissolved into something altogether darker and more dangerous. Baxter tipped his hat to her, then turned and followed Kleiner.

It took far longer than it should have to reach the harbour due to the need for repeated stops and the generally slovenliness of the drunk sailors. While Baxter hadn't had to strike any of them, it had been a near-run thing. One sailor, a former farmhand, seemed to have a notion that he wanted to try his hand with the big *Englander*. He'd backed down when Baxter hadn't flinched in the face of his drunken posturing.

As he'd expected, a steam launch was waiting for the returning sailors. Kleiner had sent one of his sailors on ahead to tell the crew to get steam up. Baxter could see a single plume of smoke rising into the still air, rapidly fading into the darkness as the sun charged towards its rest behind them.

He was acutely conscious of Esca's men still trailing him. Kleiner chattered away, unaware of the drama playing out under his nose, and Baxter forced himself to pay both attention and professional courtesy to the man.

"Well, here we are," Kleiner said as they arrived at the smartly-painted launch's mooring. The petty officers had managed to shove the drunken sailors into some semblance of a formation, albeit a sullen one, before sending them down the stone steps into the waiting vessel.

Baxter glanced back towards the glow of the city's lights, trying to catch sight of the two men hunting him. Kleiner had made no mention of giving him passage anywhere, and he knew that asking would not be appropriate.

A splash and a gale of renewed laughter brought his attention back to the sailors, just in time to see the blond head of one of the youngest sailors breaking the surface, wide panic-stricken eyes bright in the moonlight. Like most sailors, he clearly couldn't swim and his comrades were in no state to help him.

Baxter was down the steps and into the launch in a flash. He reached down just as the stricken sailor went under again, gritting his teeth as he hauled the man out of the water. He managed to get his sodden form halfway over the launch's gunwale.

A petty officer shouted something, and the crew of the launch pulled the rapidly sobering sailor the rest of the way aboard. Baxter climbed back up the steps, glowering furiously at the other men, and rejoined Kleiner. The officer had lit a cheroot, a small glowing coal marking his position on the dark quayside.

"They'll remember who they are, remember their duty, when they're back afloat," Baxter said gruffly. "Sea air and the motion of the boat will see to that, or make them all sick as dogs."

"Either that, or they will think it most entertaining to put the rest of us over the side and return to their revels," Kleiner said unhappily. Baxter knew that was highly unlikely. Right now these men had earned themselves extra duty on bread and water rations; murder and mutiny were hanging offences in most navies, and shooting offences in the remainder. "I do hate to impose on you, but I wonder if you wouldn't mind accompanying us for some of the way? I would not be able to return you here, of course, but I would be happy to put you ashore at Zanzibar as we go past. By which time I am sure they will have sobered up."

That was the question Baxter had been hoping for, but not expecting. He'd already started considering whether there was a small sailing vessel anywhere he could commandeer — it wouldn't have been the first time he'd had to do so to stay alive. Kleiner had seemed too competent to require further assistance. Perhaps he'd picked up on Baxter's desire to be away from Tanganyika and was a decent enough sort of fellow to offer assistance.

"Happy to help," he said, after taking a moment to pretend to consider it. "As a professional courtesy."

The journey in the steam launch turned out to be uneventful. Just as Baxter had predicted, once they were away from land and the temptations it offered, the defaulters subsided into a sullen silence. Some kind soul had equipped the launch with a water butt, which saw extensive use as the small vessel chugged its way north across the placid waters. He hoped for their sake that SMS *Königsberg* was not waiting too far for the rest of her complement — he would not want to be on the open Indian Ocean for long in such a small, wooden vessel.

"It seems Captain Looff put to sea in quite a hurry," Baxter commented. He and Kleiner were in the stern of the vessel, by the small brass wheel.

Kleiner shrugged. "You know how it is with captains. Always in a hurry, always springing surprises on their crews to keep them on their toes."

Baxter knew that well enough. Jackie Fisher had been famous for such behaviour, and there were any number of hard-driving captains in the service. There was something in Kleiner's tone that suggested the other man was lying, though it would not be politic to challenge him at this moment.

Before he could say anything further on the subject, the lookout in the bows called back to inform them that the lights of Stone Town were ahead. "Well, I think we can manage from here," Kleiner said cheerfully. "The men seem much subdued."

"Don't worry about going all the way into the harbour," Baxter said diffidently, mostly because he didn't want to have to answer questions about why the *Kaiserliche Marine* was providing him with transport, but also so as not to delay Kleiner any longer. "Anywhere along the beach would be fine."

"Of course, though you will get your feet wet."

"It won't be the first time, and it won't be the last," Baxter said. Kleiner spoke to the helmsman and the launch came about slightly, still on a broadly northerly heading but angled towards the lights of the British possession.

They steamed in silence for some minutes, with just the call of a sailor casting the lead in the bows and the occasional groan of discomfort. When it became clear that the launch was about to touch the sandy bottom, Kleiner ordered all stop. Baxter sat on the gunwale to remove his shoes. Having left his toiletries and some spare clothes behind in Dar es-Salaam, he was loathe to abandon anything else.

"I am obliged to you, Mr Baxter, and hope one day to be able to offer you a professional courtesy."

Baxter shook Kleiner's hand. "Think nothing of it, *Leutnant*," he said, before hopping over the side and up to his thighs in the warm waters of Zanzibar. The launch was back in motion as soon as he was clear, and he raised a hand in farewell in response to Kleiner's raised cap.

Baxter watched the vessel disappear into the darkness, hurrying to catch up with the German cruiser. With a flash of intuition, he realised why Looff had put to sea in enough of a hurry that he'd left a significant number of men behind in Dar es-Salaam. He wanted to avoid being bottled up in Dar es-Salaam. The only other navy with a presence in these waters sufficient to do that was the RN.

As the launch disappeared into the night, Baxter found himself hoping that he wouldn't find himself in a position where he'd have to fight Kleiner and his comrades. Not because he didn't think the RN would win. Kleiner and many other German officers he'd met over the years seemed like decent sorts, and it would be a waste for them to butcher each other. Others, like von Lettow-Vorbeck and the *Schutztruppe* officer Schiller, he'd have no such regrets about.

CHAPTER TEN

"Any idea what old Nosy wants?" Hensley asked as he and Baxter followed the other officers into Commander Parker's spacious office. The room was already thick with tobacco smoke, which hung in blue skeins in the air.

Baxter had made it back to his rooms without further issue when he landed a few nights before, though his feet had objected to the amount of ground-pounding he'd done in Dar es-Salaam. In truth, he was desperate to be back at sea, and not just because of the way the ground remained resolutely and unnaturally steady underfoot. He'd found the RN installation abuzz with news from Europe, very little of it good and none of it entirely clear. It seemed Austria-Hungary had been at war with Serbia since the 28th of July and things had somewhat snowballed from there. As he and Tomas had surmised, Russia had become involved, which had brought in Germany. There were rumours that France had declared, and Britain was giving strong indications that she would honour treaty obligations.

"Your guess is as good as mine," Baxter replied as he scanned the grim expressions on the other officers' faces.

Hensley's own expression had none of his usual bonhomie. Baxter knew exactly what was going through his mind, and that of every other keen young officer who'd been hoping for a bloody war.

Parker finally looked up from the papers on the desk in front of him. He didn't rise to address the officers who'd formed a rough semi-circle around him, but did lean back in his chair as he tamped tobacco into his pipe and lit it. Once it was burning to his satisfaction, adding to the cloying cloud he had already generated, he took the stem from his mouth. "Gentlemen, you may smoke if you wish."

Baxter suppressed a spurt of irritation. Parker had clearly brought them together to impart important news, but now seemed intent on making them wait. There was a rustle as cigarette packets were produced or pipes filled, the rasp of matches and lighters, the accompanying murmur of meaningless conversation as flames were shared.

"As you will be aware, our European neighbours have started having a bit of a spat in the last few days." A murmur of nervous laughter ran through the room, which Parker had clearly been looking for. "His Majesty's Government saw fit to issue an ultimatum to the Kaiser on the fourth of this month, demanding the withdrawal of German forces from France and Germany. This ultimatum has expired."

Parker cleared his throat and picked up a telegram. "Today, the Resident received the following from London which I shall read to you now. 'Tipsified Pumgirdles Germany Novel'."

More bemused laughter quickly died into silence as all the men registered Parker's grim expression. "This, of course, is a code. As of midnight on the fourth, we are in a state of war with the German Empire and her allies."

Glancing around the room, Baxter could see a mix of emotions. Excitement, perhaps, but also trepidation. One or two of the older men looked quietly confident. Baxter found himself strangely detached. Over the last few years, as his inglorious career as a mercenary had taken him from one bitter little war on the fringes of Europe to another, he'd come to the realisation that something significant was brewing. He hadn't known how it would happen or who it would involve, of course, but now the beast had finally reared its head he felt strangely relieved.

The silence that followed Parker's pronouncement was broken by Hensley. "What a ruddy ridiculous code. They could at least have chosen something more ... serious-sounding."

That led to laughter as the tension was broken. Even Parker smiled. "Mr Hensley's criticisms of our cyphers aside, are there any questions or comments? Speak freely."

"When do we attack?" another younger officer demanded.

"Attack whom?" Parker asked. "Right now, we are working on the basis that the terms of the Morocco-Congo Treaty still hold and the colonies on both sides remain neutral in this affray. *Herr* Schnee, the German consul over the water, has already indicated that he intends for Dar es-Salaam to be an open port not in use for military purposes. It should also be hoped that calmer heads in Europe will prevail, and this will turn out to be something of a storm in a teacup."

There were a few low grumbles. Now the realisation that they were at war was settling in, the younger officers were keen to see at least some action before the storm in a teacup — if that's what this turned out to be — was over. Baxter also suspected he was not the only experienced sailor in the room concerned about a lack of action while the enemy was unprepared. *That's not your decision, though, is it?* he reminded himself.

"That is not to say, of course, that we will not be busy. We can anticipate an increased demand on our bunkerage, both in terms of quantity and frequency of the need to resupply, and when last I spoke to *Pegasus*'s commander, he was of the view he may need to put in to overhaul her machinery soon. Thanks to Mr Baxter here, we are also aware that SMS *Königsberg* is at sea. I doubt very much Captain Looff will want to risk an attack on our installation, but we should remain alert to the possibility."

"And the enemy aliens currently in Zanzibar?" an officer asked. "Plenty of Germans here."

Parker shot him a sharp look, apparently surprised at the rapidity with which the hostile language had entered their lexicon. "Local troops will be responsible for rounding them up and interning them," the commander said. "We should all bear in mind, though, that until recently these men and women were our neighbours and valuable members of the mercantile community here. I know most of us — including myself — buy our suits from Perito, and while Italy has not declared, it is still officially allied with Germany. They are to be treated with the utmost respect and every courtesy."

"It's going to be a nightmare getting served anywhere," Hensley quipped. "Half the waiting staff is German."

Parker ignored the remark. "Our role is to seize the tug *Helmuth*. It was apparently chartered by some of the German worthies here in Stone Town for just such an eventuality." The commander's cool eyes swept the men assembled in front of him. "Mr Baxter, if you are not otherwise engaged, perhaps you would see to that? Mr Hensley will assist, and take such men as you deem necessary."

Baxter was about to protest that he had plenty to be getting on with, not least of which was sending a telegram to London to enquire whether his mission here was even remotely important given the outbreak of hostilities. He knew he had no choice, though. "Very good, sir."

"So glad you agree. Well, gentlemen, we have much to be getting on with. You will all have your orders before midday. Carry on."

There was something almost anti-climactic to the end of the meeting; a subdued silence as the officers filed out of the room. "Mr Baxter, a moment of your time," Parker called out, just as he was about to exit after Hensley.

"Get Dalton, a few men, and a boat — I'll meet you down in the harbour," Baxter ordered Hensley tersely, old habits of command coming back to him without effort. He then stepped back in front of Parker's desk and came to attention. "Sir?"

Parker took his time speaking, the commander staring hard at him while puffing on his pipe. "I have tolerated your excursions into Dar es-Salaam and your general lack of interest in the duties you are supposedly undertaking here — yes, I am aware that Mr Hensley has been preparing the reports — as it was clear that you were here on a more sensitive mission."

Baxter maintained his posture and neutral expression. When it became apparent that the commander expected some form of response, he said, "Sir," in as non-committal a tone as he could manage.

Parker snorted pipe smoke. He knew how to play this game as well as Baxter did, probably better. "Reservist, my eye," he muttered. "Mr Baxter, given the current situation, I require to know exactly what your mission is. And do not give me any of that nonsense about top secret orders. We are a long way from home, and you have been placed under my orders."

Baxter considered that, then dropped his gaze from the portrait of King George V over Parker's head to meet the commander's eyes. "It's a sensitive subject, sir, and potentially embarrassing to the service," he said at last. While his orders were indeed to keep his real task a secret, Parker was right that the situation had changed. While new orders would be much more quickly received in this day and age than they would have been even a few decades ago, Parker was his commander on the spot and Baxter had a feeling he would need Parker's co-operation more now. The fact that he'd seen through Baxter's ruse with Hensley also suggested the older man was perhaps more intuitive than Baxter had previously surmised. "I've been sent to retrieve an individual from Dar es-Salaam, a British national who may be collaborating with the enemy."

Parker's bushy white eyebrows twitched upwards. "This anything to do with the rather pushy … gentleman with the cauliflower ear who demanded to see me a few weeks ago?"

Baxter nodded, surprised that Parker would remember Billings. He'd almost forgotten about the former petty officer himself, given everything else that had been happening. He hadn't seen either Billings or Tomas since his return from the German colony. He was starting to get worried about Tomas, though the young man had seemed perfectly capable of looking after himself.

Before he could speak further, Parker knocked his pipe out in a large crystal ashtray. "This man you're after, does he walk with a pair of canes by any chance?" When Baxter just nodded, Parker continued in the same dry tone. "He passed through here some months ago, claiming to be on his way to Cape Town to buy diamonds. I thought there was something fishy about him. I did hear from a contact in Dar es-Salaam that he'd shown up there, taken ill."

Baxter could have kicked himself, or more accurately Saunders for requiring absolute secrecy about his mission. Parker, having been on this station for some time, would of course have cultivated contacts in neighbouring colonies — it was expected of senior officers in shore stations — and could have supplied some genuinely helpful information.

"My own information suggests he is still under guard in the European Hospital in Dar es-Salaam, sir," Baxter said. "I was on the verge of confirming that when the outbreak of war curtailed those activities."

"You understand that I cannot authorise the use of personnel under my command for any activity related to your task, not without further orders from London. I will not be able to assist you, Mr Baxter, in such a manner. Is that clear?"

"Very clear, sir," he said smartly. It was an offer, after a fashion. Parker could be ordered to assist via the Intelligence Division. Baxter doubted that such orders would be forthcoming, though. Everyone in the Admiralty would have more important things to worry about, and he suspected that Saunders would still want this kept under wraps despite the changed situation.

"Very good. Well, I imagine the *Helmuth* will not take itself into custody — carry on."

"Yes, sir." Dismissed, Baxter turned to go.

Parker spoke again when he was almost through the door. "You may have noted HMS *Astraea* is currently coaling in preparation for a patrol along the German coast," he said. Baxter glanced back, wondering if Parker was on the verge of finding make-work to keep him out of the way or whether he was sharing information he thought would be useful. His vulpine features were already turned back to his papers, though, and Baxter made no comment as he left.

Sub-Lieutenant Hensley had done exactly as ordered, assembling a detail of men under the ancient but steady Dalton and procuring a launch that bobbed gently at its moorings as Baxter hurried down to the harbour. He'd stopped at his rooms to belt on the Smith and Wesson revolver. Parker would be furious, of course, at the non-regulation weapon and belt, but Baxter didn't have the time or patience to draw a service sidearm from stores and had no real intention of using it anyway.

"Oh," Hensley said as Baxter joined him, eyes dropping to the polished walnut grip of the revolver. "I didn't think…"

He realised neither Hensley nor any of the men were armed. "Not to worry," he said brusquely. "I should have included that in the orders. I don't think there'll be any resistance, but if there is, we'll deal with it the old-fashioned way."

"Good job I brought Julius, then," Dalton said, indicating one of the smartly turned-out sailors. He was an African, burly without being big, and looked like he could handle himself in a fight.

"Well, carry on then, Dalton," Hensley said crisply. The petty officer detailed the men to the launch's oars and then the two officers went down the steps and into the stern.

"Lay us alongside that ugly tub flying a German flag, Mr Dalton," Hensley ordered, making the expedition sound grander than it really was. Baxter expected an exchange of words with the crew — no doubt a strong-worded protest, followed by surrender.

The sailors clearly knew what they were about, and Dalton needed no further instruction. The launch skimmed out across the calm water, the oars creaking in the rowlocks and the men occasionally grunting with effort. Baxter scanned the harbour until he spotted the sleek shape of HMS *Astraea*, the cruiser Parker had mentioned, moored at the coaling station. Despite the heat, both RN sailors and native labourers were busy carrying loads of coal aboard. She was an older design of protected cruiser, he knew, but powerful enough, certainly for these waters.

"What do you know of her captain?" Baxter asked Hensley quietly, indicating the ship with a nod.

"Captain Sykes. Good man, by all accounts. I'm told he can be a bit impetuous." Hensley sighed. "I'd give anything to be assigned aboard. Even cruising up and down in front of Dar es-Salaam would be better than this."

Baxter clapped Hensley on the shoulder. "Well, you'd miss out on all this excitement!" he declared, as the launch approached the German tug.

Just as Hensley had said, she was a squat, ugly little vessel, but one well suited for her appointed task and these waters. The German civil ensign flew from her flagstaff, stirred only slightly by the sea breeze. Scanning her deck, Baxter couldn't make out any armament, but then there was no reason for her to be armed. She was a peaceful vessel chartered to take civilians out of a suddenly hostile area.

Well, that's about to change, he thought grimly.

"Why do you ask?" Hensley went on. "About Sykes, I mean?"

Baxter was still focused on the ship as the launch slid towards it. The German crew had finally become aware of the boat full of British tars closing in on them, and he could make out the movement of running bodies.

"Hmm? Always useful to have an idea about the officers you might encounter."

"Well, if you do have any cause to *encounter* him in pursuit of what you're up to, do bear me in mind, old chap. I rather fancy seeing at least some action before this all blows over."

Baxter grunted noncommittally. He didn't have the heart to tell the younger man that Parker had essentially ordered him to leave the Zanzibar staff out of it.

A shout from the *Helmuth* prevented the need for any further response. "British launch, we are a peaceful vessel engaged on a civilian contract. We are not, repeat *not* a lawful prize!"

"Well, at least they know that war's broken out," Hensley said. He seemed remarkably relaxed, but there was little reason for him not to be. "Any idea if that stuff about not being a lawful prize will hold any water?"

"No idea," Baxter said, his mood unaccountably souring. "We have our orders, Mr Hensley, and one of the things you will come to appreciate is that being this far down the pecking order provides a certain amount of protection."

Dalton handed him a speaking trumpet when they were still a few dozen yards from the vessel. "German vessel *Helmuth*, prepare to be boarded and taken into custody by the Royal Navy!" he boomed through the hailer.

"Royal Navy personnel, I repeat —"

"This isn't a bloody debate!" Baxter cut across. "We are coming alongside and will take possession of your vessel!"

Baxter's volume and the vehemence in his tone seemed to stun the German sailor into silence.

"Starboard entry port if you please, Mr Dalton."

"Very good, sir," the veteran petty officer responded calmly. This could be any perfectly routine duty he had undertaken in peacetime.

The Yorkshireman certainly knew his trade, and the section of sailors under his command were well drilled. With only a few muttered commands, Dalton brought the launch alongside the tug smoothly. Julius was up in the bows and hooked on. With a confident stride, Baxter went down the length of the boat and then climbed quickly up the entry ladder.

The key here, he knew, was not to show any uncertainty or fear. The men nominally under his command would sense it, as would the German crew. He was confronted at the top of the ladder by a German merchant officer, his face beetroot-red with rage behind his bristling beard. "How dare you!" he started.

Baxter held up his hand. He'd left the revolver holstered on his hip, as he had every intention of ensuring the impounding was peacefully done. "As you are no doubt aware, a state of war now exists between Britain and Germany," he said, his tone as bland and officious as he could manage. "As such, this vessel is being impounded…"

"On whose authority?" the officer — Baxter guessed he was the ship's master — demanded. "This is completely at odds with the law of the sea and any sense of decency…"

"By order of the Resident," Baxter ground out. He didn't know for sure that was the case, but he also wanted to shut this discussion down and the Resident was the most senior member of the British authorities here. "As to laws and customs, sir, I again remind you that we are now at war."

This fact was yet to sink in with a lot of men, of any nationality, Baxter realised. It was hardly surprising, he supposed. While there had been any number of small wars in Europe and indeed globally for the last few years, they hadn't drawn in the major European powers. A lot of people on all sides would be trying to work out what this meant.

"You are of course welcome to lodge a complaint with the Resident. In the meantime, I can assure you that you and your crew will be treated with decency while you remain guests of the Royal Navy."

"*Guests!*" the man spat. He then turned his back on Baxter and crossed his arms over his chest.

He had no real choice but to accept the situation, of course. The rest of the RN party was swarming up the side and spreading out across the deck. Once they were on deck, though, they didn't quite know what to do with themselves. Baxter knew it was important not to lose momentum; he'd learned that from previous boarding actions and close fights.

Hensley, at least, was starting to organise the men into parties, even if he didn't know where to send them.

"Bridge and engine room, Mr Hensley, if you please," Baxter rapped out. "The wireless set, if there is one aboard. Quick as you like."

That spurred them on. Hensley started sending the men towards the key sections of the vessel. Looking along the short length of the tug, Baxter thought it unlikely they would receive any resistance or have to deal with attempted sabotage. The small merchant crew, most of whom appeared to be on deck and were glaring sullenly at the sailors, didn't appear to have any fight in them. The vessel herself seemed to be clean and well maintained. There was something odd, however, and it took him a moment to realise what it was. There was no smoke coming from the stack, and no thump of pistons from the smoke's guts. Even in harbour, it was normal practice to keep the boilers running at a reduced rate to provide power for the crew.

Must have engine trouble. It would explain why the tug was still in port. Baxter could just imagine the frustration and anxiety of the German civilians who'd chartered her to make good their escape.

Catching a flicker of motion from the corner of his eye, Baxter turned sharply in the direction of one of the hatches down into the vessel's interior. Everything was proceeding smoothly around him, Hensley getting the small number of German sailors in hand while other bluejackets raced to the bridge and engine room. Why, then, would someone disappear in a hurry through the foredeck hatch? Surely whoever it was would realise that there was little or no point in fighting, particularly not out of some nebulous sense of honour.

Baxter went forward and found that whoever had just disappeared below decks had closed but not dogged the hatch. Lifting it, he peered down into the inky darkness before dropping down onto the companionway. Closing the hatch as quietly as possible, he paused for a moment to allow his eyes to adapt to the dimness. Light filtered in through a grubby porthole to his right.

The cramped space smelled of rust and warm oil, hemp and tar. Crates were stacked up to Baxter's left, blocking the porthole on that side, and coils of rope were tidied away in a seamanlike manner against both sides. He cocked his head, listening for any sound that might give away someone lurking in ambush.

Nothing. Baxter reached down and drew his revolver. He didn't particularly like small arms, and, until Connie had coached him during their long transit of the Suez Canal, he had been a poor shot at best. He liked going into a potentially dangerous situation without a weapon even less.

The hatch in the opposite bulkhead stood open. He didn't rush across to it, though, but moved carefully, covering potential hiding spots with the Smith and Wesson. He'd just reached the hatch when he heard a woman scream, followed by a more masculine shout of pain.

Although Baxter had never been aboard the *Helmuth*, his years scraping by as a merchant seaman had given him an intuitive grasp of the architecture of ships large and small, and it only took him a moment to get his bearings. He went through the hatch, moving quickly but still cautiously, then down another companionway. It was stuffy on this deck, the smell of the bilges stronger. He could hear a low, angry voice coming from an open hatchway ahead. The only illumination was the flickering light of a lantern in that compartment.

Baxter stalked forward, then glanced around the hatch coaming. The man who was speaking had his back to him and was looming over a bound woman with what appeared to be a truncheon in one hand. Baxter couldn't make out what he was saying, but recognised both the language and accent.

He was about to demand the man's surrender, when the woman kicked out with one booted foot, catching her attacker on the knee and causing him to stagger. He spun back to her, swinging the truncheon. Baxter acted without thinking, firing once, the noise devastating in the confined space. The round hit with enough force to send the club-wielding man sideways into the bulkhead. He folded and lay still, but whimpered slightly.

For a moment, there was a stunned silence in the compartment. All Baxter could hear was the ringing aftershock of the shot. The air reeked of burned propellant and blood.

Sound came back slowly. There was shouting from above, the men under his command reacting to the noise of the gunshot. He glanced down and saw the woman he'd rescued glaring angrily up at him. It was an expression he was all too familiar with.

"It seems you are here to rescue me again, Marcus Alexandrovich," Mashka said in Russian. "Would you please cut these bonds so I can finish this bastard off?"

CHAPTER ELEVEN

HMS *Astraea* made an easy six knots as she cruised off the coast of German East Africa. Looking astern, Baxter could quite clearly make out HMS *Pegasus* five cables distant, her hull gleaming in the moonlight.

Glancing towards the land, it was light enough that he could make out the low, sullen mass of the mainland. The Makatumbe lighthouse should have been visible, but it hadn't been lit since the outbreak of war. There was a slight glow coming from Dar es-Salaam itself, tucked away in its bay and no doubt thinking itself safe from attack.

Baxter turned his face to the gentle wind. It felt good to be at sea again, in a proper warship and wearing uniform. While his work for Saunders in the Naval Intelligence Department was the price he'd paid to get back into this uniform, the mission on which he'd been sent had started to grate on him. Here on the gently rolling deck of a cruiser, listening to the thud of the ship's engines and the hiss of the water down her side, his head felt clearer than it had done for weeks.

He smiled to himself. The irony was that the intelligence complications that were giving him a headache were also what had brought him here. As Parker had hinted, Captain Sykes had been very amenable to the idea of landing him in in Dar es-Salaam 'to raise a little havoc'. Mashka's rescue from the *Helmuth* had put an entirely different perspective on things. The fact that a citizen of an allied nation had been kidnapped from British territory and held against her will had not only served to legitimise the seizure of the tug, but had also lit a fire under everyone from the Resident down.

The Ukrainian woman hadn't changed much since Baxter had last seen her in 1905. She'd been in her late teenage years then, though hardened by her hard life as a poorer subject of the Russian Empire. Baxter had first met her over the body of her father, during the hot bloody days of the abortive Odessa uprising. The intervening years had merely served to sharpen her somewhat, and even the relative comfort he'd sent her to as a ward of Ekaterina Juneau hadn't dimmed her zeal.

They'd only had moments to agree on a story before the RN sailors had come to investigate the single gunshot. Mashka had taken the coincidence of being rescued by him as phlegmatically as he might have expected. "It is important that the nature of our work is not known," she'd said, readily agreeing to pose as a Russian woman who'd been seized off the street by German ruffians.

Things had snowballed from there. Back at Admiralty House, Parker had interviewed Mashka personally and the Resident had expressed concern for the young woman's wellbeing. She'd played the part perfectly, appearing timid and lost, though Baxter had occasionally caught a flash of amused derision on her face. As soon as she mentioned that her dear brother Tomas was being held prisoner in German East Africa, along with at least one Englishman, Parker had almost fallen over himself to provide Baxter with the support he'd previously been denied.

She's good, Baxter mused. He couldn't imagine Parker offering this sort of help to just any stray Russian refugee who'd come along. The fact that she'd mentioned the Englishman being held in Dar es-Salaam probably helped, verifying Baxter's own story apparently independently. Mashka had also learned a lot from Ekaterina when it came to getting her own way. She'd adopted grand manners, at least around the RN officers, portraying herself convincingly as a minor noble.

Baxter had a lot of questions for Mashka, ranging from enquiries about the countess to how she knew Tomas has been taken, but there hadn't been a great deal of time before *Astraea* had been due to steam for her patrol along the enemy coastline. Baxter wondered now whether she would even be in Zanzibar when he got back, or, like Billings, would disappear entirely.

Thinking of the former RN petty officer soured his mood somewhat. Baxter hadn't seen hide nor hair of the rogue since their run-in with the Boers he now knew to be working for Esca Masing. He couldn't shake the feeling that Billings was around somewhere still, and up to no good.

"Nervous, old chap?" Hensley asked, appearing at his side almost soundlessly.

"No." Baxter knew his tone was a bit short, but he'd been enjoying the sea and the solitude.

"I bloody am," Hensley admitted with a wan smile. His hands shook very slightly as he lit a match and put it to a cigarette.

Baxter hadn't particularly wanted to bring Hensley along, but the sub-lieutenant had petitioned Parker. Reflecting on it now, maybe it wasn't the worst thing. If the war continued for any length of time, Hensley would find himself in a fight. It would be better for the men he led if he at least got some experience early.

"Chances are we won't even see a German in uniform," Baxter said. "And if we do, the thing to remember is that he's probably as nervous as you are right now. We're not looking for a fight here, so if he doesn't want to give you one, don't give him a reason."

"How the bloody hell are you so calm about this?"

"This isn't my first war, old chap." He glanced down at his watch. "Right. Captain Sykes said he was going to set a course for Dar es-Salaam bay a bit after five. Rouse the landing party, if you please."

"Yes, sir," Hensley said, smartly enough, and seemingly reassured by the formality.

"And Mr Hensley? Make sure they have guns, this time, and bullets."

The other officer smiled ruefully. "Yes, sir."

Captain Sykes had loaned them one of *Astraea*'s steam launches for the raid. Baxter didn't want the men detailed to him worn out by a long pull to the enemy shore, even if that was in the finest traditions of the Service. As well as Hensley, he had Dalton, Julius and five others. The commander of *Astraea*'s Royal Marine detachment had offered some of his people, but Baxter knew that if they came up against any serious opposition, they wouldn't be fighting, but retreating to the boat. The fewer men he had to worry about, the better.

He had been surprised when Dalton had volunteered for the landing party. The veteran seemed altogether too long in the tooth for this sort of caper. Watching him at the tiller of the launch, Baxter realised he didn't even seem particularly excited to be there. The rest of the sailors were clustered in the bow of the launch, all of them crouched low and clutching their Lee Enfield rifles. Hensley had told him that training and drilling was the way they filled their days when a ship wasn't in for coal.

Still, should have brought some bloody Marines, Baxter thought. But it was too late to worry about that now.

"Adjust three points to starboard, Mr Dalton," he said, raising his field glasses to sweep the seafront of Dar es-Salaam again. The twinkling lights of the city served to make the surrounding darkness more absolute, but he'd seen this coastline enough times that he knew it well enough. "See the lights from the hospital, Dalton?" he asked, pointing with the blade of his hand.

"I do at that, sir."

"There's a small cove about two cables to the north. We'll slip in there and wait for the bombardment to start, then make our move."

"Very good, sir," Dalton said, unperturbed.

Baxter went forward to where the men were clustered. "We'll be making landfall shortly and then waiting for the guns," he told them, making sure to look each of them in the eye. "Remember what I told you. The people here will mostly be civilians, though there may be policemen. No shooting, unless I give the order or you're fired at. We're Royal Navy sailors, and we'll behave accordingly."

That got one or two grins from the men, no doubt recalling stories some of the old salts told about pilfering their way through the belongings of defeated foes. Baxter wasn't in the mood for joking, though. "No looting. And treat anyone you meet with respect or, if they get out of hand, firmness."

The message seemed to sink in.

"If Sykes holds to his timetable, he should be opening fire in an hour. That should distract the Germans. We go in, find our people, and get back to the boat."

Baxter glanced across at Hensley, wondering if he was ready to take charge of the operational details. His training at Dartmouth would have been every bit as good as Baxter's, and more current. He didn't have as much experience, but he'd need to get it some time. And he *had* badgered Parker to get himself assigned to the mission.

"Mr Hensley, I'll leave the details to you," he said. The sub-lieutenant tried but failed to hide his surprise, and Baxter did him the courtesy of not noticing. "Carry on."

Baxter went back up the boat and took up his station alongside Dalton. He didn't want Hensley to feel like he was keeping an eye on him. The urge to double-check the younger officer's decisions was almost overpowering.

The launch continued to chug its way across the placid waters. The noise and plume of smoke from the small steam engine was a concern, but he was banking on the bombardment to cover their approach, and he doubted the Germans would be expecting a landing.

"Here we go again, sir," Dalton said, then coughed into his hand as he realised he may have spoken out of turn.

"Seen much action, Dalton?"

"Bits and pieces, sir. South Africa. Dragging them guns to Ladysmith is not something I want to repeat."

Baxter nodded. He'd not quite been commissioned in time for the Boer War, but everyone knew the story of the dismounted artillery being hauled over difficult terrain to assist in the relief of the besieged garrison.

"Yourself, sir?" Dalton asked.

"Likewise. Not South Africa, but here and there."

"I had that thought about you, sir," Dalton said. His gap-toothed grin was visible in the growing light. He sobered again, and nodded up to where Hensley was organising the men into effective units. Or at least, that's what Baxter hoped he was doing. "He'll do all right, sir."

"I don't doubt it," Baxter said. They were close to land, now, Dalton keeping the bows steady towards the spot Baxter had indicated beyond the dark bulk of the hospital. Looking further inland, Baxter could make out the masts of the radio telegraph station that would soon — if the *Astraea*'s gunnery was up to much — have six-inch shells landing on it. "A trifle to starboard if you please, Dalton. And when we tie up, I want you and the stoker to remain aboard. We may need to leave in a hurry."

"Very good, sir. My days of leaping about on land are well behind me anyway. That's a young man's game."

"That it is, Dalton, that it is."

Not far now. Baxter glanced at his watch again, conscious that it might make him look nervous. The sun would be up around six, and he wanted to be tucked away with the engines idling before then.

The hint of light on the horizon had become the glowing promise of another hot day as Dalton nosed the launch into the long aquatic grass that dominated the sheltered bay. Baxter eyed their shelter — while he'd seen it from a distance, he hadn't appreciated quite how shallow it was or how overgrown.

"This will have to do — let go the anchor," he ordered. A moment later the launch's small anchor dropped with a splash, its chain rattling for only a moment before it buried itself in the silt. "Mr Hensley, break out the rations and tea. Dalton, I want the boiler down but not out. Let's try to keep noise and smoke to a minimum."

The men went to work quietly and efficiently. Baxter was impressed. Despite their training, few of them would have seen action before. Not only that, but they had been posted to a backwater station with no real expectation of doing anything more dangerous than lifting bags of coal and operating pulleys.

The following hour dragged by. They were as ready as they could be, so there was nothing to do but hunker down in the well-hidden launch and wait for the show to start. Out in the bay there was a plume of smoke, which was probably *Astraea* moving into firing position.

The men had lapsed into a tense silence. The rising sun beat down on them. The only noises were the lapping of water against the launch's side, the rising buzz of insects, and the long grass rustling in the slight breeze. Straining his ears, Baxter thought he could make out the distant noise of ship's engines.

That relative peace was broken by the noise of distant bugles, no doubt the *Schutztruppe* being stood to, ready to defend the city as best they could. Baxter caught Hensley glancing back at him, a concerned expression on his face.

"Everyone stay here and keep quiet," he said. "I'm going to take a look."

It was a risk, but not much of one. The chances of there being patrols in this area were minimal.

Baxter hopped over the gunwale onto the mossy bank. Despite the gentle incline, it was hard going through the cloying soil and stiff grass. At least the latter provided some sort of cover; all the former did was coat the legs of his white trousers and threaten to pull off his shoes.

His field glasses were clean, though, and he swept the surrounding terrain. He could see a few sections of *askari*, the local soldiers, doubling through the town towards the sea front. There didn't seem to be any coming towards the hospital, at least.

He switched his attention back out to sea. It only took him a moment to find HMS *Astraea*. The cruiser was maintaining position in preparation for opening fire.

He was about to dash back to the boat when nearby movement caught his attention. Baxter swung back round, lowering the field glasses, and realised there was a small family of locals about ten paces from him. They'd obviously seen him and had paused their morning chores to observe this interloper. The young woman was trying to hide two children behind her, while her husband crouched down and was watching Baxter with wary eyes.

They want no part of this, he thought, and he didn't want to drag them into it.

"Good morning," Baxter said, as though he was greeting them on the street of a peaceful town. He raised a hand. There was nothing else he could do but turn and slog back through the cloying mud to the launch. "Get steam up and raise the anchor!" he called out. He didn't think the family would alert anyone, but even if they did the *Schutztruppe* wouldn't be able to respond in time.

He stepped into the launch just as the anchor — more of a grapnel, really — was hauled aboard. "Now, sir?" Hensley asked.

"Now, Mr Hensley. Dalton, full astern and then along to the hospital."

The CPO did as ordered. Steam was up, but it took a frustratingly long time for the launch to back out of the little cove, even with the effort they'd made to realign the vessel once they'd anchored. After what felt like hours but was in fact only a couple of minutes, they were clear again and Dalton had built the rudder over to send them as quickly as possible back towards the hospital. The launch's wake streamed out behind and the whitewashed building crept ever closer.

Baxter kept his eyes on the seaward side of the structure, particularly the jetty, waiting to see if an *askari* or policeman came into view. Their luck held, even if their timing was off.

Baxter didn't flinch as *Astraea*'s two six-inch guns, mounted in single mounts fore and aft, spoke. The guns fired simultaneously, gouts of flame from the muzzles bright despite the daylight. Baxter didn't have time to track the fall of shot, however, as the launch was coming up on the jetty.

It crunched into the wood, the sound almost lost in the *thump* of distant explosions. Dalton followed his orders to the letter and brought them in as quickly as possible. Julius kept his feet as the other men in the bow staggered slightly. The African sailor was first onto German soil, Hensley hot on his heels. The other sailors climbed or jumped up onto the jetty. Baxter felt a stir of pride as they went with no obvious sign of hesitation and every indication of enthusiasm, no doubt buoyed up by the sound of *Astraea* continuing to shell the city.

He caught up with them as they reached the seaward entrance to the hospital. Julius raised the butt of his rifle to smash his way through the door, but Baxter put a hand out to stop him. He tried the handle and discovered it wasn't locked. "Try not to break anything," he told the group, then swung the door open and went through.

There was a surprising amount of commotion inside. Patients who had any semblance of mobility were at landward windows, staring out towards the plumes of dust and smoke rising as the shells whistled overhead and impacted with a low rumble. Doctors and nursing staff were trying to corral them back into their beds, with limited success.

It took a few moments for anyone to realise the enemy was among them. Baxter didn't feel the need to make an announcement or try to reassure the civilians that they weren't there to cause them any harm. Instead, he took the stairs up to the first floor two at a time, Julius and another sailor hot on his heels. Hensley left two sailors to keep their retreat route open and led two more to the front door to keep an eye out.

Baxter paused at the stop of the steps to orientate himself. Although he'd been in the hospital once before, the building was still a maze of corridors. He could hear voices raised in consternation below, mostly shouting in German, and Hensley's clipped tones responding. He didn't have time to worry about it, though.

Baxter turned to the sailors on his tail. "Julius, wait here and make sure we can retreat," he said. The other man, a young sandy-haired sailor with protruding ears, looked at him expectantly. It took Baxter a moment to recall his name. "Samuels, work your way up and find a good lookout post. I want to know as soon as you see anyone in uniform approaching, but don't open fire without orders."

"Aye, sir!" they choroused. Baxter didn't like sending men out on their own, but the hospital should be safe enough and he didn't have enough sailors to go around.

Baxter advanced along the upper corridor, pistol in hand. This floor wasn't quite as busy as the one below, but there were figures at the windows and he could hear people moving around in the wards.

There was no sign of the armed guard he'd seen posted outside Arbuthnott's room, or what he'd assumed was the room in which the rogue agent was being held. Baxter paused, reassuring himself that he was in the right place and was approaching the private rooms.

There was enough noise that there was no way the guard wouldn't have been alerted, and he doubted a colonial police officer would have the discipline to maintain his post instead of coming to find out what was happening. He might have fled, of course, but it was never a good idea to assume your enemy was a coward.

Baxter raised his revolver as he got closer to the room. While he was still several paces away, a door into one of the main wards creaked open. He turned, bringing the weapon to bear before raising it as he realised it was Dr Masing.

The German physician was beckoning urgently to him, his eyes wide. Baxter was nonplussed — while they had a good relationship, one perhaps verging on friendship, they were now enemies. Seeing his hesitation, Masing hissed, "It's a trap!" as quietly as he could manage.

Baxter stepped cautiously through the door, eyes darting around as he entered. The ward, a long cool space with tall windows and lined with neatly made-up beds, was empty but obviously ready to receive casualties. Masing appeared to be alone, but Baxter kept his pistol in his hand, the muzzle aimed at the floor.

"What the hell is going on?" Baxter demanded. He knew there wasn't a lot of time — even if the colony wasn't on a war footing yet, the *Schutztruppe* were bound to respond eventually.

"*Kapitan* Schiller is here, with a dozen *askari* and some rough gentlemen with no love for the English, waiting for you. The people you have come for are not here."

Baxter stared hard at Masing's broad, open face. He appeared genuinely concerned. "Why are you telling me this?" he asked quietly. "You're putting yourself in terrible danger."

Masing straightened slightly. "I will not have my hospital turned into a battleground!" he said with some asperity, then slumped slightly. "They think you will surrender when surrounded, though I told them you were not the sort of man to just give up."

Masing was right in that assessment. Baxter wouldn't be taken prisoner again, not by anyone, and it wasn't the RN way to surrender easily.

"I do wish you had not come, that none of this was happening."

"Amen to that," Baxter murmured. "You said the people I've come for aren't here — two men: one English, one Russian?"

Masing looked away, biting his lip. While he didn't want his hospital harmed in a gun fight, he was also a loyal subject of the Kaiser and hesitant to divulge too much. Then he shrugged. "Just so. They have been moved to Schiller's plantation south of here. There's an island where he … where he and Esca…"

With a flash of intuition, Baxter realised what the doctor wanted to say but couldn't. Why Masing was willing to betray his countrymen in this admittedly small way. He reached out and grasped the German's shoulder briefly. "I'm sorry," he said. "For all of this — you're right, I shouldn't have come here. This is a hospital, not a battleground."

"I fear everywhere will soon become a battleground," Masing said, collecting himself and speaking with more firmness. "You should rectify this mistake and leave."

Baxter nodded and moved back to the door. "I hope to see you again, Doctor, in happier times," he said, before slipping back out into the corridor.

He realised that the noise had diminished somewhat. There was still an excited chatter, but the angry exchanges from below had ceased. Baxter hoped that meant Hensley had the situation under control. More importantly, the cruiser had ceased fire. While they were sufficiently far from both the warship and her target not to have been deafened by the bombardment, the thump of the guns firing and the shells whistling overhead had been an all-encompassing background noise for the last few minutes.

Baxter didn't have time to worry about that now. He went back the way he'd come, fighting the temptation to check the private room, just in case Masing was lying. He doubted the young doctor was capable of deceit.

Julius was waiting where Baxter had left him, crouched in the corridor with his rifle held across his knees. He rose as his commanding officer approached. If he was surprised to see Baxter returning without the men they'd come for, he gave no sign of it. "Fetch Samuels down," Baxter said. "Then return to the ground floor. We're leaving."

"Aye, sir." The sailor started moving, but before he could get far they heard a thump from above, the clatter of a rifle being dropped.

"Get down to Hensley — tell him to get everyone back to the boat!" Baxter snapped. Julius didn't need any encouragement and launched himself back down the stairs.

Baxter eased up the stairs slowly, drawing back the hammer of his pistol as he went. It was a spiral staircase, making it hard to tell what lay ahead.

At the top, he found himself in a hexagonal room with a tall domed roof. A number of small windows provided an excellent view over the city. Samuels lay in a pool of blood beside one of the landward windows, his throat opened almost to the bone.

One of Esca's men was crouched over the dead sailor, going through his pockets as though this was the most natural thing in the world. He looked up with a guilty expression as Baxter appeared. He licked his lips, then went for the Lee Enfield rifle that lay discarded six inches from Samuels' right hand.

Baxter did not hesitate. He fired, missed his moving target, then fired again. The bullet spun the German agent against the wall. He yelled in pain, clutching his shoulder and glaring at Baxter with desperate eyes.

Baxter levelled the smoking revolver again, taking deliberate aim at the man's head. His finger tightened on the trigger, but he didn't finish squeezing. Instead, he lunged forward and struck the wounded man in the head with the butt, dropping him.

He could hear shouts from the lower levels now, followed by one gunshot and then a positive fusillade. He'd let loose the dogs of war here, it seemed.

Baxter paused for long enough to recover Samuels' identity card from the breast pocket of his uniform blouse. He didn't like the idea of leaving the dead sailor behind, but he had the living sailors to think about now.

CHAPTER TWELVE

"Halt!" an authoritative voice shouted as Baxter reached the first landing. He ducked back into the stairwell, then risked a glance round the corner. It was Schiller, of course, the *Schutztruppe* officer he'd first encountered in the German Club and taken an immediate dislike to.

The German officer wasn't alone; standing behind him was a file of *askari* soldiers with levelled Mauser rifles.

"There is nowhere for you to go, Mr Baxter. You and your men are quite trapped!" There was a gloating note in the German's voice that put Baxter's teeth on edge. It sounded like Schiller thought he was on the verge of a resounding victory here. "In fact, they're probably already…"

Baxter leant out from cover and interrupted Schiller with two rapid shots. It caused the African soldiers to duck for cover, disrupting the neat firing line Schiller had established. Baxter launched himself across the corridor, putting his shoulder into the door opposite and crashing straight through it. Pain lanced through him from the impact — he'd pay for it later, he knew, but right now he didn't have time to worry about that.

He'd crashed through into a ward. Orderlies and patients, already distressed by the sounds of combat from below, cried out in panic at his violent arrival. Behind him, he could hear Schiller berating his men.

Baxter didn't hang around. He sprinted across the ward, scooping up a chair as he went. He used it to smash a window and followed it through without hesitation, stepping out onto the balcony that ran the length of the hospital's seaward side. Instinct made him twist aside just before an *askari* fired through the broken door, the bullet cracking past his head. He returned fire, his last two rounds before the hammer dropped on a spent cartridge.

Baxter didn't bother checking if he'd actually hit anything. The panic in the ward was absolute, patients and staff cowering away from the exchange of gunfire, and he had no desire to prolong their discomfort.

Keeping below the level of the windows, he moved to the edge of the balcony and saw that he'd be going into the water if he jumped from here. Glancing back towards the jetty, he saw the launch was still there. Four native soldiers were crouched in cover at the end of the wooden structure. Baxter grinned savagely. He guessed they'd been sent to secure the boat and had been pinned down by Dalton and the stoker. Two more men were guarding the rear door of the hospital, no doubt having driven back or killed the sailors he'd detailed to hold that position.

There was no more time to think. He could hear Schiller behind him now, yelling in incensed German. Baxter dashed along the balcony as bullets started smashing through the windows. He dived over the railing, landing on one of the *askari* pinned down at the end of the jetty. He managed to roll away from a descending rifle butt and lashed out with his foot, catching his attacker in the groin and sending him staggering back.

"Dalton! Balcony! Ten rounds rapid!" he bellowed as he staggered to his feet and swung a vast haymaker that connected with the side of a second soldier's head. A boot to the midriff sent a third man flying back into the water.

Dalton obeyed without question, turning his fire on the upper storey of the hospital as the first local soldier tentatively stepped through the broken window from which Baxter had made his precipitous exit.

Baxter didn't have time to see the effect of the petty officer's fire. A rifle butt connected with his ribs, making him stagger. The soldier he'd punched in the side of the head was coming at him, while the two who had been covering the rear door of the hospital were advancing with fixed bayonets, unable as they were to get a clear shot with their comrade locked in combat with Baxter.

He wasn't going to lose that advantage. He closed in on the African soldier and grabbed him by the belt buckle before he had time to react. Baxter then grabbed the front of his smock and lifted him off the ground, ignoring the hands that battered at his face and neck. "Hensley!" he roared, in a voice calibrated to carry across a ship's deck in the middle of a typhoon. "Back to the launch, now!"

White-uniformed RN sailors bailed out of the hospital. They rapidly overpowered the two *askari* coming at him with bayonets. The soldier Baxter was holding locked remarkably strong hands around his throat and squeezed, forcing him to headbutt the man to break his hold. Stars exploded behind his eyes as he gasped for breath.

"Time to go, I think, Baxter!" Hensley's voice was close by his ear, but all he could do was nod.

They piled back into the launch, an organised chaos of limbs and rifles and the cheerful shouting of men who had faced death and come out the other side. Baxter couldn't blame them, but he knew that they couldn't lose discipline now.

"Rifles on the hospital!" he barked. "Nobody fire unless I give the order. Dalton, get us clear of the land."

Hensley followed his lead, getting the men organised and ready to cover their withdrawal. Baxter stared hard at the hospital as they drew away. Schiller, identifiable as much from his arrogant bearing as his rather absurd uniform hat, had stepped out onto the balcony and was glaring after them. *Askari* were milling about on the balcony behind him or on the jetty, but as one or two raised their rifles to fire after the escaping launch, Schiller angrily ordered them to hold their fire.

Despite the distance opening between them, Baxter felt like Schiller was staring at him directly. Just as the colonial officer wasn't hard to pick out, Baxter knew he stood head and shoulders above the other sailors himself. He sketched an ironic salute to the German, and got similar in return.

"Why aren't they shooting?" someone muttered.

"Silence, there," Hensley snapped. It was clear from his tone that he was wondering the same thing.

Baxter broke Schiller's gaze and looked along the coastline. White flags were flying from every flagpole in sight. He was pretty sure someone had hoisted a bedsheet on one. A launch was steaming at speed out towards the stationary *Astraea*, a square of white showing at her stern. "There's your answer, lads," he said, gesturing towards the launch.

"Bloody hell — are they surrendering?" Hensley asked.

Baxter snorted. "Unlikely — probably wanting to negotiate a truce. I imagine Sykes wants to take possession of the ships in harbour, and Schnee will be keen to prevent that happening."

"Along with any further destruction to the city. Back to the cruiser, sir?"

Baxter considered that. The last thing Sykes would want while engaging in truce talks was a boatload of excitable bluejackets returning from a landing expedition. "Stand out of the harbour and make directly for Zanzibar," he said after a moment's thought. "We should have sufficient fuel."

"Aye, sir." Hensley's eyes narrowed as he looked along the jumble of sailors. "Christ — we left Samuels behind! Should we go back for him, sir?"

Baxter felt his mouth tighten. It wasn't the first time he'd lost a man, and if this war turned out to be more than a skirmish, it wouldn't be the last. "We didn't leave him behind," he said grimly, taking out the dead sailor's papers. There was blood on them. "Not in a state to go back for, anyway."

Hensley's expression changed, the excitement and tension of the raid replaced by shock and sorrow. "Yes, sir," he said dully. "I'll check on the rest of the men."

"Well, this is a pretty mess," Commander Parker said sourly, looking up from Baxter's written report. "Quite a risk for a couple of strays you didn't even manage to bring out, and a man dead. What have you got to say for yourself, Mr Baxter?"

Baxter had spent the time after they'd got back from Dar es-Salaam considering that exact question. "I made the mistake of assuming the enemy was a complete idiot and wouldn't have moved the men in question," he said bluntly. He'd never been one for dissembling. "It won't happen again."

Parker seemed slightly taken aback by his openness. "Well, then. See that it doesn't." He sat back, took up his pipe and rekindled the tobacco in the bowl. When he went on, his voice was only slightly less frosty. "At least it wasn't a complete loss and you have a lead on where these two have been taken. Assuming you trust the source."

It was Baxter's turn to be taken aback. He'd been certain that Parker would send him back to London in disgrace. That idea might have appealed to him when it was only Arbuthnott he was hunting, but now that Tomas had been taken as well, he was keen to remain.

"I believe the source is trustworthy, sir," Baxter said.

"And what makes you say that?"

Baxter had thought that through as the launch chugged back across the Zanzibar Channel. The men had been quiet after learning of Samuels' death. The excitement and adrenalin of the brief skirmish had worn off with the realisation that they were now in a shooting war and death was a very real prospect. Dalton had needed no instruction, and aside from a brief pause to speak with *Pegasus*, there hadn't been anything to disturb him.

"Dr Masing may be a German, and may see himself as a loyal subject of the Kaiser. But I did get the feeling that he wasn't happy with how the hospital was being used, and I can't fault him for that."

Parker's cold grey eyes were unimpressed as he looked at Baxter across the glowing coal of his pipe. "And?"

"Well, sir, frankly — he implied his wife has left him for Schiller, the *Schutztruppe* officer whose estate is being used to imprison our people. Politics and loyalty are one thing, affairs of the heart are entirely another."

"The heart. Yes," Parker said, unable to hide a sardonic note in his voice. "I've met this Schiller on a previous visit, in happier times. Nasty piece of work."

"That was my impression as well, sir."

"If I were you, Mr Baxter, I wouldn't necessarily be too quick to judge." There was a sharpness to the commander's tone. He sighed. "Well, what do you propose to do about this?"

Baxter stared at Parker, unsure why his commanding officer was being so agreeable. He found it hard to believe Parker was still swayed by Mashka's pleas for help — Baxter knew that even a convincing fake Russian noble would have sway for a short period of time. He wondered if Parker was giving him enough rope to hang himself, or had been leant on from London.

"First task is to find out exactly where Schiller's island is," he said, when he realised Parker genuinely wanted an answer and was on the verge of impatience. "Then we work out how to reach it."

Parker nodded. "I believe you may be in luck, Mr Baxter. I recall him telling me all about it — more or less his own private island somewhere not far from Dar es-Salaam."

Baxter nodded. That tallied with what Masing had told him at the hospital. "Some sort of expedition could be mounted then, sir," he said. "Though that would depend a lot on our orders concerning trying to maintain neutrality between the colonies."

Parker snorted. "We just bombarded Dar es-Salaam's wireless station because the Germans were still broadcasting from it, contradicting Schnee's claim that the city was to remain an open and peaceful port. I don't think anyone but our civilian masters believe that this facsimile of peace will remain intact for long."

"Yes, sir. I'll start drawing up proposals for an operation off the coast of Dar es-Salaam then." Baxter's mind was already turning the problem over — how long it would take, how many men, the number of vessels. How much time they had, before Arbuthnott and Tomas were moved again, or just quietly disappeared into the wilderness.

"Will you, indeed?" Parker said frostily. "This station is not here purely for the pursuit of whatever lofty goals the Admiralty has set you, *Lieutenant*."

Baxter tamped down a flare of anger. "Yes, sir," he said through a tight jaw. "I apologise if I overstepped. However, an expedition of this nature does offer multiple opportunities, including mapping and an assessment of native loyalty to the German Empire."

"Hmm." Parker eyed him. "Very well. Have a proposal on my desk in two days."

"Yes, sir." This was definitely not something he would leave to Hensley, though the other officer had acquitted himself perfectly well in yesterday's raid.

"It doesn't help that we don't know where that protected cruiser is," Hensley said, as they discussed the issue later in the day.

"We don't," Baxter agreed. "Short of *Pegasus* or *Astraea* being in the area, though, there's nothing we can do but stay out of the way and hope *Königsberg* doesn't spot us."

"Didn't your chum Kleiner from the other evening say *Königsberg* was heading north? No doubt looking for the rich hunting grounds around this side of the Suez Canal."

Baxter nodded distractedly. "I don't think he was telling the truth, though."

They had a map of the region spread out on a table in Hensley's slightly larger office. It showed the coast of East Africa, including the islands that were scattered along that stretch of land. "Why on earth wouldn't he?"

"Why would he tell me the truth when we weren't far from being enemies? No, for my money Looff took her south and is's lurking somewhere to the south. Possibly in the delta itself."

Hensley pursed his lips, then nodded. "I took a cruise down that way, back when I was first posted here. There are a lot of little islands between here and Mafia Island. Something like the *Helmuth* would be perfect for going and peering at them."

"Unfortunately, she's already earmarked to be a guardship for the port here. What I'm going to propose, then, is a locally hired vessel and as many volunteers as we can fit into it, provisioned for a two-week sortie."

"Would you want me along?" Hensley asked.

"We'll see what Parker says — he might not like me trying to take everyone from his command. And this will be dangerous."

Hensley grinned. "I'm told by a reliable source that wars are dangerous things."

"More dangerous than average for a war," Baxter replied flatly, but he was prevented from pressing the point further by a hammering at the door.

"Come!" Hensley snapped.

A sailor popped his head round, an apologetic look on his face. "Begging your pardon, sir, but the Russian lady is here, and she ain't happy…"

"I speak English, you know!" Mashka snapped, pushing past the orderly. Baxter almost didn't recognise her. Instead of her usual blouse, skirt and jacket — 'the uniform of the proletariat' as she put it — she was wearing what was almost an adapted RN uniform with a loose blouse and a long skirt, topped off with a broad-brimmed straw hat. It immediately put him in mind of Ekaterina Juneau. She'd been very fond of adapted Imperial Russian Navy uniforms during the Second Pacific Squadron's long voyage to destruction at Tsushima.

"Marcus Alexandrovich," Mashka greeted him imperiously, then gave a slightly warmer smile to Hensley, who actually blushed. "Mr Hensley. I trust I find you both in good health?"

Baxter concealed a smile. She had indeed learned her trade well from Ekaterina. For one, he knew her English was better than this stilted and heavily accented version, and for another, he guessed she would have been more comfortable in her usual uniform.

"Very well, thank you, uh, miss," Hensley stammered.

"Though I understand you did not meet with success in the den of thieves and murderers?" There was real venom in the way she described Dar es-Salaam, Baxter noted.

"Unfortunately not," Baxter said, then nodded to Hensley. "Why don't you give us a moment, Mr Hensley?"

The lieutenant looked slightly crestfallen, but rolled up the map and retired from the office with a modicum of good grace.

"You failed," Mashka said flatly as soon as she was sure Hensley was out of earshot, dropping her overdone Russian accent. Baxter hadn't had a chance to speak to her since his return, but he had managed to dash off a quick note with minimum detail.

"No," he replied. "The enemy had taken an obvious step to thwart us. I do, however, have intelligence as to where they might be."

"Well, what are we waiting for, then?" she demanded.

Baxter quirked an eyebrow. This was the Mashka he'd known in Odessa — headstrong and passionate.

"Running off half-cocked will get us all killed and no closer to capturing Arbuthnott." He watched her closely as he said that, and caught a flicker of anger in her eyes. "And, of course, getting Tommy back."

Mashka nodded. "Rescuing Tomaska is the important thing," she said finally. "Come. I have something to show you."

She didn't give Baxter time to respond before sweeping from the room. Grabbing his cap, he hurried to catch up. "You really have learned a lot from Ekaterina, haven't you?" he said as he caught up.

"The countess is a good teacher," she said, with real warmth and affection in her voice. That surprised Baxter. When he'd sent Mashka to ensure Tommy Dunbar got back to Ekaterina Juneau safely, it had been done in the hopes of pulling the young and newly orphaned girl out of the fires of Odessa, but he'd always suspected she would have gone back to her life of drudgery and preparing for revolution in the slums of the city.

It was good to know that he'd got one thing right, at least.

Hensley caught up with them at the front door of the palace. "Any orders, sir?" he asked smartly, fidgeting his cap onto his head and following them out into the afternoon sun.

Baxter thought he could detect a slight undercurrent in the younger man's voice. Could it be jealousy? If so, that was utterly preposterous, and not something he had time for. "Courses, please, Mr Hensley," he said coolly. "Quickest way there and back while not running out of supplies. Hired vessel, as we discussed."

"Yes, sir," Hensley said, offering him a crisp salute. Baxter returned it and sent Hensley on his way.

"He is an enthusiastic young man," Mashka said, watching the sub-lieutenant trot away. "Handsome, too."

"Behave yourself," Baxter said with a smile. "Back to business — where are we going?"

Where they were going turned out to be a somewhat shabby warehouse in a less desirable part of Stone Town, via the hotel where the Resident had put Mashka up during her stay. Major Pearce had been keen to render her every possible courtesy, though Baxter knew Mashka had turned down an invitation to stay in the Chinese Doctor's House, as the British government representative's official home was known.

They stopped in front of the hotel's grand portico. "I must change," said Mashka. "Wait for me round the back."

Baxter stared at her. "I'm going to stick out like a sore thumb in uniform."

"Do not worry, your nice uniform will not get dirty," she said wryly, then sobered. "A man in uniform can go where he likes. A woman in finery, not so much."

Baxter paced in the alley behind the hotel, aware of just how conspicuous he looked, until Mashka emerged. She had changed into more practical clothing.

"Can we bloody get on with this?" he asked, and received a sharp look in return.

"The countess has often spoken of your impatience, and her hope that it would eventually be tempered," Mashka said. "It seems she will need to continue being patient."

The mention of Ekaterina sent a jolt through Baxter. He was both surprised and pleased to hear that she often spoke of him. Assuming Mashka wasn't just trying to get a rise out of him, that was.

"I don't know if you've noticed, but there is a war on," he said, with a certain amount of asperity. "We should probably get on with this."

"I am aware — the war started for us before it did for you," she said.

Baxter held back from pointing out that it had only been a matter of days between the various declarations of war. Mashka had always been fiery, and this was perhaps not the best time to provoke her. Instead, he followed her down towards the port area of Zanzibar, keeping alert as he walked. Hensley had told him, not long after he'd arrived, that the sleepy little colonial city was for the most part safe, and he'd not had any problems. As he'd just told Mashka, though, they *were* at war and he'd already been attacked twice by enemy agents in Dar es-Salaam. If they or their compatriots arrived in Zanzibar, then the busy port would be the perfect place for an ambush.

"Calm yourself, Marcus Alexandrovich," Mashka said, as if reading his mind. "We are quite safe here — this is the British Empire, after all."

"Given that I've just got back from a raid into the German Empire, you will forgive me if I don't take that as a guarantee of safety."

"What do you think is going to happen? The *Königsberg* will sail into the harbour and shell the city flat?" She snorted. "Preposterous."

"You've seen what a warship can do to a city," he pointed out. "And what men can do when they're at war."

"*Da.*" Mashka fell silent, and Baxter was about to apologise for bringing up the spectre of the Odessa revolution when she spoke again. "We are here."

'Here' was a small warehouse, disused from the look of it. It smelled strongly of cloves and nutmeg, on which Zanzibar's wealth rested, underpinned by a hint of rat droppings and old hemp.

"Bloody hell," Baxter said, as Mashka ushered him in. "I wondered what had happened to you."

Billings sat on a shipping crate in the middle of the low, dim space, his hands tied before him and one ankle chained to a bolt in the floor. Two young men, one a local and the other probably Russian, kept him under guard. Baxter was astonished to see a look of fear cross Billings' face as the two of them entered.

"You keep that mad woman away from me!" the former petty officer snarled, jumping to his feet.

Baxter could feel a headache starting behind his eyes, and rubbed the bridge of his nose. Yesterday, he'd been back afloat, and his shore-based problems had seemed a long way away. He wished he was back out at sea now, even if that meant he was under fire. It would probably still be safer than this situation.

CHAPTER THIRTEEN

"He is my prisoner!" Mashka declared, sounding petulant, and perfectly aware that would never stand up in a court of law.

"He is a subject of the British Crown, in a British Crown colony, and you are the subject of an allied power," Baxter said patiently, as one of Mashka's men reluctantly unlocked the shackle around Billings' ankle. "And you are not, as far as I understand it, employed by the Tsar."

Mashka spat on the ground at the notion.

"I tried to —" Billings began, a note of desperation in his voice as he realised he had an ally.

"Shut the hell up," Baxter snapped. He could feel his temper rising. Even the two Russian agents took half a step back, though Mashka remained uncowed.

Baxter had no doubt she was armed, and both the men guarding Billings had pistols. The last thing he needed was for this scene to descend into violence. "I don't doubt that you feel perfectly justified — you *are* perfectly justified — in holding this man prisoner."

"You cannot tell me that you are *that* interested in maintaining the rule of law!" she snarled.

Baxter had to concede that point. He'd be quite happy to leave Billings to her less-than-tender mercies. God knew, the former petty officer had it coming. While Arbuthnott had been the architect of a mad scheme to raise tensions between Britain and Russia during the Russo-Japanese War, Billings had been his man of business. Baxter was supposed to have died in an attempt to destroy the *Yaroslavich*, a Russian cruiser bearing a close personal friend of the Tsar, and Billings had been the one to arrange that.

No, he had no more reason to want to save this man's life than he had a personal reason to see Arbuthnott brought out from German East Africa. Right now, though, he wanted every resource available — and alive — until he could get to the bottom of things. On the one hand he had his superior officer in London, convinced that Arbuthnott had sold his country out to the Germans. On the other hand he had Billings, who claimed that the rogue agent had been working to redeem himself by trying to infiltrate German circles.

"I'm not," Baxter said bluntly. "This man could be useful to us, however. We don't have time — and I don't have the patience — for settling old scores right now."

Mashka glared at him, her green eyes glittering with anger, then she snorted and almost smiled. "There is a war on, I suppose," she said. "But understand this, Marcus Alexandrovich. I *will* be taking both him and Arbuthnott back to Russia when we are done. And if he puts one foot out of line, I will shoot him."

"Well, now that we've got that settled…" Billings began.

Baxter's headache had flowered in the small, hot space. The smell of spices and decay had become cloying in the few minutes they'd been in there. "You better actually have something useful, or I will let her shoot you," he snapped, taking the wind out of the other man's sails. Billings needed to understand that he was not in control here. "Because I am *this* close to being done with this whole sorry debacle and reporting back to London that Arbuthnott is dead and, terribly sorry, but there's nothing else to be done here."

Billings licked his lips nervously. He'd been on the receiving end of Baxter's temper before and knew that it wasn't an idle threat. "I gather from Miss here that they've moved his nibs from Dar es-Salaam to some German bigwig's place in the country."

"I told you no such thing!" Mashka snapped.

"I'm not stupid, and I speak a bit of Russian," Billings replied calmly. "Thing is, I reckon I know where that might be. I'd be more than happy to tell you when I'm away from this place, with a proper meal inside me and probably a beer or two."

"And after a bath," Mashka sniffed, seemingly oblivious to the fact she was responsible for his dishevelled state.

"I really don't envy you this nonsense," Hensley said. He and Baxter were waiting to present their proposal for a cruise down the coast to Commander Parker. "I'd much rather just be at sea, shooting at Germans."

"Well, I didn't bloody ask to get involved," Baxter growled. He'd spent the last two days alternating between preventing Mashka and Billings from killing each other and working with Hensley to fine-tune their proposed operation.

"At some point, you really must tell me how you did get involved," the lieutenant said. "I'm sure it's a fascinating story."

"It really isn't," Baxter said, and was spared further discussion when Parker's aide summoned them. That had been Hensley's job until recently, but it seemed the base commander had quietly accepted the young man had a more active role and had assigned the job to Greaves.

The commander's expression was, if anything, even more irritated than it habitually was. "Whatever you are about to propose," he said shortly. "The answer is 'no'."

Baxter knew he should just accept that. Getting into a fight with a senior officer so soon into his newly fledged career would not be a sensible move.

"No?" he exploded. "We haven't even…"

"Control yourself, Mr Baxter!" Parker roared, jumping to his feet. "And recall who you are speaking to."

Baxter locked eyes with the commander. The older man was almost vibrating with rage.

"Yes, sir!" he said, looking away. "My apologies."

"Yes, you should bloody well apologise," Parker said sourly.

"If I may, sir…" Hensley tried, in a far more conciliatory tone.

"You may not," Parker said, with sharp finality. "While I am not in the habit of explaining myself to junior officers — particularly deeply insubordinate ones — I shall make an exception in this case. We have orders from the Resident that there are to be no more intrusions into German waters or assaults upon the persons or property of German East Africa. Major Pearce tells me the High Commissioner is absolutely determined to maintain the principles of the Morocco-Congo Treaty. He will be personally reprimanding Captain Sykes for the recent bombardment."

Baxter fought his temper back under control in the silence that followed. His effort was not helped by the intermittent buzzing of a fly bouncing off one of the closed windows. "Yes, sir," he said. Parker hadn't needed to explain himself, but he'd chosen to. Baxter would have to take that.

"Mr Baxter, you're dismissed. Mr Hensley, a word."

"Yes, sir." Baxter turned on his heel and walked swiftly from the room before his temper gave way entirely.

He paused outside the House of Wonders and took several deep breaths. He forced himself to put his cap on calmly and properly, rather than jamming it onto his head, and then walked at a leisurely pace across the shady square beyond the confines of the government building.

Mashka was waiting under a palm on the far side of the square, back in her Russian aristocrat guise. She twirled a parasol over her shoulder as she watched Baxter approach. She wasn't alone, of course her two followers hovering nearby.

"Trouble in paradise, Marcus Alexandrovich?" Mashka asked as he stopped next to her.

"We're forbidden from any further offensive action," Baxter said sourly. "We watch and wait."

"This is not acceptable," she snapped.

"You'll get no argument from me. But Parker's orders are clear. The Resident has forbidden any personnel from His Majesty's installation here from taking any offensive action against the forces of the Kaiser." Baxter paused, then took his cap off and rubbed wearily at his forehead.

"What?" Mashka demanded.

"My *official* orders are to undertake a feasibility survey to see if this place can be turned into a full Navy installation rather than just a coaling base."

"This sounds terribly boring."

"It is, which is why I farmed it out to Hensley. But I would be remiss if I didn't personally undertake a hydrographic survey of the surrounding waters, including potential threats to the approaches. Possibly to the south of Dar es-Salaam, for the sake of completeness."

"Your nation is at war, Marcus Alexandrovich. Surely the time for such menial tasks is past. Now is the time for fighting, not planning."

"Warfare *is* planning, Mashka," he said, knowing how pompous he sounded. "Planning and logistics. Believe me, I've been in plenty of dangerous situations that could have been avoided with proper planning — usually on someone else's part, sometimes my own. This outbreak of unpleasantness shouldn't get in the way of planning work."

Mashka seemed to consider this. "You seemed … unconcerned about rules when last we met."

Baxter plucked at his uniform jacket. "That was before I put this on," he said.

"I did not get the impression you held your Navy in high regard," Mashka mused.

Baxter had caught himself thinking the same thing of late. He'd clawed his way back into the RN, believing it was where he belonged, believing what Connie had said to him during that last bloody day in the Aegean. He'd forgotten how irritating the rules and regulations could be, the frustration of not being able to solve every problem with his fists. That, of course, was what had got him drummed out of the service in the first place.

"Well, I'm in it now, and I'm not about to throw away all the work I've put in to get here," he snapped. He took a deep breath, seeing the flare of anger in Mashka's eyes, and moderated his tone. "Which isn't to say I wouldn't have disobeyed orders to pull Tommy's arse out of the fire. Again." He stood staring into the distance for a moment. "I don't need to ask Parker's permission to undertake the survey, but hopefully I'll be able to talk him into releasing a port tender or similar for the work."

"And if he does not?"

"I've got a small budget. It should cover the hire of something for a few days."

Mashka nodded. "I also have funds, so a vessel should not be a problem. We will need men, though, and arms?"

Baxter was about to question the way she'd blithely included herself in the expedition, and indeed shut the notion down in its entirety. Not because he doubted Mashka's capability, but because the last thing he needed was the complication of a woman on a small boat. And then there was the risk of her falling into enemy hands as well. He had no illusions about the dangers they faced, and he didn't want Mashka arguing with him at every turn.

Mashka tilted her chin up defiantly, as though daring him to voice those thoughts. He was saved by the arrival of Hensley, marching briskly across the square towards them. He saluted smartly, and it took Baxter a moment to remember they were both in uniform and therefore he was required to return the gesture.

"Mr Baxter," Hensley greeted him formally, before turning to Mashka and bowing over her hand. "Miss Mashka."

There was something cool in his eyes when he looked back to Baxter, and he realised the young man was indeed jealous. He kept his own expression neutral — he didn't have time for this tomfoolery right now and had no desire to explain to Hensley that his interest in the young Ukrainian woman was purely professional.

"Anything I need to know?" Baxter asked, after Mashka had returned Hensley's greeting.

"Nothing much," Hensley said offhandedly. "Parker just wanted to talk about the report I'm preparing for you. Odd thing, really; he was absolutely insistent that I make sure my name goes on the work as well."

Mashka covered a smirk with a lacy handkerchief and Baxter tried to suppress a smile. While the lieutenant seemed none the wiser, it was clear that Parker didn't trust Baxter and wanted to make sure that an officer under his command got credit where it was due. The fact that Baxter obviously didn't care about the work didn't seem to register with either of them.

"Well, Mr Hensley, I had best consider how to proceed from here. If Commander Parker didn't give you any immediate orders, why don't you show Miss Mashka around Stone Town? I'm sure she'd be interested in your insights."

Mashka shot him a venomous look, which Hensley missed. He flushed slightly red and smiled. "I'd be delighted," he said in a rush. "If, of course, that is, if you…"

Mashka gave him a brilliant smile. "That would be delightful," she said, putting on her exaggerated Russian accent again. "Shall we start somewhere that serves vodka?"

Baxter watched them go. He had a lot to do while they were both distracted and therefore not underfoot.

He thought about going back into Admiralty House to put his case for a 'hydrographic survey' to Parker in an attempt to requisition both vessel and men. It would involve him lying to a senior officer, though, or at least omitting some truths. That wasn't something he was good at, or liked doing. The notion of hoodwinking Parker didn't bother him too much, but he knew he'd be taking men into danger on a lie.

"Fine bloody intelligence officer you're making," he muttered to himself. The problem was, as he'd said to Mashka, he needed a boat, and men to crew it. Then he smiled thinly as an idea came to him, and headed for the harbour.

Billings had told them he could be found in the Nutmeg, a rough pub that catered mostly for the crews off European ships that stopped at Zanzibar. Mashka had wanted to keep their dubious ally under guard, of course, or at least under watch. That had resulted in another argument as Baxter had attempted to weld together this strange alliance, based solely on similar, but not identical, goals. Billings had got his way in the end.

Ducking through the low door of the pub, Baxter immediately felt like he'd been transported back to London or Edinburgh, or a watering hole in any British port town. The architecture of the room was different, of course, being built from coral stone like most of the other buildings in this part of Zanzibar, and he didn't have to worry about heavy wooden beams supporting a ceiling low enough to hit his head on if he stood up straight. The smoky atmosphere, however, and the collection of burly men in various states of inebriation, was no different; the low hum of conversation and the chink of glasses made him feel almost at home. The cheerful-looking African man behind the bar only served to make the hand pumps for India pale ale and bottles of whisky and gin seem all the more familiar.

It was far hotter, of course, than your average British pub, and fat black flies lazily orbited a ceiling fan that did little to stir the close atmosphere. Baxter hadn't had time to change, and his tropical whites stood out in the dim light. A few men glanced his way, while others did their best to avoid his eye. It wouldn't surprise him if more than a few of the men were sailors from the base having an illicit drink in mufti.

Baxter ignored them all. He cut straight across to Billings, who sat at a corner table with a couple of disreputable-looking fellows. The former petty officer gave him a pained look as he sat down opposite him.

"Well, there goes my credibility," Billings complained. "You could at least have changed…"

Baxter got straight to the point. "Where's your boat?" he asked.

"Boat, Mr Baxter?" Billings asked, with every appearance of innocence.

"I have neither the time nor the patience for these games," he said flatly. "You're a sailor, Billings, and you'll want to leave in a hurry just as soon as your master is safely in your hands. Particularly with the Russians breathing down your neck. You've got a boat stashed away somewhere. And a crew. I want both. We're going to go and fetch bloody Arbuthnott."

The old salt watched him with a neutral expression. "Official operation not authorised, sir?"

Baxter could feel sweat running down his back and the stares of unfriendly patrons. He didn't want to hang around. Nor did he have the patience for a lengthy explanation.

"Do you want Arbuthnott brought out, or not?" he snapped.

"Okay, okay. Easy there, Mr Baxter. When do you want to leave?"

"As soon as possible."

"Trying to stay ahead of your commanding officer? Not to mention that mad Russian woman?"

"I'm mostly concerned that Schiller will move Arbuthnott and Tomas again — at some point even he will realise that an island isn't the best place to try to hide someone from the largest navy in the world. And if you speak of Mashka like that again, I will tan your hide so thoroughly you won't be able to stand for a week."

"Well, sir, that's no way to talk to an ally," he said.

Baxter wasn't in the mood for this. "Six this evening, Billings. I'll meet you back here."

"What, no threats of what will happen if I'm not here? Or promises to dog my every step until we leave?"

"I've got better things to do with my time, and you seem as committed as I am to seeing this through."

Billings grinned. "Got a good idea of where I'm going, sir. Maybe I don't need you along?"

"You need me to do the dangerous bit, Billings."

The false geniality disappeared. "I'm glad we understand each other, Baxter. Don't bother coming in — I'll wait for you outside. And maybe ditch the uniform, eh?"

CHAPTER FOURTEEN

Even after such a short period back in His Majesty's service, being out of uniform felt odd to Baxter. They were planning a night-time landing, however, and his tropical whites would have stood out too much.

"They'll shoot us for spies if we're caught, of course," Billings commented, watching Baxter fidget with his clothes, despite them being more comfortable than his uniform.

"Well, let's try not to get caught," he snapped.

Baxter wasn't quite sure what he'd been expecting when he'd met Billings that evening, but it certainly wasn't a small, modern pleasure boat. He hadn't seen the boat anywhere in the harbour before, which suggested that Arbuthnott's man had had it hidden well away somewhere. It was oil-fired, which simplified matters greatly, and cut across the channel between Zanzibar and the enemy coast at a reasonable speed.

"You chose well," he said, as he patted the polished brass rail in the wheelhouse.

Billings made a suspicious noise in his throat. "His nibs wouldn't want to be spending too much time on anything not befitting his station as a gentleman now, would he?"

"If you dislike the man so much, why are you sticking your neck out for him?" Billings was ex-RN; he had been a grizzled petty officer when Baxter was a freshly-minted sub-lieutenant on the same command. Arbuthnott wasn't the sort of man who seemed to command much in the way of personal loyalty, and yet Billings continually put himself in the path of danger for the rogue agent.

Billings shrugged. "He pays well," he said. "Well enough to cover a bit of risk. Man of independent means, despite everything you've put him through."

For a moment that seemed to be it, then Billings spoke again. "I know you've got your reasons for not trusting Arbuthnott. Or me, for that matter. But he's never done anything he doesn't think is in England's best interests. He's no traitor."

Baxter was unconvinced. "That's not for me to judge," he said.

"Who should judge, then? The Russians?"

"My orders are clear, Mr Billings — retrieve Arbuthnott from German territory and return him to London. And that is what I intend to do."

"Lights ahead," the lookout in the bows called out, voice low but loud enough to carry back to them at the wheel. Billings had a four-man crew, all of them every bit as rough as he was. One of them, the man on lookout duty, was sporting a magnificent black eye and moved slightly stiffly. They all seemed wary around the grizzled older man, as though he was a shell that had not yet detonated.

Baxter turned back to the chart. They had a small binnacle light on in the wheelhouse, just enough to see the chart, while the rest of the boat was in darkness. He checked their likely position based on time, speed and direction of travel, and then nodded. If he was right, then Schiller's private island should be about a mile off their port bow.

"What's the plan?" Billings asked.

Baxter glanced up at him. "I assume you've got more experience with this sort of nonsense than I have."

The other man's grin gleamed in the binnacle light. "But you're the *officer*, sir. Plans are your responsibility."

Baxter tapped his teeth with the stub of pencil he'd been marking the chart with. The German authorities knew that the British were trying to rescue Tommy and Arbuthnott, but did they suspect Baxter would be coming here? It all hinged on whether Dr Masing had told Schiller and Esca that he'd spoken with Baxter. He couldn't discount that possibility, or the chance that Schiller had beaten the information out of him. He didn't doubt the truth of what Masing had said — there wasn't a dishonest bone in that man's body, and his distress had been real. But a lot could have happened in the handful of days between the raid on Dar es-Salaam and this warm night on the Indian Ocean.

Baxter threw the pencil down. "All we can do is get ashore and see if we can find them without getting caught ourselves."

Billings pursed his lips. "I'm not sure we should be leaving the planning to the officers," he said.

"Any better ideas?"

"Short of coming back with a gaggle of Jollies, no."

Baxter actually smiled at that. A company or two of Royal Marines would be handy about now, but also in contravention of the strictures placed on Parker.

"Well, then. Let's be about it."

There wasn't much detail about the island on the chart. It was small enough that it didn't seem to have a name recorded by the RN's mapping service, only a handful of square miles. It was longer than it was broad and appeared like an inverted comma on the map, with the broader end pointing north. Billings tapped the northern end of the island. "That's where Schiller will have his house. God knows why he'd want a home there — it barely looks big enough for a cabbage patch, let alone a plantation."

"Some men value their privacy, or maybe he just likes the idea of a private island," Baxter said. "Looks like there's a beach at the end furthest from the house. We'll land there, just you and me, Billings, and see what can be seen. Your chaps can hold position there, but be ready to come to us."

"He better bloody well be there," Billings grumbled. "Getting a bit tired of this part of the world."

Baxter reflected that it was probably the first time that he'd agreed with Arbuthnott's agent.

It took them another hour to close with the island and then skirt along its eastern side. It was tucked in against a low headland that jutted out into the Indian Ocean, giving Schiller at least some shelter from the monsoon winds. Billings and his crew weren't particularly happy about passing so close between the island and the enemy coast, but that coastline didn't appear to have any habitation, and their vessel would be hidden against the deeper darkness of the landmass.

Baxter scoured the island with his field glasses as they steamed past. He suddenly had a strong sense of déjà vu, reminded of the approach to Dar es-Salaam a few days ago. There were a few lights burning around Schiller's compound, enough for Baxter to make out a wooden main building with big windows, surrounded by a few outbuildings.

The compound was close to the eastern shore, a short track leading from a wooden jetty up to the buildings. Baxter focused the field glasses on something surprisingly large tied up to the wooden structure. After a few minutes of close inspection, he satisfied himself that it wasn't a warship, just a tug or some other small steamer.

"Hard to say in this light, but there might be a couple of guards out and about," Billings whispered.

"They'd be idiots not to have set a watch," Baxter responded.

Twenty minutes later, their destination slid into view. They heard it first, the gentle hiss of waves on sand. The water was phosphorescent, the low breakers glowing with an eery blue light as they rolled up the long shallow spit of land. "Not too close, lads," Billings growled. "Don't want to beach here." He glanced at Baxter and raised an eyebrow. "Ready?"

Baxter nodded, taking out his revolver and checking it was loaded. Though if it came to a shoot-out, the whole expedition was probably doomed.

Billings produced a shotgun with a cut down barrel and stock reshaped into a pistol grip. "Let's be about it, then."

Baxter was already over the side, splashing through shallow water that didn't come up beyond the top of his boots. He strode out of the sea and onto German shores again.

The night was dark, despite the waxing moon, with enough cloud cover to diffuse its light. They made the short walk along the island in silence, boots crunching on soil that was more sand than anything else and through low scrubby grass that would offer them no cover if it came to it. They didn't have any trouble finding their target, as there wasn't much in the way of terrain to confuse them.

"All right for some," Billings whispered as he surveyed the surprisingly grand main house. The mansion had two storeys and a veranda at the front.

Baxter's attention was caught by the steamer at the jetty. There was no reason to suspect there was anything untoward about it, as Schiller would surely have supplies brought out to him, but he fumbled out his field glasses to have a closer look.

At first glance it did just appear to be a steamer, but on closer inspection Baxter could see that structures were being built on the long foredeck: flimsy wooden deck furniture that surely wouldn't serve any purpose.

Or at least, no peaceful purpose, he realised with a start. Baxter had been involved with exactly this sort of work during the Italo-Ottoman War, though, and saw them for what they were — positions for concealing guns. He could just make out the slight gleam of white paint on her bow, and while he couldn't quite read the name, he couldn't shake the feeling it was only half finished and being painted over her original identity.

"I think they're converting that tug into a commerce raider," Baxter whispered to Billings.

"Not our problem."

"No, but it could be an opportunity."

"Can we get on with it?" Billings growled, tension evident in his voice.

Baxter shrugged. "We probably should."

They took the buildings one at a time, avoiding a small outhouse, whose purpose was quite clear from the redolent smell. *Schutztruppe* were standing guard or patrolling the compound, which complicated matters for the intruders.

The second building, more of a barn, didn't contain the two men they were looking for. What it did have was a neat stack of crates in the centre of the long space. "Hello — what have we got here?" Billings murmured, a larcenous gleam in his eye. Baxter was crouched by the door, pistol in hand, as he peered through a crack in the uneven wooden planking.

"We don't have time for looting," Baxter hissed. Too late, though. The crunch of the top case being opened was startlingly loud, and he winced, expecting the thunder of approaching boots.

"You should take a look," Billings said, his voice for once devoid of that slight hint of smugness. With a curse under his breath, Baxter stole across to the pile of crates. Billings was brushing a few strands of straw from a Mauser rifle, a weapon Baxter was very familiar with. He'd hefted more than a few crates of these on and off the *Resadiye*, delivering them to the Turkish irregular forces in Tripoli.

He ran his hand over the side of the crate, just making out the Imperial German crest on the side. "This is official artillery, not Schiller's private stock," Baxter said. "And not all of these crates are for rifles — some are big enough for machine guns, maybe ammunition." He thought back to the steamer at the jetty. "He's preparing some sort of offensive operation."

"An attack on Stone Town?" Billings asked. "A raid?"

"There's at least a company of King's African Rifles garrisoning the island, so I can't imagine he'd be that daft." Baxter thought fast. "Commerce raiding, probably."

"Does any of that help us?" the other man demanded.

Baxter held up his hand as he heard movement beyond the barn. They crouched almost reflexively, and both men raised their weapons to aim at the door. But it was just a passing patrol.

"Not right now, but if things get loud this might give us the distraction we need to escape."

Billings grinned, seeing the direction in which Baxter's mind was going. "In the time-honoured tradition of the service," he said gleefully.

"Something like that. Only if we have to, though."

Moving back to his observation point at the door, Baxter saw that the pair of African soldiers had stopped in front of the mansion's veranda. That was a problem. They were casting anxious glances towards the only stone building on the island.

"That's the barracks."

"Just leaves us what looks like the labourers' quarters."

"And the main house." Baxter didn't know which would be harder to crack, the mansion or the barracks. But his gut told him that Arbuthnott would be in Schiller's residence, either because he was working with the German, or because he had enough brass neck to talk his way into being held in comfortable captivity.

The barracks lay a little bit away from the main house, forming one side of a somewhat lopsided square with the other buildings. Baxter guessed Schiller probably didn't have more than a platoon of soldiers, but even a section of ten men would be more than enough.

"Labourers' quarters first," he said as he backed away from the door. "Let's go out the back."

They climbed out through a shuttered but unglazed window at the back of the barn. Baxter dropped silently to the ground, but Billings managed to land with a bit of a clatter that made Baxter wince.

He was starting to wonder if he should have brought the old sailor along. He eyed Billings' back as he led the way towards the back of the low wooden building that was their target, wondering if this whole enterprise was some sort of a bizarre trap.

No, that didn't make sense. It was too convoluted, even for Arbuthnott. And if the two of them were working for the Germans, they would have just seized him as soon as he landed on the island. No, Baxter decided, it was just that Billings was getting too old for this business.

They pressed their backs against the rough wood. It smelled freshly cut to Baxter, the scent of resin filling his nostrils. Billings opened his mouth to speak but Baxter held up his hand. He could hear voices coming from an open window, and after a moment he realised they were speaking English.

What the hell is going on here?

He sidled up to the window. He identified three different voices, one of them Irish. He risked craning his neck to peer through. The room inside was dim, lit only by a single lantern, by which he could make out four men. Three of them were sitting around a table on which the lantern sat, playing cards and talking quietly. The fourth man was lying on a cot, hidden by blankets.

Baxter cleared his throat softly, making the men jump. "What ship?" he asked in a low voice. It was a terrible risk, as the captive British seamen — as he was sure they were — could quite easily give him away. One did in fact start to rise in a hurry, but the Irish sailor reached out to catch his chair as it threatened to fall.

"Steamer *Abigail*," that sailor replied in a similarly low tone. "Out of Mombasa, cargo for Zanzibar."

"How long have you been here?"

"Since the day after war broke out," one of the other men said bitterly. "Not that we knew about it when we touched here to ask about parts for the engine. Old *Abbie*, she's not in such a good way."

Baxter guessed their German captors had been busy putting her into much better condition, but these men didn't need to know that right now. Sailors could be touchy about strangers working on their ships without permission.

"What can you tell me about the garrison here? Are there any other prisoners?"

"Don't know about the garrison, mate. Bunch of locals, though they don't keep us under close guard. Got another prisoner in with us. Claims he's Scottish, but he sounds

Russian to me." The Irish sailor gestured towards the recumbent form on the cot. "We've done what we can for him, but he's not in a good way."

Baxter's heart thumped. That description could only be one person, and there was no reason for the Germans to be holding him and not providing proper medical care.

"There's that other cully," said the sailor who had jumped up when Baxter had first spoken. He had a broad West Country burr.

"Oh, yeah — some posh bloke. They keep him up in the main house under guard, but he's not going anywhere in a hurry. Uses a wheeled chair."

"We need to move," Billings suddenly hissed.

"We'll be back for you," Baxter told the sailors. He'd spent too long talking with the captive sailors, and could hear boots on the ground-up coral of the path that ran from this building up to the mansion.

They ducked into the shadow of the rough wood building, keeping low and close to the side of the structure. Baxter held his breath, hoping that they would manage to dodge the patrol again.

But then, luck rarely held out for forever.

CHAPTER FIFTEEN

Baxter moved as the pair of *askari* came round the corner of the building, the rifles still over their shoulders and one of them smoking a hand-rolled cigarette. There was no hope of them not seeing the two intruders, but he didn't give them a chance to react. He drove a fist into the lead soldier's gut, knocking the wind out of him, then delivered an upper cut that laid him out cold. Billings, more of a brawler than a pugilist, had taken the other man to ground and was busy trying to strangle the life from him while the African desperately clawed at his face. Baxter kicked the soldier in the side of the head, knocking him out.

Billings jumped pack, drawing a short, broad-bladed knife and starting to drive it forward. Baxter caught his wrist before he could put the blade home. "No need to kill the man," he whispered in the sailor's ear. "He's just doing his job."

"They could raise the alarm," Billings growled.

"We'll be out of here before they come to, and they'll be missed soon anyway." Baxter rubbed at his jaw, thinking. He hadn't had time to work out the patrol pattern, if there even was one. He indicated the blockhouse. "Find a way to get those men out and down to the beach."

Billings stared hard at him. "Maybe I should go and get his nibs from the mansion."

Baxter gave him a mirthless grin. "And then you'd be out of here. I'm lighter on my feet. And anyway, we don't have time to argue about it."

Billings grunted, then slipped away into the darkness, going around the far side of the barracks from the main house. Baxter hesitated for a moment, wondering if he had made the right decision. He didn't see that he had any other option, though, and it was too late to change his mind.

Baxter went to the corner of the building and cautiously peered round it. The two *askari* were at the main door, rifles in hands and looking disciplined enough. Not Buckingham Palace guards smart, but they looked alert and would probably start wondering where their comrades were soon.

Sure enough, as Baxter watched, one of the men glanced around, then murmured something quietly to his colleague. The other man shook his head dismissively, and the first shrugged and took a few hesitant steps in the direction of the blockhouse. His colleague summoned him back with a sharp word.

Baxter cursed. If they'd separated, he might have had a chance to take them both down quietly. Instead, he'd have to try his luck at the back of the mansion. He moved back further into the darkness, keeping as close to the ground as his height allowed.

He crouched, smelling his own sweat and the crushed grass under his boots. The only sound was the waves and the stir of grass in the slight breeze, and somewhere nearby the putter of an electricity generator. No expenses spared for Herr Schilling, it seemed.

He checked the revolver was still in the waistband of his trousers, then started back towards the compound, low and fast, angling for the side of the whitewashed building. He could see shuttered windows, and no sign of a patrol along this side of the building. The two men he and Billings had subdued might have been due to walk this route, of course, but he couldn't hang around to find out.

Baxter drew his pistol as he reached the side wall and then slid round to the back of the building. He had no real desire to shoot anybody, but right now he didn't have an option. With any luck, once he was inside the mansion there wouldn't be any guards. It was the middle of the night, after all, and if anyone was awake then they were probably otherwise engaged.

The rear door was not locked, not that there was any reason for it to be. He slipped through, pistol first, into a well-appointed kitchen. Heat pulsed off the range even now and despite the sweltering climate.

Baxter advanced cautiously, every sense alert, muscles taut. No sound of trouble from outside, no shots or raised voices. The creak of a floorboard beyond the kitchen door sent him dashing forward, to press his back to the wall next to a tall cupboard.

A bleary-eyed African servant came through into the kitchen, knotting an apron around her hips. She went over to the range, and Baxter realised she was there to start preparing breakfast. He started moving, hoping to sidle out past her, but disturbed a water pail. The cook turned, with an angry look on her face that dissolved into terror when she saw an armed stranger in her kitchen.

Baxter hated to do it, but he aimed the pistol at the woman and held a finger to his lips. She froze halfway through opening her mouth to scream and nodded, her whole body shaking. He covered the space between them in two quick strides, muzzle of the gun not wavering. Wide eyes stared at him, brimming with tears, and she said something in what he thought was Swahili, then switched into a rough German. Baxter thought she was asking him if he was going to hurt her.

He shook his head firmly. "*Nicht*," he said, struggling to remember what little German he had. "*Englander* prisoner, er..."

"*Häftling?*" She rattled off something fast, probably a location. When he looked blank, she pointed up urgently.

That was the best Baxter was going to get, he realised. He looked around, trying to work out what to do with the cook. He didn't think for a second that she wouldn't raise the alarm, even if she had helped him after a fashion. His eyes lit on the open door to the pantry, and he gestured her towards it. She hurried across, head down.

"My apologies," he said, as he shut her in. Better that than shooting her, at least.

Baxter knew he had to move fast. The household staff were obviously starting to go about their morning duties, and while Schiller was an aristocrat — or liked to think of himself as one — he was also a military officer. He'd be up with the sun.

Baxter went from the kitchen out into the main hall, moving quickly and quietly. The interior of the building was less grand than Baxter had been expecting. Rather than a double-height hall with a sweeping staircase up the middle, it was instead a fairly open space with a wooden staircase up one side and a few pieces of solid, plain furniture. It struck Baxter more as a military headquarters than the home of a wealthy landowner.

He took the stairs two at a time, moving as lightly as he could and wincing every time a step creaked under his foot. He paused at the top, looking down a bare landing lined with doors.

Why does it always come down to creeping around dark buildings where Arbuthnott is involved?

Baxter could hear thunderous snoring from the first room he passed, and the image of a bewhiskered Prussian colonel popped in his head unbidden. He advanced cautiously, trying to work out whether he should just start kicking doors in. All hell would break loose, but he'd be on the front foot.

No sound emanated from any of the other doors. They were either unoccupied or held light sleepers. He reached the end of the landing, glanced around the corner and saw two more doors. One of those would lead to the room with the largest windows, giving a view of Schiller's little domain.

He paused when he heard voices raised in anger. Baxter didn't need to recognise the voices to know it was Schiller and Esca Masing.

The woman's voice was coming closer, and Baxter glanced around as he realised she was approaching the door. He started to back away, but spun back and levelled his pistol as he heard the door open.

Esca emerged onto the landing, belting a gown over a long white nightdress. She snapped something in German back into the room, then flung the door closed with a slam. Baxter winced, expecting it to wake the entire building, but he could still hear the grinding snore behind him.

She stood staring at the door, breathing hard, a slender white ghost in the gloom. Then she turned and started in Baxter's direction, so angry with Schiller that she didn't even notice him until he drew back the revolver's hammer with a *snick*. Then she stopped, eyes going huge and one hand going to her throat.

Baxter knew he wouldn't shoot an unarmed woman, but the gig would be up even if he didn't pull the trigger. To his surprise, though, she didn't scream or shout for help; she merely stared at him with a strange mix of fear and disdain in her eyes. Esca would have recognised him, of course, and would have no trouble believing a British man *would* shoot a woman.

They remained frozen like that for a long moment while Baxter tried to work out what to do and she watched him, trying to guess his intentions. "Arbuthnott," he whispered, as quietly as he could.

She pointed a finger behind him. Baxter backed up to the corner, gesturing with the pistol for her to follow and then lead the way to the right room.

Esca's step only faltered slightly as she moved past him, doing her best to keep as far from him as she could in the relatively narrow space. She led him back to one of the rooms he'd passed, glancing archly at him as she pointed out wordlessly that it was the only door on the landing locked from the outside, the key still in the lock. She unlocked the door and then stood back, staring at him expectantly.

Baxter gestured for her to go first. He followed her in, closing the door after him as softly as he could. The room was even darker than the landing, the windows being shuttered, and it took him a moment to get his bearings.

"Take a seat, *Frau* Masing," he whispered, pointing to a vague shape that might have been an easy chair in one corner of the room.

"You are a fool, Mr Baxter, and will get yourself killed," Esca replied in a low tone as she padded across the room and sat down, tucking her bare feet up and hugging her robe around herself.

"I didn't know you cared," he said distractedly, as he moved to the single bed against the far wall of the room, from which the sound of gentle breathing came. "I know you're awake, Arbuthnott. Get up."

There was a beat of silence, then a deep sigh. "I should have known they would send you, Baxter. And thanks to you, getting up is a bit of a problem." It was the same plummy, slightly nasal voice, but with a more tired edge than Baxter remembered. Arbuthnott pulled himself up in the bed then swung his legs over the edge, gesturing to one knee. "It's never been quite the same since you shot me. And threw me off a ship's bridge."

Esca snorted, as though she expected nothing less.

"Given that you tried to get me killed — at least twice — you're lucky I didn't shoot you in the head," Baxter snarled. He took a breath and forced himself to calm down.

"I will be missed soon," Esca said. Baxter glanced sharply at her — it almost seemed like she was trying to warn him. Looking back to Arbuthnott, he caught the end of a look he and the Boer woman shared.

No time to worry about that now — Esca was right, Schiller would start to wonder where she was soon. "You either get up and get dressed of your own accord, Arbuthnott, or I carry you out of here over my shoulder."

Arbuthnott started pulling trousers and shirt over his flannel pyjamas, grumbling all the time. Baxter wondered what the hell he was going to do about Esca. She didn't seem overly concerned to have been caught in her nightclothes, and merely gazed coldly at him while Arbuthnott readied himself.

"You had best tie me up, I think," she said at last, as if reading his thoughts.

"She could come with us," Arbuthnott suggested, tucking his shirt in and then taking up a pair of canes and levering himself to his feet. Baxter felt a pang of guilt as he took a couple of faltering steps.

"I'm not in the habit of kidnapping citizens of an enemy state," he said flatly. "That's what got us into this mess."

Arbuthnott merely shrugged, glancing again at Esca. Baxter wondered why. There was something going on here that he didn't understand.

"We'll lock you in," Baxter told her. "I suggest you keep quiet. If things get noisy, they're going to get very loud indeed."

"It is better this way," she said, almost as though she was talking to Arbuthnott rather than him. "I will keep *schtum*."

Baxter went to the window and opened a shutter slightly, glancing out into the compound. He didn't know how long he'd been creeping around Schiller's house, but it was longer than he'd have liked. Still no sign of an alarm being raised, and no ruckus coming from the blockhouse where the prisoners were being held.

"I assume you weren't stupid enough to come by yourself?" Arbuthnott asked acidly.

Baxter closed his eyes, wondering whether it would just be simpler to shoot the man now and report back to Saunders that the Germans had already finished him off. "Of course not. Billings is with me."

"Quite mad," Esca breathed.

"Time to go," Baxter decided.

"My chair is…" Arbuthnott began, the words turning into an undignified squawk as Baxter lifted him one-handed and slung him over his shoulder. Arbuthnott was a relatively tall man, but had been slight when Baxter had first met him and had diminished further.

Baxter looked again at Esca, wondering if he should bring her with him as well. He couldn't manage both Arbuthnott and a woman who seemed to prefer to remain, however. Instead, he nodded a farewell and locked the door after himself.

"This is most undignified," the weight on his shoulder muttered as Baxter headed back the way he'd come, walking slowly and softly. No point giving the game away now, not when he was so close to escaping undetected.

"Shut up," he whispered back.

He hurried down the stairs, trying to listen for the rest of the staff. As he glanced towards the windows on either side of the mahogany front door, there was just a hint of light showing on the horizon — enough to tell him there were still guards there. Out the way he came in, then.

"Wait," Arbuthnott said. "Put me down a moment."

Baxter was about to tell him to shut up again, then relented. He put Arbuthnott's feet on the polished floorboards and supported him.

"I came here for something, Baxter, and we really can't leave without it." Arbuthnott gestured towards a door on the far side of the entrance hall. "Schiller has been tasked with operational planning by von Lettow-Vorbeck, and does most of his work here."

Baxter stared hard at Arbuthnott. He realised there was no hidden motive here — this was Arbuthnott's way of buying himself back into the good graces of the NID. He'd still be under a cloud of suspicion, given the belief that he had been working for the Germans, but it would go a long way to convincing his superiors of his probity.

And the really annoying thing about it was that Baxter knew he'd go along with it, purely on the basis that it would keep him out of hot water with Parker. Assuming Arbuthnott was telling the truth, that was, and Schiller had actually been doing something substantive here.

There was only one way to find out.

He moved forward to sling Arbuthnott over his shoulder again, but the agent — who had managed to keep his canes in his hands — shook his head. "I can make it that far, thank you."

Baxter winced at every clacking step they took across the hallway, his eyes peeled and his ears alert for any sound. Billings would be wondering what had happened to him, whether he had found 'his nibs'; either that or he'd cut and run, hopefully with Tommy in tow. Not out of any sense of charity, but because the young man would be a useful bargaining chip with the Russians.

It took an eternity to reach the study door. Schiller was confident enough in the loyalty of his staff that he didn't lock it.

The study was one of the most opulent rooms that Baxter had ever seen. It smelled of leather, polished wood and lingering cigar smoke, despite a stub in the big glass ashtray being long cold. That article sat on a large desk with surprisingly ornate carvings, increasingly visible as the eastern horizon lightened.

"I think we can risk a light," Arbuthnott said, and before Baxter could stop him he switched on an electric lamp in one corner of the room. It hummed to life, casting a sickly glow that made the rogue intelligence agent look even more cadaverous.

Baxter shut the door as softly as he could. "Just get on with it," he snapped, hand opening and closing around the butt of his gun.

"Well, make yourself useful and gather up those maps," Arbuthnott replied, gesturing at a long and slightly less grand side table that was covered with maps and charts. "I'll go through the desk."

Baxter crossed the room in a few strides. Looking down at the charts, he immediately recognised Zanzibar and the surrounding waters. Bending closer, he could see handwritten annotations correcting some of the depth soundings, along with notes on the state of the docks and the garrison.

"Bloody hell," he breathed, realising what Schiller had been working on.

"Indeed," Arbuthnott said, his own tone reflecting the seriousness of what Baxter had seen.

The door banged open with the suddenness of a gunshot. "Esca!" Schiller roared, followed by something angry in German as he came storming in. He was dressed in linen pyjamas and a paisley dressing gown, but was wearing his smartly polished tall boots.

He stopped, staring open-mouthed at the two interlopers in his sanctum.

Baxter, taken aback by Schiller's incongruous appearance, was slow to react. Surprisingly enough, it was Arbuthnott who got there first, snatching up the Luger automatic casually discarded on Schiller's desk and levelling it at the German officer.

Arbuthnott didn't hesitate to pull the trigger, and looked furious when the pistol didn't fire. Staggering slightly on his bad legs, he reached up to work the toggle lock. Schiller had started to lunge forward when Arbuthnott finished chambering a round and fired.

He didn't hit, of course, the round thudding into a portrait of the Kaiser opposite the big desk.

Baxter didn't want to risk a shot, not because of the noise — that ship had sailed — but because he didn't want to risk hitting the man he'd come to rescue. Instead, he crashed forward into Schiller, kicking out at his knee. The infantry officer was more than just stuff and bluster, it seemed. He twisted away from the attack, and while Baxter's boot connected he didn't manage to put the German over.

Schiller staggered back, recovering quickly and dropping into a pugilist's crouch, fists up to protect his face. Baxter wasn't in the mood for Queensberry rules, however. He levelled his pistol at Schiller. He saw the German's eyes widen in fear and rage, but dropped the muzzle before he pulled the trigger and shot Schiller in the leg.

The *Schutztruppe* officer, to his credit, didn't cry out. He grunted in pain as his leg folded. Baxter lowered the muzzle, ears ringing from the report. The smell of burned powder had replaced the stale cigar smoke in the air.

"Time to go," Baxter told Arbuthnott, who'd abandoned the Luger and was busy stuffing documents into a leather satchel.

"Grab those charts," the rogue agent ordered in response. Baxter could hear the pounding of running boots and voices raised in alarm, but it would take more time to argue with Arbuthnott than it would to roll up as many of the charts as he could grab.

"You *Englanders*," Schiller snarled from the floor, trying to stem the flow of blood from the small hole in his leg. "Shooting an unarmed man."

Baxter glared at him. "It's a bloody war, old chap. People get shot."

"I will remember that when next we meet."

Baxter tucked the roll of papers under his arm. "You'll be fine — but maybe don't ask Dr Masing to take the bullet out, eh?"

The boots were in the hall now, the guards finally hurrying in to see what the shooting was about. Baxter put three rounds through the open door to discourage them, then he grabbed the heavy, dark wood chair from behind Schiller's desk and put it through one of the tall windows that looked out over the narrow channel of water and Africa beyond.

"You'll have to carry me," Arbuthnott said.

Baxter lifted him by his shirt front and threw him through the broken window, with only slightly less force than he'd put the chair through it. Turning, he discharged the last two pistol rounds at the *askari* who were warily sidling up to the doorway. Schiller was shouting something in German, probably about opening fire, and Baxter vaulted after Arbuthnott as the soldiers started bringing up their rifles.

Bullets cracked overhead as he dropped below the level of the window. One caught the frame, showering the escaping men with splinters. Baxter took a moment to get his bearings. The whole compound was awake now, unsurprisingly, though there seemed to be a fair amount of confused running and frustrated shouting. That meant they had just moments to make good their escape.

A rifle barrel appeared almost directly over Baxter's head. He reacted instinctively, reaching up to grab it with both hands and pulling as hard as he could. With a startled shout, the weapon's owner came through the window, dragged over shards of broken glass. He let go of the rifle and Baxter jabbed the butt into the soldier's face, hard enough to break his nose. He whirled the long, ungainly weapon, aimed it back through the window and fired blind, then worked the well-oiled action and fired again. That second round earned a cry of pain and the sound of men hitting the floor. Arbuthnott was scrabbling around to gather up the documents he'd dropped when unceremoniously hurled from the building.

Baxter dropped the rifle and, keeping low as the soldiers started firing back from inside the study, he urged Arbuthnott away from the mansion and towards the low coral stone wall that bounded the compound.

"I assume you have some sort of conveyance away from here?" Arbuthnott asked, a little short of breath.

"A boat." Baxter fished some loose .38 rounds from his jacket pocket and reloaded his revolver as he spoke.

"Well, let's get to it then!"

"There's the minor problem of the rest of the flock to gather up." He raised his head. The sky was that strange half-light just before the sun shot up, but he could see that the stone-built barracks on the far side of the compound was a hive of activity. Soldiers were filing out in various states of undress, all of them armed, while non-commissioned officers tried to marshal them. There was no sign of activity around the blockhouse where the prisoners were being kept, or the barn with the stored weapons and ammunition.

"Forget them! They're probably already dead or taken."

Baxter shot the other man a hard look. For all that Billings was a deeply mercenary soul, he'd shown a strange loyalty to Arbuthnott. He shouldn't have been surprised that it wasn't reciprocated.

"You'll be safe enough here," Baxter told him coldly. "Just stay quiet and keep your head down. I'll get the others and fall back to you."

"Just don't bloody forget me!" the agent whined as Baxter moved in a crouch further along the wall, before popping up in full view of the *askari* who had emerged from the mansion. He fired towards them, not really caring if he hit as long as he had their attention, then vaulted the wall and sprinted for the blockhouse where he'd left Billings.

He was about halfway across the short dash to the cover of the building when someone opened fire with a machine gun.

Instinct kicked in, and Baxter hit the ground, the sharp coral gravel digging into his knees and elbows. It took him a moment to realise the wildly long bursts of fire weren't directed at him. From his position on the ground he could see the barracks building getting liberally peppered with bullets, not to mention the ground around it. The assembling *askari* were scattering for cover, one or two of them lying motionless in the dirt.

Where in hell did they get a machine gun? Baxter wondered as he scrambled back up to his feet and sprinted for cover, firing blindly as he went. Being out in the open was not a healthy place to be, particularly as rifle barrels were now poking out of the barracks' windows as the German colonial troops returned fire, the incoming fusillade barely more accurate than the machine-gun fire.

The blockhouse where the prisoners had been kept was empty. Baxter found the previous occupants and his fellow infiltrator at the next building over, the long timber barn where the munitions were being stored. There was a small door at the far end of the barn. It had been barricaded with empty crates to set up a machine-gun position from which they could fire on the blockhouse across twenty yards of open ground. Billings was crouched behind the Maxim gun and was firing it with a savage grin on his face, while one of the sailors managed the long belts of ammunition. Spent cartridges were spat out of the front of the weapon, tinkling on the ground at the tail end of every long burst he fired. The other two sailors from the captured freighter and Tommy were keeping an eye out in that direction.

"Mr B!" the latter called out as soon as Baxter entered the barn, causing the two sailors to spin round and aim their rifles at him.

"You look like shit, lad," Baxter said as he advanced into the dim space, empty pistol by his side.

Tomas shrugged, wincing with the movement. He was half-sitting, half-lying against the crate the machine gun had been extracted from, a pistol in his hand, although he didn't look like he had the strength to lift it. One eye was swollen all the way closed and his face was bruised.

Billings glanced over his shoulder, pausing fire. "Did you get his nibs?" he shouted, louder than he needed to be. But then, his ears would be ringing from the gunfire. The *askari*, emboldened by the cessation of the gunfire, increased their own shooting, heavy bullets peppering the thick wooden walls of the barn.

"I did. He's safe, for now, but we should probably get him and get out of here."

Billings, irritated by the increased tempo of incoming fire that made his loader duck as low as he could manage, responded with a long burst that he swept back and forth across the barracks.

Baxter realised that, seemingly in the blink of an eye, it was now light outside; bright shafts struck through the dusty air from the bullet holes in the wooden walls, and more flooded in around the doorway.

"No argument from me, Mr Baxter!" Billings shouted over the racket. "But we've got a whole bunch of sodgers between us and the boat."

"Surely they'll come to us?" one of the sailors demanded, a rising note of panic in his voice. Baxter had to admit they were doing well in the circumstances — the Irish lad who was on the Maxim with Billings in particular — but they were civilians. Sailors were by nature and experience hardy souls, but they weren't soldiers.

"They've probably left already, mate," Billings said cheerfully. "Or they'll be waiting where they were told to."

Baxter moved to the side of the barn nearest the mansion, crouched low and peered through one of the ragged bullet holes in the side there. He caught sight of a tan-clad leg and realised the *askari* were moving up towards them, out of the machine gun's line of fire.

"You, rifle!" he snapped, pointing at the more nervous sailor. The bark of command in his voice snapped the man into action, and he passed across the awkwardly long Mauser rifle — just in time. The first German soldier, with a corporal's stripe on his arm, was trying to sidle quietly through the same door Baxter had used. He brought the butt into his shoulder, cheek to the smooth walnut stock, and pulled the trigger. The rifle kicked like a mule, but he kept hold of the weapon, dropping the butt from his shoulder to work the bolt action before he registered that the German was down and lying still. He fired from the hip as an *askari* tried to follow his squad leader through, missing, but both Tommy and the other armed sailor were firing as well, driving the man back.

"*Feuer einstellen!*" he heard Schiller shouting, his voice quaking with rage. "*Jetzt!*"

The *Schutztruppe* ceased their firing almost at once, demonstrating remarkable discipline. Baxter had seen firsthand how untrained enthusiasts could get carried away and keep firing until they'd discharged all their ammunition. The Russian Second Pacific Squadron had been particularly bad for it.

"Stop firing!" Schiller went on in English. "Do you hear me in there, Baxter? Cease your firing!"

Billings gave the barracks a last burst. Baxter moved to the door, glancing down at the German soldier he'd shot as he went. The bullet had hit him in the chest, and while he probably wouldn't have died instantly, it would at least have been fairly quick.

He'd been in the wrong place, at the wrong time.

"What do you want, Schiller?" Baxter shouted.

"You are cut off from your rescue boat, surrounded, and outgunned. Surrender now so we can avoid any more ... unpleasantness."

"Maybe he's right," one of the sailors murmured, earning a sharp glance from Baxter.

Schiller was wrong about the balance of firepower — a machine gun was a great leveller — but he was right that they were cut off, surrounded, and running out of time. It wouldn't be long before the Germans discovered Arbuthnott, assuming he hadn't just given himself up already, and then they would burn the barn down around them.

Baxter didn't bother responding. Instead he paced across to the seaward side of the building, lifted a tarp away from a small window and peered out into the bright dawn, looking down the shallow gradient to the little steamer docked at the jetty, a whisp of smoke coming from her funnel. There were men on her deck, crouched in what cover they could find, and in the light he saw they weren't *Schutztruppe* or civilians but *Kaiserliche Marine* sailors.

Schiller was wrong about something else — they weren't cut off from the sea.

"*Herr* Baxter!" Schiller shouted, a note of irritation in his voice. "As I am a civilised man, I will give you five minutes to decide. Then we will burn you out."

"And lose all his nice gear?" Billings sneered.

Baxter crouched behind the machine gun. "Looks like they've got *Abigail* at harbour steam. How long to get under way?"

The Irishman looked back over his shoulder. "Must have fixed her machinery, then," he murmured, then he noticed Baxter's scowl. "Not long; she always gets up to heat fast when everything's in working order."

Baxter thought hard. "Billings, his nibs is lying low behind the compound wall, not far from the mansion."

"You just bloody left him there?"

"And now you're going to go and fetch him," he snapped, wiping sweat from his face with a grimy hand. "Stay low and try not to draw attention. Don't come back here, just get closer to the jetty."

"Where we belong, sir," Billings said, relinquishing the firing handle of the Maxim gun with every sign of reluctance and heading off on his errand.

"What's your name?" Baxter asked the Irishman.

"Turkington, sir."

"Well, Turkington, when I give the order I want you to rain hell on that barracks building. Just throw the entire belt at it, then run like hell after us."

"Where are you going?"

"To take back your bloody ship."

Baxter didn't have time for anything fancy. Schiller, from what he had seen, was not a patient man and while he made a great play of Prussian honour, he wasn't always a man of his word. "You up to a bit of shooting, Tommy lad?"

"Just point me at the bastards," the young man replied, sounding more Scottish than he had since Baxter had met him again.

Baxter handed his appropriated rifle back to the anxious sailor. He seemed to have more of a grip on himself now, perhaps because the firing had ceased.

That was about to change. Baxter moved to the big doors that opened on the seaward side of the barn. He cracked the left-hand one open very slightly to peer out while he reloaded the pistol. "Get ready to cover me, but don't open fire unless you have to!"

"Aye, sir!" came a chorus of voices.

Baxter grinned, feeling the rush that came from doing something really bloody stupid. The men moved up to provide him with the necessary cover.

He stepped out, running low and fast for the *Abigail*, making no attempt to hide from the armed men on the deck. Sometimes the only way was to go right at them, and this time the gamble paid off. Perhaps because Schiller had ordered a ceasefire, or perhaps because they were taken completely by surprise, the three German sailors didn't open fire. One was just swinging his rifle towards Baxter as he raced over the gangplank. He knocked the weapon to one side and punched the wiry man in the guts so hard that he threw up as he folded.

He turned towards the stern and another sailor, who was crouched in the wheelhouse. This man managed to get a shot off, forcing Baxter to duck into the scant cover of some baled wooden planks.

All hell broke loose again at that point. Baxter didn't hear Schiller give an order, but suddenly everyone was shooting. Turkington opened up with the Maxim again, a long burst of noise, as the *Schutztruppe* began their indiscriminate fire. Tommy at least was firing from the barn, pops of noise almost lost in the general tumult.

Baxter twisted away from his impromptu barricade as he heard footsteps behind him. A third sailor was coming up behind him, raising his rifle, and Baxter felt a rush of adrenalin as he tried to bring his own weapon to bear. Too slow.

His would-be killer was actually grinning as he brought the rifle up and aimed deliberately. He jerked three times, though, as heavy bullets smacked into him, sending him sprawling facedown on the deck. Twisting round again, Baxter could see Billings crouching on the shore, Colt automatic in his hand and Arbuthnott lying next to him.

No time to raise a hand in thanks, though. Baxter scrambled to his feet and rushed towards the wheelhouse, now the rifleman there had been suppressed by the peppering of bullets hitting his shelter and showering him with broken glass and wood splinters.

"*Bitte! Bitte!*" the sailor shouted, matching actions to his words by throwing his rifle out onto the deck and sticking his empty hands out through the hatch.

"*Aus!*" Baxter snapped, mustering what little German he had. "*Schnell!*"

He turned as the German uncertainly emerged from his shelter. "Get to the bloody boat!" he roared. Billings was already on his way, supporting rather than carrying Arbuthnott, and at his shout the crew in the barn started running pell-mell towards them. He was relieved to see Turkington follow the three at the door.

The German sailor was still standing on the deck, looking disconsolate. Baxter was about to ask him what the bloody hell he thought he was doing, when the penny dropped that as far as he was concerned he was a prisoner.

"Get your mate and get weaving," Baxter told him shortly. The young man blinked at him uncomprehendingly. Baxter sighed and pointed to the man on the deck who was still fighting for breath. "*Aus!* Go!"

Baxter shoved the sailor towards the fallen man, and that finally seemed to get the message across. With an absurdly grateful look, the sailor hurried off, helping his wheezing comrade to his feet.

The rescued sailors were finally piling aboard, one of them supporting Tommy. Baxter was about to start issuing orders to get them underway, but these men clearly knew their duty and their own vessel, hurrying off about their business. Turkington was the last aboard, heading into the bullet-peppered wheelhouse.

Billings and Arbuthnott were almost there but had been pinned down at the landward end of the jetty as the *Schutztruppe* realised their quarry was escaping. Baxter took up the discarded Mauser rifle and was about to open fire, but spotted that the doors to the barn had been left open. He could see the neat pile of ammunition crates inside.

Baxter took careful aim, ignoring the bullets that were starting to whine overhead, and fired; he was ready for the kick this time and kept the rifle on target. He saw a crate splinter as the round hit, so he worked the bolt and tried to fire another shot with no result.

"Try this, Mr B!" Tommy called out behind him. He turned his head to see the lad offering him a flare pistol.

"Good thinking," he said, dropping the rifle and taking the pistol. It was an older model, not unlike the flare pistols he'd used in the straits of Tsushima in 1905. Baxter snapped the breach open, checked there was a flare in place, and then brought it on target. A few soldiers had come round the structure and were closing in on Billings and Arbuthnott, but hesitated when they saw him up on the deck of the *Abigail* with what looked like a large gun.

He lined up carefully, not that it would make that much difference, and pulled the trigger. The large-calibre pistol kicked in his hand as it spat the flare out towards the shore, then the rocket in its base fired. Soldiers scattered as the projectile careened across the open space and hit one of the open doors, deflecting into the dimness of the barn.

"Well, that was a bit of an anti-climax," Baxter said, turning to look for another projectile. Billings had taken advantage of the distraction to sling Arbuthnott over his shoulder and sprint along the jetty to the *Abigail*.

"Nice idea…" he started to say to Tommy, just as the flare went off, burning a brilliant white that rapidly became tinged with orange as it caught in the packaging material that had been scattered when the escapees had pillaged the weapons stockpile. Rifle ammunition started cooking off in the heat, a pop and crackle that grew at a steady pace and sent the soldiers scattering to a safe distance.

It wasn't quite the explosion Baxter had been hoping for, but if anything, this worked even better.

"Ready to get underway, sir!" Turkington reported smartly from the wheelhouse.

That surprised Baxter — he'd been anticipating the prospect of trying to hold this position for an uncomfortably long time.

Something heavier than rifle ammunition was starting to cook off in the blaze now, actual explosions deep within the timber building. "Yes, now is probably the best time to leave. Billings, let's get her cast off."

They worked hurriedly, Baxter taking the forward lines and the old sailor the aft. A thick plume of smoke was starting to rise from the steamer's single stack, the beat of her engine and the churn of the screw almost lost in the noise as Schiller's munitions stockpile continued to detonate. There was no orderly casting off or shouted orders, just a feverish unwinding of the thick cables. Turkington already had the engines at ahead slow, the fat civilian hull wallowing forward as the slack on the lines started to be taken up.

Baxter finally heaved the line ashore and looked at the devastation he'd wrought. The barn was thoroughly ablaze now, the thump of some sort of light artillery shell detonating in between the pop and crackle of rifle and machine-gun ammunition spurting out through the walls of the collapsing building. Most of the people on shore were occupied by that unfolding disaster, men running for buckets of water and trying to stamp out flaming debris before it could set the other buildings ablaze. The day, already warm now the sun was up, was made sweltering by the blaze even at this distance. Through the shimmering air, Baxter could just make out Esca Masing standing on the veranda of the mansion, a shawl around her shoulders. Although he couldn't make out any details, he knew she was watching everything with a cool disdain.

The *Abigail* was properly underway now, blunt bow pointed towards the open waters of the Indian Ocean. Schiller had managed to drag enough men away from the firefighting to start shooting after the escaping ship. Baxter crouched down at the rear rail and returned the fire with a rifle, with no real intention of hitting anyone but rather to keep their heads down.

The coaster started to roll slightly as she cleared the little cove and headed into the channel that lay between the island and the mainland. This wasn't the endless procession of long low waves that marched across the open ocean, but Baxter already felt better as the deck moved under his feet. A few rifle rounds whipped overhead, but by now Schiller would have realised he'd lost this bout. He wouldn't want to lose the next one.

"Well, there's my barky, Mr Baxter," Billings said cheerfully. "We'll be off, then."

Baxter turned quickly, acutely conscious of the fact the rifle in his hands was empty. Billings wasn't exactly pointing his automatic at Baxter's guts, but the muzzle wasn't pointed at the deck either, which would have been the safer and politer position.

"Like hell you will," Baxter snapped, hands tightening around the rifle's wooden furniture. He was just about close enough that if he was fast, and he knew he was faster than the old pugilist in front of him...

"Indeed, you will not," Tomas said, all trace of his former cheerful Scottishness evaporating as he levelled an appropriated automatic pistol at Billings. "And do not think I will not shoot you."

"I don't doubt for a second you would," Arbuthnott said, a trace of smugness coming back into his voice. "That is, if I don't shoot you first."

Baxter's eyes flicked to the rogue agent, who was leaning against the side of the wheelhouse, the Luger he'd thought Arbuthnott had dropped back in the mansion in his hand. There was a tremor in that hand, but not so much that he would miss at this range.

"Come now," Billings said with a sly grin and the slightest glance at Tomas. "This is what we agreed, Mr Baxter."

"No such agreement was made," he snapped. "We agreed to work together to get Arbuthnott out."

"And that is exactly what I'm planning on doing."

"Where the hell are you going to go?" Not back to German East Africa, of course — whether or not Arbuthnott had been working for the Germans, he clearly wasn't on good terms with them now. Billings' vessel would be more than sufficient to get them to a British colony or even somewhere completely neutral, assuming he was able to avoid any further entanglements.

"We seem to have a bit of an impasse," Arbuthnott said smoothly.

Tomas shook his head. "No. I shoot you, Marcus Alexandrovich pummels Billings. Simple."

"Stand down, Tommy," Baxter said through clenched teeth. "There's nothing we can do here."

He knew that if they did as the young man suggested, there would be a good chance that they — and the other sailors aboard — would end up dead or badly injured. If Baxter let Arbuthnott sail away now, while he hadn't fulfilled his mission, there remained a chance for him to catch him later.

"But…"

"Do as I damn well say!" Baxter didn't raise his voice, but there was enough command there to make Tomas lower his gun. Baxter put his rifle down, not that it would do him much good anyway.

"Want me to shoot him, chief?" Billings asked, conversationally.

"He certainly deserves it, for what he's done to me," Arbuthnott said, with real venom in his voice. Baxter tensed. "But best not to — no need for any more unpleasantness, as *Kapitan* Schiller said earlier."

The boat in which Baxter had started the day had arrived alongside, and Baxter couldn't help but notice the three men aboard all had rifles either in hand or nearby.

"No hard feelings then, Mr Baxter?" Billings asked, voice mild but eyes flat and hard.

"You said that to me once before," he replied, keeping his own tone more level than he'd thought possible. "There won't be a third time."

"I don't doubt it," Billings said.

Arbuthnott hobbled past him and paused at the top of the ladder.

"I left the recovered documents aboard, and trust you will make good use of them, Mr Baxter," he said smoothly. "In particular, there is mention of a wireless station on the Rufiji that you should give careful consideration to."

Baxter breathed out, finding his calm. "I will bear that in mind."

"And when you report to your superiors in London — Saunders, I should guess — I trust you will also make them aware of who provided the information?"

Baxter stared at him flatly. "Oh, my report will be full and accurate."

"Well, that is all I can ask, really," Arbuthnott said, starting to lower himself over the side. "Good day to you, Mr Baxter."

Billings moved to help him down the side with one hand, keeping half an eye on those on deck. Tomas started forward, making a move to raise his pistol, but Baxter put a hand on his shoulder.

"This is not what Miss Ekaterina will say," the lad said darkly as Billings ran lightly down into the waiting boat. It boomed off and a moment later was heading away from the *Abigail* as quickly as possible, turning in a wide arc to head south. Baxter watched it go, then looked back towards the plume of thick black smoke emanating from the island.

He sighed, exhausted not just by the physical exertions of the last few hours but also by the endless machinations of intelligencers.

"Well, she can tell me in person the next time we meet," he said.

Turkington stuck his head out of the wheelhouse. "Where to, Mr Baxter?" he asked cheerfully, almost as though he hadn't just escaped captivity and survived an intense firefight.

"Zanzibar, if you please, Mr Turkington. There's a long list of people who will want to bollock me for this."

CHAPTER SIXTEEN

"Do you really expect me to believe any of this … this utter nonsense?" Commander Parker exploded, actually sweeping the sheathe of papers Baxter had presented him with off his desk.

Baxter could think of choicer words for the after-action report, but he didn't let the flash of amusement that came with that thought show on his face. "I'm not quite sure what you mean, sir," he said woodenly.

"That you were undertaking a 'hydrographic survey' of the waters around Zanzibar — this, I might add, despite the fact that the seabed has been examined *in detail* by men more qualified than you — and you just happened to stumble upon a British merchantman that had been captured and was being turned into an auxiliary raider? Not only *that*, but said vessel was in the possession of a German officer charged with planning the invasion of this island, giving you the opportunity to acquire vital German intelligence?"

"That's broadly what happened, sir. What some might call fortuitous circumstances."

"Some men might call it something else entirely," Parker fumed. "And what on earth possessed you to be out there in a civilian vessel, for God's sake, and to undertake a raid on an enemy garrison single-handedly in order to — what's the phrase — cut out the captured ship and rescue the crew?"

"I couldn't very well leave honest British sailors in the hands of the enemy, sir, or indeed a British-flagged ship. Finest tradition of the service, and all that."

"Hmm. Indeed." Parker sat back in his chair and lit his pipe. That ritual seemed to calm him. "Well, there's no denying the veracity of the documents you have procured, and the men you rescued are singing your praises all across the island. I imagine you're expecting a medal for all of this."

Baxter hadn't really thought about that, though given the nature of his assignment here and the fact that he'd technically failed in his mission, he doubted that would be the case. He knew Parker was venting in this way precisely because there couldn't be any sort of formal reprimand, and Baxter's account of the happenings would be what went into despatches.

"Did you get your man out?" Parker asked gruffly after the silence had stretched to the point of discomfort.

"Yes, sir, though the blighter slipped through my fingers." Baxter was still furious that, once again, he'd trusted Billings and Arbuthnott.

"I was hoping I'd be shot of you, but I assume you'll want to remain here to try to get a grip on him again?"

Baxter had shared that hope. "I've telegrammed London to ask for further instructions, but until I hear otherwise I can only assume so."

"Well, seeing as you're here you can get the intelligence you pulled out of Schiller's place in order. See if you can work out if it's anything more than pie in the sky thinking."

"It seems pretty cut and dried to me, sir," he said, for once nonplussed by his senior.

Parker's look was impassive. "Major Pearce is of the view that soldiers are often in the habit of planning for operations that will never exist. Can never exist. A thought experiment, I believe he called it, and as a soldier himself he is better placed to offer a view, eh? Captain D'Etremont, who commands the King's African Rifles company, is in agreement."

"There's a lot there for just a flight of fancy, sir," Baxter replied, indicating the papers on the floor.

"Well, that's why I'm ordering you to do the analysis, Mr Baxter — you, not young Hensley. You're the intelligence officer."

Baxter came to attention. "Yes, sir," he said crisply.

"That will be all, Mr Baxter."

He paused. He wanted to ask about the *Abigail*, but now probably wasn't the time. And he was due at another meeting that was probably going to be even less pleasant.

Baxter met Mashka in a little café in Victoria Park, just opposite the rather grand Resident's House. The establishment was owned by an Austrian, who was keeping as low a profile as possible, and wouldn't have looked out of place on a Vienna *Strasse* with its polished wood, brass furnishing and upholstery that tended towards red. Cakes and pastries, wilting slightly in the heat, were still popular despite the outbreak of hostilities. The day was hot, the high sun beating down, and Mashka was sitting at an outside table under a broad white parasol. It was early enough that she was drinking strong black tea, smoky enough that he could smell it from his side of the table. "So I am told you are a hero now," she said, as he settled into his chair.

"How's Tomas?" he asked, hoping to deflect her somewhat.

"He is recovered enough to tell me that you had made a deal with this Billings." She took a sip of her tea, her eyes cold as she looked at him through the steam.

"Coffee, please, black and hot," Baxter said to the hovering waiter, then turned his attention back to her. "We all had an agreement, Mashka. You, me and Billings. Work together to get Arbuthnott and Tommy out of German hands."

"Tomaska is certain that you had a ... a pre-agreement with Billings that he would go free with Arbuthnott. He is most beside himself, and swearing eternal vengeance on you for your treachery."

"It seems growing up in Russia has made him foolish," Baxter said. While his words were light, his voice was flat and hard. "Billings wouldn't have needed to pull a gun on me if we had an agreement."

"Unless he feared betrayal. But do you mean to say your intention was to surrender him to our custody, so he could be returned to the Empire to face justice?"

"Don't be so bloody daft," Baxter snapped, and she stiffened in her seat. Baxter took a sip of his coffee and allowed the heat and pleasant bitterness to work its way through him. "I'm an officer in the Royal Navy, with specific orders to capture Arbuthnott and return him to my superiors in London. That is what I intended to do, and will do if given the opportunity."

"So you lied to both of us!" Mashka cried, drawing the attention of some of the patrons at other tables.

"I'm reliably informed that I'm a poor liar," he said. "Therefore, you would have known it. Look, we agreed to work together to get Tommy and Arbuthnott out of German hands, and that's what we did. Tommy's safe, and I hope he will recover from his ordeal. Sometimes, you have to take what you can get."

Mashka's expression softened, and she sat back in her chair. "You are not such a bad liar," she said after a moment. "But, *da*, I would have known if you had tried. Well, it is so. Her Illustrious Highness will be disappointed, but this is life."

Baxter considered her words. Whilst she had used the proper form of address for someone of Ekaterina's station, her tone had been deeply sardonic. "When last we met, you were something of a revolutionary. Some might have called you a firebrand." He gestured at her summer dress and broad straw hat. "Now you work for a countess, with goals apparently aligned with the Russian state."

Mashka made a most unladylike noise and muttered something in what he guessed was Ukrainian. "Life changes people, Marcus Alexandrovich, and brings us surprises. Ekaterina and the rest of us have had many surprises over the years; we have all changed. I imagine your own life has not been without twists and turns."

Baxter smiled for what felt like the first time in a while. "You could say that."

He watched Mashka across the table. While she inhabited the guise of an aristocrat, he couldn't escape the feeling that the fiery revolutionary was still there. That she had not changed, merely adapted to her circumstances. That made him wonder how much Ekaterina had changed since he'd last seen her, when she'd been an agent of the Tsar's secret police.

"What are your plans now?" he asked, changing the subject.

"We have booked passage on an Italian ship leaving this evening for Crete. Once Tommy has recuperated, we will find a way back to Russia. There is an enemy to fight, after all, and war always brings opportunities."

Baxter raised an eyebrow. He wasn't surprised for a second that Mashka wanted to find a way to fight Germany, and he knew Ekaterina would also find a way to get involved, even if the Russian Empire was not in the habit of letting women fight. He didn't want to speculate on what she meant by war bringing opportunities, though.

"Was Tommy badly hurt?" he asked. The lad had refused to speak with him once Billings had escaped with Arbuthnott, flying into a high fury and retiring to the bows of the ship as they made the short journey back to Zanzibar. He'd clearly been injured during his capture in Dar es-Salaam, and Schiller's people had not treated him well. The German officer would want to know what his interest in Arbuthnott was, and how much of a danger he posed to the Kaiser's interests.

"He will be fine with rest and sufficient vodka," Mashka said airily. Baxter sensed her offhand manner hid real worry for her … what? Her comrade? He didn't think there was anything more to their relationship.

"He could stay here to recuperate, and then come back to Britain with me."

"I do not think he would like that. No, not at all, in fact. I should also remind you that you were the one to leave him in the Russian Empire." Her tone was bordering on icy again, and he thought better of pursuing the topic.

Life brings us surprises. Tommy's had been the wild veer his life had taken when Baxter had rashly decided to bring him along on what should have been a simple job watching Russian ships pass through the North Sea in 1904.

"There is nothing for him back in Britain," Mashka added, her tone softening somewhat. "In Russia, he has a good life and a family."

Baxter nodded, seeing the sense in her words. "Is he receiving visitors?"

"No. Particularly not you — he remains angry, as do I. But we women are better at hiding our anger, as it is the only way to survive in the world. I am sure, however, when next you meet, he will have forgiven you."

Baxter looked away, then picked up the fine china cup and drained the coffee down to the dregs. "I don't think any of us will be meeting again," he said shortly.

Mashka's smile was bright, lighting up her face, and it reminded him briefly of the wild girl he'd known. "The world is being turned upside down, Marcus Alexandrovich, and you are not the sort of man to stay out of trouble. I am sure we will — how do you say — bump into each other again."

She finished her own tea, placed some coins on the table and rose. "Now, if you will excuse me, I must go and say my goodbyes to dear Hensley."

"Try to break his heart gently," Baxter said.

"I shall make him worry about my heart, and that will soften the blow." She stood looking at him for a moment. "He has the potential to be a good man, if he spends less time with you."

"Well, with any luck I'll be on my way soon. There's a war to fight, after all, and it doesn't seem to be happening here."

"Well, good luck to you, Marcus Alexandrovich. You should really find the spy." She stooped briefly to kiss him on the cheek. "Until the next time we meet."

Baxter watched her walk away. She maintained a sedate pace for the first few yards, then slipped back into the stride of someone with places to be and things to do. He smiled, knowing she would describe it as the natural pace of the proletariat.

Baxter had his own things to do, though he didn't relish the prospect of his appointment with a heap of charts and papers, currently lying in an untidy heap in a locked draw in his office. If he could convince Parker and the rest of the senior officers that Schiller's plan to invade Zanzibar was not merely a planning exercise, his time here might not have been wasted.

He felt a strange sense of relief as he rose and turned back towards the palace. While Tommy and Mashka had certainly made life interesting for a few weeks, and it had been good seeing them both again, he wasn't sorry that they were leaving on a neutral-flagged ship. With them gone and his mission to capture Arbuthnott on pause, he could focus on what was actually important.

There was, after all, a war to fight. He was halfway back to his office when Mashka's last words to him finally registered.

You should really find the spy. Baxter stopped dead in the street. Of course there were German agents here, but there must be an extremely well placed one. Esca Masing had known about him almost from his arrival, and had found out more about his mission as he'd been forced to show his hand to his colleagues.

Hensley? Parker? He couldn't believe it of either of them, despite the relatively short time he'd known them. And yet, they were the only two people who had any knowledge of his real work.

Something to muse on.

That evening, Baxter went down to the harbour to watch the *Eugenia* put to sea. She was a small liner, with passengers and deck cargo, and she flew a large Italian tricolour to let any predatory warship know that she was a neutral and therefore not to be regarded as a legal target or prize. She would have the documentation to back up that claim, if a British cruiser or the *Königsberg*, the sole German warship in these waters overhauled her.

Baxter's expression was grim as he watched her go. With Europe descending into war, it was only a matter of time before that jaunty and relatively new flag was drawn into the conflict. Italy was, after all, allied to Germany and Austria-Hungary. By all accounts she wasn't a reliable ally, though, and was hungry for new territory and prestige. That had led her into the ill-considered adventure in Tripoli that Baxter had become embroiled in.

Tomas and Mashka were both aboard. Baxter had made sure of that, taking a break from his work to watch the embarkation from a distance. He hadn't tried to blend in, as that would have been a futile effort, but Tomas had studiously avoided looking in his direction as Mashka had helped him up the gangplank.

"Well, that's that then," he murmured, watching the liner's plume of smoke dwindle in the twilight. He didn't necessarily wish he was on that ship — he was hazy on the rules of war and whether it would even be appropriate — but he felt a pang of envy that they were leaving. He hadn't had any word from Saunders, and while he knew he probably couldn't expect it, he still chafed at the delay. His own communications had been necessarily oblique but, he hoped, still to the point. At this time, there was no way to know where Arbuthnott had gone or what he was now up to.

Baxter had failed in his mission, even if there had been some unexpected secondary successes.

Back to it. Despite Parker's orders, Baxter had roped Hensley into helping him go through Schiller's papers, primarily because the sub-lieutenant's German was better, but also because he knew that this wasn't something he could leave to the keen young man. Warfare was more than just derring-do and popping off at the enemy. Planning was everything, and now they had the opportunity to take a proper look at the enemy's plans.

CHAPTER SEVENTEEN

There were no fresh orders from London, either through official channels or via Saunders. Baxter felt as though he was trapped in some sort of limbo, that his odd position of being a reservist attached to Room 39 at the Admiralty meant that he had almost certainly been forgotten about. That, or Saunders had jettisoned him given his failure to bring in Arbuthnott.

"Well, perhaps war breaking out was a spot of luck for you," Hensley said, after Baxter had given vent to a rare outburst on the subject. They were in one of the larger offices in Admiralty House, having commandeered it to spread out Schiller's charts and documents.

"How do you come to that conclusion?" Baxter growled.

"Well, you're clearly the sort of chap who wants to serve," Hensley said patiently. "You're more regular service than a lot of the fellows here, most of them being a few months from retirement and dreaming of home and a quiet rose garden. Though I'm sure this will all blow over soon — home by Christmas, I'm told — while we're at war, your services aren't going to be dispensed with."

Baxter grunted noncommittally. He still had hopes that Saunders would see him reinstated into the service, with straight rank bars on his cuffs rather than the wavy lines of the reserve, but Hensley wasn't wrong. He'd still be earning his lieutenant's salary, at least, as long as somewhere within the Admiralty his return to service had been properly recorded.

"Small hope of distinguishing ourselves here, though," Hensley sighed. "Not before it's all over, anyway."

"You won't struggle for promotion, old chap," Baxter said, trying not to sound sour. Hensley was from the right sort of family and had received the right sort of education, and his career path through the RN was probably already well set. It was hard to hold a grudge against him for it, though, as he'd shown himself to be a competent officer and acquitted himself well under fire. Baxter had known a lot of officers from the same background and had clashed with his fair share of them, and there weren't many he'd willingly go into battle alongside. But he would be happy to fight beside Hensley.

"True enough," Hensley drawled. "But a gong or two wouldn't hurt, certainly with the ladies."

"Mashka forgotten so quickly?"

Hensley had the good grace to blush slightly. "I doubt I shall ever forget her," he said wistfully. "Though she's clearly above my station."

Baxter looked away to hide his smile.

"You never did tell me how you know her, and her brother. She was remarkably close-lipped about the whole thing. She just muttered something about a countess."

Baxter glanced back at Hensley. "It's a long story. Suffice to say I fell in with some wayward Russians in 1904, and got to know a couple of aristocrats tolerably well. It seems I can't escape that lee shore."

Hensley raised a quizzical eyebrow which Baxter ignored by pulling a fresh chart out of the pile of papers and bending over it.

"This all seems very cut and dried to me," Hensley said as he turned his attention back to the job at hand. "Despite what the politicos on either side might say, it's only a matter of time before we get stuck in here and I imagine the Kaiser has always had his eye on Zanzibar."

"It may be obvious to us," Baxter pointed out, "but we don't have enough stripes on our cuffs to make the decisions, and at the end of the day the military is subject to the civilian government. Represented by Major Pearce."

Hensley shrugged. "Seems to me that we'd be better off if chaps in uniform were making the decisions, seeing as we're at war and all that."

Baxter raised an eyebrow. While he had little faith in the civilian leadership of the Empire, he wasn't about to say that. "I wouldn't go around saying that sort of thing, Hensley. I've experienced autocracies first-hand, and can't say I found them particularly impressive."

"At least we could take decisive action to deal with an immediate threat," the younger officer said stubbornly.

"Well, we're just going to have to muster our arguments sufficiently well to convince Commander Parker and ultimately the Resident to take action."

As August dragged on, growing ever hotter as the southern hemisphere slid into its summer, it became frustratingly obvious that no action would be taken.

"The Resident is toeing the line," Commander Parker told them both on one of his increasingly frequent visits to what they had come to call the 'war room'. "And, to be fair to them, the German colonial authorities seem to be as good as their word, here if not elsewhere. Schnee insists Dar es-Salaam is an open port, not involved in activities of a warlike nature. After Captain Sykes' attempt to knock out the wireless station, it seems that has been put out of commission, and they've sunk a blockship in the harbour that has the dual effect of stopping our ships getting in and limiting *Königsberg*'s access."

"Any idea where she is?" Baxter asked. "At least half of Schiller's proposals involve her providing naval gunfire support for their landings."

"At large — probably the Rufiji Delta," Parker replied. "There are reports that she's taken a British merchantman, but her machinery is probably in about as good a condition as our cruisers, so I doubt we will hear from her here."

"You said 'elsewhere', sir," Hensley put in. "I take it there is news of the wider war?"

Parker gave the junior officer a sour look. "It seems all attempts at neutrality along the borders have broken down. We are receiving reports of German successes against the border garrisons around Kilimanjaro, and our own chaps have invaded Togoland, dealing with the wireless station there."

Baxter felt the familiar rise of frustration and forced it down. "Any news of the wider war, sir?"

Parker sniffed ostentatiously. "You know as well as I, Mr Baxter, that we are not an installation considered to be in need of up-to-date information. We have received confused reports of ever-larger battles in the East, and the Germans are pushing into Belgium. I understand even the army has stirred itself and sent men to France."

"They just don't want us to have all the glory, sir."

Parker and Baxter exchanged glances, a rare moment of shared understanding in the face of the younger man's exuberance. Baxter didn't know much about his titular commander's career, but any man who had been in the service as long as Parker would have seen at least some action.

"Something like that. Though it seems the pickings in the North Sea are thin, as the High Seas Fleet has yet to venture out of the Baltic."

"What are your orders, sir?" Baxter asked.

"Continue your analysis, and by all means work up some proposals for a counter," Parker said. "I can't promise we will use them at any point, but it will be well to be prepared. Hensley, I will need you back to your more … usual duties in due course. We're expecting *Astraea* in for maintenance in the next few weeks, as her machinery needs a proper service, and no doubt we will be seeing *Pegasus* in due course. The rest of the flotilla blockading Dar es-Salaam will no doubt need their bunkers topping off in short order."

The vague news Parker had brought only served to deepen Baxter's frustration at being stuck on what felt like the edge of the world. While there were further far-flung parts of the Empire, most of them were considered more vital by London and would be much better informed; and it seemed that they were just being permitted to get on with the business of fighting. Not that von Lettow-Vorbeck, the *Schutztruppe*'s commander, was the sort of man to have given them any other option.

His increasing irritation at being apparently forgotten about by his superiors in London was further compounded by the occasional visit from the East Africa squadron that was cruising the coast to control access to Dar es-Salaam and hunt the *Königsberg*, which had become something of a thorn in the RN's side. HMS *Pegasus* and HMS *Astraea*, both of them veterans built in the last century and neither particularly suited to anything other than escort or harbour duty, were frequent visitors. When the officers came ashore, often frequenting the Club, they expressed frustration at the endless patrolling with no sight of the 'shy' German, but at least they were at sea with even the slightest chance of action.

"The word is that at least one of the old Canopus-class battleships will be joining us shortly," a lieutenant from *Pegasus* drawled one evening in early September. "Then, hopefully, we'll be detached to Kit Craddock's squadron in the South Pacific and join in the hunt for von Spee's lot. They've been causing havoc out that way."

Baxter squinted at the officer. He'd been introduced to him before, but had misplaced his name in the jumble of other seagoing officers who frequented the establishment. He'd also put away a few more gins than he might otherwise have. "Any free berths, old chap?" he asked.

The officer — Jenkins, maybe? — laughed. "Afraid not. Though you shore-based chaps don't know how easy you've got it, honestly." He gestured expansively at the busy open-air bar, though his broad grin faded when he saw the savage glare Baxter gave him.

"I suppose trundling up and down the same old route with no sign of the enemy would get a bit tedious," Baxter said, forcing himself to adopt a friendly tone. No point aggravating the fellow, no matter how bloody annoying he was. A lesson he'd learned too late when last he'd worn a uniform.

"Well, quite. Though I've never quite worked out what it is you actually *do* here, Baxter."

Hensley joined the table by the slightly unorthodox approach of climbing over the back of the wicker chair. He was clearly drunk, and barely noticed when he almost overturned the chair and was saved from embarrassment or worse by Baxter putting a hand on one of the arms.

"Mr Baxter here, Harry, is a *very dangerous man* and has been sent here by Room Forty," he said, with a significant wink at the other officer. "He refuses to divulge his purpose beyond a general desire to make life difficult for the Germans."

That seemed to sober Jenkins slightly. "Intelligence bod, eh? I must confess, you don't seem the type. You might want to have a chat with Andrews, our signals officer. He keeps mumbling something about phantom German transmissions, even though they claim to have put their station out of commission."

Baxter felt himself sobering up slightly. "Has he reported this to anyone?"

"Well, the CO of course. No idea where it went after that."

"See, see there, Harry? He's caught the scent of blood, and he'll be off to cause some mayhem, mark my words."

Baxter ignored Hensley. "This Andrews is here this evening, is he?"

"Andrews? Lord, no — odd fish, that one, not a fan of bars. Or drinking, for that matter. He does love his wireless, though."

"Well, in that case, let's have another drink," Hensley slurred. "You can run this chap down tomorrow."

Baxter almost made his excuses, so he could go and find *Pegasus*'s signals officer and see what he could find out about these mysterious transmissions. It could have been nothing, of course. It could just have been that the Germans had lied about decommissioning the wireless station in Dar es-Salaam and were in fact still transmitting from there.

There was something about the way Jenkins had described it, though, that had caught his attention.

"Capital notion!" Jenkins said. "Think we're here for a few days, so I could certainly stand to enjoy the run ashore."

Baxter shrugged. There was no rush, if the old cruiser was going to be in harbour for a few days. And he'd be better speaking with the signals officer with a clear head anyway. No, better to let go of the frustrations of the last few weeks and start fresh tomorrow. "Well, one more gin can't hurt."

As it turned out, while one more gin couldn't have hurt, a couple more followed by some absinthe and a local rotgut was enough to leave Baxter with an aching head and a mouth that tasted like old leather the next morning. "I'm getting too old for this nonsense," he grumbled, after he'd plunged his head into the wash basin.

It was nothing that a solid breakfast in the local style and a few cups of coffee couldn't cure. He remembered, halfway through an extensive bowl of *shakshuka*, the conversation with Jenkins the previous evening. They'd spoken a bit more about the mysterious signals, the chances of the *Königsberg* coming out to offer battle, and the war in general. The latter was the main topic of conversation for most of the men who crowded the veranda that night. They were mostly young, freshly-minted officers like Hensley, all of them enthusiastic to hear the thump of guns being fired in anger before this whole thing blew over and the diplomats got round the negotiating table. Despite the drink, Baxter had surprised himself by keeping his peace.

The thought of making any sort of progress, of actually being able to do something rather than endlessly poring over the same documents, put a spring in his step as he walked his normal route towards Admiralty House. The path he took was slightly longer than it might otherwise have been but gave him a view of the harbour. He was about halfway along, moving at a brisk pace, when something caught his eye.

Pegasus was steaming out of the harbour. She was an old warhorse, rated a 3rd class or 'protected' cruiser as her armour mainly constituted the steel deck and coal bunkers around vital internal compartments like the engine room, but she was still a magnificent sight as she picked up speed, the wind whipping her column of black smoke away.

Baxter took his hat off and ran his hand through his dark hair, taking several deep breaths before giving vent to some choice expletives in a range of languages, yelling into the morning and startling a flock of passing porters who picked up their pace to get past the deranged British man.

CHAPTER EIGHTEEN

HMS *Pegasus* had been called out earlier than expected due to a report of the *Königsberg* at sea, it seemed. *Astraea* had received the report from a British merchantman running like smoke and oakum for the safety of Zanzibar. In Nelson's time, Baxter knew, Sykes would have taken his ship and gone in search of the German light cruiser, hoping to engage in and win a single ship action that would have made his name and garnered laurels for the station. It seemed that Jackie Fisher's maxim of the three Rs — *ruthless, relentless, remorseless* — had been successfully hammered into the navy, and Sykes had instead called for reinforcements to ensure the enemy's complete destruction.

Pegasus limped back into harbour two days later, not as a result of enemy action — there'd been no sign of the enemy warship — but because her engines were finally giving up. She'd been due to be repaired during her last visit, but that had been cut short. Commander Ingles ordered his crew, with dockyard support, to take the engines down and start the refit almost as soon as she'd dropped anchor.

"Well, it would have been a waste of time going out with her after all, but it would at least have been a change," Hensley commented when they met in the dockyard. He looked tired and grimy, having worked alongside *Pegasus*'s crew to get the machinery back into working order. It had become a common refrain from him, but for once Baxter couldn't help but agree. The heat had leeched away his energy and drive. He'd come down to the dockyard rather than going to Admiralty House, as he couldn't face another day of working up reports on the captured documents that would be duly ignored by anyone with any power or influence.

"Anything from the wireless station?" Hensley asked.

"Same answer as before — they're not a listening station, they have enough traffic of their own without worrying about retuning to German frequencies, and as far as they know there are no active German transmitters anywhere in Africa."

Baxter would have said more, but Hensley was looking out to sea, scowling. "Did you hear that?" he asked.

Baxter shook his head. "My hearing's probably not as sharp as yours," he said.

"Sign of age, I'm told."

"That, or one more fleet action than you under my belt. Not to mention a few single ship actions."

Hensley listened for a few moments more. "It's nothing, I'm sure. Probably just a thunderstorm, out at sea."

Baxter felt a chill run down his back, but he did his best to dismiss the feeling as paranoia. He rose from the bollard that had been his seat while he ate a croissant and straightened his cap.

"You're not going up to the wireless to cause trouble, are you?" Hensley asked, with no real hope in his voice.

"Just going to the post office," he replied. It was probably time to send another cable to London, just in case his last had not got through. Hensley looked at him doubtfully. "Fine. Post office, then the wireless station."

"Oh good. I'll come along, just to watch."

They were halfway to the Resident's House, where the telegraph station and post office could be found, when they both heard the noise that had caught Hensley's attention before, closer and clearer now, not unlike the sound of distant thunder followed a few seconds later by a howling noise and a splash.

"What the devil?" Hensley exclaimed, turning back to peer out to sea. He shaded his eyes.

"That's not thunder," Baxter said grimly. "That's what being on the receiving end of naval artillery sounds like."

"Then why the bloody hell are you running towards it?" Hensley shouted, as Baxter started sprinting back the way they'd come.

"Get back to Admiralty House!" he roared over his shoulder. He didn't know if anyone here had 'duty stations' in the case of enemy attack, but that seemed like the sensible place for a member of Parker's staff.

It took him mere minutes to reach the harbour front again, and in that time the initial salvo they'd heard had developed into a full-blown gunnery duel. It was *Pegasus* on one side, of course, bravely blazing away with her broadside of 4-inch guns. Her opponent could only by the *Königsberg*. Shading his eyes, Baxter could just make out a dark speck further out in the long harbour, identifiable mainly from the flash of her guns. She was standing well out, six miles or more. Looff knew what he was about, using the longer range of his main battery to engage the British cruiser while she couldn't reply effectively.

Baxter could hear shouting from the quayside, and saw a shore party from *Pegasus*. The bluejackets were piling into a launch to get back to their ship, shouting oaths and encouragement to each other as they got organised. Baxter sprinted along the quay, losing his cap in his hurry, and arrived just as the launch was shoving off.

"Make room!" he bellowed as he made a running jump and landed in the stern, stumbling across some frets and threatening to upset the vessel.

"Oi oi, lads, Jonah's whale has landed," someone quipped from the mass of sailors.

"Watch your mouth, McSwain," the chief petty officer at the tiller growled. "And get those bloody oars untangled."

"Mind if I join you, chief?" Baxter asked as he settled next to him in the sternsheets.

"If you're mad enough, than you're welcome, sir. Give way all! Stretch out!"

Once the initial confusion and chaos of getting the boat away passed, it shot forward with the oarsmen working in unison. It was overcrowded and low in the water, and the chief set the bows directly at the anchored *Pegasus* despite the shell splashes rising around her. She'd already taken some hits and Baxter could see she was on fire in a few places. Despite this, the White Ensign still flew from the flagstaff, her guns were thundering away despite being out of range, and smoke was starting to billow from her stack as steam was raised.

Despite the absurd fragility of their vessel and the very perilous situation he found himself in, Baxter felt more at home than he had done since arriving on Zanzibar. Looking along the length of the launch, Baxter could see a mix of expressions on the men's faces. Determination, anger, fear. The excited chatter had petered out as they closed on the anchored cruiser and the bluejackets realised the gravity of the situation they were willingly pulling towards. Nobody baulked, and there were no suggestions that the situation couldn't be recovered and they should save themselves. Baxter didn't doubt that there were some men who were thinking that but didn't want to appear cowardly in front of their mates, and others who had perhaps not realised just how close to death they were skirting.

A shell hit the water five yards from the launch, throwing up a spout of water that doused them. The little vessel rocked and a number of men ducked, losing their stroke, as shell splinters whickered overhead. On paper, the German cruiser's guns were only slightly larger than *Pegasus*'s, but they were more modern, more plentiful and certainly had the range, and would smash the fragile launch to kindling with a direct hit. A man vomited over the side, studiously ignored by the sailors around him.

The shells were coming in faster now, a cascade of noise and water and shell splinters and fire as more and more of them found their mark on the cruiser. The *Königsberg* seemed to be closing, but judging from the water spouts Baxter could make out between the two ships, she was not so close that she risked being hit.

Another, closer, detonation. A sailor screamed in pain. Another went silently over the side and disappeared below the clear waters, followed by a billowing cloud of red. Baxter made himself sit straight in the stern of the vessel, staring fixedly at their destination. A shell hit to port, fired at a sufficiently flat trajectory that it skipped off the water and whistled a handful of feet over their heads.

"Good practice!" Baxter shouted to the men, letting a savage grin spread across his face. "The Germans are obviously keen to stop us getting back to *Pegasus*!"

It was a weak enough sally, but enough to bolster the men. "Let's disappoint them, lads!" the petty officer shouted. "Row with a will!"

Fear as well as will carried the launch the rest of the way to the shell-torn cruiser. The noise as they got closer was deafening, both from the steady detonations and splashes of the incoming shells and *Pegasus*'s own fire. "Up the ladder and to your duty, lads!" Baxter roared above the racket. They had no idea who he was, but he had officer's stripes on his cuff and a voice that demanded obedience. Although they hadn't been able to tie on, the bluejackets raced up the side into the storm of steel and fire that raged across the cruiser's deck.

Baxter went up the side after the petty officer. He almost collided with a lieutenant-commander he vaguely recognised, and was halfway through an automatic salute when he realised they were both capless. "Permission to come aboard, sir?" he asked formally.

The officer stared at him as though he was mad, then nodded. "Granted, Mr Baxter. Though what good you or anyone else can do now is beyond me."

"Where do you want me, sir?" Baxter asked.

"Help poor Turner on the guns." With that curt order, the lieutenant-commander raced off, shouting at damage control parties to follow him and help with putting out the fires spreading over the wooden decks.

Baxter found Turner by one of the four guns along *Pegasus's* side. He was lying against a stanchion, both his legs horribly mangled, and from the twisted trail of blood that led to him he had clearly been dragging himself from gun to gun, encouraging the crews. There was no hope of co-ordinated fire, no facility for it on an older ship, and for the briefest moment Baxter was transported back to the deck of the *Yaroslavich*, where he'd helped crew very similar weapons.

"We may be done for, lads, but damn them and keep firing!" Turner shouted, voice strong despite his terrible wounds. In truth, Baxter couldn't see how much longer the cruiser could keep firing. The *Königsberg* was manoeuvring to bring her port and starboard guns, five to a side, into play in turns, deluging the helpless British ship with shells. Looking along the *Pegasus's* battery of four guns, Baxter could see most of the crews were dead or wounded, a few survivors trying to maintain a return fire while sheltering as close as possible to the ship's side. He recognised Hewitt, the ship's surgeon, moving about on deck and providing aid where he could, heedless of his own safety, though he could do little for the men but staunch the bleeding and immobilise broken limbs.

A German shell had cut away the White Ensign up in the bows, and as Baxter watched, a Royal Marine tried to hold it aloft just before his body was torn by shrapnel. Fires raged at his back, intense enough to fill the air with choking smoke.

A loader was hit a few feet from him, his arm half severed. Baxter caught the brass propellant cartridge the wounded man dropped almost without thinking, slotted it home behind the shell and slammed the breech block closed. A bluejacket, his face drawn and grease-smeared, stared madly at him. "Well, fire the bloody thing!" Baxter shouted, stepping clear just before the gunner pulled the lanyard. He moved along the deck, helping out where he could at each of the guns as they loaded and fired, just as he'd done at Tsushima. He crouched low, not worrying about trying to maintain appearances now, but he had barely managed to fire his third round when a terrible order came down from the bridge.

"Cease fire! Cease fire and strike the colours!" Commander Ingles was shouting from the open bridge, his voice almost lost in the cacophony. Baxter stopped, turning to stare back up at the bridge. Things were desperate, it was true, but they weren't far from having steam up and having the fires under control; there was still time to give the enemy a few good licks and perhaps send him packing.

Baxter caught the eye of the lieutenant-commander he'd encountered when boarding. One sleeve of his uniform was now burned and he could see scorched flesh below. The man looked bereft, and turned to the bridge. Before he could say anything, though, a loose shell detonated, causing the men nearest to duck into cover.

"Raise the white flag!" Ingles bellowed.

Baxter realised he was holding a shell, having been halfway through reloading the nearest gun. He threw the projectile over the side to reduce the risk of a further accidental detonation. "Empty the ready lockers. Over the side with it all," he told the handful of men still able to serve. The burned officer was hurrying towards the front of the ship, where two Marines now lay dead or dying, one clutching the ship's ensign. For a moment, Baxter thought the man was going to disobey orders and have the flag rehoisted, but he was shouting for anything white to be brought up to be hoisted.

Incoming 4.1-inch shells continued to pepper the cruiser, even as her own desultory fire finally tailed off and, after a moment of mad searching, a sheet was tied onto the falling flagstaff and raised. "Why are they still firing?" one of the injured men near Baxter moaned. "Surely they can see they've done us in?"

"They can't believe a British ship would strike," Baxter said, hardly able to believe it himself, despite standing on the shell-torn deck.

After another salvo, the German cruiser abruptly ceased firing. Baxter found a pair of field glasses loose on the deck, and shook the blood off them before bringing them up to his eyes. After a moment, he managed to focus on the three-funnelled cruiser as her lean, dangerous hull slid through a turn and towards the open sea again. As he watched, fire and smoke billowed from her broadside again. He braced himself, but this time the rounds were hurtling towards the shoreline, towards the spindly masts of the telegraph station on a hill overlooking the harbour. Her German ensign, vivid in the bright morning light, snapped in the breeze.

Baxter could see men running along her deck, doing something with what looked like fuel barrels lined up prominently along the afterdeck of the cruiser. As he watched, the barrels were dropped over the side, one after the other, even as the *Königsberg* engaged the *Helmuth*, which was serving as a guardship in the Southern Channel.

Are they mining the channel? The barrels didn't look like any sort of sea mine he'd ever seen, but such things could always be improvised.

A shocked silence had fallen over the deck, broken only by the crackle of flames and the hiss of water as crews continued to fight the blaze. Even those sailors still working to try to save their ship did so in a grim silence, which was eventually broken by a slightly panicked shout from the port side.

"We're holed at the waterline!" someone reported, his voice carrying clearly across the silent deck. "We're taking on water!"

Feverish activity followed this shout. Ingles and the other officers were sending what men they could to tend to the pumps, though what good those would do given *Pegasus* was already listing quite heavily to port, remained to be seen. Other men were tending to the wounded and policing the dead. Boats were putting off from the shore and nearby vessels, despite the fact the *Königsberg* was still in sight, dockworkers and sailors dashing to render what aid they could. Baxter was pretty sure he could make out Hensley, Dalton and some others from the shore installation in one of the boats.

Even if *Pegasus* could be saved — either kept afloat or towed into shallowed water to be beached without disappearing entirely — she would most certainly be out of action for a long time. Baxter looked along her devastated deck, taking in the exhausted and disconsolate men who had seen their ship, their home, reduced to a ruin in less than half an hour. He knew all too well how they felt, and that his duty now was to help out however he could.

"Andrews!" he said suddenly. The signals officer had been at the back of his mind when he'd first run after the launch, but had been forgotten in the adrenalin rush of the brief and horribly one-sided engagement. The loss of the cruiser was devastating, for both the dead and injured sailors and the RN's pride, but also because it left Zanzibar vulnerable. The *Königsberg* had shown herself capable of engaging any of the old British cruisers on the station, and there was now one fewer RN cruiser to tackle her.

"You'll probably find him down in the wireless room, sir," one of the sailors said. "He's, uh, a bit fond of his kit."

Baxter was about to dash below to find the signals officer and remove him from the ship, by the collar if necessary. Looking along the piteous shambles on deck, though, he knew he couldn't just leave these men to it.

Turner had finally lapsed into unconsciousness, or death, broken perhaps by the order to haul down the colours. Hewitt was making his way along the deck towards the injured gunnery officer, but Baxter couldn't see any other officers in his immediate area.

He turned to the handful of gunners who were still alive and uninjured. They stared back at him, hollow-faced and stunned, their faces blackened by smoke. He knew they would hate him for what he was about to say, but he also knew it was the best thing for the ship and for them.

"Right, you men," he growled, voice dangerously low. "I ordered you to get the ready lockers emptied and the shell over the side, and I expect my orders to be obeyed. Get it done, before those fires spread over here."

"What if we need to keep fighting, sir?" one of the men asked.

"This ship isn't fighting anything soon. Let's try and make sure she can get back in the fight. Come on!" Suiting his actions to his words, Baxter grabbed a shell that was rolling around loose and threw it over the side with a splash, before moving to the nearest ready ammunition locker and pulling the top round out.

It took a moment for the sailors to follow his example. He deliberately avoided looking at them, but knew from the rattle of metal and splashes that they had obeyed his order. Once they'd finished with the port battery, Baxter led them across to the starboard battery and repeated the process. "Good thinking, Mr Baxter!" the lieutenant-commander called out as he saw them working, putting the official stamp of approval on the action. Baxter wasn't convinced it had occurred to any of the other officers — not many of them would have the experience of a burning deck that he had.

Pegasus's officers and crew were managing the situation surprisingly well. The injured were already lying at the entry port ready to go into the rescue boats, and fire-fighting parties had the blazes under control. From deep in the ship's guts, though, Baxter could still hear the deep ominous gurgle of water being taken on board, and she was lying increasingly low and canted to port in the water.

Hard labour for a hot, dangerous couple of hours followed. Mercifully, one of the vessels that had sent boats across was a small hospital ship. Hewitt remained with his charges as they were gradually transferred to launches, pinnaces and anything else that would float to be transferred straight to the medical attention they desperately needed.

Those men for whom it was too late had been laid out on the afterdeck in neat rows, thirty-eight in total. Baxter lost count of the number of men who had gone over the side to the hospital ship, but he guessed a decent proportion of *Pegasus*'s complement of two hundred odd had been killed or injured.

Ingles, it seemed, was determined to salvage what he could from the situation, although he must have known that his career was over. A cable was passed forward to a tug boat, ready to move the sinking ship into shallower water. As soon as the majority of the wounded were away in the hospital ship's boats, the tug was signalled, picking up speed and taking up the slack in the cable while the cruiser's anchor was cut free. *Pegasus* jerked into motion, going on what could very well be her final journey.

The cruiser emptied as she went, moving sufficiently slowly that a relay of rowed boats and steam launches took off the rest of the crew, both the living and the dead. After the tug had taken her a mile, Baxter was almost alone on the deck with Commander Ingles, his first officer and a handful of other officers and senior ratings. The upper deck was now canted at an alarming angle.

"Well, we should be thinking about leaving as well," Ingles said, a note of deep sadness in his voice. Baxter could understand that. Ingles had been entrusted with this ship and the wellbeing of the men who sailed in her. Even if the circumstances had been different, her loss would be distressing, but being caught napping and overwhelmed while barely landing a hit in response would be devastating.

The remaining crew started going over the side and into the waiting launch, moving like old tired men. Ingles stood at the entry port and thanked each man as they went down. "You're not one of mine, are you?" he said, as Baxter's turn came.

"No, sir," he said smartly. "Came aboard when the shooting started to help where I could."

"Decent of you," Ingles said. While his tone was a bit distant and his eyes kept going to the ruin of his command, the sentiment was real enough. Baxter went the few steps down the ladder and into the launch, followed by *Pegasus*'s first officer and finally Ingles.

The launch was just about to pull away when the first officer finished taking a headcount. "Has anyone seen Andrews of late?" he asked, real urgency in his voice. "Did he get off earlier?"

He got a murmur of responses, mostly negatives and shaking heads. "A gunner did tell me he was below with his wireless equipment," Baxter volunteered.

"Bloody hell — he's probably still there, thinking he's going to salvage it."

"Never much of a seaman, Andrews — probably doesn't even realise the barky's sinking," a Marine officer said, with perhaps more levity than was appropriate for the situation. The first officer was clearly furious, mostly at his own failure of command.

Baxter was already reaching across the widening gap of water for the boarding ladder. "I'll go," he said, grabbing the ladder and swinging himself across and then up onto the sloping deck in one easy movement.

The deck was, at least, still dry — she hadn't canted over so far that water was lapping over, and the heat of the day had dried any water that had been sloshing around from the firefighting. Baxter still had to use any handhold he could find as he pulled himself towards the ship's superstructure. The ominous gurgling noise of incoming water had become a steady rumble now. Ingles may have demonstrated an insouciant *sangfroid* in his order to abandon ship, but he'd given the order just in time.

Mercifully, the nearest hatch was open and Baxter was able to clamber through into the ship's interior. The engine room was flooded and the electrical system had failed, but there was enough light through various portholes, open hatches and rents torn in the ship's structure for him to be able to see. This was the first time Baxter had been aboard HMS *Pegasus*, and he couldn't recall ever having been on any other ship of the Pelorus class. All RN ships, from the dreadnoughts of the Grand Fleet to third-class protected cruisers designed to patrol the edges of empire, had certain things in common. This included where vital compartments like the wireless room would be situated, close enough to the bridge to be accessible but well protected within the ship's citadel.

"Andrews!" Baxter bellowed, looking along this level of the superstructure. No response. Cursing, he clambered along the deck, sometimes almost walking on the bulkheads, glancing into the various compartments that opened off the main corridor.

A companionway at the far end of the superstructure led down to the deck below. "Andrews, are you down there?"

This time, he heard a faint shout in response. Definitely at least a deck below. Baxter clattered down the companionway and shouted for the errant officer again. It was dimmer down here, light filtering down from above, but he didn't let that deter him from plunging forward. As above, this deck wasn't flooded but there was water pooling on the port side. He found the signals room, a mad rat's nest of wires and other items he couldn't even begin to recognise. Wireless telegraphy had been in its infancy when he'd been unceremoniously thrown out of the service a decade or more ago, and the ships he'd been on since then had mostly lacked such newfangled systems. The one thing he would have recognised was, of course, not there.

"Andrews, the bloody ship is sinking!" he yelled. "Get yourself on deck!"

This time the voice was clearer, loud enough that he got a sense of where the errant officer was. "I can't, I'm trapped!"

Definitely below and to starboard. That side of the ship was still sitting higher in the water, even while the port side and much of the centre was already submerged. Baxter felt an unfamiliar stab of fear as he stared down into that even dimmer deck. He was a strong swimmer, but the thought of being trapped in a compartment as the ship went down was a horror that most mariners shared.

And a fate he couldn't abandon a fellow officer to.

Baxter stripped off his jacket, kicked off his shoes and padded down the companionway. He was up to his thighs in seawater before he eventually got to the bottom, and he could see that the water was already up to the starboard compartments and well above his chest height in the passageway.

"Andrews!" he shouted again.

"I can't swim!" came a plaintive cry from what he guessed was a machine room on this level. Sighing, Baxter plunged into the brackish water. While it was still just about shallow enough that he could have waded, it was faster to adopt a breaststroke over to the flooding compartment.

The signals officer had wedged himself on top of a set of shelves in the machine shop, his feet only just above the water and a look of terror on his face. He clutched a canvas kitbag to his chest as though it would be some sort of protection from the rising water. Baxter hadn't met him before, but a single glance told him he was of the new breed of signal officers who were still only grudgingly accepted by the older, more traditional members of the service. He was a small man — far too short to have waded to safety — with wire-rimmed spectacles and sandy hair that was already thinning. More interested in the technical aspects of his job than the life at sea the RN had offered him, he would probably be far happier at a shore installation.

Baxter grabbed onto the hatch coaming as the ship lurched again. For a moment he thought she'd finally settled on the seabed, but she was still taking on water. The heel was correcting itself, which meant she wasn't about to roll and trap them here with no hope of escape, but it probably also meant she wasn't far from losing all buoyancy and slipping below the water. Baxter was pushed forward into the compartment as the water level evened out, dropping behind him as it filled the machine shop further.

Baxter didn't waste time trying to coax Andrews down from his perch; he just half swam, half scrambled across to him before straightening up. "I've really never liked the sea," the fellow said, with just the faintest smile that showed he was aware of the irony.

"Drop the bag, old chap, it's just going to get in the way."

"Do you have any idea how valuable and hard to replace these components are?" Andrews snapped with surprising asperity.

Baxter stared hard at him for a moment. The water level was rising faster now, and there was no more time to argue.

"Well, let's hope they're waterproof," he said, then he grabbed Andrews by the front of his jacket and pulled him from his dry refuge and into the water.

Baxter knew that the most dangerous thing now was for the man he was rescuing to start panicking. "Just stay calm and I will keep you afloat," he said, keeping his voice conversational. "Try and keep your legs out straight behind us."

Baxter turned Andrews around in the water and started towing him back the way he'd come. The water was at the top of the hatch coaming now. "We're going to have to go under — take a breath!"

He didn't wait to see if Andrews had complied, and didn't give him time to start panicking. He dived, pulling the other man after him. Loose odds and sodds floated past his face as he dragged Andrews down under the hatch, making sure to dive deeply enough so that neither of them risked cracking their heads on the coaming.

Andrews had not so much gone limp as frozen. Baxter hauled him to the surface as quickly as possible, in case he'd tried to breathe water in his panic. There was barely enough space between the water and the deckhead, just enough for him to drag salty air into his lungs. Andrew was gasping and sputtering. Baxter felt his own fear rise again, and took a ruthless grip on it. Losing control now would be the most certain way to die.

He took his bearings. "Another few yards and we're onto the companionway," he shouted above the splashing.

Andrews' eyes were wide, but he managed to nod, breathing fast as the water level continue to rise until it was below his nose.

Baxter adjusted his grip and dove again, dragging Andrews after him. This was the dangerous time. There was very little light, and the only sound was the pounding of his blood in his ears and the low grinding, groaning noise of the ship's death cries, felt more than heard through the water. It would be absurdly easy to become disoriented and lose his way in this half-lit world and end up swimming away from salvation. He struck out as hard as he could with one hand, eyes fixed on the half-seen companionway and the rectangle of fading light at its top.

His hand caught a step, but he lost his grip as *Pegasus* lurched slightly again, though he couldn't tell if she was finally settling or starting to roll again. Baxter's lungs burned with the desire to inhale and his vision blurred. He almost lost his grip on Andrews, but managed to drag them both forward until his free hand caught onto the companionway again. Through sheer stubbornness, he pulled himself up out of the water and then heaved Andrews the rest of the way up onto the deck above.

That deck was still mostly clear of water, but he knew that wouldn't last long. Baxter dragged himself to his feet, gasping for breath, and realised the signals officer was ahead of him, staggering down the passageway to the open hatch. Before he got there, though, he staggered into the wireless room.

"Oh, for…" Baxter started to say as he forced himself into a run after Andrews. Sure enough, the officer had grabbed a leather satchel and slung it around his shoulders, along with the now-sodden canvas kitbag. He was now grappling with a crate full of equipment. "How the bloody hell do you expect to get that off the ship?"

Now that he was out of the water, Andrews seemed considerably more chipper. "Oh, I imagine we'll find a way…"

Baxter grabbed the crate from his hands and looked inside. He briefly contemplated leaving it behind. Andrews was right, though — some of the delicate equipment could not be easily replaced here in Zanzibar, and he was starting to realise how vital the wireless was to modern warfare.

With a stiff nod, he followed Andrews back out onto the deck, the bright sun briefly dazzling him. The launch carrying Ingles and the other officers was standing well off. The tug that had been towing the cruiser had cast the line off; however, he and Andrews weren't alone on the deck of the *Pegasus*.

"Good morning, sir," a sub-lieutenant said cheerfully, offering Baxter a jaunty salute. Baxter stared at him and the two sailors who appeared to have followed him aboard. "Charlewood, sir, in command of HMS *Helmuth* — or at least I will be, once we get her fixed!"

"What in blazes are you doing here?" Baxter demanded.

"We volunteered to come aboard to assess the situation now that she's struck bottom. We came across in a skiff and…"

"She's not struck bottom," Baxter snapped, just managing to bite back on "you blundering idiot". "She's just grounded in the bows. Get that man and his gear into your boat."

Charlewood was a young man, barely out of Dartmouth naval school, Baxter guessed, hence his naïve cheerfulness despite having already been under fire today. Confronted by the soaking wet and clearly angry Baxter, he jumped to with a will.

"Awfully decent of you, Charlewood, to come and get us," Andrews was saying as the two sailors handed him down into the waiting skiff and ran his equipment down the side.

"Well, we'd better see what the condition of the rest of the ship is like," Charlewood said.

"No — we're going to get in the boat and get clear of her, *sub-lieutenant*," Baxter said. His jacket was lost, long since floated away, but he was well enough known that Charlewood would know he was outranked. Even if he didn't, Baxter's manner was enough to get him moving.

Before they could get over the side, though, *Pegasus* lurched again. With a terrible grinding noise, she started to heel to port as she drifted sideways. Baxter knew, instinctively, that she was in her death throes.

"Get clear!" he yelled down to the two men on the skiff's oars. They didn't need any encouragement, and the little rowing boat shot away from the cruiser as wind and tide drove her out into deeper water.

Water was gushing over the hatch coamings in the superstructure. "Over the starboard side and swim for it, lads," Baxter ordered. "And if you can't swim, learn fast."

CHAPTER NINETEEN

HMS *Pegasus* finally sank just after two that afternoon, and even then her masts were still visible above the water. It must have been hell for her commander and crew, watching her slow settling, and her bare masts sticking up out of the once again placid waters were a brutal reminder of this blow to the RN's prestige.

It had turned out that both Charlewood and his men could swim — indeed, it was the second time that day the sub-lieutenant had had to swim for his life, as they'd abandoned *Helmuth* after she was subjected to close-range fire from the vastly more powerful German cruiser. Baxter had expected chaos when he made it ashore, but order had clearly been asserted by Ingles and his officers. The injured were either in the hospital ashore or the nearby hospital ship, and the survivors had been mustered by division and marched away. Commander Parker had appeared on the quayside, and while Baxter may not have liked the man, and indeed found him to be insufferably hidebound, he was just the man for when administration needed to be done on the hop. He strode about, trailing pipe smoke after him, putting things in motion in order to house, feed, and in some cases clothe the now berthless sailors.

The dead lay under sheets on the quayside, altogether too many in four neat rows, while graves were rapidly dug. *Pegasus*'s chaplain sat nearby, his bible open in his lap, keeping vigil over his charges.

Baxter sat on a bollard — it might have been the same one he occupied that morning, though that felt like an age ago —

and watched *Pegasus*'s end. He felt oddly drained. As far as he knew, his shoes and jacket had gone down with the cruiser, but it was hot enough that he was perfectly happy about that.

"What a bloody mess," Parker said by his shoulder. Baxter glanced up at his commanding officer, too tired to rise and salute and not exactly properly attired for it. It occurred to him that this was the first time he'd seen Parker out of his office and therefore in full daylight. His skin looked even more sallow in the bright glare of the sun, his eyes more sunken.

"Indeed, sir," he replied, when it became clear that this wasn't a passing salvo and Parker had no intention of moving on. "Can I assume that we're no longer pretending we're not at war, here in the colonies?"

There was a long moment of silence, and Baxter wondered if he'd overstepped again. Right then, he didn't care.

"You may certainly assume that, Mr Baxter," Parker said at last, tone cool but not frosty. "You may also start planning how we're going to deal with this mooted invasion. With *Pegasus* gone, and *Astraea* and *Hyacinth* on convoy duty, we're somewhat vulnerable here."

Baxter stood up and tried to straighten himself out a bit. "Has this come down from the Resident, sir?"

"Not yet, but I am more than happy to go over his head if I must. This state of affairs cannot be allowed to stand."

"I do have some thoughts, sir, but as you may know, I'm a firm believer in a strong offence."

"I expected nothing less. Have your proposals on my desk by this time tomorrow. And Mr Baxter? Speaking of bloody messes — get yourself properly attired. We have standards to uphold in the Royal Navy."

Baxter clenched his jaw. "Very good, sir."

There was no way, of course, that the residents of Zanzibar — from the Sultan who maintained his rule at British sufferance to the lowliest nightsoil boy — would not know what had happened. Many of them would have watched the short, savage fight from their homes or from the harbour. Those who were sensible would have sought shelter, of course, though it seemed the German gunnery was considerably better than the Italians, who had regularly hit the shoreline behind their targets in Ottoman harbours. There was an odd quiet throughout the normally rambunctious Stone Town, as nervous residents waited to see what would happen next.

Baxter's guess was that *Königsberg* would be steaming back to her hiding place. Looff had clearly not wanted to hang around and risk being trapped in the harbour if the rest of the local squadron had shown up, though he could have done a lot of damage if he had remained. The warship wouldn't be seen in these waters again, unless Schiller's invasion plans were put into practice. The word was that Dar es-Salaam was closed to him, thanks to the blockship sunk in the harbour mouth after *Astraea*'s raid, and the German's machinery and coal supplies were probably not in a healthy state. It would probably take a day or two, but the settlement would be back to normal sooner rather than later. Baxter had seen it a dozen times elsewhere in Africa and further afield.

He smiled grimly. Agents of any civilian shipping line, particularly those of neutral nations, would not be having a peaceful time of it right now. He expected a lot of the European civilian population would be keen to leave.

Back at his lodgings, Baxter considered his options. Unlike Hensley, who seemed to have a plentiful supply of money and could always turn himself out neatly, Baxter was down to what might be referred to as 'sea-going clothes' or the blue undress uniform he'd arrived in, which was patently unsuited to this climate.

He stood looking at it for a moment, then sighed and unpacked the stiff-collared shirt and tie that went with the frock coat, laying them out for the morning. While he had some hard work ahead of him, the prospect didn't bother him. Not if it meant they could finally go on the offensive. He knew that there would be little point in trying to work through the night. Action, even brief fights like the one today, took a lot out of even experienced hands, and the adrenalin come-down would hit him soon. Better to be at it early.

He was, in fact, just about to retire when someone knocked on the door to his rooms. Baxter had come to recognise Hensley's somewhat peremptory rap, and was tempted just to yell at him to go away. The young officer had been working like a trooper the last time Baxter had seen him, setting to the task of looking after the bereft sailors with a will. It would be churlish to send him packing.

"I come bearing a gift, and a request," Hensley grinned when Baxter opened the door, brandishing a bottle of Johnnie Walker whisky.

"You'd better come in, then," Baxter said, stepping to one side. A stiff drink suddenly seemed like a good idea. Then he put an arm out to block the door. "Depending on what the request is."

Hensley grimaced, and indicated the man standing behind him. Baxter hadn't seen him in the darkness, but as he came forward he recognised Sub-Lieutenant Andrews. He'd almost forgotten about him as soon as he was in the skiff.

"He's the last lost lamb I need to find a home for," Hensley said hopefully. He clearly expected Baxter to grumble about it, but as it happened he didn't even need the whisky to overcome any objections. Not that Baxter was going to mention that.

"By all means, come in," he said, clearing the way. Andrews stepped through, blinking owlishly behind his glasses. He was still in his uniform, looking more than a bit rumpled, and had the leather satchel he'd rescued from *Pegasus*'s wireless room clutched protectively across his chest. "I'll find some glasses."

"I was remiss in not thanking you earlier, Mr Baxter," Andrews said formally, once everyone was seated. The lodgings weren't really set up for entertaining. Baxter leaned against the edge of the rickety table, Hensley lounged in a low-slung wicker chair and Andrews perched on a three-legged stool. "You quite literally saved my life, at great risk to your own."

Baxter hadn't thought twice about going back for the lieutenant, and not just because he had useful intelligence. He waved the thanks away.

"That's Baxter for you," said Hensley. "He's a one-man landing party, rescuer of stray sub-lieutenants and all-round fire eater." He swallowed his whisky in one deft movement.

"Well, all the same, Mr Baxter…"

"It's just Baxter," he said. "And you're a comrade, Andrews. Hensley here would have done the same."

"Oh, I can assure you, I most decidedly would not," Hensley drawled, making Baxter wonder if he'd perhaps been drinking with the various officers he'd been lodging *Pegasus* survivors with. "Not a heroic bone in my body."

Baxter snorted. "Heroism, for the most part, is nine tenths circumstance and one tenth not having time to think." He swallowed the rest of his whisky. He didn't know where Hensley had found it, but it was a remarkably smooth one.

"When last I saw him, Jenkins mentioned you were onto a German transmitter, a powerful one not in Dar es-Salaam."

"Well, yes, Baxter," Andrews said, slightly taken aback by the sudden change in subject. He swallowed a larger gulp of the smooth amber nectar than he'd perhaps intended, and coughed. "Why do you ask?"

Hensley shot a bemused look at Andrews. "One of the better ways to find the enemy, old chap, is for them to tell you where they are. Even better if we know what they're saying to each other."

"Oh, well, quite." Andrews placed his glass down carefully on the table and drew the satchel over to him. "All of my observations are in here."

"Give me the short version," Baxter said, before Andrews could get the papers out and start talking in detail. "Are they using the Dar es-Salaam transmitter, even though they've claimed it's out of commission?"

"Oh no, I think they've at least temporarily disabled it. Though if I know old Taubmann, he won't have done anything permanent to it even if he was ordered to burn the lot."

"Know him well, do you?" Baxter asked.

"Oh no, never met him, but we used to chat whenever *Pegasus* was in range. Before the war of course." Andrews actually smiled impishly. "Amazing what you can get away with when you're the only one who knows how the device operates. Captain Ingles called it my 'infernal machine' and had as little to do with it as possible."

"But we digress," Baxter interjected.

"Oh, I do that sometimes. Where was I? Ah yes. My transmitter. That is, the one you're interested in. The German one. It's in the Rufiji Delta, or at least I think it is. Perhaps a touch up the coast or along the river."

"Are you sure it's not just *Königsberg*?" Baxter asked. "Rumour has it she's berthing there now Dar es-Salaam is closed to her."

"Oh, no no no — far too powerful. Definitely land-based."

"Odd place to put a wireless station," Hensley said.

"No, not really," Baxter said thoughtfully, then sipped his whisky before continuing. "Being away from a population centre is going to pose problems in terms of supply, particularly fuel for the generators. But if you want to keep your wireless network at least slightly functional when your cities are vulnerable, then in the *veldt* makes some sense."

"Bravo, Baxter," Andrews said, becoming more loquacious with the drink. "It's certainly powerful enough to reach the German squadron in the South Pacific, so even with the Togoland and Dar es-Salaam transmitters out of action they can send orders."

"What do you need to pinpoint its location?"

"Ah, well, there's the rub. There's a relatively new technique, but we need two receivers in different, fixed locations, able to receive long wavelength transmissions. I understand that we currently have none in Zanzibar, and I don't think the Cape Station is going to redirect a cruiser to support us."

Baxter crossed his arms and glanced at Hensley, who nodded. "*Königsberg* did hit the wireless station here and damage was done. It's not catastrophic, but it will take time to repair. The only other wireless, of course, is currently at the bottom of the harbour."

"What about the items you retrieved from *Pegasus*?" Baxter asked, turning his attention back to Andrews.

"I've laid them out in Admiralty House to dry and will need to examine them. Some might have survived and could be used to help repair the station." Andrews brightened. "Good job I got you to bring them out, really!"

Baxter looked away before his glower could dampen the signal officer's sudden enthusiasm. "That gives us one wireless. We need a second one, perhaps on Pemba Island?" Pemba was the most northerly island of the Zanzibar archipelago.

Andrews considered this. "They may still be a little close together, particularly given the probable direction of the transmitter, but I could at least narrow the area."

Baxter clapped his hands together, his fatigue of a few minutes' ago forgotten. "Well then. It's not everything we need, but it's a start."

"The other thing we'll need is old Nosy's permission. I don't think your excuse for the assault on Schiller's island is going to fly again."

"I have some hopes there," Baxter said. He realised the prospect of sleep was long gone, and started pulling on his uniform. "I'm going to Admiralty House to consult the charts and do some thinking."

Hensley stood up, appearing more sober than he had done when he arrived. "I think I will come and help."

Andrews looked conflicted, caught up in the enthusiasm but also clearly exhausted. Baxter solved his conundrum for him. "You stay here — we're going to need you fresh and ready to work tomorrow."

As Baxter had expected, it didn't take long for Zanzibar to come back to life. By the time he and Hensley finished their work, it had been the small hours of the morning and both of them had caught up on a few hours' sleep on cots in Admiralty House. They were woken by the ululating call to prayer from the city's main mosque, and when they emerged into the early morning light they had found the cafes and other businesses in the area busy preparing for the day's long labour as though nothing had happened. While a steady stream of European civilians left over the following days, taking ship on anything available, they were fewer than Baxter had expected. Much of the relatively small, mostly British population either thought the danger had passed, or that the balance of risk lay with remaining safely ashore while the *Königsberg* was at large and able to continue her predations.

Both the King's African Rifles detachment and the RN personnel had been shocked out of complacency by the devastating assault. Parker made an appearance down on the harbour every day, while Captain D'Etremont of the King's African Rifles was regularly seen putting his men through their paces, clearly calculated to put the civilians' minds at ease. The infantry tried digging trenches to cover the approaches, but rapidly found that after half a foot of loose soil they hit the coral on which the city stood, and were forced to put up sandbagged positions instead.

Barely a day had passed before salvage work began on the sunken cruiser. The enemy's brazen foray into a British-controlled harbour had finally convinced someone that perhaps a converted tugboat with a 3-pounder gun may not be sufficient defence. Over the following days, some of HMS *Pegasus*'s main battery of 4-inch guns and a few of her 3-pounder secondary guns were brought up. Much of the ammunition would not be usable after even a short immersion in water, but Zanzibar had been receiving shipments of shells from Cape Town to enable the cruiser squadron's resupply and by the time weapon mounts had been fabricated to turn naval guns into a shore battery, more would have been forthcoming.

Baxter was altogether too busy to see most of this, engaged as he was in planning possible counters to the threat of German invasion and trying to convince the chain of command that such a response was necessary. He was on hand during some of the salvage work, a delicate process involving divers and a ship-mounted crane to bring the heavy guns up.

"I was having another look over the *Abigail*," he commented to Hensley as they watched the first of the 4-inch guns being brought up. It emerged from the harbour like some strange sea creature, breech first and streaming water from the barrel. He idly wondered if that was one of the guns he'd loaded and fired during his brief contribution to the battle. "The Germans have done a good job converting her, given their facilities."

"Do you think she'd take one of those beasts? There'd be a certain justice in using one to blast the blighters limb from limb."

Baxter glanced across at Hensley, surprised at the vehemence in his voice. They'd both been at the funeral services for some *Pegasus* sailors who'd lost the number of their mess earlier, and emotions were running high. Most of the officers were well known and liked in Stone Town.

"She may not be strong enough, and I doubt we could poach one. A three-pounder, however, may be another matter."

"And we still haven't clarified who she even belongs to and whether she can be pressed into service. Andrews is on Pemba Island playing with his cylinders and retorts, sending the launch daily to demand more of this, that and everything else. I'm just astonished Parker released a work detail and generator to him."

"At least one thing is going well," Baxter said, after silently watching the salvage for a few moments. While the wireless telegraph station had been hit by *Königsberg*'s shelling, as far as he understood it from Andrews, the damage had mostly been done to the masts which 'even the chaps who staff it should be able to fix'. That had freed Andrews up to start building a rough secondary receiver on Pemba. "Leave the *Abigail* to me."

"What a state to be in; we've got a harbour full of RN personnel and not a bloody ship between them," Hensley said. They'd considered any number of options, including *Pegasus*'s surviving boats, but it came down to needing a ship that could carry supplies, armament and a wireless set. He gave Baxter a suspicious look. "You're not going to steal her, are you?"

"Where the ruddy hell would I hide her?" he said over his shoulder as he strode away, though as soon as he said that any number of inlets and bays around Zanzibar's coastline sprung to mind. Baxter dismissed the notion with a shake of his head — impractical, and not something a King's officer should even be contemplating.

On his way back to Admiralty House, sweating under the beating sun and receiving sympathetic glances from locals and the more lightly dressed Europeans alike, he encountered Parker, also on his way back.

"Good morning, sir," he said, saluting smartly. The base commander looked like he was having anything but a good morning, but returned the salute crisply. Baxter fell into step with him, as Parker showed no intention of slowing down. He moved at a rapid pace, despite the fact that at least one of his knees obviously gave him problems.

"Baxter. I gather things are progressing well enough with your various endeavours."

"Some are going very well, sir, certainly in terms of information-gathering." As usual when there might be unfriendly ears listening, he spoke as circumspectly as possible. It was a habit he wished some of his colleagues, Hensley included, would get into. "As to what we do with that information, I understand from Mr Hensley that there are still some impediments."

Parker glanced across at him with narrowed eyes. "The matter is still being considered, Lieutenant," he said coolly. "As I'm sure you're aware, even in wartime the correct legal processes should be followed. And there is still pressure from the civilian authorities here not to provoke an escalation in violence between the colonies."

Baxter almost shook his head in disgust. British cruisers had shelled German ports, and a German cruiser had sailed right into Stone Town's harbour and sunk a warship there, and yet their political masters still clung to these outdated notions and the letter of a treaty that had been honoured more in the breach than in compliance.

"While the information gathered will be useful, sir, without some means to act on it that utility will be limited."

"I'm well aware, thank you," Parker said acidly. "Believe me, I am taking this matter seriously. I must also consider the good of the service in our relationship with both the civil authorities, HM Government back in London and, of course, the Sultan of Zanzibar himself. Now, Mr Baxter, don't let me keep you from your duties."

Baxter gave Parker's back a hard glare as he marched away. It occurred to him that Parker was keeping very close control of the reports coming to him, as was his right as the installation's commander and only proper given the chance of intelligence being leaked. He'd been tempted to ask whether Commander Ingles could bring any influence to bear or even authorise an operation using what was left of his command, but his gut told him that Parker hadn't even briefed *Pegasus*'s former captain and that any mention of it would be construed as going over his commander's head.

Baxter turned in a circle, scratching his chin and feeling the weight of his wool frock coat. If he couldn't push forward with anything else, he could at least do something about his attire.

He headed deeper into what was considered the European quarter of Stone Town. Perito and Sons was tucked away in an alley between relatively tall, pale coral stone buildings that huddled close together to provide as much shade as possible. From the outside the tailor shop looked unprepossessing, aside from the magnificently carved doors that Baxter had become quite used to in his time on the island. Stepping into the cool interior was akin to being transported all the way to one of the grander cities in Italy. The large, airy space contained a small fortune in mirrors and polished mahogany woodwork, with red velvet furnishings and polished brass fittings completing the look. Bolts of cloth were on display, and the proprietor himself greeted every guest as they arrived.

Baxter doffed his cap as he entered and received a half bow of acknowledgement from the portly little tailor. Perito already had a customer. In fact, from the look of things, he'd had a number of customers of late.

"Commander Ingles," he greeted the officer currently being measured. It was an oddity of the service, Baxter reflected. A few days ago, even though his rank was Commander, Ingles would have been called 'Captain'. Now his command was sunk, that was no longer appropriate.

"Mr Baxter. I see you are in slightly less of a dire strait that I am, but still in need. It seems the war has been very kind to *Signor* Perito."

The tailor smiled and bowed again. "You are most lucky to have arrived before the lieutenant, Commander Ingles. It takes much cloth, a very great amount, to clothe him. But do not worry, Lieutenant Baxter, I have your dimensions and should have just enough."

Baxter took a seat while he waited for Perito to finish darting around Ingles' tall, spare frame with his tape measure. HMS *Pegasus*'s officers and men wouldn't have had time to gather their belongings when the ship was abandoned, and it seemed the officers had followed their usual practice of descending on the tailors. "I gather you've got my signals officer squirreled away on Pemba Island," Ingles said unexpectedly. "Playing with another of his infernal devices."

Baxter fought to keep his expression neutral, though he was genuinely shocked by such a flagrant breach of good sense, let alone security rules. At least Ingles hadn't actually said anything about wireless or direction finding. "That's right, sir," he said carefully, then an idea came to him. Perhaps he could turn the situation to his advantage. "We're hoping to find a way to hit the Germans back for what they did to *Pegasus*, sir, by finding where they're lurking. Though what we could do if we *do* find them is the question, given our limited means here."

"Are you, by Jove?" Ingles said, a note of interest in his voice. "Never thought Andrews would ever be that useful to anyone. But I suppose you're right; we don't have a lot here. Not with old Peggy gone."

Baxter loathed that he was doing this, hated what he had to say. It smacked altogether too much of the sort of thing Arbuthnott would do. Or Ekaterina, for that matter — though she might even be proud of him for it.

"There's always the Cape Squadron, of course," he went on airily. "But it would be good if we could hit them back ourselves, and soon. Even if that old coaster we captured was released to us for use, though, there are political considerations…"

Ingles straightened up. Perito, ignored, tutted to himself that his measurements were being thrown off again.

"You're far too junior to be worrying about such matters, Mr Baxter," Ingles said severely, and for a moment Baxter thought he'd overstepped and the old captain was on to his games. "So you leave them to me. You do what you need to do to get that old tub ready for war and find these blighters."

Baxter managed to conceal his relief. He'd taken a gamble, seeking to put an idea in a senior officer's head without appearing to go outside his own chain of command, and he risked operational security by talking even in roundabout terms in a public space, although Perito's was often seen as an extension of the RN facilities. It was the sort of behaviour he loathed, but he couldn't see any other way to move things forward.

CHAPTER TWENTY

Zanzibar had finally woken up to the fact that there was a war on. It had shaken off the last vestiges of peacetime lethargy, and Stone Town now reverberated to the crash of marching boots and gunners practising with the 4-inch Peggy guns that had been salvaged from the wreck. Pemba Island, however, seemed almost entirely untouched by war.

Baxter watched the long white beaches and low tree-covered hills slide by as he took the steam pinnace salvaged from *Pegasus* on a supply run to the little martial outpost at the far tip of the island. They passed an occasional dhow or other local small boat, but the supply run had become usual enough that it excited no response or even a glance from the fishermen. Seabirds turned lazily overhead, their cry the only noise aside from the splash of water against the sides and the small steam engine that pulsed under their feet. They had passed some small settlements on the way, including Chake Chake, the largest, but they were often only visible as a collection of smoke plumes.

Baxter consulted the chart in the small wheelhouse. Their destination was Kigomasha, the most northerly village on the settlement and the location chosen for the receiver. He paced along the short length of deck, ignoring the slightly concerned glances from the small crew. This was one of the bluejackets' more pleasant duties: a gentle cruise to an exotic island, a bit of offloading upon arrival and then perhaps a meal, which made a nice change to the usual fare available in the mess. Baxter was tense, though, for a reason he couldn't put his finger on, and that tension was spreading to the men.

"Not far now, sir," Dalton said pleasantly. The old petty officer was at the wheel, and had done this supply run several times since the receiving station was established. "I imagine Mr Andrews and his boys will be glad to see us."

Baxter grunted and stared out to sea, eyes peeled for the dangerous low shape of the *Königsberg*, which was still out there somewhere. The German cruiser hadn't been seen since the attack on the 20th September, and opinions varied wildly as to where she was and what Looff was up to. Some suggested she was running east, trying to find and join von Spee's squadron. Or perhaps she was ranging around the end of the Suez Canal to play havoc with Britain and France's seaborne trade coming through that vital artery that wound its way through the desert. Neither of those sounded likely to Baxter, on account of her supply situation and the likely state of her engines.

No. *Königsberg* was still in these waters, lurking in the Rufiji Delta.

Baxter raised his field glasses and swept the channel to the west. German East Africa leapt into focus. Zanzibar felt absurdly vulnerable, lying bare miles off that enemy-held coast. That was the way Britain had always existed, of course, clinging to the edge of an often hostile shore, but here the enemy had de facto naval dominance. At least until the Cape Squadron cruisers returned.

But what capacity did they have to use that naval dominance? That was the question he hoped Andrews would help answer.

"Smoke ahead!" Julius, up in the bows, called back.

"Maybe they've got a firepit going," one of the other sailors said hopefully. The last crew that had come up this way had spoken at great length and in great detail about fish slow-cooked over an open fire.

There was too much smoke even for a large bonfire, let alone a cooking pit. The plume was big enough that the smoke could be seen from several miles away, so there was still some time before they would arrive.

"Full ahead, Dalton," Baxter said calmly.

"Full ahead, aye." The chime of the engine room telegraph punctuated the sentence, and a moment later the pinnace started picking up speed. Judging from the density of the smoke, it was probably too late to prevent disaster befalling Andrews' little party, but they may still be in time to salvage something.

"Could just be a fire, sir. That generator didn't look to be in the best condition, and you know what tars can be like away from shipboard discipline."

"I do indeed, Dalton," Baxter said. He resisted the urge to raise the glasses — there was still a headland to round — and instead took another turn up and down the pinnace. Silence had fallen over the little boat, and the sailors went from lounging comfortably to standing upright and alert.

Baxter blew out a long breath. The smoke showed no sign of abating, and he fancied he could hear a faint popping noise. "Clear away the main gun," he ordered. "Action stations."

There was, of course, only one gun, the 3-pounder Hotchkiss mounted on the foredeck, and only so much the little boat could do in terms of going to action stations. The men responded in a lively fashion nonetheless. Two sailors readied the gun while the four other sailors — who until a moment ago had been expecting to be nothing more than porters when they arrived — disappeared below to grab Lee Enfield rifles and ammunition from the small arms locker before parading on the foredeck. Baxter had been pleased to see Julius, the African sailor who had handled himself well during the Dar es-

Salaam raid, was part of the crew, and was doubly glad of it now. He hadn't flinched in the face of the enemy.

The pinnace slid round the small headland, casting something approaching a bow wave and with white water streaming down its side as it reached twelve knots. Baxter could see the metal lighthouse at Kigomasha now, even without the field glasses, and that at least seemed intact. The plume of smoke, though, seemed to be rising from the wireless station that had been established not far from the lighthouse. They were still a mile or more away. Raising his glasses, Baxter could make out an unknown vessel, of a type not dissimilar to his own, lying off the beach to the north of the lighthouse, and figures moving around a raging inferno that could only be the wireless station. He realised the popping noise he could still hear was rifle fire, which meant at least some of the small shore party was still fighting. He could make out little flecks of white that were probably bodies in RN uniforms, lying sprawled in the scrub.

"Load rifles!" he barked, unable to keep a note of anger from his voice. "Main gun, load HE!"

The sailors all knew what was what, now, and the lazy humour that had characterised the voyage disappeared. They may not have been as well trained with the rifles as a Royal Marine or a soldier, but they'd drilled enough that they loaded the strips of .303 ammunition smartly. The Hotchkiss's crew operated smoothly, slotting the brass-cased high explosive round home and clanging the breach closed.

"Helm, two points to starboard," Baxter called out, the orders reflecting the clarity of his thought and analysis of the situation. This was what he had been born to, despite what his father and the RN might have thought. They were closing on the beach where the German pinnace lay. Baxter could see men retreating to their boat, a white-uniformed prisoner among them, while four other prisoners were kneeling on the sand with their hands behind their heads. Other enemies — *Schutztruppe* rather than sailors, he thought — were retiring in good order behind the sailors making for the pinnace. None of them gave any indication of having seen the RN pinnace descending on them.

The rearguard, then. Baxter gave the order as the range closed. "Main gun, target bearing thirty degrees, range eight hundred. Shoot!"

The Hotchkiss fired, slamming back on its mount, the gunner riding the recoil through the padded shoulder mount he leant into as he sighted.

Baxter watched for the fall of shot and saw the shell burst in the scrub ten yards wide of the small enemy rearguard. The 3-pounder didn't throw a big shell, and had been obsolete even in 1905 when Baxter had commanded a boat not too dissimilar to this one against far more heavily armed Japanese torpedo boats. The detonation, however, was enough to throw the rear guard into confusion.

"Adjust three degrees right, range ... five hundred. Shoot!"

The shell landed just in front of the soldiers this time, and Baxter thought he saw at least one man go down.

"All guns, engage at will!" he called out. "But don't you bloody dare hit any of our men. Helm, lay us for the pinnace."

The sailors with rifles opened fire. Even in the relatively calm water here, the pinnace wasn't the most stable gun platform and all they really achieved was kicking up little spouts of sand and dirt, and further startling the German sailors and soldiers. The Hotchkiss thumped out a regular beat of HE shells, the block slamming open to waft cordite smoke back along the deck as it spat out the brass case to be replaced by a fresh shell.

Baxter's instinct, as a trained gunnery officer, was to be up on the foredeck directing their fire, but he knew he needed to keep an eye on the wider situation. He stood tall beside the wheelhouse, using his field glasses to pick out specific details.

They were close enough that Baxter could identify Andrews in the party of *Kaiserliche Marine* sailors, being dragged along unwillingly by a massive German petty officer. His heart sank slightly when he saw *Leutnant zur See* Kleiner, the officer who'd been good enough to give him a lift from Dar es-Salaam and had therefore saved him from Esca's hunters, in command of the party.

The Germans may have been caught by surprise, but they were recovering quickly. The *Schutztruppe* rearguard were sprinting pell-mell for the beach and their escape route, while Kleiner's party was already splashing out through the breakers for their pinnace. There was movement on that vessel as well, the crew running to its own armament. Kleiner was shouting something to the two sailors who were guarding the four prisoners. One of them started running after his comrades, while the other hovered over the prisoners, rifle half-pointed at one of them, as though he was contemplating murder before escaping.

"Julius, take that bastard out," Baxter snarled. He knew the African sailor was a better marksman than him and probably most of the other sailors.

"Aye, sir," Julius said, rising slightly and taking careful aim before sending a heavy round clean through the German's centre mass, knocking him flat on his back. The prisoners threw themselves flat; Baxter could see more white uniforms emerging from the direction of the lighthouse, firing as they came.

The German pinnace had a machine gun in its stern, which opened up with a long stuttering chatter of fire. That first burst went high, cracking overhead, but the second chewed into the pinnace's bows or rang off the polished brasswork, small explosive shells blowing holes in his command. Baxter glanced forward, seeing the gun crew crouching behind what cover they could. The Hotchkiss didn't have a gun shield, so there wasn't much.

"All rifles, fire on that gun!" Baxter snapped. He was about to order the main gun to fire on the German boat as well, but the enemy shore party was tumbling over the side of their pinnace, some men running to the forward gun while others disappeared below. They were close enough now that Baxter thought he could hear Andrews' voice, raised in uncharacteristic anger.

"Course, sir?" Dalton asked, as another burst of machine-gun fire tore up the water around the pinnace.

Baxter took stock. The German pinnace was already getting up steam. Kleiner was visible in her stern, shouting at the *Schutztruppe* and waving his arm, encouraging them to run for the vessel even as it started moving. The machine gun fired again, this time managing to wound one of the Hotchkiss gunners. Baxter didn't have time to check on his condition. The enemy vessel was picking up speed, Kleiner realising that he didn't have time to wait for the men in the water, but it wouldn't be fast enough.

"Three points to port," Baxter ordered. That would put them on a course to cut across the long curve towards the open sea that the German boat was starting to take. "Lay me alongside."

There was a steady fire going between the two boats as they closed. The German machine gun appeared to have jammed, and one of the gunners was hit even as he tried to clear it.

Baxter ran to the foredeck, pausing briefly to check on his own gunners. The wounded man was being tended to. Baxter knew they couldn't risk the gun at this range anyway, and the riflemen were doing a sufficient enough job keeping the enemy's heads down.

Dalton knew exactly what he was doing, and didn't need any more input from Baxter. "Brace!" Baxter shouted as the pinnaces' courses converged. He actually saw the look of shock and surprise on Kleiner's face just before the two vessels crunched together, staggering both crews.

Baxter had been ready for the impact, but he still almost lost his footing. He recovered quickly and jumped between the two boats. Kleiner was pulling himself up, and Baxter took the opportunity to punch the German officer in the face. Pain flared through his hand but Kleiner went down. He spun, hearing movement behind him, and kicked a uniformed sailor over the side just as Julius landed three paces away and tackled a sailor trying to ready a Mauser rifle.

The shooting had stopped now, replaced by the desperate grunt and crash of men locked in hand-to-hand combat, struggling for their lives. Baxter dropped into the wheelhouse — more of a recess in the deck behind an armoured shield — to confront the helmsman, the big German sailor he'd noticed escorting Andrews.

The petty officer straightened and turned, bringing a weapon to bear. Baxter found himself staring down its broad mouth, then ducked aside as the trigger was pulled. The noise and heat was devastating in the confined space. He felt the wind of the flare's passage past his shoulder, then brought his fist up in an uppercut aimed towards the German's square jaw.

His opponent, it seemed, was a brawler. He managed to get a forearm in the way and deflect the blow before unleashing a flurry of meaty fists into Baxter's ribs in return. He wasn't as big as Baxter, but broad and strong, and they were fighting in a confined space. The scrap rapidly got dirty, neither of them able to swing a decent punch. They grappled, Baxter managing to turn the man and get an arm around his throat. The German sailor reached back, thumb probing for Baxter's eye.

"You could just give up, you know," Baxter gasped, leaning his head away from the grasping hands as he managed to brace his foot against the forward bulwark of the wheelhouse. He got his other hand onto the top of his opponent's bald head and twisted when the German didn't do the sensible thing and give up. His neck went with a sickening snap and his body went limp.

"I surrender! *Bitte!*" someone shouted from below, before the stoker emerged with his hands raised and eyes wide as he stared at his dead comrade.

Baxter gasped in a lungful of air. He realised the other sounds of combat had died away, aside from someone moaning in pain. The silence was eery, despite the fact the boarding action could barely have lasted longer than a few minutes.

"Mr Baxter!" Andrews called out from the small cabin, voice slightly plaintive. "Is that you?"

There was a surprising amount to do after the short, sharp fight. The wireless station was a dead loss, the tall masts that had gone up under Andrews' care now flaming pyres that threw heat off for yards around. The tents the shore party had been living in were just burnt-out skeletons and the generator was a husk. Kleiner had been thorough in his destruction, as was only proper from his point of view.

There were the prisoners to be secured and kept under guard. Baxter got everyone off both pinnaces as soon as the Germans had surrendered or been subdued and split up the different groups. The *Schutztruppe* who'd been left in the water had already surrendered to the British sailors ashore. They couldn't be faulted for that, after seeing their escape route disappearing and being confronted by vengeful armed men at their backs. Waist-deep in water was no place to mount a last stand with no purpose.

"I should never have given you a ride back here," Kleiner said miserably as the two men stood together, watching the precious installation finish collapsing into the inferno at its core.

"Well, I'm glad you did," Baxter said, clapping him on the shoulder. "No doubt it gave you a chance to reconnoitre our coastline. And you did achieve your objective."

Kleiner shot him a dark look, then smiled thinly and shrugged. "Such is the nature of war, it seems," he said, voice tired. "Will you accept our parole and let us go?"

Baxter arched an eyebrow at that. It was a strange thing, hearing that idea raised on a hot shoreline thousands of miles from home. Parole was a concept from an earlier age, when men could more easily be trusted to keep their word and not take up arms again.

"Not for me to decide, I'm afraid," he said. He didn't know what the official policy on the matter was; it would be one of the many things this unexpected war had thrown up. While he had no doubt that Kleiner was a man of his word, the last thing he needed was an official reprimand for letting prisoners go.

"What is your intention, then?" Kleiner asked, voice cold again.

"We'll bury our dead, though we can't take too long over it as we both have wounded, and then return to Zanzibar." Baxter stared hard at him. "Impress upon your men that I don't want any hijinks or notions of escape. You'll find me to be a fair man, but do not confuse that for weakness."

Kleiner avoided his gaze. Baxter had spoken mostly for his benefit, as any officer worth his salt would be looking for a way to turn this situation to his advantage. Even with the shore party added to his crew, Baxter barely had more men than there were prisoners, and that could turn nasty quickly. He'd separated the African *askari* from the European prisoners, and everyone in his party was going about with rifles. He'd even remembered to belt on his Smith and Wesson; that had been left in the cabin during the fight. The guns on both the pinnaces were manned and trained on the shore as the final deterrent.

"Let's get some graves dug, Dalton," Baxter called out. Andrews had lost two men from his party, and a third RN sailor had died during the boarding action. More Germans had lost their lives, and there were severely wounded men on both sides. "And look sharp. We can't be too long about it."

They steamed south later that day, Dalton in charge of the German pinnace with the White Ensign flying from its flagstaff. They left behind a little row of forlorn graves next to the burnt-out remnants of the wireless. A deputation had come out from Kigomasha once the shooting had died down and the fire had subsided, and arrangements had been made to keep the graves safe from animals or other interference until a burial detail could come up and remove the dead to a proper cemetery. That discussion had been hindered by a language barrier, as Julius was from a different tribe and only had a limited command of the local language. Baxter, while he had a smattering of a half dozen languages from spending his early adulthood travelling the world on his father's ships, hadn't yet had a chance to spend much time learning Swahili and hadn't been able to help.

The two pinnaces were somewhat overcrowded as they finally turned their bows south, and the journey was considerably more subdued than the pleasant cruise of the morning. The green-clad hills of Pemba seemed more sinister in the fading light, even though it was friendly territory, and every man's thoughts dwelled on the dead they'd left behind. The RN sailors were also on edge, given the number of German sailors and *askari* troops they had packed into the cabins of the little steam vessels. Baxter had the prisoners locked in and armed guards posted at each door, despite Kleiner's repeated offer of parole and protestation of good behaviour. "We'll make the transit as quickly as possible to minimise your discomfort," he'd promised the disconsolate young officer, who he kept out on deck so he couldn't formulate plans with his subordinates.

Baxter's mind was preoccupied to an extent with the wounded men stretched out on deck under the inexpert care of their comrades. Now the manic activity of the action and its aftermath had passed, however, he kept turning over the events of the last few hours. He found it hard to believe that the *Kaiserliche Marine* had just stumbled upon the wireless station, nor would they have been able to use direction finding, as Andrews had built it solely to receive. So how had Looff found out about it, quickly enough to despatch a raiding force?

At least the fact that a single pinnace had been sent suggested the cruiser was not currently seaworthy, wherever she was laid up. It seemed likely that Looff would have considered the station a sufficient threat that he would have come and shelled it flat if he could, rather than risking a handful of men so close to British forces.

Andrews himself sat on the afterdeck, surrounded by notebooks and loose sheafs of paper weighted down with empty 3-pounder cartridge cases. Baxter had, at first, thought that the deaths of the men, some of whom had been nominally under his command, had been weighing on him, but he soon realised the signals officer was more concerned with the destruction of his receiving station.

"I was so close, Baxter," he said now, looking up from his papers. "Herr Kleiner attacked while I was narrowing it down. Remarkably chatty, whoever was running that transmitter, but that's a perennial problem with the Germans."

Baxter was starting to realise that Andrews operated on a different plane to most people and that he had to adjust his approach accordingly. "You previously told me that it was utterly disastrous, the whole enterprise a loss."

"Yes, well, that was in the, ah, heat of the moment," Andrews stammered. "And, in many ways, the loss was devastating. My triangulation of the location will not be that precise, indeed it could be several miles out, and there was that second rather odd transmission on a shorter wavelength I managed to pick out two or three days ago that I intended to triangulate…"

Baxter had started to think of the implications of that when one of the sailors came hurrying back from the bows.

"What is it, O'Reilly?" Baxter barked.

"Beg your pardon, sir, but we're taking on water forward," the sailor said, with a sharp salute.

Baxter nodded. While the damage from the German cannon had been around the pinnace's bows, it didn't surprise him that the stress of the impacts might have led to a leak being sprung. "Thank you, O'Reilly. I'll be forward directly," he said, then turned back to Andrews. "A search radius of even a few miles is a lot better than the entirety of the Rufiji Delta, so as far as I'm concerned this hasn't been a disaster. Now, while I prevent us sinking, why don't you get what you've got on this other wireless signal in order?"

CHAPTER TWENTY-ONE

The planking had indeed opened in a couple of places, and shrapnel had driven through the side not far above the waterline, probably from a near miss that burst on the water. Nothing that couldn't be handled by regular pumping and bailing, and Baxter's crew were delighted when their prisoners were put to work on that duty.

Organising that work to keep the pinnace afloat for the few hours it took to return to Stone Town, running down past smaller islands haunted by ruins and Zanzibar's hills that seemed impossibly green with fruit trees and clove plantations, occupied his mind fully. They steamed back into their home harbour in the late afternoon, all of the RN sailors feeling a justified stir of pride as both their comrades and local people stopped to stare at the small returning convoy. There was inescapable administration work when they landed — repair and resupply for their own pinnace, the captured vessel to be inspected, arrangements to be made for the prisoners to ensure they were kept both secure and as comfortable as they could be. Baxter fielded a torrent of questions from his fellow officers, ranging from the quartermaster needing to know details of who had died and how many extra mouths he had to feed, to officers from *Pegasus* wanting to know every detail of the brief fight. It was a victory, even if it was a very minor one.

Commander Parker didn't come down to the harbour, but Baxter sent a runner with an initial report he'd briefly scribbled in a notepad on the way back. An hour after he'd landed, he received a return missive to report to Admiralty House along with Sub-Lieutenant Andrews.

"A great deal of excitement," Parker said drily, looking at him over his pipe, a cold expression in his eyes. Baxter guessed that the wheels he'd put in motion when he spoke to Commander Ingles had finally turned sufficiently that the base commander was aware of exactly what he'd done. He braced for what he guessed was coming.

"I imagine you are to be commended, Baxter, even if the capture of a single pinnace and a handful of Germans is not exactly Trafalgar, eh?"

"Just doing my job, sir," Baxter replied stoically. Playing the bluff sailor — what he was, at heart — would be his way through this interview. He was too tired for anything else.

"Any indication of why the Germans descended on Mr Andrews' installation, and indeed how they even knew it was there?"

"My belief, sir, is that they must have known the significance of the work we were doing. That was a risky operation for them to undertake."

"You sound like you admire the enemy, Mr Baxter."

"I respect him, sir. Only a fool doesn't." Baxter immediately regretted adding that last point, as it skirted the edge of insolence, and Parker's sharp look told him that the point hadn't been missed. "As to how they were aware, I believe Mr Andrews has the answer to that."

"I do? Jolly good," the signals specialist said.

"Well, spit it out, man!" Parker snapped, his patience obviously wearing thin.

Andrews flinched. "I did detect a brief, shortwave transmission three days ago," he said. "Though what it has to do with —"

"In code, I assume?" Parker interrupted.

"From what I could pick up of it, yes, I think so. Tricky business, picking up —"

"And not one of our own wireless transmissions?" Parker cut across Andrews again.

"Oh no no, definitely not a wavelength we use in the service, and there aren't other transmitters on the island. Official ones, that is to say…"

Parker leant back, looking pensive. "We have an enemy spy on the island, and one well enough placed to know details of our deployments."

"That was my conclusion, sir," Baxter said. "I also think I know where this agent is located and how he's getting the information. Not just about the wireless transmitter, but some details of my own assignment that I believe were then passed to German officers."

Parker struck a match and stared hard at him as he lit his pipe. "Do tell, Mr Baxter."

"I take full responsibility for this, sir, but some details of Mr Andrews work were inadvertently discussed in earshot of an Italian civilian."

"While I understand that you might want to fight the world, Mr Baxter, we are not at war with the Kingdom of Italy, even if she is technically allied to our enemies."

"I'm aware of that, sir, but men spy for things other than patriotism. Greed, most often."

"Well, we'll deal with any malfeasance on your part in due course." Parker almost sounded pleased by that, but then made the slip Baxter had been expecting from him. "And how were details of your assignment leaked?"

"Well, sir, to be frank, I believe that was you. Inadvertently, of course."

His conclusion was inescapable, both his own culpability and Parker's. Not to mention Commander Ingles, who had said far more than he should have when Baxter had spoken with him. The Germans had known far more about his work in East Africa than should have been possible, particularly so soon after his arrival. Schiller was exactly the sort of man to be running an operation here, probably without the permission or knowledge of his civilian superiors given the desire most seemed to have to maintain cordial relations between the colonies. *Frau* Masing had probably been drawn into his machinations, as few men would suspect a woman of being an intelligence agent, and she had every reason to hate the British.

Baxter laid all this out to Parker, but took no pleasure in watching his pallid face grow greyer. "The blighter has been operating under our noses for years," he said when Baxter had finished. "The one place every Royal Navy and Rifles officer is almost guaranteed to visit, and feel like they can speak freely."

"Without being as noisy as somewhere like Pierre's," Baxter agreed. "I'm afraid we've all been rather lax."

Parker rose, his expression stormy. "Well, we're all going to have to do better, aren't we?" he snarled, stalking to the map. "This throws the entire operation into doubt. They'll know we're coming."

Baxter had been mulling this over. He knew he was partially responsible for this, just as he'd admitted to Parker. He hadn't liked what he'd had to do, manipulating Ingles to move things forward, but just like every other damn officer on the island it had never occurred to him that someone would be listening.

Parker took a few puffs on his pipe. "But then, if this latest debacle hadn't occurred, then we may never have known there was an enemy agent here."

"We can also use this to our advantage, sir," Baxter said, inspiration striking him. Any fighting officer worth a damn needed to be able to deceive the enemy, but this sort of operation needed an experienced hand. It was the sort of thing Ekaterina would do, and he found himself wishing either she or Mashka were here to advise.

"I'm listening, Baxter," said Parker.

"Well, Mr Andrews has certainly now lost all of his possessions. Twice. It's probably time to visit the tailor."

The plan took a couple of days to prepare and was simple enough, but it caused Baxter a certain amount of anxiety, simply because he wasn't the one to execute it. He didn't know that much about the intelligence world, despite working for Naval Intelligence, but he was still the most experienced hand on the island. If he was right, and either Perito or someone in his establishment was listening in to the casual conversation of British officers while they were getting measured for new suits, whoever the spy was would almost certainly be made suspicious by Baxter going in for a new suit or uniform and casually dropping some juicy intelligence so soon after he was last in. No, it had to be Andrews, escorted by Hensley, who'd taken the fellow under his wing.

Baxter waited in Admiralty House, along with Parker and Ingles. No other officer had been indoctrinated into the operation, not because he thought they might be traitors, but because everyone on the station seemed to be an incurable gossip. Ingles paced around the office in a way calculated to suggest that he didn't have a worry in the world, though Baxter presumed that Parker had no doubt found a way to intimate that he had accidentally revealed some sensitive information to an enemy agent. Old Nosy himself demonstrated admirable coolness, tackling the seemingly endless pile of paperwork that a station commander had to deal with.

Baxter watched them both from the corner of the room he'd been exiled to, as a junior officer in the company of the two most senior officers on station. He wondered idly whether Parker would have made a good captain at sea. He certainly managed to appear imperturbable under pressure, but then he also had a bad habit of flying off the handle. Would the battle in the harbour have gone any differently if their roles had been reversed?

Probably not.

Hensley and Andrews' return, at least half an hour after the agreed time, was presaged by cheerful voices raised in a high, spirited discourse. They burst into the room like a couple of young officers who'd been engaged in hijinks and had forgotten to whom they were reporting. Which, Baxter mused, they were. Neither of them could have been long out of Dartmouth, and they certainly didn't have the sea miles behind them that even Baxter had, let alone the two older men.

Parker surprised him by adopting a slightly avuncular tone. "Well, gentlemen?"

Hensley threw his cap on a chair and actually beamed as he ran both hands through his mop of blond hair. "That was actually quite fun, sir," he said with a grin.

"Did you get the information out convincingly?" Ingles snapped, showing the frustration bubbling beneath the surface.

That sobered Hensley slightly. "I believe so, sir. It seemed to go swimmingly."

"And did anyone seem to be paying particular attention?" Parker asked.

"Old Perito just did his usual routine, and will make Andrews here look positively dapper if allowed. There were others around, including one of his sons."

"Which one?" Baxter asked sharply. He found it hard to reconcile the cheerful little Italian with being a secret agent. His sons, however, were a different matter.

"Ah, the older of the two, I think. Slicked back hair, always seems to be impatient to be off and doesn't pay that much attention."

"Doesn't sound like the sort to be a spy," Ingles said.

Baxter suppressed an incredulous expression. "Sounds exactly like the sort to be a spy, sir," he said, hoping he'd managed to hide his surprise at the captain's naivety.

"Well, then," Parker said. "Andrews, get yourself up to the wireless station and keep an ear out for any unauthorised transmissions."

Andrews brightened immediately. "Though I do have to point out, sir, that it's very unlikely —"

"Yes, yes," Parker cut him off. "Still, probably worth you following orders, eh?"

"Yes, sir. Very good, sir!" Andrews stammered, grabbing his cap and heading for the door.

"And not a bloody word about this. To anyone. It's about time we started taking this war seriously, gentlemen, and behaving accordingly."

"Of course, sir, not a word."

They waited for Andrews to hurry out. Hensley, sensing the base commander's mood, for once kept his mouth shut. "Well, I suppose now we wait to see whether or not they take the bait," Parker said.

Baxter cleared his throat. "If I may, sir? As Andrews has pointed out, the chances of him actually picking up any transmissions are minimal. I'm not sure we can risk waiting to see, given the stakes."

"I remain unconvinced that this invasion force is actually going to materialise, and between the shore batteries, the auxiliary and the pinnaces we at least have some form of force to oppose them."

"Assuming *Königsberg* doesn't sally out, that is correct, sir," Baxter conceded.

"And as you have surmised yourself, the enemy cruiser is probably bereft of fuel and machine parts, and is therefore unlikely to put in an appearance."

"I may not be right, sir, and it's always best not to underestimate the enemy," he said. It didn't do to argue with a superior officer, but he knew his time on the island was limited anyway. "We may be better going on the offensive. We may even be able to do something about *Königsberg* before she can come out of her lair. Ships are always at their most vulnerable when caught at anchor."

Baxter resisted looking at Ingles when he said that, but he could almost feel the shot go home.

"There is something to what Baxter says," the shipless captain said. "There's nothing worse than being on the back foot all the time, and the service has always won through by being aggressive. Even when our enemies hid in their ports, we didn't sit in our own safe harbours and wait for them to come to us."

Parker looked between Baxter and Ingles. "Very well. I'll speak to Major Pearce about authorising an expedition."

"Why don't you leave that to me, Commander?" Ingles said, in a tone that suggested the question was more in the way of an order.

A tense silence fell over the office, broken by Parker's icy command. "Mr Baxter, you're dismissed."

Baxter left the office quickly and quietly, choosing discretion over valour and making sure that he got well clear of the area before the two senior officers had the row that was clearly brewing between them. That was something he wanted no part of.

There was work to do, of course, there always was, but there was also the waiting. Baxter was well used to long periods of waiting, not knowing what was going to appear over the horizon, but he found them easier to handle at sea. There was nearly always something to occupy the attention, even in steam-driven ships that didn't require the careful tending of sails, and long days of calm steaming could blend into one moment of *now* with the wake stretching out behind and the unknown forever ahead. Here on land, though, the waiting soon became intolerable, despite the fact he knew how slowly the wheels of naval bureaucracy could turn. Whether or not their gambit with the supposed spy had worked gnawed at him, along with the constant threat of an invasion flotilla showing up before his superiors had decided to act.

And, he had to admit, there was also the possibility that the whole enterprise had been a figment of Schiller's imagination, and there would be no attempt on the island. It was equally possible that the heat and grinding pressure of being in a war without knowing what was going on had led them all to jump to conclusions about the possibility of there being a spy on the island.

Coincidences, after all, happened all the time. It was a big world, as Baxter knew better than most.

"It's the infernal waiting I can't stand," Hensley commented the following morning, staring out of the office window at the placid harbour. "I mean to say, I wasn't exactly happy to be posted here last year, but at least we had some sort of routine that made things bearable. Paperwork, such as it was. Parade the men weekly. Drinks in the Club or Pierre's, coal the occasional visitor, the occasional visit to — ah, well…"

Baxter snorted. "What would Mashka say?"

Hensley actually blushed slightly. "Don't tell her I said that, will you?"

"I doubt either of us will see her again," Baxter said. He hadn't thought much about Mashka or Tomas, or the woman they worked for. Not to mention Billings.

Hensley sighed. "I know. I've just … never met anyone quite like her."

Baxter couldn't help but smile. Hensley didn't know the half of it, or that she wouldn't be shocked by the idea of young officers visiting brothels. Disappointed, certainly, and also pleased to be proven right about the aristocratic classes.

There was a knock at the open door. "Commander Parker requests the pleasure of your company, gentlemen," an orderly said.

Baxter felt a rush of adrenalin. *This is it.*

CHAPTER TWENTY-TWO

Just like the day they found out that the war had broken out, the commander's office was crowded with white uniforms and stuffy with tobacco smoke. Parker wasn't seated behind his desk this time, but was standing by a chart pinned to the wall, along with Commander Ingles. The chart they were staring at was one that Baxter and Hensley had been working on, and he could see their pencil marks on it still.

Baxter recognised some other senior officers from *Pegasus*, including the commander of the Royal Marine contingent and Ingles' first officer. The rest of the complement was made up of some of the base's officers. The only other man not dressed in the RN's tropical white was Captain D'Etremont, the commander of the King's African Rifles contingent on the island. He stood out as much as Baxter in his khaki uniform, and was also holding forth at length.

"I really don't see what all the fuss is about," he was drawling as Baxter and Hensley arrived. "With those guns you chaps pulled off your sunken boat, and my men, this island should be safe as houses."

The army officer didn't get much agreement from the sailors he was imposing on. While the RN's purpose for years may have been keeping the Empire together and policing it, they all still felt the finest tradition of the service right down to the marrow — find the enemy's ships, and take, sink or burn them. *Pegasus*'s crew had been trying to do exactly that, and no doubt other ships of the Cape Squadron would be back on patrol shortly. After the lethargy imposed by the civilian authority's ban on offensive action for the first few weeks of the war, the officers stationed on Zanzibar seemed to have woken up and found their offensive spirit.

"The shore guns and your troops will of course be invaluable if the enemy does get this invasion force out to sea," Ingles said, "or in the unlikely event that the force is too much for us to handle."

"Assuming it even exists," D'Etremont broke in, a smug smile spreading over his narrow face. Baxter had encountered him once or twice, though the King's African Rifles officers usually drank in a different establishment to the RN. He didn't much like the man.

"Assuming it exists," Ingles concurred. "Determining the veracity of which, gentlemen, is the purpose of the exercise that we are proposing to undertake and can now brief you on, now that Mr Baxter and Mr Hensley have deigned to join us."

Hensley opened his mouth to speak, but Baxter managed to grab his forearm and very slightly shook his head. He had a sense of the way this meeting would go, and didn't much care as long as the mission went ahead and he was on it. He didn't want that jeopardised by Hensley shooting his mouth off.

"*My* intention is for a strong reconnaissance of the Rufiji Delta and waters further north," Ingles went on. His voice sounded tired. While many of *Pegasus*'s former crew appeared to be fired up for revenge against the German cruiser that had ambushed them, Baxter couldn't help the feeling that Ingles was just … broken. "It will consist of the coastal steamer *Abigail*, the steam pinnace that we were able to salvage and the recently captured enemy vessel."

"Who will command, sir?" Ingles' first officer asked, a note of hope in his voice. Ingles, of course, would have every right to take that role himself, but Baxter doubted he would want it, and may even be prevented by the fact he'd lost his own command. The letter of the law was not something he'd ever paid much attention to.

"I was hoping you might, Walsh," Ingles said. "I'll give you as many men as can be spared from the salvage work, including some Marines under Childers here."

Lieutenant Childers, a little terrier of a man with a bristling moustache, looked delighted at the suggestion. Including Marines in the party meant there would be landings, and there were few things the Jollies enjoyed more.

"If I may, sir," Parker cut in smoothly. "Given that Mr Hensley is familiar with the Rufiji from his peacetime pleasure jaunts, and Mr Baxter has, ah, some experience with this sort of caper, I'd like to propose that they join the expedition along with some picked men from my own command."

Ingles nodded gracefully — he could hardly turn down help from a man who'd gone back aboard his sinking ship to pull out an officer he'd left behind. "Walsh, I'll leave the dispositions to your discretion. I want you at sea no later than nightfall tomorrow. Questions, gentlemen?"

The briefing broke up an hour later — a long, hot, stuffy hour that hadn't been able to dampen the sudden energy in the room and the good mood among the officers, even those who would not be undertaking the expedition. Eventually, everything had been agreed to the senior staff's satisfaction and everyone knew what they were doing.

As always, having dawdled for weeks, there was now absolutely no time to waste. The men of the modern RN may have been less beholden to tide and wind than their predecessors, but the infernal rush remained.

"What the bloody hell was that all about?" Hensley muttered sotto voce after they had finally filed out of the office. He at least waited until the crowd of officers had dispersed. "We did most of the bloody work on that."

Baxter just held up his hand for peace until they'd descended to their impromptu war room.

"That was a bit of arse covering," Baxter said, once he was sure they were alone. "After a fashion. Ingles' command may be at the bottom of the harbour, but he's still the senior officer here. Parker would have had to confer with him, particularly as we needed some of his crew, at which point our proposals were, well…"

"Thrown out of the window."

"Modified," Baxter corrected him tiredly. "Ingles is just as done for as *Pegasus*, and he knows it. But he'll want as many of his people to come out of this smelling of roses as possible, and he'll have seen this operation as a way to do that. Risky, but if it goes to plan everyone comes out of it looking good."

"But we should be getting the credit. Dammit, man, you've done most of the work on this."

"I'm here from Room Thirty-nine, Hensley," Baxter said. "I'm sure my superiors there wouldn't want too much attention drawn to what I'm getting up to. And at least Parker has got us and some of his people involved."

There was more to it than that, of course. Baxter hadn't told Hensley of his own underhanded machinations, and had no intention of doing so. As far as the sub-lieutenant was concerned, this was as much of a surprise to Baxter as it was to him.

Hensley paced the length of the room. "At least Walsh is good," he said at last. "Decent hand at gin rummy as well. Two extra boats, though, and more men than we'd expected."

Baxter raised an eyebrow. "I've never heard an officer complain about having more men than expected," he said.

"We'll need to rework the supply situation, but this should mean we have more of a chance of success, not less."

Baxter held his hand up as they heard footsteps, heels loud on the polished wooden floorboards. Lieutenant-Commander Walsh, previously first officer of *Pegasus* and now, apparently, the commander of this operation, knocked politely on the doorframe.

"At ease, gentlemen," he said as he entered the room, though only Hensley had made an attempt to straighten up. Baxter had run into the commander on a couple of occasions here on the island, usually while one or both of them were a little drunk, but Walsh hadn't left much of an impression. He was of middling height, urbane, and either more competent than he appeared or from a wealthy family to have advanced to commander at a surprisingly young age. Baxter hoped for the former but expected the latter.

Silence fell for a moment. The king glowered down at them from a wall, and the only sound was a fat black fly turning lazy circles around the sun-dappled space.

"I'm well aware of the situation, and that between the two of you, you've planned this entire operation," Walsh said eventually, sounding self-conscious and a little awkward.

"That's our job, sir," Baxter said. He was getting a little tired of this talk of fairness. Wars, after all, were rarely just.

"Well, yes, indeed," the commander said, looking slightly surprised. Baxter guessed he'd come down here with every intention of making that exact point. Walsh paused again. From what Baxter had seen, he wasn't someone usually lost for words, but he'd come in here with a plan of action and now found himself struggling.

"Where do you want us in the expedition, sir?" he asked, throwing his new commanding officer a lifeline.

Walsh brightened slightly. "We've agreed that personnel from the base will man one of the pinnaces. Mr Hensley will take command of that. I want you with me on the *Abigail*, Baxter, as second in command."

That was something, at least. While Baxter knew he couldn't expect justice and equality in the service, and other such notions that Mashka had spoken of endlessly in the past, he had to admit that the way Ingles had seized control of the operation still rankled, even though Baxter had been the one to put the idea in his head.

"Very good, sir. When do you intend to leave?"

"I want to be approaching the enemy coast at around dawn two days from now, so I'm putting to sea mid-afternoon tomorrow."

"If I might, sir?" Baxter said, then waited for the nod to continue. "I understand the Resident intends a raid on Perito's this afternoon, which should plug one source of information. But we have no way of knowing if the enemy has other sources in these waters, coast watchers or other local informants. I suggest we try to leave in the hours of darkness."

Walsh pursed his lips. "I had thought to steam north when we left harbour — that should fox our enemies for a little bit. I want as much night as possible when we're closer to the African coast."

"With respect, sir, I think steaming away from our intended destination isn't going to fool anyone," Baxter said. "We could put to sea this evening and then run in during the night."

Walsh's gaze was cool and assessing, then he nodded. "That does mean we've got our work cut out for us," he said. "The pinnaces at least have their armament, but the armourers are still adapting the mounts the Germans constructed on the *Abigail* for our three-pounders."

Baxter nodded. "Well, there's probably not a moment to be lost, then. Sir." He could almost see the expedition's commander adopt the decision as his own.

"Mr Baxter, I'll ask you to see to the outfitting and supply."

Hensley held his tongue until they were sure Walsh was well on his way.

"I'm pretty sure something happened there, old chap, but I'm not entirely sure what it was."

In that brief interaction, Baxter had taken the measure of the man and worked out how to handle him. A hard horse officer wouldn't even have given him leave to suggest something, so it was encouraging that Walsh had actually listened. He'd perhaps agreed too quickly.

"Here's something I wish I'd known years ago," he said. "There are ways to manage your superior officers to ensure you get what you want. I don't like doing it, but sometimes it's necessary."

Hensley grinned. "I shall observe closely, and learn how to do it."

Baxter grabbed his cap. "Don't even think about trying it on me," he growled. "Come on. We've got work to do."

The little flotilla was ready to put to sea just as the sun was preparing for its plunge below the western horizon. It had taken a lot of hard work to get it to that state. Looking along the quay, Baxter was struck by what a pitiful force it was to take out into potentially hostile waters. If *Königsberg* found them, they were done for — the cruiser was certainly faster, and had demonstrated the capacity to hit her mark at several miles' range. The only hope was to avoid her, which, given the punishing nature of the environment she operated in and likely supply issues, probably wasn't going to be a problem. Their mission, after all, was not to hunt for her.

The men hadn't been told what the mission was, of course. The less they knew, the less likely it was that someone would let something slip while ashore. They couldn't hide the preparations, of course, but the word was being put around that the vessels were being outfitted to join the repaired *Helmuth* as guard ships.

Walsh emerged onto *Abigail*'s deck, looking as tired as Baxter felt. They were the only two officers aboard, with Hensley in command of the captured German pinnace and an even younger chap called MacGregor in command of the third vessel.

Baxter saluted smartly. "We're ready for sea, sir."

"Very good, Mr Baxter," Walsh said as he returned the salute. "Dashed fine work getting her ready."

"Thank you, sir, but I can't take the credit." That was true enough — all of the bluejackets had worked like troopers. *Abigail* was barely recognisable from her peacetime state. The *Kaiserliche Marine* had already painted her battleship grey, and now she mounted two 3-pounder Hotchkiss guns along the foredeck and a Vickers machine gun abaft the wheelhouse. Both could be concealed if necessary, using means the Germans had already installed, but that would only really be useful for commerce raiding and that wasn't what they were about.

It had been hot, hard work, but the sailors had set to with a will. Baxter probably wouldn't have earned himself any friends just by driving them through the blazing heat of the day, but he'd pitched in with them frequently, particularly during the delicate operation when a quarter ton of light naval artillery was lowered into place on the adapted mount. That had been nervous work indeed, and Baxter had had to nip in a couple of times with one of the armourers to make adjustments on the fly. That had been done through the simple expedient of wielding a sledgehammer one-handed in the confined space on one occasion.

"It bodes well for the success of our enterprise," Walsh went on. The nearest bluejackets, who were busy belaying loose equipment and otherwise preparing the little ship for sea, suddenly took on the exaggeratedly casual look of men trying very hard not to appear as though they were listening in. They all knew they weren't just going on guardship duty; sailors had a way of grasping when something was afoot even if they didn't know the details.

"They're certainly a fine body of men, sir," Baxter said, seeing as the sailors were listening. It wasn't a good idea to try to suck up to a crew, but it *was* important that they knew they'd done good work.

Shadows were sliding quickly across the deck, and the light that bathed the harbour was rapidly darkening to orange as the sun disappeared behind the town at their backs. Hensley and MacGregor walked along the quayside. Baxter and Walsh went up to meet them.

"Well, gentlemen, you know your orders," the commander said crisply. He'd gone from being second in command of an old cruiser on a backwater station to commanding a small force, even if it was one of the more irregular flotillas that had put to sea under the White Ensign. But if he was feeling any nerves, they were well hidden under his professional demeanour. "As soon as it's fully dark, we'll go and pick up the Marines and the last of our supplies, then put to sea directly with as little light and noise as possible. *Abigail* will lead, followed by *Ruby* then *Heidi*. As soon as we clear the harbour, we'll go south until we've cleared the island and then south-

south-east. It's not going to be comfortable in the little boats, I'm afraid, but it'll just be for the day. Any questions?"

There were none, nor should there have been at this stage. While they'd spoken, the last light had faded and the sky had darkened from a rich orange to purple and finally a twinkling darkness. The lights along the harbour were coming on and a few people were still about.

"Carry on," Walsh ordered, and the small group broke up as quickly as it had formed.

It didn't take long to raise steam — the boilers had been ready for an hour or more — and with the quiet efficiency that typified the service the three boards untied and pushed off from the quay, *Abigail* in the lead. When there were already several yards of water between the boats and the dock, Baxter heard someone shouting his name. Some unnameable instinct made him move as far forward along the converted coaster's deck as he could go, without looking to see what the commotion was. Walsh emerged from the wheelhouse. "I think that chap's got a telegram for you, Mr Baxter," he said.

"I'm sure it's nothing urgent, sir." He'd spent days waiting for a telegram, hoping for orders that would bring him back to Britain, back into the war. He couldn't think of anyone else who might be sending him a telegram — as far as he knew, his father was still alive but wouldn't know where he was, and he didn't think Mashka and Tomas were likely to try communicating with him. For all he knew, Saunders might be sending him orders to keep looking, as bizarre as that might sound now that war had broken out, but it was just as likely to be orders recalling him. "It can wait until we're back."

"Very good, Mr Baxter," Walsh said, his mind no doubt already moving on from the issue.

Baxter stood up in the bluff bow of the steamer, staring ahead. He'd barely thought about Mashka and Tomas since they'd left. Arbuthnott and Billings had barely been on his mind unless he was concerning himself with what Saunders would demand next. Since *Königsberg* had brought the war to this harbour, he'd been living exactly in the moment, and that was where he needed to be.

HMS *Abigail*, as she now was, wasn't a large ship — a little under a hundred feet long and with a shallow enough draft that she could navigate rivers and small harbours, as well as make her way along coasts. She hadn't been designed with a large crew in mind, so with twenty sailors and the space needed for the Jollies, a lot of the men had had to sling hammocks in what had been her cargo hold. That meant they were up on deck unless duty took them into the sweltering space below — Baxter certainly didn't envy the stokers — but even with the crowd of sailors there was almost complete silence. Looking back, Baxter could make out the two pinnaces, mostly from the faint glow of their binnacle lights.

Their course took them past *Pegasus*'s wreck. Baxter suspected Walsh had chosen this route specifically to remind his men of why they fought, though he suspected they didn't need that. Warning buoys had already appeared around the vessel, and the skeletal shapes of her masts sticking forlornly out of the water could just be made out against the backlighting of the town.

The ship's complement had assembled unconsciously along the side facing the wreck. Baxter straightened and moved to the railing. "Off hats," he called out softly, removing his own cap. A susurration of fabric told him that the men had followed the order without hesitation.

The eery, lonely sound of the warning buoy's bell slipped aft, and the informal, impromptu parade slowly drifted apart. Shortly after passing the sandbank that *Pegasus* had grounded on, their course was adjusted towards a less frequented part of the seafront in the long and comparatively shallow crescent harbour.

The sombre moment as they passed the sunken ship was soon forgotten as they tied up again. Baxter could hear whispering coming from the men; there was a palpable sense of excitement despite the fact they appeared to be mooring again.

The brisk voice of Lieutenant Childers, the Royal Marine commander, sounded from the shadows as soon as the gangplank had been swung out. "First file forward and aboard quick as you can!"

There was the rumble of running boots, and someone said, "Blimey, it's the Jollies. Wondered where they'd naffed off to."

A file of ten Marines came up the gangplank at the double, causing the wooden structure to flex uncomfortably. As well as their Lee Enfield rifles and packs, each man carried more supplies for the journey — crates of tinned food and small butts of the vitally important rum. They were all in borrowed King's African Rifles uniforms, as their kit was currently soaking at the bottom of the harbour. Baxter got the naval infantry below as quickly as possible while smaller groups of Marines boarded the pinnaces that had tied up behind *Abigail*.

"Few sacks and such left, old boy," Childers declared as he came up the gangplank, the last of his men off dry land. He touched his swagger stick to the brim of his cap as he passed Baxter, who grabbed the nearest sailors and set about getting the last of their supplies.

The whole operation was carried out in a rushed silence, with just the occasional muttered command and the sound of running feet, hard breathing and the clatter of kit being moved. Baxter didn't know whether the Germans had agents in Zanzibar — that was the sort of thing Parker should have known — but it was better to be safe than sorry, and this was good practice for the sailors anyway.

With the last of the forces and supplies aboard, they put off once again and Walsh took his small flotilla on a wide arc to head south. They had a local pilot aboard, a taciturn Arab who kept them to the clear channels between the sandbanks.

"Shame we can't use the Southern Channel," Walsh commented, his face eerily underlit by the low light in the wheelhouse as the Arab murmured instructions to the quartermaster on the wheel.

"I'm pretty sure those were just empty barrels the Germans put over the side," Baxter said. He'd said the same thing to Parker after the attack on *Pegasus*, but everyone from the Resident down had thought it prudent to listen to the warning *Königsberg* had transmitted in the clear as they steamed away. *Avoid the Southern Channel.*

"You think Looff was just having a joke?" Walsh asked.

"It wouldn't be the first time deception has been used in warfare."

"Well, all the same, perhaps its best if we keep a careful watch in case any of those barrels have floated away and turn out not to be empty."

Baxter nodded, and called a few men over to brief as he headed to the side.

"How're we supposed to spot a mine in the darkness?" one of the men muttered.

"Look for white water, or anything that doesn't look right," Baxter ordered, though he couldn't help but agree.

Despite the fact that Baxter was pretty certain that the *Königsberg* had not in fact laid mines on her way out, he did know that minelaying was an important part of German strategic thinking and they were sailing close enough to the supposedly mined channel that danger could exist. Tension was spreading over the deck and more and more men lined up to keep an eye out.

The broad expanse of the Indian Ocean lay before them, dark and mysterious under a canopy of glittering starlight and a crescent moon. All eyes were on the gentle waves marching past them, though.

"There!" someone called out breathlessly, and Baxter snapped round to follow the pointing arm. He squinted at the white water in the darkness. "Just waves on a sandbank," he said after a moment. "But sharp eyes to see that."

The distraction meant that they didn't see the barrel-shaped object ahead until it was almost too late.

CHAPTER TWENTY-THREE

"Ten feet off the port quarter!" came the shout, louder than Baxter would have liked even though they were far from land now. He hurried forward, expecting to see another shoal, but instead saw what looked like glossy black metal breaking the waterline. He wiped sweat out of his eyes and looked again. He was trying to pick out a black object against a black surface.

He caught it again; there was something about the contour and sheen that made it stand out even against the water. He sprinted back to the wheelhouse.

"Possible mine off the port now, sir; we're almost on it."

"Two points to starboard, O'Neill, and then all stop. Mr Baxter, boom the bloody thing off."

Baxter was already running forward, grabbing one of the long stout poles that were normally used for pushing far less lethal objects away from the hull.

He eased the pole forward, eyes searching for the slightly curved spikes of the detonators. Nothing — the surface appeared smooth. That didn't mean they weren't there — if it was a mine, it might just have flooded on one side and turned over, hiding the horns.

"Gently, lads," he said, as more booming poles appeared on either side of him. He made contact, with a *thump* that made him wince. *Abigail*'s course was changing, and he could hear the clatter of a signal lamp informing the pinnace *Ruby* to adjust course as well. The sea's current seemed to be pushing the object towards them, almost as though it had a malicious will of its own and had chosen to put an end to this expedition before it could truly begin.

Thump. Another boom, further down, keeping the object away from the hull. Baxter moved aft so he'd be in position to fend it off further down. The cylinder turned in the water as someone else caught it high on the convex upper surface, and Baxter held his breath.

Then he saw the word *Benzin* in faded white lettering, and what might have been a crude drawing of a flame, and breathed out. "False alarm, sir," he called over his shoulder. "Looks like a barrel."

He was careful to fend the bloody thing off, all the same.

The hour before dawn found them creeping along the coast towards the Rufiji Delta, having made good time through the night. *Abigail* had proven herself to be sufficiently fast that she didn't hold back the pinnaces. The journey wouldn't have been a pleasant one in the little boats, exposed to the long swell of the Indian Ocean, the waves that had marched across thousands of miles of open water and found themselves unimpeded by island or coastline. Baxter had experienced similar taking a similar vessel across the South China Sea, although the company he'd kept for that voyage had more than made up for any momentary discomfort.

"We should probably see to some breakfast, and then prepare to run it with the early light," Walsh said, emerging on deck looking positively bleary. He'd taken the tiny cupboard that was called, with a certain amount of humour, the captain's cabin, but he didn't look like he'd got much rest. Baxter had slung a hammock on deck and, for the handful of hours he'd been off watch, had slept soundly enough.

"Aye, sir," Baxter said. Their complement didn't run to a cook, but they had a cook's mate at least who would be capable of brewing tea and frying bacon in the tiny galley.

"I really don't like running in in daylight," Walsh said, rubbing a hand over his unshaved jaw. "Particularly with the sun behind us."

They'd already had this conversation during the run south, talking in hushed tones so as not to disturb the men trying to sleep on deck. "I don't think there's any other option, sir. If the Germans have been careful to conceal this wireless station, it's going to be hard enough to pick out in daylight."

"And if that ruddy cruiser is out and about?"

"Then we run like hell. Sir."

Walsh nodded. Away from Commander Ingles and a clutch of officers he'd known and worked with for years, he was starting to demonstrate a disturbing level of indecision, which made Baxter worry for the expedition if they did run into any opposition. But then, it wasn't unusual for men to find their resolve when the shells started flying.

"I assume you'll want me on the guns if there is any action, sir?" he went on.

"Bit small for you, aren't they?" Walsh asked. "I thought anything under four inch isn't to your taste."

Baxter shot him a sharp look. He hadn't, to his knowledge, mentioned that particular foible to anyone since he'd arrived in Zanzibar. "I've learned to adapt, sir," he said, patting the walnut grip of the revolver he now wore.

Walsh nodded, his own expression reserved. Then he obviously came to some sort of decision. "I've heard of you, Mr Baxter," he said quietly. "Through Bradshaw and one or two others."

Baxter didn't respond. It was only a matter of time, even in a service as large as the RN, before he would run into the officers who'd successfully blackballed him before, or people who knew them. This was not opportune timing, though.

"And I have to say, I think they were mostly talking rubbish — for what it's worth. I'm glad to have a fighting officer as my second on this."

That surprised Baxter. While Walsh had seemed capable enough, he certainly belonged to the class of officer who'd always looked down on the son of a merchant skipper. He'd been prepared for anger, and now found himself taken aback. "I'm glad to be here, sir."

Walsh nodded firmly, his expression communicating that this would be the last that would be said on the subject. "I'll see to the men's breakfast, sir," Baxter said.

"Very good." Walsh looked at the dark mass of the coastline. They could already make out where the heavy mangrove swamps were broken by the various channels of the old river as it finally disgorged into the sea. To the east, Mafia Island was just visible, placing them between two potential enemy forces. "Well, this does seem to be it."

"It does indeed, sir."

Walsh had laid out his intentions before they'd set sail, so there was no need to bring the pinnaces alongside to confer further. Once the men had eaten, Baxter made the signal to the smaller vessels, a prearranged flag rather than the signal lamp being used.

The pinnaces took the lead after that, steaming line abreast towards the broad mouth of the river and its many channels. Walsh had decided he wanted the small force to stay as close together as possible. While that reduced the amount of coastline they could search, it meant they would be able to support each other. Hensley waved his cap as his command, the German pinnace captured from Pemba Island which they'd named *Heidi*, steamed gamely past *Abigail*'s starboard side before drawing in front of the freighter's bows so they could take soundings and hopefully prevent her beaching on any of the sandbanks. The consensus was that the Germans could very well have mined their harbours and other waters, and *Heidi*'s crew had more of a chance of spotting the mines without detonating one. *Ruby* steamed to starboard so she could cover the far bank of the river.

Baxter looked down at a chart he'd spread out on the deck behind the wheelhouse. Andrews had marked the search area he'd narrowed down with his direction-finding work, and Walsh had shown himself to be a capable navigator. They therefore had a good fix on their own position, and a reasonable idea of where they needed to be.

"Shouldn't take us too long, even if we have to creep up there," Walsh said. "I'll take the con, Baxter. I want you up in the bows, keeping a sharp eye out."

"Yes, sir. Should we close up to action stations?"

Walsh pondered that for a moment. Baxter had run through the same considerations that were going through his commanding officer's mind. They didn't know when or even if they would meet the enemy, so being on high alert for hours could very well tire the men. At the same time, they needed to be ready for action at very short range and probably with very little warning, and being at stations would keep the men alert.

"Very well, Mr Baxter, action stations it is."

The men had been in high spirits since they'd left Zanzibar, glad to be underway again. The dark, oppressive mangrove swamps on either bank and the many islets they manoeuvred around soon put a dampener on the mood. The almost overwhelming reek of rotting vegetation didn't help matters, even further out in the deeper channel where *Abigail* had to steam. In reality, being at action stations didn't mean that much either. The two Hotchkiss guns and the machine gun in the stern were all manned, and anyone not otherwise engaged with running the ship lined the rails, keeping a sharp eye out both for the enemy and any obstacles in the water. It was hard to maintain focus, though, through the long morning that followed. Baxter ended up standing the men down in shifts so they could rest their eyes, eat and drink, and with any luck, get some sleep.

"*Ruby* signalling, sir," the signals rating assigned to *Abigail* said not long after the last of the crew had had their lunch of cold corned beef sandwiches and hot, sweet tea. Baxter lowered his field glasses, having been scrutinising the river ahead. *Ruby* lay about a hundred yards off their starboard quarter, hugging the tree-lined bank. He caught the end of a rapid set of flashes from its signalling lamp: *Masts sighted, bearing two ninety degrees.*

Baxter's heart started to beat harder. He adjusted for *Ruby*'s different position when she'd taken her bearing, but didn't see anything — just a mass of mangroves and a bend in the river. Walsh came hurrying forward. "Tell *Ruby* to confirm that bearing," he snapped, when he couldn't make out the masts either.

"Wait," Baxter said, shading his eyes then bringing his glasses up. *Abigail* was proceeding at barely four knots, just enough to make headway against the river's sluggish current, and as the helmsman followed the bend of the river the angle changed sufficiently for Baxter to be able to make out what *Ruby* had seen. "Got them, sir — it does look like a radio mast, maybe two miles ahead." He squinted, trying to disaggregate the masts from the trees. "I think there might be a ship there as well — I can see smoke and what might be ship's masts."

Walsh reacted faster than Baxter had expected. "All stop!" he called back to the wheelhouse. "Let go the anchor! Signal *Ruby* and *Heidi* to come alongside."

The clatter of the signals lamp was almost lost in the rattle of the anchor chain. A seaman had been detailed at the winch for exactly this sort of situation, when it became necessary to stop as quickly as possible. *Abigail*'s way came off her gently, slowed first by the current and then by the anchor digging into the river bed only a scant few feet below her keel.

"Any thoughts on what she is, Baxter?" Walsh asked, voice tense. The two pinnaces were turning and steaming back towards the command ship, but Baxter hadn't taken his eyes off the masts.

"I see a single mast, sir, and smoke from one stack. It's not *Königsberg*."

"You're quite sure?" Walsh demanded.

"She might be lying at an odd angle and only have one boiler going, but I'm pretty sure, sir."

Walsh chewed his lip thoughtfully. "We'll send *Ruby* ahead to reconnoitre."

"Might I suggest waiting for nightfall, sir?" Baxter didn't like suggesting it, given the time pressure, but darkness would allow them to make a stealthy approach and possibly take the installation without too much noise. At the same time, he couldn't help feeling that time was ticking down on the German invasion force leaving — assuming it wasn't already underway. The delta had so many channels that they could quite easily miss each other in exactly the same way that the RN force hoped to avoid *Königsberg*. "The pinnace would be spotted quite easily."

"I know that, Mr Baxter, but it's worth the risk to make sure we're not about to sail into *Königsberg*'s guns. I'm also not keen on hanging around here too long — if we get bottled up we're not fighting our way out."

"Yes, sir. We could use *Heidi*, though, given they might think she's from their own cruiser." Baxter knew he was pushing his luck, questioning his commander and making suggestions, but while Walsh was clearly a capable officer when it came to the day-to-day running of a warship, it was increasingly obvious that he was out of his depth.

Walsh rolled his shoulders as he thought, then wiped sweat from his face and nodded. It was the early afternoon, and both heat and humidity were rising. "Good idea, Baxter — why don't you repair aboard and take her round?"

"Happy to, sir," Baxter said, though he knew he'd have to put up with Hensley's sulking.

Baxter went down the ladder and into the waiting pinnace as soon as it was alongside. Hensley had brought it round in a tight arc behind *Abigail*'s stern so her bows were pointed upriver. "Waiting for orders, sir," he said after he and Baxter had sketched salutes at each other.

"Still your command, Mr Hensley," Baxter said. "Take her upriver at your discretion — I'm just here for the reconnaissance."

"Very good, sir," Hensley replied, his tone warmer, and started issuing orders to his crew.

It felt odd being on the German pinnace, even if it was flying British colours. The vessel wasn't so different from British and Russian vessels of a similar type that he was familiar with, but just different enough that he found it strangely unsettling.

"I would get the flag down, though," Baxter added quietly once they were underway. It took a moment for the sub-lieutenant to work out what he meant, then he scrambled back past the wheel to haul down the ensign, which had just started snapping in the wind of their passage.

It didn't take long for *Heidi* to round the long bend, skirting close to the massively gnarled routes of the mangroves. Their view opened up ahead, the mangrove swamps giving way to more open trees and then scrubland. An islet lay ahead, with what looked like a small shore battery on it, and beyond that a wireless station that didn't look so different to the one the Germans had just burned on Pemba Island. A modern shallow-draught cargo vessel lay at anchor in the river between the islet and the German station, a German flag at her stern and her single stack venting enough smoke that Baxter guessed she had either recently arrived or was preparing to move on.

Baxter took his time to scrutinise the scene as the pinnace chugged across the river. Their presence had certainly been noted, and he could see men moving to man the light gun — probably a one-pounder, from the look of it — at the guard station. There were also men on the freighter's deck and at the radio station. Baxter heard the distant sound of a bugle calling people to attention.

"Well, that's torn it," Hensley muttered.

"They'd have spotted us here sooner rather than later," Baxter said, not taking his eyes from the Germans. They didn't seem unduly panicked, which suggested they were going through the motions even though they'd probably recognise the pinnace. Baxter could even make out someone at the shore battery waving to them. He processed a number of factors quickly, coolly. How long it would take them to get up to the station, and how long the other vessels would take to catch up.

How many men he had aboard — including five Royal Marines with a score to settle — and how many Germans were likely to be ahead. How quickly that freighter would get moving, particularly given the increasing volume of smoke coming from her stack.

Most importantly, how long it would take the enemy to realise the pinnace was not, in fact, friendly.

"Mr Hensley, put us about, but calmly, and bring us into position to signal *Abigail*," he said. "And run up the German ensign."

"Yes, sir," Hensley said. He seemed reassured to have an experienced officer aboard now that they were in sight of the enemy.

Baxter waved back to the shore battery, glad that the German navy's tropical uniform was also white. A moment later, the red and gold of the *Kaiserliche Marine*'s ensign broke out at the flagstaff, drawn out by the breeze as the pinnace came round and moved across the broad bend.

"Hold us here," Baxter ordered, then moved to the signals rating at the lamp, making sure to block him from the view of anyone upriver. "Make to *Abigail* — have sighted wireless station and German freighter making preparations to depart. Am engaging. Requesting support."

Hensley's head snapped round at that. Dalton, at the helm, grinned. "Those aren't our..." the sub-lieutenant started to protest.

"I don't want that freighter getting away, or the wireless station getting a signal off to the cruiser. The enemy clearly think we're friendly, so I'm taking the initiative."

"Signal sent, sir," the rating said formally, once his little lamp had finished its racket.

"Put us about again and bring us between the freighter and the shore battery, Mr Hensley."

"Shouldn't we wait…?"

"Not a moment to be lost, Hensley!" Baxter clapped him on the shoulder, almost sending him over the side of the pinnace.

Baxter could just imagine how Walsh would respond to that terse signal and the fact he hadn't waited for orders. Sometimes, though, an RN officer had to make decisions based on their own initiative. And that's exactly what he planned to tell his court martial, assuming he lived that long.

CHAPTER TWENTY-FOUR

Hensley took *Heidi* upriver at three quarters ahead, trying to minimise any impression of hurry. "Everyone stay below decks or keep low — particularly you Jollies," he ordered the Marines. "Easily now though, men. We're just a boat full of Germans out for a pleasure cruise."

Baxter dropped into the small wheelhouse. He didn't know if there were any German officers on station as big as he was, but there wasn't any point taking the risk. That was the sort of thing a keen-eyed sentry could pick up on.

Glancing back, he could see the smoke plumes from *Abigail* and *Ruby*, and guessed it wouldn't be long before the Germans spotted them as well. He crouched down to look into the cramped cabin that took up most of the length of the pinnace, currently stuffed with sweating sailors and marines.

"Stand by," he said. "As soon as Mr Hensley gives the word, get up on deck and prepare for action."

"The Germans are signalling," Hensley said quietly.

Baxter raised his head again, and saw someone at the islet battery waving a pair of flags in a distinct pattern. "Surprising — I would have thought they'd be a bit more lax halfway up the Rufiji."

"We *are* about to demonstrate why you shouldn't take such things for granted," Hensley pointed out. "Orders, sir?"

"Ahead full. Walsh should be coming round the bend immediately behind us. We might be able to make them think we're being chased. And Hensley?"

"Baxter?"

"This is your boat to fight when the shooting starts, remember that."

The younger officer looked briefly uncertain, then nodded. Baxter admitted to himself that he felt the urge to take direct command, but the lad had to learn sometime.

The shore gun fired a blank round to underscore the signal, which was then repeated by the soldier with the flags.

"That's right, you blighter, tire your arms out," Dalton muttered.

Glancing back, Baxter saw *Ruby* come charging round the bend, the sluggish brown water creaming at her bows. The appearance of a second vessel, this one flying British colours and obviously ready for combat, sent the Germans on shore into a flurry of activity. The signal flags were discarded as men ran to trenches. The light gun's crew were desperately reloading.

"Now, sir?"

Baxter watched the shore gun intently, waiting to see which way it was swung.

"Wait for it." They were close enough to the sandbagged gun post for Baxter to see the weapon was a belt-fed 1-pounder — what the Germans would call a 3.7-centimetre weapon — along the same lines as the one mounted on *Heidi*. The gun was being pointed down towards *Ruby* as she came on. "They still think we're friendly."

Heidi was passing the islet now, barely twenty yards from the guard position. Baxter could see a mixture of European and African faces, some in the uniform of the *Schutztruppe* and others *Kaiserliche Marine*, no doubt from *Königsberg*. The nearest *askari* was staring at the pinnace intently as they steamed past; then he spun on his heel and shouted something. His cry was drowned out by the *pom-pom-pom* beat of the Maxim gun firing, sending shells hurtling down the river towards *Ruby*. She returned the fire, the bigger shell bursting just short of the sandbagged position even as the water around her was churned up by exploding shells.

"Now!" Baxter snapped. "Get that gun silenced!"

The sailors and marines came up from belowdecks as quickly as they could, although the pinnace was not designed for going to action stations rapidly. Two men ran to the gun while the marines levelled Lee Enfield rifles over the railing. Baxter lunged for the German colours and hauled them down. Even a pragmatist and firm believer in Fisher's three Rs like him knew it wouldn't do to open fire under false colours.

Schutztruppe were running along the bank, coming from a little blockhouse behind the trenches, while others turned from their positions around the Maxim gun to point rifles at *Heidi*. They seemed uncertain what to do, though.

Hensley cleared that up for them just as the signals rating bent the White Ensign back to the flagstaff and hoisted it the couple of feet up. "Open fire!" he shouted.

The main gun thumped to life, hammering shells into the German gun position. They were past the sandbags, which hadn't been built up along the sides of the islet, and after a quick correction they were landing on target around their German counterpart. Even if the bursting charges were small, they wreaked havoc among the gun crew. *Ruby* was still firing, the shells howling overhead, though one did crash into the log-built blockhouse and took a bite out of the wall.

The Royal Marines had opened a disciplined fire on the enemy riflemen, knocking some down but mostly keeping their heads down, which was what was really needed now anyway.

"Straight on, Dalton!" Hensley ordered sharply, as the bo'sun made to turn the pinnace so the Maxim could stay on target.

They were past the shore battery and running along the length of the islet towards the freighter. They'd done their work, though, silencing the gun for now and sowing confusion among the small garrison. *Ruby* was hammering up behind them and *Abigail* had finally come into view.

Baxter could see men on the freighter's aft deck, waving and shouting towards them. "It looks like they still think we're Germans!" Hensley called out cheerfully.

Baxter saw a look of panic on their faces. "*Nicht schiessen! Nicht schiessen!*" someone who might has been the skipper was shouting. "*Minen!*"

"Hold your fire!" Baxter roared to the Maxim gunners. "Nobody shoot at that freighter! Signal *Ruby* and *Abigail* to pass that on."

"What's the problem?" Hensley demanded from where he crouched not far from the gun.

"They're carrying bloody mines," Baxter said, then rose to his full height as he turned to face the freighter and raised his voice to shout as clearly as he could. "Reduce steam! Do not raise your anchor. You are now a prize!"

The German skipper stared down at him as the pinnace churned past, and Baxter knew what he was thinking. He could cut his cables and run, hoping the British would not be mad enough to shoot at a vessel packed with high explosive. "We will fire on you! Reduce steam and raise a white flag immediately!"

The fight went out of the German civilian, and he just nodded before turning away.

Heidi was past the freighter now, and the German wireless station was just ahead. There were *Schutztruppe* taking up firing positions around the long building, using whatever cover they could find, but they didn't seem to have dug trenches here.

"Hensley," Baxter said, pointing at the khaki-clad soldiers. The pinnace's commander needed no further encouragement, getting the Maxim gun thumping again and bringing his Marines over.

Baxter glanced back, making sure the freighter was now flying a white flag and had remained at anchor. *Ruby* was cruising slowly past the German shore battery, pouring rifle and 3-pounder fire into it, while Walsh seemed content to stay at range ready to lob fire at anything requiring it.

"Jetty?" Hensley called back to him.

"Jetty," Baxter agreed. "I'll lead the landing party, if there are no objections? We'll take the main building."

Hensley grinned at the slightly flippant question. He was clearly excited, and probably a little scared, but handling himself well. "Jollies, go along with Mr Baxter when we run in!"

"Yes, sir!" the lance corporal in charge of the small section replied, managing to sound like he was on a parade ground even as he fired his rifle. "Fix bayonets!" he ordered the men under him.

Dalton brought *Heidi* in with similar smartness and precision as the long blades were drawn and fixed to rifles with a rattle, running up alongside the short wooden jetty and easing back the engine speed as he did so.

Baxter reached up, grabbed the jetty as the pinnace slowed towards the ladder, and pulled himself up, rolling to his feet and sprinting along the uneven boards. The Marines followed his lead, jumping up rather than bunching up around the ladder. The river bank was low enough that the Maxim could keep firing, and Hensley had the gunner peppering the area to the right of the wireless station.

Baxter could feel his heart thumping in his chest as he sprinted across the open ground, the Marines pounding after him. He didn't stop to think, or even draw breath; he just crashed shoulder-first into the door of the long, low building. It was flimsier than he was expecting and he crashed straight over, a bullet that might have hit him slamming over his prone form and into the far wall. A marine was through on his heels, a guttural war cry in his throat as he bayoneted the German who'd fired while the unfortunate man was still trying to work the bolt of his rifle.

The bayoneted man screamed, clutching at the blade buried up to its hilt in his guts. The marine pulled it free. The agonised screaming filled the dark space, until he drove down again, this time into the man's throat, silencing the howl. Baxter rolled to his feet, slightly shocked despite his own long exposure to violence. The other marines poured into the log building while the handful of occupants threw down their weapons and raised their hands, the dark gleam of fixed steel bayonets sapping their courage.

"That's the problem with them Mausers," the lance corporal said. "Slow action, even if they shoot straighter and further. Jones, Higgins, keep your rifles on them blighters. You two, start shooting on the blighters outside."

Baxter was about to go back out, but in the tense silence that had fallen in the wireless station he heard the rasp of a lighter mechanism. He snapped back round, scanning the circle of terrified faces that looked pallid in the light of a single bare bulb. Looking past them, he realised there was a further area at the far end of the building that had been partitioned with a blanket slung over a line.

He raced toward it, drawing his revolver, and tore the partitioning fabric down. A German was crouched over a large bucket into which papers, notebooks and charts had been loaded. He was cursing to himself as he tried to coax a flame from an American zippo lighter. Even the blanket coming down didn't distract him from his desperate attempt to burn his secrets.

Baxter thumbed back the revolver's hammer. "Don't," he said.

The German — an officer, Baxter thought — looked up at him with large fear-filled eyes. Before Baxter could say anything else, though, he clicked the action one last time, and a rich orange flame flickered into life. Baxter didn't hesitate, pulling the trigger. The revolver cracked, kicking in his hand, and the officer went over backwards, clutching at his wounded shoulder while the lighter skittered away into the darkness. Baxter stepped over him, grabbed up the lighter and pocketed it before anyone else could get any bright ideas.

When he got to a slitted window to peer out, it seemed that the arrival of *Abigail* had brought the fight into its final act. Glancing out of the door he'd smashed through, Baxter could see the *Schutztruppe* on his side of the river retiring in something approaching good order, subjected to the occasional round from *Heidi*'s Maxim to keep them moving. The garrison on the island didn't have that luxury, though they kept up a steady fusillade for a few minutes before *Abigail* came as close as she dared and levelled the blockhouse with several well-laid 3-pound HE shells.

All the while, the German freighter kept her white flag flying, though Baxter noticed the crew had surreptitiously put a boat in the water and were making ready to run for it. He almost let them go, on the basis that they would otherwise be prisoners they didn't have the facilities to deal with, and it wasn't as though every German in the vicinity wouldn't be alerted by the racket they'd made. Then Baxter walked down to the riverbank, ignoring the occasional pop of rifle fire, and drew his revolver. He shot into the water in front of the launch; the .38 round made a pitifully small splash compared to the ordinance that had just been flying around, but it got their attention.

"I believe you men surrendered. Now, out of the boat."

Baxter wasn't sure if he'd be willing to shoot at unarmed men just trying to escape — with the exception of Arbuthnott — but the German sailors decided not to test him or the Marines who had come up along the riverbank. They may not have understood English, but the pointed pistol and rifles got the point across.

"Baxter, *Abigail* is signalling. You're to report aboard immediately."

Baxter felt his jaw clench. It was time to face the music.

Hensley gave him a lift back to the converted coaster, while *Ruby* landed its marine complement to finish securing the telegraph station. Baxter went up the side, ready for a fight with Walsh, but was surprised to find the commander in a remarkably buoyant mood, despite the fact his right arm was slung across his chest with blood showing through the heavy bandages around his upper arm.

"One of the last shots that pom-pom got off," the commander said as he awkwardly returned Baxter's salute with his left hand. "Burst not a foot from me. Dalton thinks the arm is broken, but it seems both adrenalin and morphine are excellent for dulling the pain."

"Very sorry to hear that, sir. Any other casualties?"

"Few scratches here and there, but nobody killed, thank God." Walsh stared at him for a moment, as though he was trying to remember something important. It seemed to come back to him. "Though I do seem to recall ordering you to reconnoitre the river ahead, not launch headlong into an attack."

"Sorry, sir," Baxter said, keeping his tone bland. "I saw that supply ship getting up steam and thought it best to use my initiative. Given that she's loaded with mines, that was probably for the best."

Walsh blanched slightly. "Mines, you say? If those had taken a hit, things would have gone very differently!"

"And if the cargo had been delivered, I'm sure bad things would have followed."

"To put it mildly." Walsh suddenly looked a bit faint, and Baxter guessed the adrenalin and morphine were wearing off. Baxter helped him down onto an upended ammunition container. "I don't think I'm going to be in a fit state to command, Baxter, which means *Abigail* and the expedition are yours. Given that we've more than achieved our mission here, it'll be up to you to get us back to Zanzibar safely."

Baxter straightened. "Yes, sir," he said dutifully, though he had a notion that at least some of them wouldn't be heading back just yet.

CHAPTER TWENTY-FIVE

Baxter assembled what were now his senior officers on *Abigail*'s foredeck an hour later. It wasn't a large group — Hensley, MacGregor and the Royal Marine Lieutenant Childers — though he also included Dalton, somewhat against protocol. He'd spent the time having a first look at the recovered papers, along with MacGregor, who had at least some knowledge of written German, while the others had finished securing the freighter — *Caroline* — and corralling those enemy forces who hadn't been able to escape. Everything had been done in a hurry — while the enemy may not know exactly what had occurred, there was a good chance they had been alerted by the gunfire and there could be an expedition on its way to investigate the racket.

He hadn't liked what he and MacGregor had been able to work out, not even slightly. The bucket he had saved from burning was something of a treasure trove, including a code book, but probably the most important document had been a map with current dispositions on the Rufiji marked out. He had that spread out on the deck between them now; the space to do that was one of the reasons he was having this conference on deck rather than in the privacy of the cabin. That, and it was infernally hot below deck.

"As you know, once we have finished the demolition of the wireless station here, we will have achieved our orders. More than achieved them, with the capture of the *Caroline*." He looked around the circle of faces. They all looked tired, but exultant at a job well done. Everyone but Dalton, whose habitual lugubrious expression remained unchanged. "What

I'm proposing now goes well beyond the scope of our orders, but the course of action is, in my estimation, necessary for the defence of British possessions in the area."

The younger officers exchanged glances. "I'd be happier hearing that from Commander Walsh, sir," MacGregor said earnestly. He was a fellow Scot, sandy-haired and freckled, his accent placing him from somewhere in the north-west although he clearly did his best to hide it.

"Commander Walsh is currently unconscious, and will need to be returned to Zanzibar as soon as possible." Baxter was no medical man, but he'd seen enough wounds to know that it needed to be properly treated if the arm was to be saved. "I'm in command." His tone brooked no dissent, and MacGregor blanched slightly and nodded. "The commander's condition and that of other wounded men — both our own and the enemy's — means that someone will need to take the prize back to Zanzibar. That someone is you, MacGregor."

MacGregor actually looked slightly crestfallen at that. While returning with a captured merchantman and news would be a feather in his cap, now that he was barred from the further operation he clearly regretted opening his mouth. The truth of the matter was that someone *did* need to take *Caroline* and the wounded to Zanzibar, and Baxter had worked more closely with Hensley and Dalton, who were the other options.

"I can give you a few men to stoke and steer, but not as many as either of us would like," he went on, voice flat. "You'll manage, though."

"Are the prisoners going back as well, sir?" Childers asked. The Royal Marine officer seemed completely unbothered by the idea of continuing the mission without permission and steaming further into enemy territory.

"No — we can't spare the men to guard them, and I don't want to risk them seizing the freighter back. We'll leave them here with some supplies and no boats. Someone will be by for them in due course, I have no doubt."

Childers nodded, apparently satisfied. "Do we have a plan for when we get upriver?" Hensley asked, crouching to tap the map where someone had pencilled in '*Königsberg*' in small, neat lettering. "We now know where that blasted cruiser is hiding, or at least where she was when the chart was marked. I assume you're going to try to find a way to get at her?"

Baxter raised an eyebrow. The Rufiji split into a gnarled tangle of channels as it entered its delta. At the depth to which they had penetrated, there were three main waterways, all of them interconnected. The small flotilla that was now under his command lay in the middle of the three, and if the map was accurate the comparatively powerful German cruiser lay in a channel to the north-west, well out of danger of anything the RN had in the area — including his own force.

"No, we're going to turn south-south-east and follow this channel," he said, tracing the channel they were in as it took a sharp turn south. "*Königsberg*'s certainly a threat, to us and to Zanzibar, but I'm increasingly convinced her fuel and repair situation is critical. According to this chart, there is a *Schutztruppe* encampment here, and orders had been issued to gather up shallow draft vessels capable of carrying men and equipment. German command seems to think our cruisers are still some distance away. This leads me to believe that the flotilla's departure for Zanzibar is imminent."

The other officers exchanged glances. "Begging your pardon, Baxter, but I don't think I've got enough men to assault a full encampment of *Schutztruppe*."

"And I don't propose asking you to, Childers." The Marine's familiarity irked Baxter slightly — they were technically the same rank, but they only knew each other in passing and Baxter was in command. "Our goal is to disrupt the operation, by destroying whatever craft the enemy have gathered there, and denying them use of the channel for as long as possible."

"And how do you propose we do that? By sinking *Abigail* as a blockship?"

The idea would have merit, if there weren't so many channels in the river. "We'll need her to get home. However, the Germans have thoughtfully provided us with some mines. I propose to make use of that gift."

Realisation dawned on their faces. "Don't suppose it's too late to unvolunteer for this, sir?" Dalton asked.

"I wasn't aware that this was a volunteer-only job, Dalton, and even if it was, it is too late."

"Very good, sir. The thought never occurred to me anyway."

"Right. We've got a lot of work to do and not a lot of time to do it in. Let's be about it, gentlemen."

They didn't see the enemy for the couple of hours they spent reorganising and resupplying, which surprised Baxter. Looff had shown himself to be an enterprising and aggressive commander, so even if the cruiser couldn't navigate round to this position — either because of her draught or her supply situation — he would have expected at least some boats. There were also German soldiers scant miles away, possibly under the command of Schiller, with access to vessels. While the disconsolate German prisoners looked on glumly, *Caroline's* holds were plundered for coal and the crated mines, which were brought aboard *Abigail* with a great deal of trepidation and more care than was probably warranted. *Heidi's* ammunition locker was also replenished from the shore installation.

"Where are you, you bastards?" Baxter muttered, scanning the dun landscape and the sluggish brown water that flowed past his anchored command. *Abigail* was alongside the German freighter, so cargo could be transferred directly, but this also made her extremely vulnerable. While most of the crew and the Marines were engaged in what the Russians had called the feast of coal — seasoned with the lethal explosive charges of the mines — plenty more were keeping a very sharp lookout so they could cast off as quickly as possible if threatened.

"You've got a tricky job ahead of you," Baxter told MacGregor just before they parted company. "It's a good couple of miles before you reach a section where you can turn round."

The Scot nodded. "At least the current will help us, sir," he said, then gestured to the wounded men on the deck. They were taking four injured enemy servicemen, including the man Baxter had shot in the shoulder, as well as their three casualties. "I'll be careful, and get these men to hospital as soon as I can."

Baxter nodded, and before MacGregor could make a move to salute, he stuck his hand out. "Good luck to you."

The junior officer smiled slightly and shook his hand. "And to you, sir. I … I wish I was going with you."

"I don't doubt it, and you'd have been welcome. Your job is just as important, though. If nothing else, Ingles and Parker need to know where the *Königsberg* is and we can't risk a wireless broadcast."

"I understand, sir," said MacGregor. He saluted smartly, and Baxter returned the salute.

"Carry on, Mr MacGregor."

Baxter went across the ramp separating the two freighters, then gestured for two bluejackets to draw it back across. He stepped up to the rail and looked between the two pinnaces that had resumed their upriver positions, off *Abigail*'s port and starboard bows respectively. He waved to the commanders — Hensley back in *Heidi*, and Dalton now in command of *Ruby*. "Carry on!" he shouted, once he had their attention.

All three vessels had steam up, and as soon as he gave the order the two pinnaces raised their small anchors and started heading upriver again. He wanted them as far ahead of the more cumbersome coaster as possible, while still in range of support from her heavier armament.

"Helm, ahead one quarter."

"Ahead one quarter," the sailor at the wheel confirmed, pushing the engine telegraph forward. *Abigail*'s twin screws started turning, churning up the water, and she eased forward into the current, taking up the slight slack in the lines mooring her to the captured freighter.

"Cast off bow line. Cast off stern line," Baxter ordered, and the cables were thrown back across to the handful of British sailors on *Caroline*'s deck. She was away, forging slowly forwards, and MacGregor was already giving orders for the freighter's anchor to be raised. He and the men under his command did find a moment to cheer their compatriots on their way. Baxter raised his cap in response as *Caroline*'s anchor rattled up out of the ooze and the freighter started to drift backwards, current and engine working together.

Baxter went forward from his station just abaft the wheelhouse. One of the 3-pounder Hotchkiss guns was cleared away for action, a shell already loaded and the crew trying to suppress smiles of anticipation. He leant out over the rail and looked back. The freighter was already well on her way, sliding backwards through the water, and the German prisoners seemed to be keeping well clear of the wireless telegraph station, as they'd been warned to do.

Baxter moved back to the 3-pounder. "Mind if I lay it?" he asked the gun captain, a weatherbeaten Geordie who, for some reason, went by Jock to his comrades.

"Course not, sah," he said, giving Baxter a grin that was more gum that tooth.

Baxter got his shoulder into the gun's mounting and brought the heavy weapon round, sighting in on the telegraph station. It would, perhaps, have been easier just to douse it in the generator's diesel and light a fuse, but he'd wanted to be well underway before they gave such an obvious indication of their location.

"Sir, looks like there's a German running back to the station," Jock said. "He's shouting and waving. Can't tell what he's saying, though."

Baxter raised his eye from the sight in time to see not one but two Germans sprinting into the telegraph station. He held fire, as killing them wouldn't achieve anything and it wasn't as though they'd be able to save the transmitter. He wondered if they thought he'd left a bomb on a timer in there and they had a chance to disarm it.

He ducked back to the sight. If they weren't out soon, he'd have to shoot before the slowly changing angle became too acute. "Helm!" he shouted, without taking his eye from the sight. "Point to starboard but stand by to correct to port on my order!"

"Point to starboard, aye!"

The two Germans emerged again, both clutching squirming bundles of fur, and Baxter realised they'd gone back in to rescue what appeared to be kittens. "Bloody idiots," he said, but held his fire anyway.

"Wonder why they didn't just tell us," said one of the gunners.

"We're baby-eating Britishers, mate — of course we'd have eaten the bloody things," Jock commented.

Baxter was only half-listening. As soon as he was sure the two foolhardy officers were clear of the area, he adjusted the angle slightly. "Firing," he said, and pulled the trigger.

The Hotchkiss jarred back into his shoulder and he tasted and smelled cordite. His ears rang from the detonation, and he got his head up just in time to see the shell slam into the building. He'd managed to put it exactly where he wanted, through the open doorway the Germans had used, and the whole building lit up as the small charge detonated.

That detonation was lost in the larger blast of the mine they'd carefully moved into the middle of the building, going off a split second later. It lifted the roof of the building, sending two of the fifty-foot-tall radio masts toppling and showering the two Germans, and their rescued cats, with debris even though they were a fair distance away. The diesel that had been liberally sloshed over the interior and exterior of the building caught fire after that, the flames rapidly rising up the third mast that had somehow remained upright despite the force of the explosion.

"Lovely shot, sir," Jock said approvingly. "Welcome to lay my gun anytime."

"Decent of you," Baxter said drily as he straightened up and raised his field glasses. The devastation of the station was complete, but the Germans all seemed unharmed. When he set out to do a job, he was a firm believer in being thorough.

CHAPTER TWENTY-SIX

The mast and building were still burning as night fell, though by this point it was an orange glow on the northern horizon. The fire and the light seemed to have disturbed the local wildlife, and they could hear deep roaring coming from the undergrowth and see flocks of water birds silhouetted against the glow as they flew backwards and forwards.

"You really don't fool around when it comes to destroying things, do you?" Hensley said as he came up the ladder from *Heidi*. Baxter had sent him to scout further ahead during the last hours of daylight, in the hopes that the German ensign the pinnace flew would have the same effect as it had had at the wireless station. He'd returned unscathed, at least. "Won't that have alerted them to our presence, though?"

"I doubt anyone who heard the skirmish is in any doubt we're among them," Baxter said. "That couldn't be helped. Right now, though, they're all wondering what the hell that was and hopefully getting quite worried."

Baxter led Hensley aft. *Abigail* was anchored again, as there was very little water under her keel now and he didn't fancy trying to take her further upriver in the dark. "Well?"

"It's as you suspected, sir," the sub-lieutenant said, his tone altogether more serious and professional. "There's at least two companies of German colonial troops camped about three miles upriver from us. The Marines thought the encampment might have been big enough for a whole battalion, but you know how prone to exaggeration they are. The Germans have amassed a proper transport flotilla. I counted at least three fishing boats, a tug, and a customs cutter, the latter two armed.

There may have been something larger further upriver, but I couldn't get close enough for a proper look."

Baxter whistled. That was quite a force, and demonstrated how serious the enemy was about taking Zanzibar. "Shore defences?"

"Now, there's the rub," Hensley said unhappily. "There's at least one light gun at the encampment, well dug in and aimed towards the river. It's almost as though those clever blighters knew that was the main direction we might attempt an attack from. We also spotted earthworks a bit downriver on the opposite bank, though I think those are machine guns or a pom-pom at most. We're not going to be able to sneak up on them, I'm afraid. There was definite activity on shore and on the boats, though hard to say if they were getting ready to get underway or had been rattled by your destructive tendencies. Sir."

Hensley added the last word almost as an afterthought when Baxter shot him a dark look. Night had well and truly fallen at this point, the evening chorus replaced by the quieter, more sinister sounds of the wilderness in the darkness. The burning telegraph station didn't provide a lot of light, just enough to cast everything into jumping shadows.

Baxter found his signals rating. "Make to *Ruby* — come alongside and report aboard."

"What are you thinking, sir? If I might be so bold?"

"I'll explain the plan when Dalton gets here," Baxter growled. "I don't like repeating myself."

Hensley lapsed into silence and Baxter paced back and forth across the deck a couple of times. He didn't like formulating a plan without having seen the lie of the land and water himself, but he knew he had to learn to trust junior officers. He wondered if demolishing the wireless station in such a spectacular fashion had been a good idea, given it had been akin to kicking a hornet's nest. It was a nest that had already been nudged, though, and it was too late to do anything about it now.

Baxter gathered the two pinnace commanders together as soon as Dalton was aboard.

"We're going to have to mine the river in the dark, and that's going to fall to you two. We'll bring *Abigail* up as far as we can to provide gunnery support, guided by *Ruby*, then you'll both go ahead and lay as many mines as possible in the deeper channels. Even if it keeps the enemy bottled up here until they can sweep them, it'll buy us some time to prepare the defences."

Hensley nodded. "Not planning on shelling the encampment then?"

Baxter's patience with the constant questioning was starting to wear thin. It was partially his fault, as the two of them had worked together as equals. At the same time, Hensley probably needed to know, even if Baxter hadn't quite made his mind up yet.

"I'll have a look myself at first light," he said, tone short. "We might engage in some long bowls and see if we can hit the ships. We don't have the artillery to do much to a well dug-in infantry force."

"Understood, sir," Hensley said. "I'd best go and familiarise myself with these mines."

"Get your Jolly contingents up onto *Abigail* as well — you'll need all the space you can free up for this."

After that, there was little for him to do. The night was close, cooler than the day but still muggy, and the crew were either standing around talking in nervous whispers or trying to get some sleep. After a few minutes' discussion between themselves, his two subordinates started getting the mines, still in their crates, over the side. Baxter had examined them briefly after they'd brought them aboard. They didn't appear to be official *Kaiserliche Marine* issue, the crates lacking the expected armoury nomenclature, and Baxter guessed they were either special appropriation for these shallow waters or had been privately purchased. They seemed simple enough to operate, and safe enough to handle until the primer lanyard was removed. Nonetheless, he was reassured to see how carefully the sailors were handling the weapons.

It took about an hour to finish the operation, by which time the fire behind them had burned itself down to a dull glow and they had to work by the light of carefully shielded lanterns. *Abigail*'s deck was crowded, the white-uniformed sailors stark against the Marines in their khaki battledress. Baxter knew they would not be able to fight the ship in those conditions, and the infantry would be subject to terrible casualties if they came under fire.

"Mr Childers — get your men below, if you please. I know it'll be hot, but better they're overly warm than dead."

The Royal Marine lieutenant hurried to obey, giving his men permission to discard their jackets as they went grumbling down the companionways into the hold. A few minutes later, the sailors who had been below came up on deck, all but the stokers labouring away down in the engine compartments. That was a much better state of affairs.

Baxter gave the order to raise anchor and inch the coaster forward. The current here was marginally faster, requiring a few more revolutions of the engine, and Baxter sent every man on deck who wasn't otherwise engaged up into the bows to keep watch for sandbanks or mines. "Don't everyone go yelling at once if you do see something. Report it quietly to PO Watson, who will report it to me."

They managed the first bend, bringing them onto a south-westerly heading, without too many issues. The river kept turning, and consulting the chart in the glow of the binnacle light Baxter saw that it would run south-south-east and bring them out into a relatively broad stretch of water barely a mile downriver from the encampment.

"If we can get that far and bring our artillery into direct play, we might do some real damage here," he murmured.

"Sir?" the helmsman asked. Baxter was distracted by a runner arriving from the bows, sent by Watson.

"Beg to report we've got about three feet of water under us," the runner said. "Less on the starboard bow."

Abigail was following *Heidi* as closely as possible, though not so close that if the pinnace stopped suddenly it would be ploughed under. The pinnace did draw a bit less water, and had perhaps missed how quickly the sandbank was shoaling.

"One point to port and forward as slow as possible," he told the helmsman, wishing he had the steady Dalton on hand. The petty officer was sensible enough to use the speaking pipe to the tiny boiler room rather than using the brass-bound engine telegraph with its associated bells and other noise.

Baxter went forward, trusting long experience and instinct to keep his footing in the dark. They were running entirely without light, as they were closer to the encampment.

Julius was in the bows with the junior officer, using an old-fashioned lead and line to measure the depth. The water was an inky black, but when Baxter peered over the edge he was pretty sure he could make out a hint of a sandbank. The appropriated German chart was excellent, but sandbanks were tricky, shifting things.

The coaster was more or less holding station, the low revolutions he'd ordered just enough to maintain headway in the current.

"I think this is the highest point," he told Watson. "Julius, good work with the line."

Baxter headed back to the stern. "Ahead one half," he said, leaning out over the rail and watching the water with rapt attention as the yacht started to ease forward again. "Come another point to starboard."

The helmsman obeyed immediately. The sandy bottom seemed to rise up into view to starboard as he looked over the rail, and Baxter felt his heart rise into his throat. It would be disastrous if they grounded now. Even if they managed to get the steamer off, the noise would be devastating.

"Another point to starboard!" he snapped, breaking his own orders about volume.

Rising, rising.

"Barely a foot, sir!"

"Two points to port!" Baxter ordered, not really knowing what combination of factors made him settle on that course. Judgment, intuition, or just the sum total of years of experience.

The copper-plated hull kissed sand, crunching and hissing. *Abigail* slowed, but still had momentum. A cool detachment came over Baxter as they reached the crisis point. "A point to port, sharply now," he said, pitching his voice just loud enough to reach the wheelhouse.

The steamer was slowing, but not stopping. The noise, even from below the water, was hideous.

He breathed out explosively, realising he'd been right about the lie of the sandbank. With a last grinding racket, the coaster slid free, launching ahead again.

"All stop!" Baxter snapped, realising they weren't quite out of danger yet. "Half astern."

The vessel slowed, though for a second Baxter thought it would not be enough. Having shot clear of the obstruction, they were heading straight towards another long, narrow sandbank lying off the port bow.

"Belay that — three points to starboard and ahead full."

"Make your bloody mind up," the helmsman muttered as he obeyed the terse command.

Abigail hadn't quite slowed far enough to be going astern, and started to pick up forward momentum again. She slid past that second sandbank, and Baxter finally relaxed as the hint of river bottom receded into the darkness and they were sliding through deeper water.

"All stop. Drop anchor," he ordered. There was just enough starlight for him to see that they were not far from the final turn into a broader channel, which would bring them into view of the encampment. He was pretty sure he could hear faint voices and the hum of machinery. The anchor splashed into the water and stuck almost immediately, bringing *Abigail* to a gentle halt.

Baxter went back to the bows, and took up one of the shuttered lamps. He cracked open the shutter just enough that a little light showed, and then raised it, dipped it and raised it again. He heard the putter of the pinnaces' small steam engines increase in pitch slightly as they pulled away, heading out into the open water to undertake the mining work.

Baxter made himself stand still in the bows for a little while. He wanted desperately to be out there in the small boats. Not because he relished the idea of handling mines, but because he would be doing *something* rather than simply waiting.

As the night wore on, the collection of men in the bows dissipated, wandering off to rest or eat. With Baxter's permission, Childers brought his men up by fives to stretch their legs and use the head.

The night was very still, with just the chirrup of noise from night creatures to disturb it, and the faint murmur of the camp. The pinnaces were under orders not to stray too close to the German positions and to start laying mines further out, working their way back to *Abigail*'s position. Baxter tracked the time by the moon's position and an occasional glance at his watch by the binnacle light. He was too on edge to sleep, but had to resist the urge to pace impatiently or check each station regularly.

Childers wandered across at around four in the morning when Baxter was up in the bows, listening out for the pinnaces. They should have been back well before then. "Can't sleep either?" he asked affably enough. "Me neither. Never can, before a fight."

"You think there'll be a fight?" Baxter asked.

"Five minutes in your company, Baxter, and I know there'll be a fight."

Baxter held up a hand to silence him, craning his neck to listen hard. "Here they come," he said, finally catching the faint sound of steam engines and even the splash of a mine being deployed. "Looks like you may have been wrong, Childers."

He regretted saying that almost immediately. There might have been a keen-eyed sentry in one of the land positions, or a lookout on the ships, or someone had heard the engine noise just as Baxter had. A bugle rang out upriver — the unmistakable noise of the alarm — followed by the sound of a machine gun firing.

Baxter's response was instinctual. "Up anchor!" he shouted. "Helm, full ahead! Gun crews to your stations!"

The sailors went about their work with a calm professionalism that made him proud. Within moments, he could hear the rattle of the anchor chain being winched back aboard. *Abigail*'s bows were pointed into the current and she started moving forward as the engine room got them up to speed. Baxter could feel the anchor dragging and then breaking free, and the coaster leapt forward gamely, feeling for a moment like a much lighter, smaller ship. The gun crews didn't need to go far to ready themselves, crouching around their lethal charges with a supply of 3-pound HE shells ready to fire. From the stern of the ship, Baxter could hear the rattle of a machine-gun belt being readied.

All the while, Baxter could hear at least two Maxim guns roaring away, joined by the thud of heavier weapons firing. He thought he could make out the pinnaces' armaments in the cacophony.

"Where do you want me, sir?" Childers asked crisply. They were both distracted as a flare was sent up from the German machine-gun position, lighting the sky a brilliant white. While *Abigail* was picking up speed, Baxter still chafed at the time she was taking to come round the river bend and into action.

"If we put some fire on that German machine-gun position, could you take it?"

"I can take it with or without your tars trying to hit it, sir!" Childers declared cheerfully.

"Then get your bloody lobsters in the boats and be on your way — don't get 'em up on deck until the boats are in the water, though."

"Happy to!" Childers dashed off, shouting for his men to ready themselves for a landing party. Baxter detailed some of the gun crews and anyone else he could lay hands on to get *Abigail*'s two small whaleboats, both of them rowed rather than steam driven, into the water on the freighter's port side.

They were close now, almost to a point where he knew he would be able to see what was going on courtesy of the steady pop and fizzle of flares being sent up by the enemy. He forced himself to walk calmly back to the wheelhouse.

"When I give the word, I want a turn to port of just under ninety degrees and then slow ahead," he told the helmsman, then realised that Watson had taken over the wheel. "I don't want us to lose headway, but let's give the gunners as stable a platform as we can."

"They'll need it, sir," Watson said with a grin.

Baxter was already moving off. *Abigail* had finally come round far enough that he could see what was going on, and what he saw didn't please him.

CHAPTER TWENTY-SEVEN

The scene on this broader section of the Rufiji was lit in an eery, wavering light by the flares that were being sent up from the machine-gun position. That was on the west bank of the river, around three quarters of a mile away. There were two machine guns firing from it, the long flare of muzzle flash visible despite the monochromatic light that bathed the scene. Both weapons were firing at *Heidi*. The pinnace appeared to be motionless in the middle of the water, painfully exposed to fire from every angle.

"Daft blighters have run aground," said one of the gunners on the forward 3-pounder.

Ruby was closer, less than a hundred yards away. The pinnaces should have been travelling parallel to each other, laying mines on either side of the river wherever it was deep enough for a vessel to pass. Dalton had turned his command and the Hotchkiss was thumping away at the machine-gun positions, with limited success, as was the machine cannon on *Heidi*.

What worried Baxter was what was going on further up the river. A fairly tubby vessel with a low freeboard, slightly larger than the pinnaces and with an outsize funnel, was already underway from her moorings not far from a fairly extensive encampment on the east bank. It was hard to make out details at that distance, as it was still moving outside the pool of white light cast by the cascade of flares, but he guessed it was one of the customs cutters he'd seen in Dar es-Salaam. It opened fire, a rapid series of flashes and shells kicking up furious white water around *Heidi*, but didn't appear to hit it. Baxter recognised the weapon from his own bitter experience in 1906, a truly obsolete revolver cannon. The motley collection of civilian vessels assembled to transport troops wasn't on the move, but he could make out something larger further up the river, just as Hensley had reported.

"Watson, execute turn to port!" Baxter shouted to the wheelhouse. "Number one gun, lay on the machine guns. Number two gun, the cutter. Number three gun, stand by." No point burning through the Vickers' .303 ammunition until it had something it could shoot at usefully.

Baxter would rather have concentrated everything he had on one target, but there were too many targets to choose from and they could all do with an immediate pasting.

Watson was prompt in following his orders. He brought the bows round, spinning the wheel until *Abigail* was steaming at almost ninety degrees to her previous course, slowly cutting across the expanse of water at an oblique angle.

"Fire!" Baxter shouted. The Hotchkiss guns went off together, adding their noise and muzzle flash to the cacophony of light and sound. Baxter was too busy to watch the fall of shot. "Fire at will!" he ordered the crews.

They weren't far from the west bank now, the whaleboats bobbing along at the side of the freighter sheltered from enemy fire. Childers already had his men going over the side, either lowering themselves over the railing or clambering down the ladder. Baxter went across to him so he could be heard over the thump of the guns. "Off you go, Childers," he said.

"I can only get fifteen men into these," the Marine officer replied, gesturing down to the boats. They were already jammed with men and rifles, the men on the oars — a mix of sailors and Marines — trying to wield the long implements despite the crush.

"I'll get *Ruby* up to take the rest," Baxter replied. "Do what you can until they can reach you."

"Yes, sir!" Childers said cheerfully, then touched his cap brim with his swagger stick and clattered down the ladder into the lead whaleboat.

The two heavily laden boats shot away from *Abigail*, the oarsmen pulling as hard as they could but with only a minimum of co-ordination. They didn't have far to go before the men could start wading ashore, just a few hundred yards along the bank from enemy fortifications.

"Signaller, make to *Ruby*. Come alongside and take on Marines."

"Aye, sir!"

Baxter took a moment to raise his glasses and assess the situation as best he could in the flickering light. It was, he had to admit, a little on the hot side. The customs cutter was closing in on *Heidi*, firing furiously but so far ineffectually. The bigger vessel was definitely a tug boat, and judging from the thump of her gun firing and the howl of the shell passing overhead, she mounted something reasonably significant. The tug seemed to have identified *Abigail* as being the main threat, and her second shot threw a hefty spout of water up just off her stern, dousing her decks with water.

"That's a bloody destroyer's gun!" someone shouted, and Baxter had to agree. Probably an old 22-pounder, so considerably heavier than anything at his disposal.

Ruby was alongside; the second contingent of Marines seemed keen to get aboard her and off the ship receiving the heavier fire. Baxter leant over the railing and shouted for Dalton's attention. "Put fire on the machine guns as you run the lobsters in, then support *Heidi*!" he ordered once the petty officer looked up. He didn't wait for an acknowledgement — Dalton knew his business.

There was a round from the tug, close enough to send shell splinters ringing against *Abigail*'s unarmoured side. A second heavy gun fired mere seconds later, too fast for the 22-pounder to have been reloaded. That would be the field gun dug in with the *Schutztruppe*, the shot going wide.

"Helm, hard a-starboard!" he ordered. *Abigail* answered, bows swinging ponderously round — she certainly didn't handle like a torpedo boat or pinnace. Baxter waited for his moment as the bows came all the way round to point directly into the current, the ship slowing dangerously. The tug fired, the range low enough that the shell came in on an almost flat trajectory and blasted straight through the funnel, before detonating over the wheelhouse. Baxter felt the freighter sag away from the turn almost immediately. The shore gun fired, closer this time, and machine-gun rounds were rattling into and through her sides.

"All guns, fire on the cutter!" he roared as he sprinted back along the deck. The wheelhouse was a mess, blast and shrapnel having caved the corrugated iron roof in. Somehow, Watson was still alive and on his feet as he fought to control the wheel. Blood was streaming down his face and one arm was hanging limp. Baxter ducked under the sharp edges of the metal roof and threw himself onto the wheel, hauling it all the way round to put the freighter back into her turn, zagging back across the river on the opposite tack.

More sailors were appearing now, some helping Watson out of the wheelhouse and one replacing him now that Baxter had the ship under control. He stepped out to see that *Heidi* was in a sorry state, having taken several 1-pound shells from the cutter's revolver cannon. Hensley's boat wasn't returning fire, but given the storm of steel tearing up the water around her, that wasn't surprising.

Abigail's gun crews had swung their weapons around — it was tight but there was just enough space between them for the long barrels to be swung — and opened up on the cutter again. The machine gun was silent, though. Baxter swung round, fearing the worst, but saw that the two-man crew was hunkered down behind their weapon, looking at him expectantly. "Well, bloody fire then!" he roared, gesturing at the cutter. "Get that bloody boat off my river!"

His blood was up now, the rush of adrenalin singing in his veins. The Vickers opened fire, the galvanised machine gunner grinning fiercely behind the firing yoke as he sprayed bullets into the cutter, which had closed to within a hundred yards of *Heidi*. Probably more by luck than skill, the stream of bullets raked across her bows and, as Baxter watched, a shell hit her wheelhouse and demolished it.

He knew he couldn't get distracted by one fight, that he had to keep a grip on the whole engagement, and he dragged his attention away from the cutter as it was hit again and again. Keping track of the engagement became harder, though, as the last flare from the Germans on the west bank guttered out in the river. He could hear screams and shouts from that direction, and guessed Childers had just gone in with cold steel while he had the element of surprise.

Without the light from the flare, the night was just a confusion of muzzle flashes splitting the darkness and briefly illuminating the area around them. The cutter at least seemed to have ceased firing, but the tug and the field gun ashore were still sending shells downriver. His own gun crews had ceased their fire, having lost the target he'd ordered them to unleash on.

"Hold your fire," Baxter ordered the gun crews. The machine-gun position had fallen silent and the sounds of combat there had died away, so he could only assume the Marines had taken it. Without nearby muzzle flashes, his eyes were starting to adjust to the starlit night and he thought he could make out *Ruby* closing on them.

"Mr Baxter, sir," Dalton's voice floated out of the darkness. "You're sailing towards the minefield."

"Three points port," Baxter ordered the helmsman. "Dalton, can you get to *Heidi*?"

"Aye, sir. We'll get her off the sandbank."

"If you can't do it quickly, just get the crew off."

"Aye, sir." The shadowy, half-seen shape in the water turned and started away towards the beached pinnace.

Baxter thumped a fist into his open hand. The Germans were still firing, but the tug didn't seem to be coming any closer. With *Abigail* and the pinnaces not shooting back, they'd lost their targets and were firing blind and wild into the night. He had no way of communicating with the Marines ashore until *Ruby* got back, unless he took *Abigail* in close enough to shout across, and that could give away their position. It was odd that the encampment or tug hadn't put up a flair yet, and he grinned as he imagined Schiller or some other *Schutztruppe* officer furiously yelling for a flare gun to be found.

A sensible man, he knew, would cut and run at this point, once everyone was back aboard. He didn't like the number of shallow draft vessels that were still afloat, though, and the tug would be able to carry at least a company if she was packed full.

He looked at his watch. Not long until dawn, either.

"All guns, train on the muzzle flash from the tug," he ordered quietly. "But hold your fire until my order."

319

"Can I interest you in taking a crack yourself, sir?" one of the gunners quipped, and Baxter grinned again.

"I'll leave it in your capable hands."

The bright trail of a flare's rocket propellant finally went up from the encampment. The flare popped to life, drifting under its tiny parachute and casting its white glow over the German positions and the two British pinnaces. It had been fired at such a steep angle, though, that *Abigail* was still half lost in shadow.

"Shoot!" Baxter ordered the Hotchkiss crews.

The light guns started firing at once. The German guns had the advantage in both weight of shot and the range with which they could throw a shell, but the latter at least was negated by the close range of the engagement — less than a mile now — and the British crews were plying their lighter weapons faster. They were firing alternately, the heavy thump and crash of the gun's discharge followed almost immediately by the clang of the breech being opened and the smoking spent case being ejected and replaced. Close the breech block, repeat. The guns, long considered obsolete as an anti-torpedo craft weapon because of their small charge and low muzzle velocity, were starting to make their mark on the unarmoured tug. Raising his field glasses, Baxter could see holes appearing in the hull and superstructure and men lying dead or injured around the long gun she mounted. The Vickers' crew hadn't waited for orders this time and were peppering the area around the tug's artillery with bullets.

"Number three gun, target those fishing boats!" he ordered. They were doing good work, suppressing the enemy gun crew, but the German troop transports were the priority target.

Heidi was firing again, her crew able to work the unprotected Maxim machine cannon on her deck again now they weren't subjected to the torrent of shells from the customs boat, and Hensley had the presence of mind to be firing on the fishing vessels as well, the small shells tearing up the wooden boats. With a roar, the machine-gun post came back to life. Baxter spun round, but the flames spitting from the gun's muzzles were aimed squarely at the German encampment, hosing fire across the fishing boats, field gun position and the tents beyond.

There was now a positive storm of fire pouring into the Germans, but they were firing back gamely. Rifle fire crackled along with the two machine guns, rounds splashing into the water around the pinnaces as *Ruby* closed on *Heidi*, firing her 3-pounder almost directly over the stranded vessel.

Abigail paid for Baxter's decision to switch machine-gun fire from the tug to the boats, as a shell from the tug scored a direct hit forward and blew a massive hole in the coaster's bows, sending a shower of hot metal fragments whickering across the deck. Men cried out in pain and both forward guns fell momentarily silent. "Number three gun, hit that bloody tug!" Baxter called out, running forward to help where he could. He kept one eye on the water as he dragged an injured man to one side — nothing to be done for him now — to allow more sailors to get to the gun. He didn't know how many men he had left standing, but as long as both the furnaces and the guns were fed, and there was someone on the wheel, they'd do all right.

First one then the other Hotchkiss came back into action. Looking forward, Baxter saw that the bows were a tangled mess of metal, but well above the waterline. Another flare went up from the German camp, this time angled over the river, and by its light Baxter saw that the fishing boats had been reduced to matchwood.

But where was the cutter? Its gun had fallen silent, but that didn't mean it had sunk. Baxter moved to the rail, scanning the night beyond the illumination of the battle, and finally caught sight of it.

"Hard port!" he bellowed, seeing the sturdy little vessel drifting towards *Abigail*'s port quarter. The sudden turn threw the gunners off, giving the Germans a momentary respite. The freighter was slightly slower to respond, which suggested she might be taking on water.

Baxter ran to the bows, stepping over sharp-edged torn metal, pistol in hand in case this was an attempt by the cutter's crew to board. It was nothing so bold, though — the little vessel had been shattered by shell and machine-gun fire, and a lot of men were lying dead or injured on the cramped deck. A few survivors just stared up at Baxter as the river current brought the two vessels together, while others wrestled with the wheel, trying to get any steerage at all.

Rather than slamming straight into each other, the cutter hit *Abigail*'s bows at a sharp angle thanks to the turn. Baxter winced as the hulls ground together. Then the cutter slid free, the men on board shouting something up to him that he didn't catch. They probably wanted a line thrown so they didn't just drift further along the river, but he couldn't help them now.

Abigail staggered as she was hit again, this time in the stern — dangerously close to the engine room and boilers. Baxter turned on his heel, swiftly assessing the situation. *Heidi*, he saw, was being abandoned, the men scrambling across to *Ruby*. He saw Hensley wading across the sandbank that had done for his first command, his face covered in blood.

Childers' Marines were still firing on the encampment, and Baxter imagined their delight at having this opportunity. There was little they could do to the well dug-in field gun, which was still sending shells towards his command. The tug was still coming on, .303 rounds clattering against her sides and superstructure, sweeping the area around her gun clear. Right now the Vickers gun was the only weapon bearing after the hard turn to avoid the cutter.

Most importantly, the invasion flotilla was mostly sunk at its moorings. The freighter wasn't designed for the hits she was taking, and wouldn't be able to take much more of them. They'd accomplished their goal here, however.

Baxter hurried back to the stern and ordered the gunners to cease firing. He cupped his hands around his mouth, took a deep breath and roared, "Childers! Back to the boats!" as loud as he could. Given he'd bellowed commands across decks in the middle of Pacific cyclones, that was fairly loud. The shore guns kept firing for a few more moments, then fell silent. There was no other acknowledgement from the Royal Marine, so he had to assume they'd heard him.

He collared a sailor hurrying by laden with fresh cloth belts of machine-gun bullets. "Jump down to the engine room as soon as you've delivered that and report back on their status."

"Aye, sir!"

"Helm, forty-five degrees starboard and ahead one half!" he called into the mangled wreckage of the wheelhouse. The sailor was having to crouch under the torn-up roof.

The turn would bring them back towards the river bend they'd come round to enter the action, hiding them from the enemy guns, and from there back up the Rufiji. But he didn't think for a second that it would be that straightforward, and he couldn't order *Abigail* back downriver until *Heidi* and the boatloads of Marines were back, which would mean at least two trips unless Childers had taken an unlikely number of casualties.

The turn he'd ordered brought the main battery, such as it was, back into play just as glorious golden light slid like liquid across the landscape, the sun announcing its presence and what would be another long, sweltering day. "Fire at that bloody field gun!" Baxter called to the gun crews, forgetting any semblance of discipline as another shell smashed into the ship's unarmoured side and detonated under his feet. Number one gun, the foremost weapon, fired, the shell arcing over the entrenched position and exploding in the increasingly battered-looking encampment. Number two gun fired, but with a horrendous crash flew clean off its mounting and went cartwheeling into the river, taking the gunner with it. Baxter swore as he realised what had happened — the detonation in *Abigail*'s guts had obviously weakened the mounting. Miraculously, the gunner surfaced a moment later, spluttering and shouting for help, and his mates quickly slung a line to him.

It was definitely time to go.

Ruby was steaming fast towards them, running ahead of the tug that had picked up speed again. The German gun crew was taking advantage of the sudden chaos that reigned on the British ship's deck to run forward and bring the comparatively heavy 22-pounder to bear. If that hit, Baxter knew, it would more or less be over for them.

The long gun swung to bear. "Anyone with a gun, shoot at the tug!" Baxter bellowed. He showed the way by levelling his revolver over the side and pulling the trigger, even though the tug was still several hundred yards away. Just as the hammer snapped down, sending the futile .38 round in the general direction of the enemy, the tug's bow disappeared in a thunderous explosion and plume of water.

"My mine! That was my bloody mine!" Hensley could be heard exclaiming in the stunned silence that followed the detonation.

The cloud of vapour and debris cleared in a moment, fragmented wood and metal splashing down into the water. The river was so shallow here that the weapons were more or less bobbing on the surface, rather than lurking several yards down in the depths, but the German crew probably hadn't been expecting this. Tug ships were tough little vessels, designed for hard labour and getting in close to much bigger, heavier ships, and the small mine didn't have much of a charge. It had still blown a significant hole in the ship's bow, through which water was rushing, causing her to sink by the bows very quickly. Even as he watched, she seemed to hit the bottom and she hung up in that awkward angle, the stern kept afloat by the quick closing of watertight doors. Most conveniently, she'd sunk in a position that masked the German field gun, her crew having sailed into its field of fire in their eagerness to close with *Abigail* and bring their big gun to bear at point-blank range.

"She'll be salvageable," Baxter said, as Hensley was helped up the ladder. The subaltern was a mess, his head wrapped in a dirty bandage and his white uniform stained with blood from a half dozen cuts and knicks. "But not quickly. Hot work?"

"Warm enough, sir!" Hensley said, obviously in high spirits despite his injuries and the fact that his first command was currently stuck in an African river, in enemy territory, and was now well ablaze.

"Get below and get those injuries seen to," Baxter ordered gruffly, though he felt an odd sense of pride in the young officer.

"Not much of a below to get to, sir," a rating reported. "That last shell's made a bit of a mess. A lot of our supplies are gone."

Looking around, Baxter saw that a lot of the wounded men who had gone below to be treated by the medical orderly assigned to the voyage were now back on deck, looking dazed as well as bloody.

There was a crackle of rifle fire from the east bank of the river, *Schutztruppe* deploying along it to fire on *Abigail* now that their fire had been blocked by the stranded tug. Men ducked as bullets started cracking overhead. He didn't trust his remaining Hotchkiss to fire, for fear of it further tearing up *Abigail*, and the crew didn't look overly keen on being there.

"Everyone get down!" he barked. "Number three gun, fire on the infantry."

Dalton was angling *Ruby* away again, without waiting for orders, bringing his gun back into action to fire on the figures darting around in the bush. *Abigail*'s Vickers gun added its fire, but Baxter knew they couldn't have much ammunition yet. The enemy was demonstrating the effectiveness of their tan-coloured uniforms, however, and the fire was only partially effective.

Baxter swore when he saw a machine gun was also being set up about eight hundred yards away, where it would be able to sweep the deck clear of British sailors just as they were negotiating the bend. Baxter raised his field glasses, ignoring the bullets cracking past, and was pretty sure he saw Schiller in command of the unit setting up the Maxim. It was certainly a European officer with a limp.

The machine-gun post that Childers had taken had opened fire again, hammering arcs of bullets into the opposite bank.

The Marine officer had either not heard Baxter, or more likely disobeyed orders to provide more covering fire.

One of the whalers that had taken the Jollies ashore was pulling hard for *Abigail*, sailors at the oars and packed to the gunwales with returning Marines. "Helm, one quarter," Baxter ordered, slowing the steamer further to allow the muscle-powered boat to catch up. The *Schutztruppe* were finding their range, bullets striking *Abigail* and tearing up the water around *Ruby* and the whaler.

Baxter ran to the side just as the first Royal Marines came up the side. "Where's the other boat?" Baxter demanded, grabbing the most senior Marine he could find, who had sergeant's stripes on his sleeve.

"Mind your manners, Jack," the NCO snapped, then realised who he was speaking to, drew himself to attention and delivered a parade-ground worthy salute. "Beg your pardon, sir. The other boat is sunk, seeing as it was shot a number of times. Mr Childers has asked me to inform you that he intends to cover your withdrawal for as long as possible, then make his way overland to friendly territory."

Baxter whipped round to stare hard at the machine-gun post, now three hundred yards away across bullet-torn water. He knew the sailors in the whaler would go back for the Marines if he ordered them, but given the increasing intensity of the fire coming their way, that would probably be a suicide mission. Being on the pinnace or the steamer wasn't much more healthy, in truth, but at least the combined fire of the machine guns and *Ruby*'s 3-pounder was disrupting the *askari* now shooting at them.

"They're bringing that gun round," Hensley remarked. Baxter turned back towards the enemy, and could see a team of

Schutztruppe toiling to wheel the field gun round to where it could bear on them again. That made his decision for him.

"Damn them," he muttered, though he wasn't sure exactly who he was damning. "All right — whaler crew back aboard, leave the boat. Full ahead and follow the river!"

He raised his cap to the Royal Marines on the bank, and saw the distant figure of Childers wave his swagger stick in response.

The sailors didn't need any encouragement to get back into the comparative safety of the steamer, abandoning the whaler that was taking on water from a number of holes.

Looking around, Baxter couldn't see his signaller, and the signal lamp was shattered. "Dalton, full steam ahead for the river bend!" he bellowed to the pinnace's commander. It was looking unlikely that *Abigail* would make it, even with Childers' cover, and the pinnace wouldn't be able to take everyone. This way, at least some would make it out safely.

Even as he gave the order, though, the placid waters three hundred yards downriver from them exploded into a torrent of shell splashes. Great clods of earth were raised from the bank and an ancient mangrove toppled over.

"Where in God's name did that come from?" Hensley exclaimed.

Baxter raised his field glasses, staring hard. He thought he could just make out three smokestacks, far away on the westernmost spur of the Rufiji. He certainly saw the flash of guns firing, and now that he was paying attention, he could hear the distant rumble of the artillery. A moment later, the salvo fell into the river, corrected slightly further towards the British ships, which continued to sail into danger.

"It's the bloody *Königsberg*," he breathed. "They must be in touch with Schiller's mob somehow, wireless or even a telephone line, or just heard us shooting."

"Well, that's us done for, then," Hensley said phlegmatically. "It's only a matter of time before they can get our range."

Baxter thought fast, staring intently at the distant ship, or rather just her upperworks. Another set of flashes, and the salvo landed at about the same place. "Two points starboard, ahead one quarter," he ordered, buying time before they sailed into the maelstrom. Without a proper rangefinder, even the now obsolete models he'd trained with, it was difficult to estimate range, particularly in these conditions. He dredged up what he remembered of the cruiser's armament, what he'd seen in Zanzibar.

"That's her maximum range," he said at last. "That must be as close as she can get without beaching."

"Doesn't help us, given that she's still commanding our way out. If we can steam through the gauntlet, the river turns and might keep us out of range, and I imagine she only has so many rounds for the main gun."

Baxter grunted. *Königsberg* didn't throw an enormous broadside, five 4.7-inch guns, but they fired fast and with commendable accuracy. He didn't doubt that her gunnery officer would be able to zero them in on a relatively predictable course along the river, and he didn't give much for *Abigail's* chances, let alone *Ruby*.

The field gun fired again, having been laboriously manhandled into position, and while Childers' machine guns were suppressing the enemy infantry, the *Schutztruppe* were still making their presence known.

Baxter ignored a dousing of water from a near miss, and turned to scan the eastern bank of the river. The chart was gone, lost when the wheelhouse had been partially demolished, but he clearly remembered...

"There!" he snapped, pointing with the blade of his hand to a much smaller, narrower channel that aimed almost directly north, cutting off the fat curve of the river that *Königsberg* commanded with her guns. Those at least had fallen silent, though he didn't doubt they'd speak again if the British ships dared her challenge.

Hensley peered. "Just an inlet, old chap, barely more than a bay."

"No — it's a channel. No idea how deep it is, and we'll be perilously close to the German infantry."

Baxter's adamant tone seemed to persuade Hensley. "I'll take that over being shelled to pieces or surrendering."

That thought hadn't even occurred to Baxter. He wasn't about to haul up a white flag, and even if *Abigail* was sunk under him, he intended to keep fighting. He knew there were a lot of men on board he couldn't ask that of, though.

"Are you fit enough to keep serving?" he asked.

"Never better, old chap," Hensley said. "For as long as old *Abigail* lasts."

That reminded Baxter. The field gun was still shooting at them, and he didn't want to be subjected to that sort of fire in the narrow confines of the channel — particularly if they did run aground.

"Mr Hensley, you have the con — get us up into that channel. And tell Dalton to go ahead of us."

"Aye, sir."

Baxter ran forward to the remaining 3-pounder. "Get clear, lads," he said as he examined the weapon, leaning against it and pulling it this way and that. He thought there might be a little give in the mounting, more than there should be, but he didn't think it was about to go flying overboard. He wasn't going to ask these men to risk it.

"You'll need a loader, sir," one of the men said truculently, grabbing a shell from the ready ammunition locker the Germans had bolted to the deck not far from the concealable weapons mount. "Though we're a bit low."

Baxter nodded his thanks. "Load shot!" he ordered, settling himself against the padded shoulder brace and leaning into the gun to swing it round on the mounting, one of the other sailors assisting as he brought the weapon to bear on the field gun. He found it by its flash and the detritus kicked up by the muzzle blast. The shell screamed mere feet over his head, as though the gunners were targeting him personally. He didn't flinch, but adjusted the angle. Hensley had brought them up to half ahead, the water creaming along the hull as *Abigail* settled onto the heading he'd chosen.

He adjusted again, glaring down the sight at the gun. This was ridiculously close range at which to have a gunnery duel, and it was only a matter of time before the field gun hit them again, possibly lethally. He pulled the trigger, riding the recoil into his shoulder and watching the fall of shot. The round burst short and a little to the left, close enough that it sent the enemy gunners diving for cover. "Load! Smartly now!"

The gunners were well trained, fast, and the German troops seemed just as capable, scrambling back to their weapon. Baxter felt sweat running down his brow but didn't want to take his eye from the sight as he adjusted to account for this ship's motion. "Loaded!" someone roared in his ear, and he fired.

There was nothing dramatic, such as an explosion in the gun's ready ammunition supply. The small shell must have hit the mounting or possibly a wheel, slewing the German field gun round and turning it over, scattering the crew like broken dolls around it.

"That'll do," Baxter said grimly. He knew he'd probably just personally killed or injured a fair number of enemy soldiers, but it was them or his own crew. He slapped the Hotchkiss's hot barrel. "No more firing unless I give a direct order."

Up in the bows, Baxter could see just how narrow the channel was. Tall and wide-spreading trees reached out to meet in the middle without ever quite touching. It could almost have been peaceful in the dappled light, the banks and foliage diminishing the noise of the fighting they'd left behind. The machine guns had finally fallen silent, which hopefully meant Childers and his men were already on their way back towards British territory — hundreds of miles away at this point.

Ruby had slid past *Abigail* and steamed a bit ahead, and Baxter could see Dalton staring worriedly into the water. If anything, the channel was even shallower than they'd expected, banks of mud showing over the surface here and there. Baxter detailed men to keep a sharp eye both on the water and both banks, then moved back to the now roofless wheelhouse. Hensley was leaning against the structure, looking pale from blood loss and shock. As Baxter approached, the younger officer slid down onto the deck.

"I think I need to rest a moment, Baxter," he said drowsily.

"No you don't," Baxter snapped, hating the fact he needed to be harsh but knowing it was necessary. Hensley's eyes snapped open at his hard tone, and he started to try to struggle to his feet.

Baxter put a hand on his shoulder. "You stay there," he said, softening his tone. He knew he couldn't let the young man drift off, as he probably wouldn't come back, but he also didn't want him losing more blood or risking pitching over the side.

He beckoned a walking wounded rating over. "Don't let the lieutenant nod off, d'you hear?"

"Aye, sir," the rating said. His arm was in an improvised sling, a bloody bandage around his forearm, but he seemed alert enough.

Baxter rose, looking around. There was work to be done, as *Abigail* should probably be lightened. Without knowing why, he drew his pistol and swung the cylinder out. He'd fired a few rounds, but ejected all of the remaining cartridges, the brass tinkling to the deck, and reloaded.

Childers had mostly sent his walking wounded back with the boat, but all the Marines still had their rifles, and the Vickers gun in the stern was still crewed, the men's faces tight with watchfulness.

"You Jollies get to the railing," he said. "Anyone with a gun, shoot at anything moving. Don't wait for an order."

Tired faces turned towards him. "We're almost out of this," he said, raising his voice so everyone on deck could hear. "And you've all done bloody good work. I don't intend to falter at the last, and we will get each other home."

He didn't exactly get a rousing cheer in response, and hadn't really been expecting one. The sailors and Marines did move with a bit more spirit to their duties. Baxter could hear bugles and shouted commands, still relatively distant, and the sound of a body of men moving through the undergrowth.

He spotted the medical orderly, moving among the wounded who were up on deck. There were a fair few carrying injuries of one form or another, but fewer than he'd expected given the intensity of the action. "Get the wounded over to starboard; give them as much cover as you can. Anyone who can walk and shift a heavy load, start getting everything you can over the side. Water stays, and bullets."

"Even the rum, sir?" a plaintive voice asked.

"Even the rum." Baxter grinned. "Save one cask, though. I think we've all earned a tot."

The men set to with a will, and soon he could hear the splash of their previous supplies going over the side or being tossed out through shell holes in the hull. He'd love to lose the quarter ton of gun on the foredeck, but he didn't think that could be done safely and they'd just have to settle for the remaining ammunition. Anything to raise the coaster a little higher in the water.

He stiffened, half raising the Smith and Wesson as he caught movement in the shadows under the trees. A rattle of ammunition belts being shifted told him the Vickers crew was ready, and grim-faced Marines poked rifle barrels over or under the railing.

Rifle shots rang out from the shadows, bullets slamming into the hull and superstructure. A Marine slumped silently, dead so fast from a bullet in the head he didn't have time to cry out. The machine gun roared to life as soon as they came under fire, the stream of heavy bullets tearing up the undergrowth, and the riflemen opened up with a rapid rattle. Baxter fired almost blind, jerking his pistol between flashes of movement.

He could hear someone shouting in German, exhorting his troops to keep firing. There were more *Schutztruppe* in the undergrowth than there were British sailors and Marines shooting back, and they had a lot more cover. The Vickers gun probably wasn't hitting a lot beyond chewing up the foliage, but that at least was serving to disrupt the attack.

Baxter didn't want to bring the Hotchkiss back into play, but he didn't think there was much choice. "Number one gun! Fire at will into the treeline!"

The 3-pounder fired almost at once, the shell hitting the solid trunk of a mangrove and showering hot metal and splinters into the surrounding troops. All the while, the unarmed sailors were feverishly hurling everything over the side, bringing *Abigail* up in the water very slightly. It would be enough; it had to be enough.

Baxter reloaded his revolver. His fire wasn't adding much to the gun battle, but it made him feel better. He was halfway through slotting the little bullets into the hot cylinder when he saw Schiller himself. The German officer had emerged onto the riverbank, waving his men forward before levelling his Mauser automatic directly at Baxter.

"Blighters are going to try to board!" Hensley called out. He'd dragged himself over to the railing and had taken up a fallen Lee Enfield.

Baxter ran forward, looking over the side. *Abigail* still had water under her and was still forging ahead, but she was barely a foot from the oozing mud of the bank. Baxter felt the heat of a shot whip past his head, and knew it was Schiller. Hot anger coursed through him, and before he could think he'd jumped over the railing. His boots sank into the mud, but fury drove him forward. The look of surprise on Schiller's face turned to panic as Baxter charged him down. The German levelled the Mauser and fired, missing by an inch. An *askari* reared up in front of Baxter, trying to knock him back with his rifle butt, but a rifle round knocked him over.

Schiller turned to run, too late.

Baxter reached the German officer, ignoring everything else going on around him. He grabbed Schiller by the shoulder and spun him round. His opponent tried to bring up his pistol, but Baxter slapped it out of his hand before lashing the barrel of his revolver across the smug, arrogant face, sending him spinning into the mud.

"For God's sake, Baxter, get back on the bloody boat!" he heard Hensley shout. He glared around, but the attempt at marshalling a boarding party had failed in the face of sustained rifle and machine-gun fire. The native troops didn't seem overly keen on trying to rescue their officer and had taken cover again. Baxter stooped, slung the German over his shoulder, and ran along the riverbank, the cloying mud dragging at his feet. With a grunt, he hurled Schiller up onto the deck, then staggered and lost his footing. *Abigail* slipped further away, and a bullet kicked up mud next to his knee. Baxter rose again, forcing himself onwards. Voices shouted encouragement over the noise of the Vickers gun, and hands reached down.

A slight turn was coming up ahead. Baxter's legs were leaden after the adrenalin rush of his mad charge onto the land, but he forced them to pump onwards. The freighter lost a little way as the helmsman, ducked low in the wheelhouse to keep his head, followed an order to turn. Baxter launched himself across mud and water. His hand caught the rail but his muddy boots scrabbled for purchase. Then sailors were grabbing his forearms and shoulders and dragging him aboard.

Hensley was back on his feet and offered Baxter a hip flask. "You're quite mad, you know?"

Baxter looked down at the unconscious Schiller lying at his feet, then shrugged and gestured around at the trees. "We're not out of the woods yet, Mr Hensley, and that cruiser is still out there. We've got a lot of work to do if we're going to keep the old girl afloat." He lifted the hip flask and took a welcome slug of brandy. "So let's be about it, eh?"

EPILOGUE

Cold rain lashed at Admiralty House, warping Baxter's view through the small window. Beyond the glass, London hunched under the downpour. It had been colder and damper than this when he'd left earlier that year, but somehow the city seemed glummer. The country was at war, reeling from a series of shocks and blows, amongst which the surrender of a RN ship in harbour hardly seemed to have registered. Talk of it all being over by Christmas had all but died away.

Saunders cleared his throat. The Naval Intelligence Department officer had gained an extra stripe on his sleeve since Baxter had last seen him, making him a lieutenant commander.

"Well, it wasn't quite what we sent you to do, Mr Baxter," he said, looking up from the report he'd been reading. He tapped ash from his cigarette and took a drag. The report was considerably fuller than the one Baxter had presented to Ingles and Parker when *Abigail* had finally limped into port, containing as it did a lot more information regarding his activities in pursuit of Arbuthnott. He *had* left one or two trivial details out, including how much he'd had to take Parker and Hensley into his confidence, and the involvement of Mashka and Tomas.

"I suggest next time you send someone more qualified for intelligence work," Baxter said, unable to hide the sourness in his tone. "Sir."

"Not quite what we sent you to do, but you achieved quite a bit anyway," Saunders said patiently, obviously trying to mollify him. "I agree with your analysis that this Captain Schiller would indeed have launched his invasion before the Cape Squadron could replace *Pegasus*. And while it is unfortunate that Mr Arbuthnott remains at large, you at least extracted him from German hands. With any luck he will retire somewhere quiet and trouble us no more."

Baxter didn't bother responding, guessing that Saunders believed that no more than he did. He certainly hoped that was the last he'd see of either Arbuthnott or Billings. If he did see either of them, he was resolved to shoot first and move on.

"I'm sorry I couldn't bring him in," Baxter said. "For what it's worth, I'm inclined to believe Billings, that he hadn't turned traitor. Arbuthnott truly believes that what he does is in the country's best interests."

"Indeed? If that is the case, it would be the better if he actually consulted us before launching into one of his mad schemes." Saunders crushed the life from his cigarette and slapped the manilla folder closed. "You've certainly caused quite a stir. Ingles made a glowing report of the actions, though he was at pains to note the role of Commander Walsh, Lieutenant Childers and the rest of the former *Pegasus* crew. Parker was more grudging. You did exceed your orders on a number of occasions, and brought a lot of injured men back. Not to mention the number killed."

"I brought them all home." The deaths had been weighing on Baxter. Between the storming of the wireless station and the attack on the invasion flotilla, he'd lost nine killed across the three vessels. Childers and the section of Royal Marines who'd stayed behind to cover their retreat had still been missing when he'd left East Africa.

"You did at that, Baxter," Saunders admitted, drumming his fingers on the stiff cover of the folder. "Not to mention being instrumental in the capture of an enemy agent."

The Zanzibar Constabulary had stormed Perito and Sons the morning after the small flotilla had sailed and found a small wireless transmitter. In a way, the blow was devastating for many of the officers on the station, as while all the evidence pointed to the older son being the spy, all the Peritos were in custody awaiting trial.

"Nobody is quite sure what to do with you. Parker suggested a court of inquiry might be in order, and certain of my colleagues think you should just be quietly discharged. Others have suggested we pin a medal to you first."

"And you, sir?" Baxter said. He'd been apprehensive during the long journey back from East Africa, after bidding a fond farewell to Hensley and Andrews, and a more formal one to Parker. Strangely, now he was actually in Room 39, he felt almost relaxed. He guessed that if the Naval Intelligence Division was going to have him discharged from the RN, he wouldn't even be here.

"It seems you were right. The country needs fighting sailors, and you've shown yourself to be exactly that sort."

Baxter stepped across the room to stand in front of the fire, staring into the blaze. As much as he'd occasionally suffered in the heat in Africa, it had got into his blood and he'd been uncomfortably chilled since his return to the British Isles. He'd adapt, though. He always did.

"On that subject, sir, Sub-Lieutenant Hensley conducted himself very well under fire, as well as showing himself to be a sharp young man."

"I'm sure he has a bright future ahead of him, once his commanders stop trying to get him killed. This Andrews is of more interest to us, however. Is he really as good as your report suggests?"

"Better," Baxter said. "I don't pretend to understand the technical side of things, but we wouldn't have succeeded without him."

Saunders didn't say anything further, instead writing intently in a notebook.

"My commission?" Baxter asked bluntly after a few moments, tapping the rank insignia on his sleeve.

Saunders seemed slightly taken aback by his directness, but then a man who moved in his world would likely not encounter that too often. "It's being considered," he said simply. What he meant was quite obvious. Baxter had been commissioned into the Reserve, originally, as a stopgap so he could return to active service. He had technically failed in the task set for him by Room 39, though.

Baxter clenched his jaw, but took a moment before speaking. "And what are my orders, sir?" he asked.

"Oh, I think we'll stash you somewhere where we can lay hands on you, as and when we need your unique set of talents," Saunders said. "I hear Scapa Flow is, well — not *exactly* lovely at this time of year, but the Grand Fleet has an insatiable demand for officers right now."

A NOTE TO THE READER

If it can be argued that Europe stumbled into the devastation of the First World War, then the spread of Europe's war to Africa was even more halting and at times farcical. This can be seen from the peculiar code — *Tipsified Pumgirdles Germany Novel* — that alerted British colonial authorities to the outbreak of the war, to the strange period immediately thereafter where the civilian authorities tried to leash local military forces and the attempts by some officers to adhere to older forms of war, such as the notion of parole and of giving notice of an intention to attack. This last was disastrous on a number of occasions, not least the landings at Tanga that failed in part because the British commanders deemed it appropriate to let their enemies know they were about to break the truce.

Dismissed at the time as a 'game of tip and run', the First World War in East Africa — indeed, across the entire continent — has perhaps not received the attention it warrants, though there are some worthy tomes on the subject and good analyses in texts on the wider conflict. It should be recalled that the first British soldier to fire in anger was a member of the Gold Coast Regiment in Togoland, and the German *Schutztruppe* under the able but ruthless leadership of Paul von Lettow-Vorbeck didn't surrender until three weeks after the Armistice. Europe's war in Africa would be costly for all involved, but in particular for the local population who suffered terrible deprivations and casualties through direct involvement in the conflict, as soldiers and porters, and the disruption to food supplies and vital services.

While in some respects, the First World War owed much to an earlier age, it was also a deeply technological war. Military aviation, after a stuttering start in the Italo-Ottoman War of 1912, came into its own — barely a decade after the Wright brothers made their first flight. Long-ranged and highly destructive artillery ruled the battlefield. This was no more true than at sea. While the torpedo, mine and submarine had all been invented or perfected in the nineteenth century, they reached maturity in the so-called Great War. Naval aviation developed from a few floatplanes to experimenting with aircraft carriers as we understand them. Vitally important, often not fully understood or exploited as well as it should have been and perhaps less glamourous was the role of wireless communication. Wireless telegraphy — radio, as we now know it — played a vital role in the intelligence game through the interception of broadcasts and using the enemy's transmissions to locate them.

This is a world in which Baxter has once again been forced to dip his toe, much against his will. It has got him back into a Royal Navy uniform, however, and while in 1914 few might have guessed it, the war is going to be a long, hard conflict. It's unlikely that Room 39 is completely done with him, however.

As usual, I have tried to keep as close as possible to the history as it happened and remained true to historical figures and places featured. These include Paul von Lettow-Vorbeck, the *Schutztruppe* commander, SMS *Königsberg* and her commander, and both HMS *Pegasus* and *Astraea* and their respective commanders. I hope I have done them all justice. The raid on Dar es-Salaam and the Battle of Zanzibar were both as depicted, saving Baxter's involvement. Commander Parker and much of the base establishment are of my own creation. To the best of my knowledge, there was no German plan to invade Zanzibar — much as they might have wished to claim the spice island — or a British expedition up the Rufiji at this time. While the German colonial establishment almost certainly had coast watchers and agents in and around the city of Zanzibar (this was, for instance, how Looff knew *Pegasus* had put into Zanzibar and was therefore able to trap her there), I have found no suggestion of a sophisticated spy network within the city. Such things are, of course, not outside the bounds of possibility and are therefore, I think, fair game.

On the subject of names, I have maintained my previous practice of referring to places as they were at the time. In particular, the customary use seems to have been for 'Zanzibar' to refer to both the city and the island it was on, rather than the more correct Unguja Island and Zanzibar City. I have done my best to differentiate the two in the text.

Thank you for taking the time to read this, my fourth historical fiction novel — I hope you enjoyed reading it as much as I enjoyed researching and writing it. If you enjoyed it, it would be great if you could drop a review onto **Amazon** and **Goodreads** — these can be a great help to authors. You can find me on Twitter (**@ReaverRedemptor**) and Facebook (**Tim Chant Author**) for short rambles about my hobbies, other interests and writing.

I'm also developing a blog, mostly about naval history and my great-grandfather's career in the Royal Navy, which can be found here: **timchantauthor.com**.

Sapere Books is an exciting new publisher of brilliant fiction and popular history.

To find out more about our latest releases and our monthly bargain books visit our website: **saperebooks.com**